Get Behind Me Satan
The Novel

Mike Yousif

xulon
PRESS

Get Behind Me Satan
Mike Yousif

Printed in the United States of America

ISBN 978-1-60791-518-8

Scripture taken from:

The HOLY BIBLE, NEW INTERNATIONAL VERSION®. Copyright © 1973, 1978, 1984 by the International Bible Society. Used by permission of Zondervan.

The Amplified® Bible, Copyright © 1954, 1958, 1962, 1964, 1965, 1987 by The Lockman Foundation. Used by permission. (www.Lockman.org)

www.xulonpress.com

Table of Contents

I dedicate this book to the Lord Jesus Christ.

A Special thanks to my loving wife, Sharon,
who endured with me the intense
hardship and Spiritual Warfare during the writing of this book.
And to my son Johnny, who sacrificed time with Daddy in order
to complete this project.
He is a gift from God.

Just another Wednesday

Jim, who is a bachelor in his mid thirties, woke up to the alarm clock at 7:30 a.m. Next to him, sitting on a chair, is a demon named Daemon. Jim is not aware of the demon's presence. Demons and angels move at the speed of light, too fast for humans to see. However, the supernatural beings can read and influence the human thought process.

Jim thought, *Oh no. I stayed up late last night, and now I have overslept for half an hour. I'm gonna be late for an early meeting this morning.*

Daemon said, *Why don't you call in sick today?*

Jim agreed and picked up the phone to call, and then he thought, *No, I've called in sick too many times already,* and hung up the phone.

Daemon replied, *What are they going to do, fire you? The job sucks anyway.*

Jim thought, *Yes, it's true the job does sucks. But I need the money.* As he walked to the bathroom, rubbing his eyes and yawning, he tripped over a bottle of liquor. The floor was cluttered with bottles, food wrappers, and take-out boxes.

Looks like she messed up the place good, said Daemon.

Why does she have to come on a weeknight anyway? thought Jim.

You didn't mind it when she showed up unexpectedly, Daemon reminded him.

Jim smiled as he headed towards the shower. He got dressed quickly and thought, *No coffee this morning. I'll have to get it on the way to work or at work.* Then he headed out towards his car. Daemon followed.

He got into the car, which was in the driveway outside his nice suburban house, and closed the door. Daemon got into the car through the door on the passenger side with no problem. As a spirit being, he could go through doors, walls, and so forth. Jim turned the ignition and the radio started. The newsperson reported that there was an earthquake, as usual, somewhere in the world that doesn't usually have earthquakes; the newsperson also said that earthquake occurrences were increasing in number and magnitude.

Jim said, "Personal assistant," and a voice from the dashboard said, "Good morning Jim. What would you like me to do for you?" Jim replied, "Check my calendar." The automated voice said, "Synchronizing calendar, please wait… synchronization complete. You had a meeting at 8:30 a.m. which has been cancelled, no reschedule time is specified."

Jim was excited over the report and said, "Great," then he thought, *I'd have been very late for this one.* Then he said, "Dial Cindy," The voice said, 'dialing Cindy, please wait… speaker phone on… connected." A voice over the speakerphone said, "This is Cindy, can I help you?"

Jim said, "Hi, its Jim. I just wanted to confirm that the eight thirty meeting has been postponed."

"Yes, and I am trying to get all parties to agree on a good mutual time. I will update your calendar when the time is set."

"Thanks, talk to you at the office." Then he said, "PA, switch to radio."

Daemon said, *I told you not to worry.*

He felt relaxed and listened to the radio. As he got on the freeway another driver cut him off.

Daemon said, *Are you going to let him get away with that?* Jim sped up his car and caught up with the other driver, which turned out to be a female. He gave her the finger and Daemon said, *That's my boy!* However, the other driver looked back at him, shrugged her shoulders and raised her hand in an apology. He smiled and felt bad now, for what he did. Then he hid himself in the traffic to avoid further embarrassment.

He arrived at his work place and got into the building where he works. He opened the main door and got in, while Daemon went in through the glass door. He used the elevator to get to his floor and passed by his floor receptionist's desk, where other employees and their demons were unusually hanging around and surrounding her. He thought, *Why are these guys here? But, that's good for me; she didn't notice me coming in late.*

Daemon said, *There's something good, though, going on down there, you should come back and check it out, later on.*

He was almost at his office when a colleague passing by said, "You're late again, Jim."

"There was a traffic jam on the freeway."

Daemon said, *That works every time. I taught you well my boy.*

As soon as he got inside his office, his best friend, Jack, who is about the same age, popped his head inside the door and said, "How are you doing buddy, have you checked out the front desk yet?"

"No why! What's happening?"

"C'mon you'll have to see it for yourself." Then they both walked together towards the front desk. Their two demons were walking behind them.

Jack's demon said to Daemon, "The harvest is so big I am doing Jack on a part time bases. But be careful, the enemy is still out there. I saw one the other day."

Daemon replied, "Jim's circle of friends and family are all controlled by our brothers. So I don't have much exposure to the enemy."

"Watch out for them, they infiltrate and brainwash our subject."

When the two men got to the front desk, they saw the receptionist who was wearing a low cut blouse exposing big cleavage. Jack asked the receptionist if he had received any mail. The frustrated receptionist replied, "For the third time Jack, no!"

Jack thanked her, and they both left. Jack asked, "Did you check the twins?"

Jim replied smiling, "Yes, they're great. That explains the big crowd earlier."

"Yeah, I'll see you at lunch then."

Jim and Jack's demons asked the secretary's demon, "What's her story?"

"She just got divorced, and I told her to make an investment in a boob job. The new puppies cost her a couple of thousand dollars, on a payment plan. She is looking for promotion at work and someone to pay for the boob job."

Afterwards, Jim came across the building electrician, Tom, while he was walking the hallway. Tom told Jim that he was having an extramarital affair and he thought that his wife might already know about it. "However," he said, "I'm not sure, but I think she is having an affair too, man. It could be great if we could do swapping one day with other couples."

"Aren't you afraid of catching a disease, there are all kinds of scary bugs out there?" Jim asked.

"No man, we are using condoms. Let me know if you are interested in swapping!" Tom replied.

Later, Jim talked to his mother on the telephone, and she invited him to dinner that night. He said, "I already have a date at eight tonight."

"Why don't you come in at seven then, I just wanted you to meet my new boyfriend. You can leave right after you eat," she insisted.

"Mom, you just divorced dad not six months ago!—"

She cut him off and said, "I'm not wasting any time, and I need someone besides me here."

"I knew you were playing the field, but I didn't know you were going that fast."

"Listen, I've invited your younger brother, Steve. I don't want you to make a scene," she said.

"OK, then I'm definitely not showing up."

"C'mon now, he is your brother, try to be open-minded about his lifestyle. Do this for me."

"Ok, mom I will show up at seven, but I can't stay long."

At lunchtime, Jim and Jack got together and walked to the cafeteria. Jack said, "You're a lucky man, do the two girlfriends know about each other?"

Jim replied with a whisper, "Of course not, and I don't want you to tell anyone about this secret."

"OK. OK…"

Then they arrived at the cafeteria counter and started selecting their meals. Jim picked up the fish special.

Jack asked, "Didn't you eat fish the other day?"

"Yes!"

"Better watch out for mercury!"

Jim put the fish back and picked up the beef plate.

"Watch out for cholesterol and mad cow disease!"

Jim, feeling frustrated, put the beef dish back and picked up the chicken plate.

Jack laughed and said, "Bird flu!"

"C'mon now, what about you, what are you going to eat?"

"I'm going to be safe and take the salad special."

Jim, taunting him back, said, "Well then, watch out for E. Coli and salmonella," and they both laughed.

Daemon commented to the other demon, "We've done a good job messing up Earth and the creation."

After they sat down at a table, Jack said, "Look at that guy over there." Jim looked in the direction where Jack hinted with his eyebrows. He saw a guy, looked like in his mid-thirties, who was saying grace before he ate. Jack continued, "Look at that Jesus freak! Who does he think he is, acting like he's all holy and religious?"

"What a jerk!"

"We're honest people, we're good people. We pay taxes, tip the waitresses, if they're pretty. We haven't killed anyone; I even went to church last summer for a wedding."

When the man finished praying, Jim took another look at him and said, "Wait a second. I know that guy. I met him at the company picnic last year. His name is John and he was a nice guy."

"Did he try to talk you into religion? They must pay him to do that or why else would he waste his time on that junk?" Then Jack looked at John with disgust and said, "I don't know why; I just don't like him."

Jack's demon looked at Daemon and said, "This unsaved man doesn't know why he hates the gospel! It's because he's mine."

Then Jack said, "Look over there. Your girlfriend, Sheila is having lunch, too. Who is she with?"

Jim looked quickly and said, "I don't know, she might be a new employee." Then he looked back again and said, "I think that's the lady that cut me off on the freeway this morning."

"Never mind about her. When will you see Sheila again?"

"This weekend," Jim answered.

"What about the other girlfriend, I think her name is Pat?"

"I'll be seeing her tonight. Again, just make sure you don't tell anyone."

"Lucky you," Jack sighed, "I wish I could be single again; marriage stinks. Here you are, having a high adrenaline rush from dating two women, and a thrill of doing the forbidden thing."

"Not really. I have to lie all the time to both of them. Sometimes they both want to go out on a Saturday and I have to come up with new excuses, a brother's birthday or mother is sick. I have to remember what I have said to whom, or what version of the truth I last said."

"Measly inconveniences to achieve that kind of thrill and pleasure. I feel like I'm trapped, but divorce is messy. Remember Dave? After the divorce, he lost his house and children and now he pays alimony. I heard that his ex cleaned him out and now is sleeping with a new guy."

"I don't know," Jim mused. "It seems like you got a good deal. A nice family, warm home-made meals, a loving wife, two cute children—"

"Boring. I'd give up all of that and my soul, too, to get what you have and some action. And if I can't have a divorce, then I'll just have an affair. Everyone else is doing it. It's hard to give up all the available females and remain exclusively loyal to only one woman. It is against the male sexual instinct. It just doesn't make any sense. Ask a male dog, he'll tell you."

The two demons perked up their ears and surrounded Jack.

Daemon said, "Did you hear that? Work on it. All you have to do is present the opportunity."

The demon replied, "Yeah, I heard a lady on the fifth floor that said the same thing yesterday. I'll have to get them together!"

On the other side of the cafeteria, Sheila, Jim's girlfriend, was talking to a coworker named Diane.

Sheila said, "Aren't Christians supposed to be good people? I wonder why my neighbors get dressed up every Sunday and go to church, yet the grass in their lawn is about one foot high. Not only that, but there is always messy garbage outside. How do you explain that, Diane? I'm not likely to read the Bible, nor books of Christian theology to learn about God, but I'll read Christian lives."

"First of all, just because someone is a Christian, it doesn't mean that they are perfect people. Moreover, just because one Christian is behaving badly, that shouldn't stop you from becoming a Christian. Just this morning, I was on the freeway and without knowing it, I cut off someone. I apologized to the man and felt so bad afterwards. My conscience bothered me until I prayed and asked God for forgiveness. See, if God says that I'm a saint, that doesn't make me sinless; it makes me blameless."

"I tried the religion thing many years ago and I didn't like it then, and I don't want to do it again," Sheila retorted.

"Yes, me too, I did try religion, and didn't like it either. Then, I met Jesus. Why don't you come with me to church or a Bible study, and I'll explain more to you?"

"Are you trying to make me like the Christians living on my left and right, who don't talk to each other because they are from different denominations? And what's with all these different denominations, why so many, and aren't you all worshipping the same Jesus? I have one family next door that fights all the time. Sour people, haven't smiled in years. What do you guys baptize them in, lemon juice?" Sheila snickered at her own joke.

"That's a shame. Even though people cannot recognize us as Christians by our outward appearance, our unique language, principles, and values should give us away. Our Christian culture should reveal us as being in the world, but not of the world. Unfortunately, not all Christians understand the fundamentals of following Jesus. Jesus said 'Build your house on a rock and not on the sand, and—'"

"Yada, yada, yada and the three little pigs used different building material to build their houses and the wolf came to huff and puff," mocked Sheila.

"You know, the wolf is the devil, and he will test the foundation of everyone."

"No thanks. That's not for me. I believe in God, and I believe that you can find Him anywhere and you don't have to sit in a building made by man to find Him. The church is nothing more than a club for people who cannot or don't want to mentally evolve."

Diane didn't pursue the conversation any further after that.

Later on that afternoon, Jim and Jack saw one of their colleagues being escorted out of the building by security.

Jim asked Jack, "What is his story?"

"They fired him because he was watching porn at work. Do you believe this guy? He should be watching that stuff at home, like the rest of us. I guess he couldn't wait until he got home."

"You watch porn at home?"

"Of course I do, who doesn't? In his defense though, he was doing it on his lunch hour. I think he is going to sue the company for invasion of privacy. Those company IT techies, they can track the web sites you visit, and I guess he got caught," Jack informed.

The terminated employee walked away shamefully with his head down, but the demon behind him was very happy. He said to Jack and Jim's demons, "We are making great headway with porn, brothers." They gave him a high five from a distance.

"I can't believe that a man lost his job because he looked at a computer screen pixels, those little dots!" said Jim. Daemon thought, *He will lose more than his job; we're aiming for his soul, too, if we can keep him addicted to porn until he dies. Unfortunately, I could never get you hooked on porn.*

* * * * * *

At seven p.m., Jim showed up at his mother's house for dinner. After informal introductions with the new boyfriend, Doug, they all sat down around the dinner table. There was Jim, his mother and her boyfriend, and his younger brother, Steve, at the table. Also present were their demons in the background, surrounding them. Steve, a young man in his early twenties, looked sick, pale and bald, with many blotches on his face. Everyone knew he was an AIDS victim. He was quiet and everyone avoided looking at him. His mother, in a show of support, said, "It's your life, son, you can do whatever you want with it. I'm sure they will find a cure one day for this horrible disease."

Jim couldn't hold back his feelings and said, "I told you to leave this life style, and now you're going to die."

Their mother Judy got upset and replied, "You have no right to be judgmental!"

"It's just that when we were kids and we went to church, I remember the preacher saying that homosexuality was wrong."

Judy replied with a soft voice, "Honey, that was a cult, and we were listening to a cult leader. We shouldn't have let them lay any of their Bible thumping bull shit on us. I wish we never went there."

One of the demons looked at Daemon and said, "What's going on with your human? You haven't done a good brainwash on him."

With a nervous tone, Daemon replied, "Oh, it's nothing, guys. Before I took him under my wing, this family went to church, and I guess the seed was planted early on about the homosexual sin. It's hard to erase early teachings, as you all know. Nevertheless, it's harmless. I have it under control. It's amazing though, how two brothers have different weaknesses. While you have the younger brother under the spell of homosexuality, I have my subject under other spells."

Steve's demon said, "That is why we want to start early, in kindergarten, to reprogram the kids' minds to our radical sexual agenda. We used to start brainwashing them at age thirteen a century ago, then at age nine about fifty years ago, and now we need to start at age six to get to them before the enemy gets to them. We must undermine the faith teachings that the kids get at home. Just like Hitler with Nazi Germany and the Soviets controlled the kids by getting to them at a very young age. It is easier when the parents are divorced and have no time for their children. While the children watch TV and play video games, we send them our messages, with the help of Hollywood and the homosexual-biased media, of course. We're planting the seeds of homosexuality, and Hollywood is watering it. They help us spread all kinds of evil and wickedness throughout the world, and before they know it, we'll have a perverse generation."

Daemon asked Steve's demon, "How come your slave doesn't say anything?"

"His conscience is bothering him. He knows that his life style caused the divorce of his parents. Also, he will die in a few months, so it's normal to feel like this."

Then Judy's boyfriend, Doug, said, "Even Jesus supported homosexuality. I was driving along the freeway today and I saw a billboard quoting Matthew 8:10. I looked it up and found out that a Roman leader with a high position asked Jesus to heal his servant. When Jesus wanted to go to his house, the Roman said, 'I'm not worthy for you to come under my roof…' Obviously, they were a homosexual couple. And Jesus still healed the servant and didn't condemn either one!"

Jim had no response to that. However, Judy was pleased.

Doug's demon said, "Twisted mortals, we have to twist scriptures for them because their conscience is bothering them. The Roman centurion didn't want Jesus to come into his house because he knew of the authority that Jesus had over the wind, sickness, and death, just like the centurion had authority over a hundred men. He knew that Jesus was no regular Jew, but a miracle worker. Has nothing to do with homosexuals."

Doug, feeling good about Judy's approval, continued, "My neighbors are a female couple raising an eight-year-old boy, and they told me that even Jesus supported the gay life style. You know the Bible says that Naomi and Ruth were lesbians; they loved each other as Adam loved Eve. The neighbors' adopted son has all the support of his elementary school, where they are teaching them that being gay is an acceptable and perfectly healthy alternative sexual life style. They read to them traditional stories with a transgender twist like 'Jane and the beanstalk' in class. I'm surprised that an educated person like yourself would have such prejudice against gays."

Doug's demon said proudly, "I told him to look up homosexuality and Christianity on the Internet, so he made his research just to score some points with the mother, because she has already told him about the situation of her son, Steve. It's a good thing that he didn't see and read the part in the Bible that says all those who die while still a homosexual are damned and destined to the Lake of Fire.

We've become very aggressive recently about promoting homosexuality, to make it look like a moral lifestyle. No more Mr. Nice Gay. The Gay community now says 'Stay out of our bedrooms.' What occurs in those bedrooms is spilling over in disease into the general population. I'm glad he didn't mention the part about the special health risks associated with homosexuality."

In the background, Steve's demons looked at Daemon and said, "Steve was molested when he was a little boy and no one knew about it. The incident created an emotional hole. The first seven years in a child's life are innocent; he was pure in heart, naïve, and sensitive. All I had to do was tell him that he was born to be a homosexual, and he believed me. Now he has a short time to live. After that, he will arrive at the gates of Hell. This plan is guaranteed to work as long as we keep the enemy away from him. At the same time, we arrange for him to be with the wrong crowd who encourage each other in sin. After that, I'll be able to graduate to a new assignment."

Judy's demon said, "The AIDS disease is one of the many great inventions we came up with. Sodom and Gomorrah revived; do you guys remember the fireworks of these two cities? What a show!"

Judy calmly said to Jim, "See, they are even teaching children in the first grade to be understanding when other kids have two moms or two dads. Six-year-old children are more tolerant than you are!"

Jim blew up and said, "He's the reason you and Dad got a divorce."

Outraged, Judy glared at him. "How dare you bring that up?"

Jim held up his hands in a calming gesture. "I apologize, everyone. Maybe we should just eat now."

Judy's demon said, "To think that this family was going to church just a few years ago—"

Doug's demon asked, "How did you break them?"

"They built their faith on a house of sand. The preacher they admired was caught in the act of adultery. Many of his followers abandoned the faith. What a great way to collect souls - preacher scandal. If we attack the shepherd in the pulpit, the sheep will run away and scatter. We did the same thing with their leader and his disciples scattered. Unfortunately, he was resurrected. That wasn't on the agenda," Judy's demon replied.

Daemon said, "I hear our leader still hasn't recovered from that day."

"No, he hasn't. Anyway, this family and others became calloused because this painful experience pulled them away from the faith. And when they grew calloused and hopeless, they fell into the grip of depression. Judy couldn't return to her Lord and recover her mental and emotional health. Once a dog has been scalded with boiling water, he will even fear cold water. I love it when a Christian makes a one-hundred-eighty degree change in their course of life and faith."

Jim felt uncomfortable with the atmosphere there, so he ate quickly and left his mother's house to head out to his date with Pat.

* * * * * * *

When Jim arrived, he parked his car outside her house and Daemon said, *Let's get ready to party.*

Jim knocked on the door and Pat, a gorgeous blond woman, answered the door. She was wearing a tight black silk dress that caressed her hourglass figure. A lot of smoke came from the inside of the room. There was also another demon in the house.

"Hello, come in," Pat said.

Jim and Daemon went inside and the two demons high fived each other.

* * * * * * *

It was late when Jim drove home, with Daemon in his usual place in the front seat next to him. Along the road, he noticed a young girl on the curb, dressed up like a hooker. She was wearing a red mini skirt, high heel shoes, and a fur coat that covered only a bra. She seemed afraid as she waved at oncoming cars, trying to flag down a ride, and frantically screamed, "Stop, please!"

When Jim started to slow down the car, Daemon said, *What are you doing, are you crazy? You never stopped for hitchhikers before!* Still, Jim slowed down and stopped the car. The girl got in and Daemon moved to the back seat. The demon who accompanied the young girl also sat in the back seat next to Daemon and said, "Hello, brother."

The girl, in her late teens, said, "Please help me, my life is in danger. Just drive away from here."

He drove away quickly and asked, "So what happened?"

"My pimp is going to kill me any minute now because I wouldn't sleep with this creep!"

"Why not, isn't that what you do?"

"He was asking me to do some weird stuff!" she replied.

"You are a hooker. What do you mean weird? Why don't you try drugs? They will make it easy for you."

"I don't do drugs anymore. My friend died from an overdose a few weeks ago," she responded sadly.

"How did you get into this business in the first place? What made you start thinking about doing this kind of work?"

The young girl kept silent and wouldn't say anymore as she looked out her side window.

Then her demon said, "I had this girl, Carol, molested by her stepfather when she was thirteen."

Daemon said, "That's the way to do it."

"As long as Carol won't forgive her stepfather for what he has done to her, I'll be able to hang around her."

"What are your plans for her?" asked Daemon.

"I tried to get her killed a couple of times," the demon said.

"And?"

The demon pointed to outside and above the car. Daemon looked up through the roof of the car and saw an angel sitting above them.

Daemon looked back at the other demon and said, "Oh no, what's he doing there?"

"Her mother became a born again Christian and she's been praying for Carol from two thousand miles away. God has honored the mother's prayers and the spirit of the Lord is moving on her behalf. Meanwhile, I got stuck with this angel, who has been protecting her day and night. She used the same drugs that the other roommate prostitute used. That one died and this one didn't. I can't explain it. The mother's prayers gave Carol more time."

"You should get some backup," Daemon suggested.

"No, I requested backup to stop her mother from praying, to get rid of this angel. Then I can destroy Carol. I gave our leader the filthy and disgusting things Carol does, so he can go up and accuse her to the creator. But I still haven't gotten a green light because He promised the mother He would protect Carol."

"Well, did they send backup to discourage the mother?" Daemon asked.

"Yes they did, but she has built her house on a rock."

Finally, Jim asked, "Where do you want me to drop you off?"

"I have been thinking about going back to my mother. Just take me to the train station on Main Street. I'll stay at a hotel tonight."

Stuck between Life and Death

The following morning, Jim was still in bed and had just woken up to the alarm clock, and said, "I shouldn't have stayed up late last night."

Daemon, who just came back from another assignment, said, *You're hooked on her and can't stop seeing her. Just enjoy the sex addiction.*

Jim began another day at work. This Thursday started out just like any another day, until he got into the elevator and saw John, already inside and by himself. Jim thought, *Oh no, the praying man and religious nut. Everyone at work runs and hides from him because he speaks about Jesus,* then he said, "Good morning. John, right?"

John replied, "Yes, how are you, Jim? It's been a while."

"Yes, I don't usually come to this floor…"

Daemon, standing behind Jim, felt uncomfortable in John's presence. While they were talking, the elevator shook and stopped between floors abruptly!

Jim panicked and said, "I'm scared of tight spaces. I don't like this at all."

The Holy Spirit informed John, *This is one of my sheep; his lost soul is crying out for help. Swing the conversation to the subject of spiritual things, and start witnessing to him with the message of the gospel.*

"May I ask you a question?" John said. "Do you know where our souls go after we die?"

"That's heavy. I'm not sure!"

Daemon advised Jim not to talk to John, and reminded him, *This is the Jesus freak, don't talk to him.*

John's assigned angel, Raphael, made himself visible to Daemon, to stop him from interfering with John witnessing to Jim. The following conversation between the spirits occurred at the speed of light, compared to the conversation between the two humans.

Raphael asked Daemon, "What are you doing here?"

"I'm doing the work of my master, Lucifer, the prime minister of heaven."

"Satan the Devil is your master; he's a liar and father of lies, and a deceiver from the beginning."

Daemon furiously said, "Don't insult my master. He is the shining morning star, favored among all, until your master cast him down to earth. He is an angel of light, and son of the morning."

"He is the father of the night," Raphael responded.

"Jewels and stones of fire were on his garment."

"They will turn up in the Lake of Fire."

"He is the perfect anointed cherub—"

"Until iniquity was found in him," Raphael interjected.

Daemon said, "He is beautiful and wise, surpassed in beauty and wisdom."

Raphael replied, "He is hideously beautiful and has foolish wisdom."

"He is the god of this age."

"The Lord God is one."

"He's the bearer of light."

"My God is the maker of light," replied Raphael.

Daemon said, "He is all power, all knowledge."

"He isn't omnipotent, omniscient, or omnipresent, like my God."

"He had the authority and rulership in the holy Mount of God."

"He was banished from heaven when he revolted and was overthrown by God, condemned to perdition," Raphael reminded him.

Daemon became furious with Raphael. His head turned into a roaring lion. He puffed up in size as he shook the elevator. All of a sudden, another angel appeared and joined Raphael.

Daemon said, "Oh, great, so there are two of you against one of us!"

Because Daemon shook the elevator, the two men thought the elevator had been repaired and was going to start moving. But it didn't. Instead, there was a dead silence, and that caused Jim to panic even more, so he pressed the Emergency button a couple of times. On a slower pace, a simultaneous conversation went on between the two men trapped in the elevator.

John said, "You know, our teachers and leaders prepare us to go through this life. They teach us how to go to college, get a job, get married and climb the labor ladder, buy a house, then have children and retire, and then start shopping for a casket. They don't prepare us for what happens after death. Even more, they discourage us from thinking about death or discussing it, because they don't know. But they do tell us that death and taxes are two sure things in this life. Thank God for the Bible that opens our eyes to the truth about heaven and hell. Confucius and Plato talked about the past and present, but as far as what happens after the grave, they hoped that there would be life after death, but they weren't sure."

"I was a Christian when I was a boy and went to church with my parents. I was turned off by religion; I never grasped the meaning of being a Christian. And when I started going to high school and college, they taught evolution and I became even more confused," said Jim.

When John heard the evolution topic come up, the Holy Spirit encouraged him to expose the false doctrine.

"You know, evolution is an atheist excuse for saying 'there is no God.' It all started with Darwin and his theory, the Origin of the Species. Darwin's theory allows atheists not to have to explain why we're here. Atheists want us to think that we're nothing more than smart trousered apes. I wonder whether apes have become humans, or is it the other way around, humans are becoming apes? Evolutionists believe that humans are nothing more than sophisticated animals, slower than some animals and more intelligent than others, but far from distinctive.

"People like the idea of being related to animals because they can indulge in immorality and never evaluate their behavior. Look at animals. They mate when they feel like mating, programmed by hormones. We humans, in contrast, can master the desires of our bodies and the 'animal instincts'. Humans can examine every action and decide if a civilized person would take it.

"Angels are spiritual beings, animals have bodies only, but man has body and spirit. If a man thinks with his conscience, he is an angel, but if he lets his body control him, he becomes an animal. One thing is for sure: without God, our similarity to the wild kingdom becomes more evident. The Bible teaches that we're unique creatures, touched by the finger of God and that we're a little lower than the angels. I prefer that, over us humans being a little better than the apes."

Jim surprisingly smiled, as his mind was no longer focused on the elevator situation he was in.

John was encouraged and continued, "Evolution made it okay to exploit the weak. It teaches that the more death there is, the more progress, and the better the selection of humans. It considers poor humans as weeds, waste, and dead weight of society, labeling them as useless eaters depriving the earth of resources. They want to kill off the poor by sickness and disease, and create a race of thoroughbreds. And then you have the Natural Selection concept, which promoted survival of the fittest. But the fittest still die at the end, because life isn't only in the physical. There is more to it."

"You know, I never thought about that before," said Jim.

"You probably never heard that World War II started because Hitler wanted to preserve the best type of human beings, the fittest, to make the Nazis a superior race. Hitler adopted the concept of one man stronger than others, with the right to step over the weak. He thought he was doing the world a favor by eliminating the weaker, inferior races from the face of the earth. His followers thought they were doing good for humanity by hurrying the natural selection. This led to anti-Semitism, getting rid of Jewish blood, a bad heredity, from the human race gene pool. The Jews topped his list, and in the Holocaust, he exterminated six millions of them."

"That's horrible. I never realized the seriousness of the concept of evolution!" said Jim.

"Oh yeah, Karl Marx followed that move with the introduction of communism, socialism, and atheism. In the twentieth century alone, atheism in both of its forms of fascism and communism was responsible for killing far more people than all the religious wars of the previous nineteen centuries. They believe that an ethical life can be lived without religion. If a society is to succeed, it can't trust everyone to do the right thing. Who will monitor those who monitor the masses to do the right thing? It needs to rely on a more reliable system, like the Bible."

"But why do they teach evolution in schools?" Jim asked.

"In the 1920's, a teacher was prosecuted for teaching evolution in the classroom. Now, Darwin's evolution is a new religion protected by atheists, and other theories are excluded. Evolution is a carefully protected state religion, just like communism was in the Soviet Union, and speaking against it has now become a blasphemy. The false theory is still taught everywhere by mixing poison with science in textbooks. They figured if you tell a lie long enough, students would believe it. Especially first graders, they believe everything. The teaching of evolution in public education has affected teenagers with an increase in violence and suicide and has promoted immorality and mortality. They removed God from schools so they can play God themselves."

Jim wasn't really interested in this conversation, but he was confined in an elevator with nowhere to go, so he asked, "What about the evidence they present, as far as discoveries of bones?"

"The evidence isn't present; it didn't fossilize. Fossil records don't support Darwinism, and the theory should be discarded. The missing link isn't missing. It never existed, and the only thing missing is what's between their ears. Scientists preach the gospel of evolution in the museums, their church. Using our tax dollars, they tell people that dinosaurs lived millions of years ago. If I say that kissing a frog turns it into a prince, you'll say that's a fairy tale. But if I say it takes a billion years to happen, you might believe it. And recently, they just found live tissue on a dinosaur skeleton. They recently found charcoal deposits in the South Pole, which means that there was a jungle there in the past.

"Darwin himself said that his macroevolution theory would be true only if we could find millions of transitional forms of fossil records. Transitional forms are in-between stages that lie between species. Transitional species are still missing and nowhere to be found. There is no transition between species; instead, there was an explosion of life.

"The Grand Canyon, for example, has evidence of a catastrophic burial caused by the flood. The evidence is running strongly against Darwinism and scientists are now leaning towards God's intelligent design. Microevolution, on the other hand, is adaptations within a species like horses, zebras, and donkeys, and that's acceptable.

"Darwin didn't have knowledge of the complexity of DNA information that we have today. DNA contains billions of coded digital formation. Who puts it in there? The DNA codes have a mechanism that protects it from too much deviation from the origin of code. If Darwin would see all the DNA and scientific new facts, he would retract his theory."

Jim thought, *Get me out of here*, and pressed on the Emergency button a couple more times. A voice came out of the speaker, "Hang in there, guys. We're dispatching an electrician."

"See, if they void God out, then everything is permissible. And if there are no moral absolutes, then there is no right or wrong and the attitude of 'anything goes' prevails. Today's culture rejects the very idea of absolute standards; everything is relative. A Christian culture, on the other hand, rejects relativism in favor of the absolute standards of the unchanging word of God. If some things are right, then other things are wrong and must be rejected. Creation reveals the power, wisdom, and glory of God. Christians reveal the grace and love of God."

"Are you the only one who doesn't believe in evolution?" Jim asked.

"Oh no, many people and scientists believe in creation. There's no contradiction between science and the Bible. All of the early scientists were Christians. People and scientists are intimidated into believing Darwinism. Just because everyone believes something, it doesn't mean that it's right. The world thought that the earth was flat, and when someone suggested that it was round, they didn't treat him fairly."

Meanwhile, Daemon said to the two angels, "It was out of the ordinary to see and talk to you guys here and now, and one day we'll settle this once and for all. But right now, I have to go and assist my subject human. I feel he's losing the argument, as your mortal is trying to brainwash him." Daemon switched off the conversation with the angels and joined Jim again. Daemon quickly said to Jim, *Ask him about the missing link, carbon dating, and all the archaeology proofs I have staged.* So Jim did exactly that, and asked John the question.

John answered, "Carbon dating isn't a reliable aging technique! If you were able to take those evolution scientists to the first day of creation and ask them how old Adam was, they would say that he looked like a perfect specimen in his twenties or thirties. A one-day-old man created by God! We believe that nothing is impossible with God."

"Yes, but the scientists don't believe in the Bible, and no one was there to see it, So—"

"Those same scientists believe that there was a Big bang, billions of years ago. Was anyone there to see it? Both scenarios, evolution and creation, require faith because no one was there to see it. The Big Bang theory says that the universe exploded from nothing. Can you get a dictionary from an explosion of the printing press? As a Christian, you probably know that Jesus turned water into wine in a few seconds, a process that would usually take weeks, not to mention that the grapes were missing. So, if God can do all this, then the Bible is true and He created the universe in six days."

"What about Mother Nature?" Jim asked.

"Mother Nature can only produce patterns, not detailed meaningful information. Did Nature know how to calculate the exact distance between Earth and the sun for life conditions to exist on Earth? Or did it just so happen that the sun is exactly ninety-three million miles away from the earth, so that it wouldn't be so hot that humans would burn up to a crisp, or be too cold, and freeze? And who created the sun to give us daylight and the moon for light at night, so we can see? The moon is at the right distance so tides wouldn't destroy the coastal cities. If the oceans were deeper or higher by a few feet, they would have upset the oxygen and nitrogen balance, and the biosphere couldn't be sustained."

Daemon, frustrated with the witnessing encounter of a Christian who learned to give every man an answer, instructed Jim not to listen to John anymore and said again, *He's a Jesus freak*. But they were stuck in the elevator and had nowhere to go.

John continued, "Nature always destroys and doesn't put things to order. It is easier to destroy things than to build them. The second law of thermodynamics states that everything tends towards disorder and chaos. If you leave something alone for a while, it will rot, rust, die, fall apart, or break down. Nothing gets better by itself; it gets worse. If you put a car outside, exposed to all weather conditions, and come back a hundred years later, it's not going to improve. You don't see a car from the early 1900's, unless someone preserved it."

"What proof is there that God did all this?" Jim wanted to know.

"God's existence is proven by the creation in the world, the universe, and nature. God reveals Himself to man through the things He has made. He left clues in them, from the black hole to the amoeba, and anyone who cannot see that has to intentionally close their eyes to the facts. The human body is complex and it has a hundred trillion cells in it, and the cells themselves are complex.

"God is a divine mathematician whose mind is revealed in the precise mathematics of the creation. His divine hand sets the universe in motion. The amazing solar system could only have been designed by the power of an intelligent and powerful being. Did you know that the word 'universe' means a single spoken sentence, 'uni-verse'? And God said 'Let there be.'

"Moreover, science and technology were inspired by the animal kingdom for insight and design. Emulating the animal kingdom led to the invention of new amazing concepts. The brain surgeons study the woodpecker, the architectural engineers study the beaver, and aviation engineers study the birds. Helicopters were designed by studying the dragonfly; sonar was designed by studying bats. The bee brain processes more information than the fastest existing computer.

"Now compare this to what they teach; that life started from a complex chemical organic soup! What was the source of information? Chemicals don't have information. Life made from organic soup is a lie. We're not simply the end result of ancient mud puddles struck by lightning. Some say that we evolved from sea creatures. I refuse to believe that my great-great-grandfather was Sponge Bob."

Jim chuckled.

John continued, "They say that life came together by chance and time, a mindless random chance process, which is unscientific. They watered down the truth and lied because they don't want to face how sinful they are. Instead of the origin of the species, they should be interested in the future of the species. The future belongs to God, and the best is yet to come. Evolution's monkey business, the Big Bang, and Random Chance are all fairy tales for adults."

Jim was very intrigued as he listened to John, and completely forgot about his fear of being stuck in an elevator. Daemon, however, became desperate, so he summoned other demons in the building to have the elevator fixed as fast as possible, to stop this conversation before John removed the blindfold that Daemon had put on Jim.

A demon was dispatched to solve the problem. The demon got the electrician to move quickly to fix the elevator. The electrician got a dispatch and ran quickly to the elevator. This was the same person who was talking to Jim about wife swapping the day before. The electrician, Tom, couldn't fix the elevator from his floor, so he had to go up ten flights of stairs. The whole time he was going up the stairs, his demon said, *Go faster, you piece of blubber, you're going to lose your job if you don't fix it quickly. There is a VP in the elevator.* Tom ran up the stairs as quickly as he could.

Tom finally fixed the elevator and it moved to the next floor safely. Shortly after that, Tom had a heart attack and collapsed to the floor. People nearby saw what was happening to him and called for an ambulance. However, the demon was surprised at what happened to Tom, and with excitement said, *Are you dying, man?* Then he patted him on the shoulder and said, *Go down that quicksand, don't be afraid of sinking in it.*

The heart attack was massive and Tom died before the ambulance arrived. His soul came out of his body, saw the demon, and asked, "Who are you, man…ghost or whatever you are?"

"I'm your worst nightmare," replied the demon.

"Oh my God, help," Tom's soul cried.

"It's too late for that. You had your chance and you blew it."

The demon started to take Tom's soul down when angels intercepted them.

The angel said, "We'll take it from here. He has to face the White Throne judgment first."

Tom's soul asked, "What does that mean?"

The demon said, "It means you'll have to go to Hell, wait a while there, then go to your final destination."

"Where would that be?"

"You'll see. I wouldn't want to go where you're going. This is where we part, fool. He's all yours, guys," said the demon as he looked at the angels. "As for me, I'm out of here. This mission is complete. Time for me to find a new assignment."

Meanwhile, the elevator started moving again. John and Jim exited the elevator and were shocked to see Tom dead on the floor. Jim said, "I can't believe it. I just talked to this man yesterday!"

"Yes, it is unbelievable," replied John.

Then the Holy Spirit communicated with John, *That's why I asked you to talk to Tom yesterday, when the opportunity presented itself.*

John sadly thought, *I'm very sorry, I thought I had plenty of time. I was going to talk to him later about the Lord.*

This is your territory, my son. I brought you here to shine My light in this dark place.

Then Jim said, "John, why don't you walk with me to the front desk? I want to check my mail box."

When they arrived at the front desk, the receptionist was still dressed like the day before, with very revealing cleavage. Jim wanted to observe John, to see how he would act in that situation. He wanted to see if John was just one of the fake Christians who spoke godly but acted worldly, who talked the talk but didn't walk the walk.

John was caught by surprise, since this wasn't his floor. He took a quick glance at the receptionist's cleavage, and turned his face away to the other side, where there was a bulletin board. He cast down all imagination and replaced these thoughts with information he read on the bulletin board. He occupied his mind and shut the door on sin and the enemy. He didn't feed off the flesh.

Meanwhile, Daemon and the receptionist's demon both threw fiery darts and arrows at John and said, "Lust of the eye and lust of the flesh."

However, when the darts arrived at John, they were immediately extinguished and deflected by the invisible barrier and shield of the Holy Spirit surrounding him. John had guarded his heart. He took heed as to what he saw and what he heard. He wasn't ignorant of Satan's devices.

Disappointed at the failure, Daemon said, *Why don't you just look at them? Your God made them. Admire them the same way you admire the birds and the bees!*

The Holy Spirit reminded John, *It is written, if you look at a woman to lust after her, you would be committing adultery in your heart.*

John thought, *yes Lord, Jesus said that to show that we're all sinners, and no matter how much we claim to be good, we actually sin a lot, especially in the present days, when women dress down, showing a lot of skin.*

Daemon said, *You don't have to lust after her, just look and admire. There is no harm in looking!*

John ignored those thoughts and continued to read the bulletin board, but became uncomfortable with the situation. Meanwhile, Jim was picking up his mail from his mailbox, but watched John through his peripheral vision.

John turned to leave and said, "OK, I'll talk to you later, then."

"Wait and I'll walk with you," said Jim, impressed by John's manner.

The two demons talked among themselves, "C'mon, let's tell him what we were going to tell him if he would have looked and lusted. We have nothing to lose now."

Daemon said, *Hey John, these boobs are better than your wife's. I know that you glanced at them quickly, so make a comparison when you get home.*

As John started leaving, the Holy Spirit said, *Make a note, John, to have Diane talk to this secretary's poor soul, to show her the truth, to witness to her and get her out of the grip of her demon.*

Daemon said to the other demon, "Did you hear that? The enemy is coming to your doorstep soon."

"I'll be on guard and watching out for them," replied the demon, then pointed at John and asked, "Who is this guy, anyway?

Nobody's resisted like him yet. Even the women are checking the receptionist out. You know, even King David looked at Bathsheba when she was bathing naked and kept looking until he lusted in his mind. His covetousness drove him to action and had her brought to him, and after he stole her from her husband, he committed adultery with her that night. When he found out later on that Bathsheba was pregnant, he lied and murdered her innocent husband, Uriah. David broke all of the Ten Commandments there, and dishonored God and his relatives. Then God took David's newborn son from him. Two people died from that one look, and David is the one they said was a man after God's own heart! Who is this guy, now," pointing at John again, "and what's his story? Somebody should report him."

"I'll be reporting him to our territory leader. He has stepped into my domain and I'm not happy about that. But tell me, how is the secretary doing?"

"She has got a couple of offers, but she is waiting for a good catch. Someone has to pay for these new boobs."

As they walked away, Jim looked at his mail and said, "Here, look at this big advertisement on the back cover of the magazine about a cave man. What do you think about that?"

"People lived in caves over the past few thousands of years, and if it was a rainy day, maybe they spent the day doodling on the cave walls. Some of God's prophets lived in caves. It has nothing to do with evolution. Osama Bin Laden lived in caves; it doesn't mean that he's an evolving cave man!"

Then John thought, *Man didn't come out of the cave, but he is heading to the cave, and will be crying out for the mountains and the rocks to fall on them in the Great Tribulation, if they don't repent.*

Then he said, "Christians don't believe in evolution, but we do believe in transformation. The only evolution we believe in is the transformation of an unbeliever who gets into the church of God crawling like a slimy caterpillar, walking strangely and looking weird. Then the word of God cocoons him, and after a while he comes out as beautiful as a flying butterfly, praising and worshiping God. By the way, the caterpillar's metamorphosis takes only days, not billions of years."

Then John invited Jim to come to church with him or to a Bible study one day to talk more about the many questions Jim seemed to have.

Jim asked, "Which church or denomination do you belong to?"

"The Bible-based church of love."

Jim seemed puzzled.

John continued, "I go to the church that preaches Jesus Christ."

* * * * * *

Later that day, John was driving home from work and listening to the radio in his car, which he usually did. He only listened to gospel stations, and maybe jazz sometimes.

At the stoplight, he noticed a homeless man with a dog on his lap. A driver stopped his car and gave the homeless man a can of dog food. The homeless man looked at the can of food, smiled, and said a few words that John couldn't make out.

John thought, *You gave something for the dog, but gave nothing to the man!* John tried to get some money to give the beggar, but the light turned green and the line of cars moved again. John thought, *People are saving the trees, the birds, and the whales, while people are starving all over the globe. As if these creatures are more important than man is. We should care for the environments and the animal kingdom, but human life comes first. Human life is more valuable to God than the rest of the creation.*

Then the radio program host said, "Welcome back; we have a caller. Hello, you're on the air."

The caller said, with a broken accent, "Hello, my name is Ali. I'm a Muslim living in this accursed western country. I'm very upset right now. My daughter is thirteen years old. She just came home from school and she tells me that they gave her a shot for some STD disease. She says that she had no say in the matter and that it was mandatory. Maybe your children and teenagers are having sex at age thirteen, but our girls stay virgins until marriage, or they may be killed, according to our customs. If we don't have these customs, then our sisters and daughters will turn out like your sisters and daughters, fornicators."

"Listen, my friend," replied the radio host, "I agree with you that this should be voluntary and a teenager should be able to choose. As for your teenage daughter or your sister, you shouldn't kill people because of adultery or fornication. Most religious leaders want to take living men and move them towards death, but Christ wants to take dead people and move them towards life."

"Well, you always criticize Muslims. Why don't you walk the streets and see how your Christian women are dressing up?" the Muslim continued. "The clothes that the Christian girls are wearing, a silk worm can make at lunch break. Our women cover all their body up to the neck. We help the poor and fast, while you spend billions on diet plans. And at night you go to nightclubs, drinking alcohol and sleeping with strangers for a one-night stand. How can your Christian God be pleased with this kind of filth that His followers practice?"

"Listen friend, I see your point. Let me tell you though, that God isn't pleased with the people you described. Just because people are born Christians, doesn't mean that they are true born again Christians. And please, don't base your opinion of God on what you see on the streets and the movies. Why don't you try to go to a local Bible-based church first, and you'll discover a much different society, a minority who have dedicated their lives to God and based their values on the Ten Commandments.

"Muslims believe that Moses was a prophet, and you believe in the law and the Ten Commandments that Moses received from God. And you should know that true Christians still observe these commandments. Now, you sound like a devout Muslim, and a dedicated one. I know some Muslim friends that are more decent and holy than some Christians. And if you are a descendant of Ishmael, then you should know that God has promised to bless him into a big nation. But you have to worship the God that gave that blessing," the radio host stated.

"We're blessed with oil."

"Yes, but God has more for you. Esau gave up his birthright for a cup of lentil soup; don't give up your blessings for some oil wells. God sent Jonah, whom you believe in, thousands of years ago to warn your ancestors to repent. And now, God is using satellites to send you His message.

"This message isn't for all the Muslims, but there are a few confused Muslims that God is calling to come out of that mess and give their lives to Him. They belong to Him. People from all the nations of the world will be kings and priests in heaven and will rule with Jesus in the future."

"What the hell are you talking about?" the Muslim asked.

"Don't you see what the devil is doing? From the beginning, he put friction between Ishmael and Isaac. And later, between Esau and Jacob, who later was given the name Israel. And to this day, their descendants fight because God blessed and Satan wants them all dead. When the Arab's attacks on Israel failed, Satan had Muslims killing each other," the radio host explained.

"Muslims are united under the one true prophet."

"Jesus told a parable of a man who planted a vineyard and rented it to farmers and went into another country. When he sent a servant to the farmers to collect from them the fruit of the vineyard, they beat him and sent him away without anything. Again, he sent to them another servant and they stoned him. And he sent many others—some they beat and some they put to death. Last of all he sent his beloved son to them. But those farmers said, 'Here is the heir; let's put him to death, and the inheritance will be ours.' And they took him and killed him. The point is that Jesus, whom the Quran calls Isa Al Masih, represents the son in this story. He was the last one that God sent to the world. Any other prophets after him came too late—"

"Don't tell me that your Jesus is the only way!" the Muslim cut in.

"This is what the Lord Jesus said, so if you have an issue with this, you can take it to Him. I'm not trying to insult your Prophet Mohammad. He was like David and Solomon, a political and military leader with many wives. He was like Moses and Joshua, who united tribes and led them in battles. He was like Elijah and many other prophets, who destroyed idols and dealt with the corrupt political and economic powers of his day. So He had a lot in common with the Old Testament prophets," the show host replied.

"No way! You are getting nowhere with your religion. If you talk about Jesus in public, they will put you in jail. The very institution of your religion is nonsense, and is falling apart. Your God is dead, Fred. Back home where I come from, the holy Koran is taught in our public schools twice a week, from elementary through high school. While you, on the other hand, cannot take a Bible to your school, let alone teach it to your kids. We're taking our Allah to other countries, spreading and converting, by force if we have to. Our prophet Mohammad came on a horse with the sword in his hand and conquered while your prophet came on a donkey surrounded by palm branches. Your Christianity is weak and is an endangered religion. It is going out just like Judaism, while our religion will dominate the world," the Muslim stated.

"Oh no, you're wrong about that. He's the Son of God. He was crucified, died, and was resurrected and now He sits at the right hand of God in heaven, still living and working. The difference between Christ and every other religious leader of history is that He has conquered death and has the power to give eternal life to all who believe in Him. No other leader from the past is still alive, leading and loving His followers, and giving them victory over the grave. As for the Bible, Mohamed didn't question the accuracy of the Bible. Koran points to the Bible as truth over a hundred times."

The Muslim replied in rage, "You are making me angry. No wonder my brothers are blowing you up all over the world. I would do the same if I got the chance. And if the west ever weakens, what we'll do to you, will make what the white man did to the African-Americans and the American-Indian look like a picnic. Get a grip, get a life, and most importantly, get a god that gives a ****." Then the man hung up the phone.

The radio program host said, "The church is under attack, and it is reaching a climax just before the Lord Jesus comes back for us. There is a new censorship, and speech restrictions on radio and TV. Even the church service itself will have to refrain from offending other religions or mention that Christ is the only way to salvation. The FCC could suspend our radio and TV station licenses as a consequence for violating this new law. I, the radio host, apologize if I offended any Muslim. And if my remarks are going to affect this program or the station, then I'll step down, but I would ask that the station not to be shut down, for it is the last light in this dark world.

This is the last week that we can mention the blood of Jesus Christ, but we have cassettes and videotapes of old programs that you can purchase and we'll make them available to you. Sadly, conservative talk radio stations will be shutting down soon."

As John arrived home, disgusted at what he heard regarding the censorship, the radio program host said, "We're going on a break, but please stay tuned. There is a new law that will take effect this Saturday and it will affect all of us Christians—" John parked the car, turned off the ignition, and went inside.

John's wife, Mary, a fair lady in her early thirties, greeted him and said, "I've been feeling bad all afternoon and I don't know why. I ordered pizza for dinner, I hope that's OK?"

"Yeah, sure honey, where is Gracie?"

Mary replied sadly, "She is upstairs. She's upset about being teased at school. Would you talk to her this time?"

"Not again! I'll talk to her."

John went upstairs, knocked on her door, and said, "Hi, honey, it's me. Can I come in?"

"Yes, Dad," she replied.

"Hi, what happened? Your mother said that someone teased you?"

"Yeah well, other students are calling me names, laughing at me, and saying hateful comments such as, 'Why don't you just go to a Christian school where everyone thinks like you do, and leave God out of here?' I haven't said anything to them; I didn't carry a Bible and walk around with it. God forbid if I should carry a Bible in school. They say literature is interesting, and the Bible is dull. They attack me just because I don't dress up like them and try to keep my conversation clean. It's really bad, Dad, when most students think what's bad is good and what's good is square. Even children of church folks say that Christianity is old fashioned and chase after what is exciting and acceptable to the world. They embrace pleasure without concern for God's eternal laws. They say that abstinence doesn't work, so the parents give them condoms since they can't control themselves. I haven't had sex!" Gracie explained.

John shook his head and said, "Yes, and we're proud of you, honey. And I would prefer you didn't get in trouble, but if you ever do, I'm here for you. Today, new age young people have strong sexual temptations. Giving condoms to a teenager to sexually experiment is like giving someone on a diet a cookbook." Gracie smiled and John thought, *Modern liberals are spreading their views of sex under the deceitful title of sex education throughout the school system. This type of human biology education is designed to replace the moral values that we teach our young people, and is causing sexual promiscuity.*

"Sweetheart, I know it is getting harder and harder to be a true Christian. The devil is trying to choke us to death. But we have confidence and hope in the Lord to keep going. And your mother and I, we're very proud that you are keeping the faith and holding onto your Christian values. The Lord Jesus loves you very much."

"Thanks, Dad. I mean, these kids should learn to fear God. The school and church should be preaching to them that message. Instead, we see 'no fear' on tee shirts everywhere. I mean, for real Dad, these teenagers don't fear anyone anymore. Not the police, the authorities, the teachers, the principal, no one. They're even starting to look weird with their tattoos, body piercing, black makeup, funky hairdo, and black clothing. And the Christian's kids adopt the latest trends and fads of the world in their dress, language, and morals. By their language and lifestyle, it is impossible to tell which kingdom they belong to, the kingdom of the Hell or the kingdom of Heaven."

"You know, Gracie, in the sixties, there were shows on TV where kids would look at their father as their spiritual and moral leader. They asked him for advice in all matters of life. Nowadays, the father is being portrayed as the village idiot. And the devil knows that once he gets the fathers out of the way, it is easy to work with the mother and the children. Also, in the sixties, when the father or the mother came inside the house, the party was over, no questions asked, that's how much kids respected their parents. We have been conditioned and brainwashed by Hollywood to accept and excuse evil and sin. They continually shock people's minds until they no longer are shocked, after it is repeated so many times.

"Fear of the Lord is a healthy fear, and the beginning of wisdom. Statistics show that children who are brought up in a wholesome religious atmosphere are more likely to develop the resistance to juvenile delinquency that is destroying our society. The modern-day western education system's goal is to undermine the scriptures, Christian ethics and morality. They want to undermine the faith of people and to rob them of their trust in the Lord Jesus Christ and the Word of God, and to teach the way of heathenism and godlessness," John explained.

A demon whispered in Gracie's ears, *Your parents are holding out on you. It is so much fun to have sex. You should go for it, it's good. Everyone is doing it.*

Gracie said, "For real Dad, I don't have any fun. I feel like I'm missing out on things."

"Honey, don't think that you have missed something by being in a home with conservative Christian values and convictions. The truth is, you haven't missed anything except a lot of heartache and trouble. It is true that there may be a short-lived pleasure to sin. But the problem is that the fun wears off very quickly, and all one is left with is the pain and regret of sinful choices. Believe me, sin will cost them more than they would ever want to pay, and take them places they don't want to go, and keep them there longer than they want to stay. Sin promises pleasures, but produces pain. It promises life, but delivers death. However, because sin does seem to offer enjoyment, it takes strong convictions and rock-solid values to resist. Holding on to our belief isn't always the easy choice, but it's always the right choice. We have higher ideals than the world.

"You know the story of Abraham's nephew, Lot, who pitched his tent just outside the evil city of Sodom. Soon, he owned a house right in the middle of town. We have to be careful that we don't get closer to the gates of sin than we ought to. After that, all it takes is time and a foothold or two, and Satan will entangle us as he did with Lot, whose family was wrecked when God destroyed that city. As for your friends, you'll graduate one day and your friends won't matter. You won't see them ever again. So why worry about them rejecting you or excluding you from their circle?" John reassured her.

Gracie said, "I have to be around these guys all the time and go through a lot of peer pressure. They call me a geek."

John replied, "There will come a time when we stand before God, and all these memories will fade away and their sentiments and peer pressure will be so unimportant. And I'd rather be called an oddball and see the face of Jesus in heaven, than be a popular person going with the flow and end up in hell."

Gracie hugged her dad and said, "That's not the worst of it. One of my teachers asked us to participate in a project where we write an essay about making a contract with the devil. We have to bargain with the devil to do something for us, and in return, we're to deliberately give up our souls to him. And we're not allowed to reject the devil in what he proposes. I've already decided that I'm not going to have anything to do with this project. I'm not going to conform to the world, but change it." Just then, the doorbell rang. She continued, "Thanks for the faith boost, Dad. The pizza is here and I'm starved."

As they walked down the stairs, John prayed, *Oh Lord, help Gracie to always live for You, and to make her mind up to do right anywhere, anytime, and under any circumstances. Help her draw the line between the world and your kingdom and against the temptation to play footsy with one foot on each side. I don't want her to get the worst of both worlds and the best of none.*

Shortly after, John and his family gathered at the dinner table. John started to pray as usual, and the demon said to Gracie, *Aren't you sick of the same boring prayer, day after day, after day…?*

Gracie repeated out loud some of the words that her dad was praying, and said, "Yes, Lord, " confirming her dad's prayer to shake off the demon. She also prayed that the Lord would seal her mind from the influence of the devil and his deceitful thoughts and ideas.

Then the demon tried again and said, *Who are you praying for? Why do you pray for another kingdom to come? Don't you like my master's kingdom here on Earth? Everyone in school likes this kingdom. Why do you have to be a stick in the mud?*

Gracie ignored these thoughts, and when her dad finished praying, she said, "Amen," then continued, "Hey, Dad, do you notice that the pizza is round and the box it came in is square, and each pizza slice is a triangular shape? Could we use this to explain the trinity?"

John smiled and replied, "We trained you well, darling."

Then Mary said, "I saw this man today who was carrying a sign on the front saying 'I'm a fool for Jesus' and everybody laughed at him. When he turned around, there was another sign on his back saying 'Whose fool are you?' I thought that was cool."

While they were eating, John found himself staring at his wife's breasts. The demon took advantage of the situation and said, *Remember what my two brothers told you this morning?*

Mary noticed and asked John, "Did I drop some food on my blouse?"

John blushed and replied, "I'm sorry, I was just thinking of something else."

The demon said to John, *I'll remind you again when you are with her in bed. We're waiting for that day when you drop your shield of faith.* Then said to Gracie, *Your show is about to start, you'd better ask them now.*

Gracie thought, *Not yet,* and then she said, "Have you guys heard the joke about the Christian horse? This man bought a horse from a Christian, who told him that this horse is spiritual and follows only certain commands. He said 'If you want him to go, you don't say "gitty up" you say, "praise the Lord," and if you want it to stop, don't say, "whoa," say "amen".' So the man took his new horse home for a ride and remembered to say 'praise the Lord' to get him going.

"So he started going. It was a nice ride at first, and then the horse started galloping and sprang into action. The man said 'stop,' and it started going faster. Then he started saying 'whoa, whoa,' but the horse didn't stop. Then he finally remembered to say 'amen,' and the horse stopped right at the edge of a cliff. The man, relieved from plunging into his demise, said 'praise the Lord' and the horse started going again, but off the cliff."

Everybody laughed.

Then Mary said, "Earlier today, I had an organic peach. It cost a lot but it tasted great. I wonder when Jesus was on Earth and He tasted honey, would He have thought 'I'm glad I created bees to make this delicious honey'?"

Gracie said, "What about milk? Do you think He said 'I'm glad I created cows to make milk'?"

After dinner, the demon reminded Gracie again, *Ten minutes until the program starts, you'd better ask now.*

Finally, Gracie asked, "Dad, everyone in my class is watching this program on TV. Can I watch it too? I'm the only one who hasn't seen it, and when they ask me about the details of the program and I don't know anything about it, they say, 'What planet are you on?' Please, Mom?"

"Well, now, is the show on one of our normal faith TV channels?" asked John.

"No," said Gracie, disappointed.

John asked again, "Is it a nature program?"

"No. Dad, you know what program I'm talking about."

"Yes, I do. And, if it is as worldly as I hear from my colleagues, then you'd probably be better off not watching it. If Jesus were here in the living room with us, would He watch this program? My house is the embassy of the kingdom of God on this earth, the Bible rules here, and God comes first. You know, some Christians don't even allow TV sets in their homes."

Gracie pouted, then looked at her mom and said, "Mom, this isn't fair!"

Mary replied, "I'm sorry, baby, your dad knows best. Fill your mind with things eternal instead of shallow, purposeless, worldly things."

"But they're going to have that famous actor as a guest star on tonight's episode."

John said, "Don't idolize anyone on TV or anyone else; the TV superheroes of my generation are now on TV commercials advertising life insurance, laxatives, and arthritis medication."

Mary giggled and added, "And back pain medication."

John turned the TV on and switched to the faith channel. There was a short newsbreak, where the announcer said that bees were disappearing, and dolphins were committing suicide on the beaches. Then he said that the doomsday clock had been moved backward one last minute and it was now one minute before midnight because of the global nuclear threat. Then he said those events confirmed the signs for the return of Jesus Christ, and Christians were to go through these turbulent times with patience because God was in control.

A preacher came on next, who said, "I'll send you a dollar to bless you, and you can send me ten percent of the blessings you receive afterwards. Or, you can send me ten percent of your income right now and God will multiply your offering by thirty times, sixty, four hundred fold, I guarantee it, folks. By sowing a seed, you'll be twisting God's arm to bless you and reward you back. I'm also building a cross. Send me the name of four people to nail on the cross and send an offering for twenty dollars. I'll also send you a handkerchief for healing, a shawl for prosperity, and oil for anointing. You know the rapture is coming soon. Why are you holding onto your money? Give it to me. We've got it all, folks, healing, blessings, baptism, communion, prosperity, just call this number on the screen..."

John said, "This man sounds more like a used car salesman than a preacher. It's deceivers like this that cause people to blaspheme God. Immoral and crooked preachers taking offerings by manipulation and force, tricking senior citizens like that. They make a business out of accessing God and provide a way for healing and to buy forgiveness. Thieves and liars commercializing religion, they will have to answer to Jesus." Then he switched the channel.

Mary said, "I was reading a book last week that said one of the signs of the end of times is that preachers will be greedy for money." Then she asked, "How do we know who to donate money to?"

"The Holy Spirit will guide us. Thank God for the Holy Spirit."

The phone rang. Mary picked it up and said, "It's my sister," and started talking on the phone.

A few minutes later, Mary said, "John, Martha says Hi. She says that she is going to the mountains to ski. I told her that I heard that there was going to be an exceptionally high snowfall this winter. And I don't feel good about this trip. What do you think?"

John confirmed the same thing, being driven by the Holy Spirit who gives His followers the advantage of warning them of danger.

John switched the channel and watched another preacher, who was very old, and said, "...what kind of a god would be pleased by killing unarmed Christians and shed their blood? They can defend themselves sometimes and strike you back. But, because of the love of Jesus, they refrain from doing that. I'm not pleading for the Christians only; I know where they are going after you kill them and die, you're just freeing their spirits to go to Heaven. But you who persecute them are going to hell unless you repent.

"As for you, persecuted Christian brothers and sisters, let me encourage you, for you are blessed when people hate you for His sake. Be glad, for they persecuted the prophets before you. Continue lifting up the cross. Jesus said 'in this world you'll have tribulation.' Endure and strengthen yourselves. And you know that the blood of the martyrs is the seat of the church, and precious in God's sight is the death of a martyr.

"And I'm not talking about martyrs who strap a belt of bombs on themselves or trucks and blow up others; Christians, Jews, and sometimes their own brothers, too. Our book says if you do that, you end up in Hell. Your book says that if you do that, you go to heaven. Two contradictory concepts; only one can be right. You believe in the God of Abraham, and already know that God wasn't pleased when Cain killed Abel. Our lives belong to God, and no one has the right to take a life. And if anyone told you that there is a heavenly reward in killing, then they have deceived you."

A series of pictures of Christians around the world, being tortured, appeared on the screen as the preacher continued, "As for those of you who don't believe that God exists, and killed those defenseless Christian men, women, and children, the look on their faces and in their eyes is haunting you and you're having nightmares, you can't sleep with guilt. You need to turn to the Lord Jesus, He can let you live again without guilt, if you repent and give your life to Him. But if you obey the devil and the government that rules your country and promotes killing Christians, you'll be bloodthirsty and want to kill more and more, and you'll turn into a monster that belongs in the fire of hell. God loves you and doesn't want you to go there."

Mary, who was disturbed by the pictures said, "The western nations have the freedom to choose the free call of salvation, yet they reject it, while the brave men and women of godless nations endanger themselves and some get killed to receive Christ."

John shook his head and thought, *I hope the west starts to read the writing on the wall and return to God. Otherwise, He will remove His protecting hand if they keep biting it, causing them to fall. It didn't matter if the empires had been so strong for so long with high walls and nuclear weapons, they still fell.*

The preacher reached for a glass of water with a frail and shaky hand, took a sip and continued, "You may not agree with what the western nations are doing around the world, and by the way, God is not American or European. I'm not talking to you as a westerner, but from one child of God to another, man-to-man wherever you live and where Christians are persecuted. Don't choose to be a child of the devil. God loves you, but He hates your sin. God's arms are open for you right now.

"As for you western Christians, when you became born again, you became soldiers and enlisted in God's army, not in a Sunday school picnic. You are not going to get the Medal of Honor just for showing up in church service, as spectators and for a good show. Don't be preoccupied with the latest fashions and diet plans like the world around you, while your brothers are in chains for Christ to advance the gospel, suffering and witnessing for Jesus our Lord. One reason they are able to push on is that they have Christian brothers and sisters faithfully supporting them through prayer on the home front. Fellow believers, we should never underestimate the power of our words offered up to God on behalf of the brave souls on the mission field. God hears those words and grants His workers the ability to remain encouraged and faithful to the cause.

"The gospel message is one of peace, but it is a declaration of war, as far as Satan is concerned. We need people who catch fish and defend the faith and the moral issues of our time. Here is how you can help: by sending Bibles to new believers around the world, donate Bibles, pray for the persecuted around the world, and invest in the Kingdom of God. Here is the phone number and website—"

Then the TV station went blank. John changed the channel and all the other channels were working fine, except the faith channel where the preacher was talking. John accidentally switched to the TV channel showing the program Gracie wanted to see.

Gracie said, "OK, let's just watch a little bit." After watching for a couple of minutes, it was obvious that the show was filthy and demoralizing. Even Gracie asked for the channel to be changed.

John said, "TV has left no room for the imagination. Almost everything is exposed and anything goes. 'Sex sells' is their motto; there is no shame."

John, moved by the Holy Spirit, called the number that the preacher left on the screen to make a donation. The call wasn't going through at that number, and then the phone line went down. So he used his cell phone, and the demon blocked the airwaves so that the call wouldn't go through. When Gracie used her laptop to get to the preacher's web site, she got a porn page and she screamed and put her hands on her eyes. John rushed towards Gracie to see what was going on. Before he got to the laptop, he realized what it was from the seductive and sensual voices coming out of the laptop, and stopped it immediately. Gracie said, "I'm sorry, I must have typed the web address wrong!"

"No," said John, "you typed it right!"

Mary felt angry and asked, "Why would this preacher give out such a web site?"

The Holy Spirit told John that the family needed to pray right then.

Gracie said, "Our antivirus is up to date. Did our laptop catch a virus?"

"No, honey, the world has caught a virus called sin. It started in the Garden of Eden and we all got it. There are two ways to inoculate, which means get rid of the virus, either by the blood of Jesus Christ and the cross, or by the fire of hell. I think I know what's gone wrong here. When life becomes frustrating and uncomfortable, we can be sure that Satan is nearby, waiting for an opportunity to attack. We need to have a family prayer." The family huddled together and started praying.

The demon thought, *OK I'll go, but I'll be back later*, and disappeared. After they finish praying, the phones and the Internet worked fine.

Gracie realized that she was the one who dragged the demon home with her and opened the door for him and she repented. John prayed that the porn image be removed from Gracie's mind. The Holy Spirit granted his request, so he put his hand on her head. Afterwards, Gracie didn't remember what popped up on the laptop screen.

* * * * * *

That same night, Jim had another date with his sex toy, Pat, but for some reason he didn't feel like going. He went anyway, and when he arrived at her driveway, he parked the car and sat there for a minute, as if there was something telling him that this was wrong. There was something different about this time. He felt different after John talked to him that morning.

Of course, Daemon, sitting next to him in the car said, *C'mon man, think of the booze, the drugs, and the best sex of your life. You've got to have that!*

Jim was still not moving.

Nobody is perfect. You have your needs, God understands.

Finally and reluctantly, Jim walked towards the house door and stopped there again.

Just think about this moment, don't worry about the future or the consequences of your actions. Think about pleasure, now.

He knocked on the door hesitantly. Pat opened the door wearing sexy lingerie with only a see-through robe on top, and welcomed him as he went in.

Daemon said, *Now that's a body for sin.*

Pat's demon asked Daemon, "What's wrong with him? I'm getting bad vibes from him."

Daemon sadly replied, "He has been brainwashed by the enemy. They planted the seed."

"Oh no! How did you allow that to happen?"

Daemon defensively replied, "I couldn't help it."

"Well you've got to choke it out of him and snatch it away. Make sure that the seed doesn't take root. You know the drill; a little trouble or persecution will do the trick."

"I was thinking maybe if he gets wealth, I could deceive him and keep him worried about his investments!" Daemon replied.

"That'll work, too. You know, I don't think this night will go well."

"Yeah, me neither."

Organized Evil

It is Friday, and Daemon left Jim momentarily to report to his leader. The leader's headquarters were in an abandoned building somewhere in the city close to a cemetery where demons usually hang out. The windows were boarded up and the only light coming in was through a few small holes in the wall.

Daemon stood in the line of demons waiting to report. The demon standing before him said, "I'm plotting rain for a revival meeting at the stadium to keep them from hearing the gospel."

The demon standing behind Daemon said, "Good work. We have to keep these miserable creatures blinded and running in circles. Anyone remember Samson, or maybe you studied about him in school? He was one of those that God blessed with a supernatural strength…"

Daemon said, "I hate those gifted guys like Solomon and David. We always have to send the best of our brothers and work overtime to bring them down."

"Yeah, anyways, this guy was a regular Joe, nothing special, but he was killing our human agents left and right. Then we sent him a gorgeous special agent, Delilah, and after many trial and error attempts, it turned out his great strength was in his hair and in his obedience to God. Once he gave up the importance of God's command, we had his head shaved at the devil's barbershop. Then we had his eyes gouged out and had him bound with shackles and grinding at the mill in a prison, running around in circles like a blind donkey. And that's how we like our humans. Unfortunately, he repented later on, and when his hair grew back, the number of our slaves that he killed just before he died was more than when he lived. But that was still good news for us because many souls headed towards Hades that day."

Finally, it was Daemon's turn to talk to the leader and he reported John as an enemy of the kingdom of darkness.

The leader said, "Yes, I got reports on Diane, too. I have them both on my black list. I'm going to send backup demons to take care of them both, to watch how they live and pick up on their weaknesses, then persecute and discourage them."

"Thank you, Master," Daemon replied.

"By the way, the humans are going to demolish this building next week. So I'll send you an all-demon-bulletin to inform you of my new headquarters."

"OK," said Daemon and headed back to Jim.

* * * * * *

Later that day, John's manager called John into his office. As John arrived outside his manager's office, he recognized another department manager leaving his manager's office. He noticed that this man was angry and gave John a dirty look. The man had a demon following him who said, *Welcome to the lions' den, praying man.*

John didn't know the reason for the aggressive attitude coming out of the man, so he proceeded inside the office.

John's manager said with all seriousness, "Hi, John, have a seat. I need to talk to you."

"Thanks." John sat down. By now, he was puzzled as to what could have happened that made everyone act in a hostile way.

"You have been slacking off lately," said the manager.

"Not true. I met all of my deadlines, and you know that."

"This is awkward. I'm being pressured by other managers because of your praying in the cafeteria in public, and talking about the Bible with other employees."

"It's a silent prayer; it shouldn't bother anyone," John stated.

"Look, you're one of my best employees, John, and I don't want to lose you. But I'm getting too much pressure from other managers."

"This is my right. There is no law against it," John replied.

"There was another employee, a Muslim, I think, on another floor who also prayed three or four times a day on his breaks, and his manager had a talk with him about it, too. He was fired a month later because he lost a contract due to his unsatisfactory performance, which cost the company a big client. He is now suing the company for intrusion on his privacy, which is an absolute lie. The company is going to settle out of court for a lot of money. This put a bad taste in our mouths about religion. We don't want to see that happen again."

"But that's not the case with me," John explained. "I only talk to people about the Bible on my break time, and I don't talk to anyone about it unless they start the conversation."

"OK, let me put it this way," said the manger as frustration built up, "I don't want to see you go, but nobody is irreplaceable. I hope I'm making myself clear."

John sadly replied, "Yes sir, and I apologize for the stress you had to go through on my account." John left the office, feeling really bad for what just happened.

Behind John's manager stood a demon who had been called for backup. Seeing John's tenacity, he said, *I see why Daemon is all disturbed by you.*

* * * * * *

That evening, Jim received a message on his answering machine at home from Pat, telling him that she wasn't interested in pursuing the relationship and that he shouldn't call her anymore. This, of course, upset Jim and ruined his evening.

Daemon had a conference call with Pat's demon and asked, "What happened here?"

The demon replied, "Jim didn't perform well last night, so Pat decided to dump him. She has already found a Christian at the club tonight."

"She found another guy already?"

The demon excitedly replied, "We got lucky with a backslider who is looking around for some action, and I got him hooked. After that, I can also get his future ex-wife and their two children. You know how it is with broken families. The father leaves and the rest of the family become vulnerable to us, easy prey."

Daemon anxiously asked, "What about Jim? This news will crush him, and I might end up losing him."

"You should get some backup from our Special Forces, like the loneliness brothers, or even better, a brother who specializes in suicide. They'll help you get rid of him. They'll have him kill himself, so you can get reassigned to someone else."

"I don't know about that. There's this Christian that has planted the seed in him already and that's messing up my plans."

"Why don't you choke the seed out of him? This is a good opportunity to add pressure into his life and snatch the word out of him. You know the routine," the demon replied.

"I don't know. He still has the other girlfriend, Sheila. I'll try something, but I don't like these changes."

Disturbed by the news, and with his confidence shaken, Jim called Sheila to arrange for a date for Saturday, to make sure that he at least had one girlfriend.

A Day to Witness

It's Saturday and Jim went on a date with Sheila to the local mall, first. Sheila was the materialistic type and loved shopping for expensive items. She told Jim that to live a good life and have a secure future, she needed to have a spouse; two or three children; a spacious new home with a three-car garage; own two shiny new cars, preferably BMWs; a vacation home on the lake; and a high-status position within the company earning a six-figure income. Then she asked Jim for advice on what she needed to do to get promoted at work. Jim missed Pat who was the opposite of Sheila. On the one hand, Sheila was self-centered and expected Jim to give her the world and make her happy. On the other hand, Pat was into sex games, didn't want a relationship, and had no plans for the future.

John, Mary, and Gracie were also at the shopping mall that day. They passed by a store where there was heavy metal satanic music playing in the background. The store sold black leather jackets and all kinds of tattoos and piercing. John looked inside briefly, and it looked like a club where demons would hang around. Gracie noticed a man coming out of the store with purple hair, body piercings, and tattoos all over his body. Some of the tattoo designs were spider webs and upside down crosses. The man's pants were hanging down to his knees. Also noticeable was a big knife in his side pocket, and a pack of cigarettes tucked into his shirtsleeve up by his shoulder.

Gracie said, "Look at this guy's tattoos, Dad."

"I don't know about tattoos. Since our body is the temple of the Holy Spirit, we should not use it as a billboard. After all, we don't own it. It is the property of God and we're just using it for a while. In the past, slaves were tattooed with the name of their master, and army soldiers were marked, too. And God did say in the Old Testament that we shouldn't put any marks on our bodies. Now I'm not saying that people with tattoos are bad people. There are some saved Christians who had tattoos before they were saved and just can't get rid of them. We won't judge. You know, Brother Joe at last summer's picnic had tattoos all over his body. When he gets his resurrected body, he won't have any markings on it. The tattoo business is preparing the world for the mark of the beast when the Antichrist comes in the tribulation period."

Later, while they were walking along, a saleswoman working out of a kiosk in the middle of the mall stopped Mary and said," Can I ask you a question?"

"Yes, sure, if you let me ask you a question afterwards."

"OK. Can you try out these two lotions and tell me which one you prefer?"

While she tried the lotions, John said, "I'm going to check on Bill at mall entrance number two. Meet me there when you're done."

"OK." Mary looked at the saleswoman and said, "I like this one."

"Great, well today, you can have two for the price of one," the saleswoman replied.

"OK, I'll take two, then. Now for my question," she said as she was getting her credit card out of her purse. "If you die today, would you go to heaven or hell?"

The saleslady was shocked, looked at Mary, and said, "I haven't really thought about that."

"Well, do you believe in God?"

"Yes, I do!"

"Have you been living by the standards of the Ten Commandments?"

"Ten Commandments? Isn't that legalism?"

"The 'thou shall nots', are like an x-ray to the doctor; it shows the flesh what went wrong. But the x-ray can't fix the problem; only the doctor can fix it. Similarly, Jesus' grace is the only thing that can redeem our sins. Besides, the laws are there to protect you; you don't want your neighbor to steal from you!" Mary explained.

"I know that good guys go to heaven and bad guys go to hell."

"That's not true, to think that you have to be perfect to get to heaven by your own efforts. You don't pass a grade to get to heaven. We start out unclean and egotistical, and then we become born again and Jesus piggybacks us to heaven."

"Come to think of it, I have been keeping the commandments!" said the saleslady as she bagged the lotion bottles.

"Well, let's see then. Have you ever told a lie?"

"Um, maybe in the past."

"Remember, time doesn't erase sin. God sees our past sins as though it were yesterday. If you have told even one lie, then you are a liar. Be honest now."

"OK! Yes, I lied," the saleswoman admitted.

"OK, then have you ever stolen something? It doesn't matter how small or inexpensive the item was. If you have stolen one thing, then you are a thief."

"Um, when I was a kid."

"Have you committed murder? Remember that harboring hatred in your heart is also considered murder," Mary asked.

"The Bible says that? I never heard that before!"

"Jesus said, 'whoever looks upon a woman or a man to lust after her or him, has committed adultery already with them in their hearts.' Have you done that?"

"I have definitely done that," the woman said with a smile.

"How about the Sabbath, have you kept it holy?"

"Wait a second, are you Jewish, what's this Sabbath business?"

"The Sabbath is a holy day of the week you keep to honor God, usually Sunday."

"Oh, OK! I was just wondering," the saleswoman said.

"Have you always honored your parents, have you put God first in your heart, loving Him with all your heart, mind, soul and strength? Do you love your neighbor as much as you love yourself?" Mary asked.

The lady thought to herself, *Most of us have trouble loving our loved ones, let alone loving our neighbors.* By now, the woman was losing interest, so Mary had to sow her seed quickly and get out of her way.

"Have you ever used God's name in vain, by using it as a curse word or misrepresenting Him? Do you value anything more than God, creating an idol? Do you pursue money more than God or give work more priority than God? Have you ever desired anything that someone else has? —"

"Oh, you're one of those 'Brimstone and Fire' denominations, aren't you?" the saleswoman interrupted.

"No, I'm just telling you what the Bible says about who goes to heaven or hell. If you have broken even one of these Ten Commandments, then you have sinned against God and cannot enter Heaven. On Judgment Day, every sin you have ever committed will be used as evidence of your guilt. You'll be damned forever and lose your soul. Without God's mercy, you'll go to Hell. The scriptures tell us that unless we repent, we will perish."

"All I know is that I'm a good person, better than some of the people I see walking around here," said the lady, as she looked at people walking by her kiosk.

"If you say that you are basically a good person, then you've become self-righteous. If you refuse to admit your sins, then you'll never seek God's mercy. God's goodness will make sure that justice is done; He will not overlook your sins. He will punish all liars, thieves, adulterers,—"

"Ok, so I have a few faults of my own. I'll just try to avoid doing that."

"I told you, you can't clean up your life. No good you do can wash away your sins, only God's mercy can do that. Jesus came to this earth to take the punishment for us. When Jesus died on the cross, He stepped into the courtroom and paid the fine for us. Because we violated the Law, His suffering was necessary to satisfy it. The moment we repent and trust the Savior, God forgives our sins and grants us everlasting life," Mary explained.

"Well, in my defense, my grandma and mother have been praying for me, so I feel that I'm OK with God."

"No, sister, that's not true. Have you heard of Jesus' parable of the ten virgins and the oil?"

"Yes, I asked the clergyman when I was a young girl about this because I thought it was selfish of the first five virgins not to share their oil. And he said that he'd tell me when I got older."

"May God forgive him. If you were smart enough to ask, you were ready to receive the answer. You see, the oil represents the Holy Spirit and that is something you can't share. You have to acquire it yourself; it's a one-to-one relationship. No one can pray you into heaven," Mary explained.

At that moment, the lady's demon came back and with shock said, *I leave you for one minute to attack this guy standing outside the mall, and when I come back I see you listening to this enemy. I don't believe it. C'mon, get her the hell out of here!*

So she said, "OK, look, I like to be free from any commitments right now."

"You would think that you are acting freely which is part of Satan's trap, but actually you are taking your orders from the ruler of this world, the devil."

The lady's countenance changed, she hardened her heart, rolled her eyes as she was getting impatient and said, "Please, I have to go back to work. You don't have to buy this if you don't want to."

"That's OK, I'll buy it. Here is the money. Thanks," Mary handed her the money and left.

After they left, Gracie said, "Mom, did you notice the lady was wearing a cross on her neck with Jesus on it crucified?"

"Yeah, Satan likes that. People see a doctor when they're sick and take two tablets. But people are allergic to the two tablets of the Bible which have the Ten Commandments written on them."

"How can I witness like you, Mom?"

"You start by acquiring the knowledge about God and His truths, study the Bible, and memorize scriptures. So when you have an intelligent conversation or witness to an unbeliever, you can teach the Word of God and be confident. But remember, it is hard to teach and preach when our lifestyles don't support our teachings."

"Do you think your message was a little harsh?" Gracie asked.

"Jesus didn't try to develop non-confrontational, no-strings-attached relationships. He wasn't a seeker-friendly savior. I've seen people spreading the modern gospel message and promising a road of roses for those who come to Christ, while some of us who came to Christ are experiencing painful thorns. They find out where a sinner hurts and tell them that the Lord Jesus will make it better. Clever wolves telling people what they want to hear, not what they need to hear. Many new converts feel disheartened when tragedy strikes, and may feel angry with God and those who promised them the so-called "good news." This lady doesn't realize that we're expressing love and concern for her eternal welfare, rather than merely proselytizing for a better lifestyle while on this earth. God has eternity in mind when He deals with us. He sees the blessings of living an eternal life," Mary replied.

Now on the other side of the mall, outside entrance number two, Bill, who was in his late thirties and John's best friend, was passing out Christian tracts about the mission of the local church he attended and their service times. The tattooed person came across Bill, who handed him a track. There were three demons following the man. One of them screamed and said to the man, *Don't listen to him! Punch him in the face!* The man's face turned red and he made a fist to strike Bill. Another demon said, *Wait, don't hit him. I have a better way to get him out of commission without getting you arrested.* The tattooed guy gave Bill the tract back, gave him a dirty look, and walked away from him.

Meanwhile, John was still inside the mall and had stopped by an ATM machine to get some cash. He waited for the person ahead of him to finish his transaction. The man had a problem with the machine, so he banged on it. When he looked back to see if anyone noticed, he saw John standing behind him. Embarrassed, he said, "This is a broken world and it sucks," as he took his cash and bankcard and started to walk away.

John responded, "I hate it when that happens, too, and I know that it is a broken world, but God plans to fix it soon."

"Don't be ridiculous, there is no God," said the man as he kept walking away.

John followed him, leaving his spot in the line, and said, "Excuse me, sir, if you don't mind me asking, why don't you believe in God?"

The man replied with a question, "Do you have children?"

"Yes, I have a thirteen-year-old daughter."

"Well, somewhere in the world at this moment, a God-believing family like yours, who prays and does everything right, has their young daughter, like yours, abducted and raped and probably killed. Can you tell me how a good God allows for this to happen?"

"You're looking at this scenario from one side. The man who is committing the crime is a person who doesn't believe in God, I assure you. And he has been influenced by the devil to do this act," John replied.

"Let's suppose for a moment that this other imaginary character does exist. Why did God create him then in the first place?"

"God created him initially as an angel; he rebelled and became the devil."

"If I were God, I would destroy the devil," the man said.

"Satan is a spirit. You can't destroy a spirit. A spirit lives forever. However, God can restrain a spirit and put it in confinement, and that's where Satan will end up. If a king or president had an uprising against him and he killed the revolting leader, then his aides and nation will always wonder if the revolting person was right. But in a freedom model, God allows the challenger, Satan, to prove his point and in the end fail and go to hell."

"Are you on drugs, man? Stop talking twilight zone and come back to earth. You're just talking fantasy. I believe in carrying a gun and protecting myself and family," said the man as he walked away again.

"What if the doctor told you that you have cancer and you have six months to live? How's the gun going to help you?"

The man froze in his spot. John got closer to him. The man replied, "Well, thanks for the horrible image. I'm beginning to dislike you."

"No, you dislike the Holy Spirit inside me that is confronting you. And He will be talking to you in the next couple of days, so you can search for the truth."

"What is truth?" the man asked.

"The truth is the fact that we're all sinners and destined to death and eternal damnation. Then Jesus came along and saved our souls from hell by believing in Him, calling on His name, and accepting His sacrifice on the cross for our salvation."

"What about the man who raped the girl; what if the rapist repented? Is Jesus going to forgive him, is Jesus going to allow serial killers into His heaven?" the man asked.

"No one gets a visa to heaven before they clear things out with God and arrange their heaven papers here on Earth, by their sincere repentance and by their receiving forgiveness. Heaven will be filled with ex-liars, ex-thieves, ex-adulterers, and yes, ex-killers."

The man was going through a tug-of-war between the Holy Spirit, who was trying to convict him of his sin, and a demon that had one hand on the man's mind to shut the door of his understanding, and the other one on his heart to harden it. Both were fighting for the man's soul.

"You wasted ten minutes of my time," the man said.

"Those were the most important ten minutes in your life. Nothing else you're doing is more important than saving your soul. I'm trying to save you from the fire of hell. The Holy Spirit is in me and is knocking on your door, and if you ask Him, He will come into you," John replied.

"Oh, so if I don't believe like you, I will go to hell. Do you see how narrow-minded this is, all these other people of other religions are going to hell?"

"It's in your hand to keep your name in the Book of Life or have it erased. Let me give you an example. Suppose your employer requires that you wear a uniform in order to be employed there? Wouldn't you do that in order to keep the job? It is their job and these are their requirements. The same thing with God. He made us and these are His requirements to be saved," John explained.

"This is all ridiculous; I wish you people would all just disappear," said the man as he started to walk away, followed by his demon who won, for now.

"We will one day soon," said John, then thought, *And what's left is people like you that you'll have to deal with, and it won't be pretty.* John kept his ears wide open to make sure the man didn't follow him and get physically violent, as had happened before.

On the other side of the mall, Bill stood outside mall entrance number two and passed out church literature. He talked to one person who said, "My wife and I were going to a church for years, and then those Christians, they interfered in our lives and made a bad influence to the point where it almost cost us our marriage."

Bill said, "I'm sorry you had a bad experience. But you still need spiritual food. Have you tried other churches?"

"We've been getting our spiritual food here and there by watching some Christian TV stations and radio."

"You know, the Bible says when you see the end is drawing near, don't abandon the assembly of the brothers and your meeting together," Bill reminded him.

"I'm comfortable with my arrangement right now. Why did I have to run into you?"

"Would you rather be comfortable here and lose your rewards in heaven? If statistics show that the devil is gaining ground over the church, then we need to help. Jesus doesn't need our help; He can do everything Himself. But He chooses to use our help. And if we don't respond to help His purpose, then He will find someone else and we lose the blessing. Remember Esther, she answered the call of God and stopped the annihilation of the Jews, by going in front of the king, her husband, in his court, breaking the rules. She took the risk of being executed herself. She trusted God and He blessed her. If she hadn't taken the risk, God would have found another person to accomplish His purpose. He already conquered the devil on Calvary and left us with a commission to spread the news. The Lord wants you back in His army. You might be a hole in the net for catching men. If your friends and neighbors look at you, they won't come to church either, because they'll think that it didn't work for you," Bill replied.

The man nodded his head and said, "I know, you're right. I'll tell my wife now. We'll give another church a try. Thanks for telling me."

"Great, and maybe you could become a counselor to other couples who are thinking of divorce. You know the Christian divorce rate is as high as the secular unbelievers' divorce rate. It is discouraging."

The man thanked Bill again and left. Bill looked at him walking away and thought, *I don't understand how Christians backslide at this day and age, when we're so close to the end.*

Then Bill looked at the crowds and said, "Lord, please send more efficient shepherds and workers, for the harvest is big."

When John arrived where Bill was, he saw him having a conversation with another person. So he stood by and listened in.

"Your God says that when He comes back, He'll destroy anyone who doesn't believe in Him. What kind of God is this?" asked the stranger.

"A good God," answered Bill. "I lived in my father's house until the age of twenty. And I remember as a teenager this phrase was mentioned a lot, 'I brought you into this world, and I'll take you out.' God has created this wonderful world for us to live in it. And people turn around and tell Him that there was a big bang and their great-grandpa was an ape, when He specifically said that He made us in His image. If I were Him, I'd be upset, too," Bill replied.

"You mean to tell me, whoever doesn't believe in Jesus goes to hell?"

"Yes. That's right."

"I see. You're one of those 'my-way-or-the-highway' crowds. That is so narrow-minded and abrupt. Sorry, but your controlling, freakish thinking is showing!" the man said.

"Well, let's say for example your child is going to put his hand in the fire and he asks you if that would be OK, what would you answer him? Do you beat around the bush by saying 'maybe,' or 'I'm not sure.' Or a do you say a solid No?" Bill asked.

"Yeah, but are you saying that a good person, all around, still goes to hell?"

"Good question. I guess someone like Hitler, by your standards, deserves to go to hell?"

"Yes. Absolutely!" the man said.

"What about a person not as evil as Hitler and not as good as Mother Teresa? Somewhere in the middle."

"Um, I don't know."

"Then where and who draws the line on when your good deeds are not equal to your bad deeds? The Bible says if you broke one of the commandments, you deserve hell."

"Look, all religions lead to God; they all have a road and a way to get you there," the man said.

"Yes, but one leads to God's redemption and salvation in heaven, and all the others will lead you to judgment by Him."

"I don't even believe that there is a God."

"Do you think that you know everything?" Bill asked.

"Um, no, I don't."

"Do you think maybe you know half of everything?"

"No."

"Let's assume you know half of everything. Is it possible that God exists in the half you don't know?" Bill inquired.

The man shrugged his shoulder.

"How do you decide right from wrong?"

The man replied quickly, "I do, I'm God of my universe."

"Well, I'm the God of my universe and I decided that I'm going to shoot you. How do you like that? The Bible says every man did what was right in his mind."

"I don't believe in the Bible. It's just one more ancient volume pulled together from the ramblings of a bunch of desert poets," the man stated.

"Well, have a good day, then."

"What, are you leaving? I thought you guys wanted to make converts of everyone. Did you lose the argument?" the man asked.

"No, but the Holy Spirit told me not to waste my time on you by arguing and it's clear you are not willing." Bill was right; the man had already hardened his heart, but his demon had instructed him to tie up Bill's time by debating and arguing, so that he wouldn't witness to other people.

"You've got that right," said the atheist. "I'm not willing to kneel to or worship anyone. You won't see me do that ever. I'll follow my own design and philosophy."

"If you don't kneel on this earth, then you're right, I'll never see you kneel where you'll be going. But I assure you, you'll kneel one day," Bill stated.

"End time's prophecy hog wash and scare tactic. You Christians put the fear of God in people in order to control them. You obviously have too much time on your hands. You and your religious sector need to mind your own business and let people do what they want. You are intruding on my life and I don't want God in my life or anything to do with Him. The gospel is only for those who lack money, those who are despairing in life's difficulties," said the man, and he left.

"God created us to be able to choose, and He honors our choices, even if we don't want anything to do with Him. He won't force you to spend eternity with Him." Then Bill looked at John and said, "Wide is the way that leads to destruction. People get offended by the truth and resent Jesus and become future objects of wrath. It's OK to be spiritual and believe anything, as long as we don't talk about Jesus."

John shook his head and said, "Don't get upset and disappointed if they don't listen to you. Shake the dust off your feet and keep going. God is in control. So, how are you doing?"

"I'm OK, praise the Lord, brother. This wasn't so bad, but earlier I encountered a dangerous and scary-looking tattooed man and I was very afraid. I thought he was going to punch me."

While he was talking, the tattooed man came back with a mall security guard. The tattooed man said to the guard, "This is the man with the hate speech."

"Excuse me, sir," said the guard to Bill. "You're under arrest for breaking the law."

"Breaking the law? All I did is pass these church tracts!" Bill replied.

"You are breaking a new law that took effect today. It is a new hate crime law that prohibits preaching in public and offending people. This man claims that you offended his life style."

"How would I offend anyone by passing a tract? I know the law took effect! But I didn't break it," Bill insisted.

"You Christians are disgusting, unloving, and intolerant and I hate you. Why don't you take your religion crap and shove it?" said the bitter tattooed man.

John said, "I wish we could have put a stop to this law from passing! I don't know how we couldn't win in preventing it from taking effect."

A demon thought, *The judge changed his mind at the last minute, thanks to our brothers in high places. The decision was made quickly and unexpectedly to get a few of you in jail and make you an example to others. That'll teach the rest of you to stay put, hunkered down, and shut you out.*

As they were talking, a police car pulled over and parked next to them. One of the officers who was arresting Bill said, "We've got another live one. There is one in every mall, a religious fanatic extremist." Then he looked at Bill as he put the handcuffs on him and said, "Why don't you leave your religion at church and at home? Don't bring it out here. You are free to practice your religion in your home and in your Christian community, period. You don't have the right to speak your viewpoint; keep your religion to yourself." The officer snickered. "But you do have the right to be silent."

The other officer said to his partner, "I don't want any trouble here. Let's just do this by the book, OK."

John assured Bill, "Don't worry, I'll bail you out." Then he looked at the officer and asked, "Which police station are you taking him to?"

"The one on Main Street."

Then, John noticed that the tattooed man had a huge knife, the size of a machete, which made it illegal, on his side, but he wasn't being arrested.

When the police car pulled away with Bill in it, John prayed, "O Lord Jesus, help Bill just like you helped the Apostle Peter when he was in jail. We're helpless, Lord, and we need you. Give us the courage to stand firm."

Then Mary and Gracie came out, and Mary asked, "Where is Bill?"

"He was just arrested. They took him away in that car," replied John sadly, as he pointed at the police car.

"Why was he arrested?" Mary asked, shocked.

"It's the new law against hate speech, if you offend anyone's viewpoint or life style, they'll arrest you."

"We tried our best to put a stop to that! All the picketing and demonstrations we held—"

"No, obviously it passed and took effect today," John interrupted.

"Mom," said Gracie, with anxiety in her tone. "Mom! The lady you just witnessed to, she is with a security guard, and they seem to be looking for someone. I think maybe they're looking for us!"

"Oh my God," said Mary, after she looked inside the mall through the door. "Let's go, let's go to the car, Hurry!" Mary out of panic said, "I'm scared, John!" John hid his fear and replied, "Don't worry, God is with us."

The three hurried to their car in the mall parking lot. Gracie walked first while John and Mary walked behind her to block her from view, because the lady would be looking for a mother and her daughter. Once they got to the car, Gracie got in first in the back seat and scrunched herself down so she wouldn't be seen, then Mary, then John got in quickly and just sat there. The security guard and the woman came outside the same mall exit through the door and looked around. The security guard was talking on the walkie-talkie in his hand. Mary scrunched down too, so that she would not be seen.

Mary said with a shaky voice, "Oh my God, oh my God, help us, please. Help us, O Lord, we're strangers and aliens in this world, and we need you. We have no one else to go to but you. Protect us from the evil one, but lead us not into temptation. We know that you won't take us out of this world, so we ask you to protect us while we're here." Then she looked at John and asked, "What is happening to this world; whatever happened to the freedom of speech?"

"I agree that punishing behavior is right. But punishing thought is wrong, and it goes against the freedom of speech. If they are going to regulate speech, belief, and thought, will they come up with thought police next? Freedom of speech is restricted against the truth of the gospel, but it is OK for filthy speech. I wonder what would happen if there were a Bible hate speech law. So many people are so bitter, against Christianity in particular. Satan is tightening his grip. Jezebel is on the loose."

Gracie asked, "Who is Jezebel?"

"She was an evil queen, a Baal worshiper in the Old Testament, who hunted down the prophet Elijah. Dogs ate her flesh before she was able to kill Elijah and her carcass was as dung upon the face of the field, and no one buried her. This is fulfillment of the signs of the end that the Lord gave us. So we should lift up our heads, for our deliverance is near," John explained.

Gracie looked up through her back seat car window and said, "They're gone; we can leave now, Dad."

And they drove away.

* * * * * *

John dropped off Mary and Gracie at home, and then went to the police station to bail Bill out. When they exited the police station, Bill asked, "Where did you park your car?"

"I couldn't find a spot here, the place is packed. I had to park a block away. Business is good here today."

Bill said, as they walked towards the car, "Thank you, brother, for bailing me out. You know, the Apostle Peter was in jail sleeping awaiting his execution when an angel appeared and opened the doors of the jail cell for him. You are my angel today, arranging for my bail."

John looked at Bill's face and asked, "What happened to your eye?"

"I'm a thorn in the kingdom of Satan and a soldier for Jesus Christ, and a soldier is expected to be wounded in battle. I'm glad to suffer for Jesus because He suffered for me."

"That's right. When Satan gives us lemons, we make lemonade," John replied.

"They want us to keep our mouths shut and only discuss religion in a special building one day a week. This is a time when it is easier to talk to God about people than it is to talk to people about God. I tell you, the Christian brothers turned the jail station to a preaching station. But Christians who are on the front line working for Jesus to advance the Kingdom are on Satan's black and hate list, and he's inflicted on us the most brutal attacks. In these uncertain days, God is looking for some strong and steel-like saints, Christians with iron in their souls!"

John admired Bill's courage and thought, *A couple of hours in jail has produced faith and character in him. He became a genuine velvet-covered brick, soft on the outside, but strong on the inside. Oh Lord, use adversity to bring about that kind of maturity in me. Give me the power to be bold, and courage to be able to witness and stand my ground. Amen.*

"When threatened, we pray for help from on high and we'll stand firm while rejoicing," continued Bill. "Thousands of angels clap for us when we stand up for Christ. At least I only have a black eye. The early Christians and apostles were severely persecuted, yet they still rejoiced for their reward is great in heaven.

"Now I know that it's not a natural reaction to 'leap for joy', when we're mistreated because of our faith in Christ! But I know that God sees and hears what others say and do to us because of our faith. Jesus told of the parable of the farmer who went out and hired laborers at six a.m., nine a.m., and twelve p.m., then he went out and hired more laborers at three and five p.m. because his harvest was too big. Then he paid them all the same wages at six p.m., we're the generation of the five p.m., at the last hour and the last harvest, and our reward is the same as those who worked before us. There's a large harvest and a heavenly reward waiting for us."

"Amen. But really, what happened to your eye?" John repeated.

Bill touched his eye ever so gently as it seemed to be painful to the touch and said, "There was a man in the jail cell who was describing the horrible conditions on the street outside, drive-by shootings, mugging, and rape. A man who was sitting in the corner, who later on I found out was blind, said, 'I wish I could see all that.' So I started sharing the words of God with them. Some of them started mocking me and ridiculing me. But the blind man was encouraged by my speech; the soil was right in his heart. So they asked him why he was in jail and the blind man answered, 'I was carrying a sign that said 'the end is here, Jesus is coming.' They laughed at him and one man said, 'End times doom and gloom. You people prophesy based on what you see on the news. First, it was Saddam Hussein in the nineties and when he was neutralized, you came up with new dangerous men. In the first decade of this century, it was North Korea and Iran. What happens if these threats are removed, are they going to go after China? They're just selling books, that's all there is to it. The world goes around on and on.'"

John said, "In the last days, scoffers will come, scoffing and following their own evil desires. They will say, 'Where is this coming he promised?' Ever since our fathers died, everything goes on as it has since the beginning of creation."

"Exactly, and I said to the man, 'I see what you're saying, and I'd rather people read these books than the books of the devil's agents who are attacking Christianity and poisoning the minds and putting doubts in their faith. And if you don't want to read either side's story, then read the Bible. Everything you need to know is in there, from the beginning to the end. As for prophesying based on events, Jesus did say watch and pray. So you'd be asleep if you don't watch world events and see where we are in the end time prophetic clock and at the same time being ready all the time for Jesus' coming.'

"The man said, 'If you believe in the Bible!'

"Then another man asked me, 'Preacher, did this man sin or did his parents sin for him to be born blind?'

"And I answered, 'Neither he nor his father sinned, but this is for God to be glorified. This man will manage his life until Jesus comes.'

"A man asked, 'What kind of a cruel God does this?'

"And I replied, 'His plan is bigger than all of us.'

"Then the blind man said to me, 'I feel the anointing and the presence of the Holy Spirit on you, brother. Can you heal me?'

"Everybody started laughing and I said, 'Yes, I'll pray for you.' So I prayed and said 'Lord, I don't want to put you on the spot,' and then I thought, 'How can anyone put Him on the spot?' When I finished praying for him, the man said, 'I can see.' It was a miracle right there in the jail cell. Now the rest of the guys attacked us and beat us up, and said that the man was a liar and was never blind in the first place. The guards had to separate us into a different cell."

John didn't expect that the blind man would see, and said, "Praise God, nothing is impossible to Him."

The two continued walking down the street and Bill went on, "Suffering isn't the worst thing that can happen to us. Disobedience to God is the worst thing. I'd rather be insulted and persecuted than spend eternity in hell. Faith is under fire, and we're not just going to stand by and watch them muzzle the gospel and silence the church. Our laws guarantee the freedom of religion. I respect and obey the authorities, but when it interferes with God's business, I say no. We're commanded not to speak or witness, but we must obey God rather than men. We work for God and that's where we get our marching orders from. No earthly government or parliament has the authority to overrule God."

John said, "Remember the midwives in Pharaoh's time? They disobeyed Pharaoh when he asked them to kill all the newborn male Jews, and the Lord blessed them for that. Then you have the Magi; they disobeyed Herod the king when they didn't go back and report to him where the baby Jesus was living. The more persecutions they inflict on us, the sooner our deliverance gets near. Hallelujah... So, how do we proceed from here?"

"We maintain our gracious Christian witness. We'll just have to be careful; we can't stop witnessing. First century believers did it and passed the baton of faith on to us. We need to move beyond the defensive line of Christianity and move on to the offensive to advance the kingdom, fulfill the great commission, and tell others about Jesus. Our Shepherd will never lead us where His strength cannot keep us. He will never lead us down a path that He hasn't first walked down Himself. We have courage, not because of who we are, but because of whom we serve. We need supernatural power to be bold and to be able to withstand persecution. We're in the witness protection program now, and God Himself is our protector. I hope it'll be safe to worship in church."

John turned around a street corner and said, "Are you joking? They'll be censoring the Sunday sermons coming from the pulpit in every church. Every Christian hater will flock to church to get a pastor on a cell phone camera, and record anything negative regarding homosexuals or radical Islam. Then they'll submit that to the authorities as evidence of hate speech. If they can put a couple of pastors in jail, the whole church freedom concept will change completely. Pastors will walk on eggshells and tiptoe around any controversial subject. We'll have to monitor who comes to church, something never done before. You know, it is easier to join a church right now than to join any club. We'll have to go from inviting people to church to screening them. God help us."

"Abortion activists say 'keep your hand off my reproductive organs.' Gays shout, 'stay out of our bedrooms.' Christian ministers would be within their right to say 'stay out of our pulpit.' This country better change course or severe judgment is on its way," Bill replied.

John said, "God always tested His people before entering into a promise to a breakthrough. The Jews were asked to go through the desert and face giants before entering the Promised Land. And we're going through a test phase right now before the rapture, to see who has the strong foundation and who is just sitting on the fence."

Bill said, "One person said that I was a fanatic to go witnessing on the streets. There are those who say all you have to do is believe in Jesus and you're saved. They promise a smooth flight, but those who are already on board are suffering turbulence. Name it and claim it and it's all yours - health and happiness. The church wonders why there is a silent exodus of people slipping out the back doors and the big catch is disappearing. It's because new converts respond experimentally, simply to see if the wonderful life is as good as Christians make it to be."

Finally, when they arrived at where the car was parked, they found two guys stealing the tires off of John's car.

"Hey, that's my car and those are my tires. Stop!" screamed John.

The two thieves grabbed one tire that they already took off the car and ran with it. John started running after them, when Bill stopped him and said, "Wait, John, stop. Come back here. What are you doing?"

"That's my tire!" replied John as he started walking back.

"Come here, John." Bill put his arm around him. "Look at them." John turned around and looked at them running. "They don't even have a car; and they're running away with a tire. Look at how ridiculous they look."

Bill burst into laughter. John started to see the humor and he laughed, too. They both laughed for a couple of minutes. Then Bill said, "Oh, that was a good laugh. Look, they were working on the second tire, too. They can only carry two tires; let's get the spare tire mounted and get out of here."

While they were mounting the spare tire, John said, "Now I have to go and buy a new tire."

"I'll pay for it. Our deliverance is near, my brother. When we get to heaven, we won't need tires or money. The more evil I see, the more assured I am that Jesus is on the way." Then they got in the car and drove away singing, 'I'm a friend of God, He calls me friend. I'm a friend of God.'

John became more confident that night because of Bill's chains, and was now much bolder to speak the word without fear.

Time for Church

Sunday morning, Jim reluctantly got ready to go church, acting on John's invitation to him.

Daemon tried to discourage him from going and said, *Why do you want to waste your time? You could be sleeping in; your body needs the rest. You know you have to wear a special dress code to go to church. There'll be new, annoying people to meet there.* Jim continued dressing up. When hassling Jim didn't work, Daemon said, *OK, you want to go, fine, I'll show you how phony Christian are.*

Jim did get to church, where he met John. In contrast to the mall, the presence of God was tangible in this place.

While they were talking, John said, "Excuse me, I have to go to the restroom. I'll be right back."

While Jim was standing there by himself, a member of the church, wearing a name tag, approached him and said, "Hello, is this your first time here?"

"Yes."

"It's a nice church; they play bingo and serve food sometimes."

Daemon connected with the demon associated with this man and said, "Hey, do something to discourage Jim from coming back here. I have to convince him that Christians are fake people."

The demon whispered in his subject's ears, *Hey, you didn't make your quota this month and you need to sell more new policies.*

The man then asked Jim, "Excuse me, do you have life insurance?"

"Yes I do, through my employer."

"If you need additional insurance or if you ever need a stocks and bonds consultant, just give me a call." Then he reached into his pocket and gave Jim a business card and said, "I do very well for my clients."

Then the man left and Daemon thought, *Strike one.*

When John got back, Jim said, "I'm glad you're back." He told John what happened and asked, "Do Christians do business here?"

John apologized for the incident and said, "Don't let this discourage you, not everyone is like that. One time, Jesus made a whip and drove a bunch of merchants out of His father's temple over two thousand years ago. Not much has changed. And please don't make an opinion about God based on what you see and hear at church today. Just because people become Christians, it doesn't mean that they are perfect people and don't sin. We're a bunch of sinners who meet here to learn the ways of God. Everyone makes mistakes."

The two men sat next to each other in a pew in the back so John could answer any questions Jim came up with. Then the service started and a speaker said, "Aren't you glad you're in this church and belong to this denomination and not the one down the block?" People clapped and cheered. Then he said, "Aren't you proud of the leader of this church?" pointing at the pastor. Again, people clapped and the pastor accepted the praise. Daemon and nine other demons stood up, shot their arrows at the pastor, and said, *Pride of life.*

Daemon thought, *Strike two. This is going very well!*

Jim whispered, "I thought you said denominations didn't matter?"

John was embarrassed and replied, "Don't pay attention to that, he's a visiting pastor. I have been to too many churches, big and small of different denominations, and none of them are perfect and without fault. So, to answer your question, I really don't know why this pastor said that."

Daemon, after consulting with other demons, thought, *I know why, we gave him a little success and it got to his head. He hasn't prayed at home for days, busy with reading books, counseling people, going to seminars, visiting other churches. He's too busy with the business of the King, so he lost his affection for the King. He is going down a slippery slide.*

Then the same pastor asked people to contribute to a project the church was working on, and he asked people to stand up and declare in public how much they were going to contribute. People stood up one at a time from the different corners of the church and announced how much they were going to contribute and their names were broadcasted. Some said a hundred dollars, and some said two and five hundred dollars as people cheered and clapped.

Daemon said, *Strike three!*

Jim noticed that John wasn't participating in this event.

Daemon said, *Your buddy here is too cheap to donate!*

After a few minutes, Jim was curious and asked John, "Why aren't you participating in this auction?"

John answered, "I don't want to lose my reward with God by declaring how much I give to the church publicly. I'm going to put my contribution in an envelope and discreetly put it in the donation box later on."

Daemon said, *Now that you've heard these hypocrites, I know that you're just itching to leave. You have work tomorrow. C'mon, let's go."*

Jim agreed and did want to leave, but he was too shy to get up because everybody would see him go.

Daemon picked up on that thought, *If you leave and never come back, you don't have to worry about what they think.*

Jim saw the same point and said to John, "Excuse me, I'm going to use the restroom." He stood up, and walked away with no intention to come back. When Jim was almost outside, a very attractive young woman with tight clothing came out of the women's bathroom and gave Jim a very sexy smile. Jim smiled back and got aroused by her beauty and perfume. The woman went back to the church service. Jim couldn't help but follow her back into the auditorium to see where she was sitting. He sat next to John again, but kept his eyes on her.

Daemon went to the demon associated with the woman to inquire about her. The demon said, "She already has a boyfriend and she only comes to church to please her mother. She likes to tease other men, and she hasn't met the new face yet, Jim!"

Daemon said, "I'd like you to discourage this because I don't want my slave to come back to church again on her account!"

The demon said, "No problem, brother, we work together. I'll take care of it."

Shortly after, the young woman had a cramp that caused her to stand up and leave with her mother at her side. When they left their pew, the young woman noticed Jim, but wasn't friendly at all this time.

Daemon said, *You shouldn't think about her anymore. She is not interested in you.*

Then the ushers started collecting money for tithes and offerings.

Daemon said, *Look at these fools; they're giving away their hard earned money to this preacher who probably drives a better car than they do. It's highway robbery; they just want your money here. You have to pay for membership, just like any other club.*

The pressure mounted as the ushers approached and got closer to Jim. Jim thought, *What should I do now? I don't have any cash on me.*

Just roll your hand to make a fist as if you have money in it, and when the ushers come, pretend like you are putting money in the basket, answered Daemon.

Jim did just that.

Later on in the service, ushers came out for collection again.

Daemon mocked, *They are just making sure that if you have any spare change, they will clean you out and send you home. At least when you gamble you have a chance of winning, but the situation here is lose, lose, and lose. By the way, that guy from the third floor invited you to a gambling night tomorrow. I think you should go.*

Jim thought, *I don't gamble!*

Yes, but you go to Las Vegas! replied Daemon.

That's different, it's just entertainment. You're the one who told me that it was OK to gamble there, and that it wasn't really gambling, just pure fun!

Yes, he's right, I did tell him that, I forgot, thought Daemon, then said, *Let's leave this subject now and go back to the ushers. Here they come, let's leave now.*

No, I already did that once. It's too late to leave now, anyway. No, I'll just do the hand lump thing, Jim thought.

As the ushers got closer to John and Jim, Jim noticed that John didn't put anything in the basket, so Jim didn't have to lie and pretend to put any money in the basket.

At the end of the sermon, the preacher prayed the sinner's prayer and invited unsaved people to respond to the message they had heard that day and give their heart to Jesus Christ.

Daemon distracted Jim from listening to that invitation by saying, *Hey, you know the project that you're working on has a deadline that is approaching. You need to meet that deadline.*

Jim got preoccupied with that thought and missed the preacher's invitation to give his heart to Jesus. John didn't try to pressure Jim into that because accepting Jesus had to be sincere and from the heart. If he accepted the call because of pressure, he would get out of it just as easily.

Later on, the pastor introduced a visiting missionary who gave an encouraging report about the progress of their missionary activities in a foreign country. The missionary said that they had a shortage of neckties for the missionaries there, and requested every brother to donate their neckties and said that he would deliver them personally. The pastor took off his tie, then all the men started taking off their neckties. John couldn't believe that this was happening today, of all Sundays.

Daemon had a field day with that one and said, *Well, isn't this precious? First they tried to sell you something, then they tapped into your wallet, twice, and now they're taking away your clothes. How about that? Now just imagine for a minute here if there was a shortage of pants in that country. Just look around and imagine for a second how ridiculous these people would look if there were a shortage of pants, just imagine that.* Jim started giggling to himself. Daemon continued, *OK, I think you've seen enough. I just wanted to show you what becoming a Christian would entail and how they are only after your money. I'm telling you, man, we'd better leave here soon before it gets worse. And let's not come back here again.*

Jim nodded in agreement and waited for an opportunity to leave.

Daemon muttered, *I'll be damned if I let you contribute to this effort. My brothers are fighting fiercely over there, tooth and nail against those missionaries. Ah, I guess I'm damned anyways.*

The Holy Spirit advised John not to give up his necktie because it would be a hindrance and a stumbling block for Jim and would put Jim on the spot. John just sat there and didn't participate like the rest of the brothers. And just before Jim wanted to stand up and leave, John said, "God will supply all His servant's needs. They should just give the spiritual food and the rules of the Kingdom and stop finding new ways to have the flock give money. The Holy Spirit will lead the flock and tell them when and how much to give."

John was disappointed at the church service that day and thought, *The pastor shouldn't pressure his flock to tithe or attend every church meeting. Instead, he should have faith in God to provide for his ministry in finance and membership.*

"I'm done here. Would you like to leave now?" John asked.

Jim was relieved and replied, "Yes, sure."

Then Jim asked, "What is this Rapture thing that the preacher was talking about? Is it that vicious type of dinosaur we see at the movies?"

John smiled and said, "No, it isn't a dinosaur at all. It is actually a moment of time when Jesus decides to snatch His church, which is made up of born again believers, out of earth to go to heaven. It is a private party affair, invited guests only, extended to those who responded to the hope of Jesus Christ's glorious appearing."

"After they die?"

"No, while they are alive and in the blink of an eye. Dead righteous people will be resurrected at that time, too. Jesus the shepherd will take care of His sheep and take them to Heaven," John answered.

"Well, I have never heard that before."

"I can tell you all about that, if you like. Why don't you come to our Bible study on Wednesday night?"

Daemon said, *No thanks, we'll wait until we see this mysterious and goofy Rapture, and then believe in Jesus.*

"Maybe," replied Jim then asked, "I was always puzzled by God being three persons in one. What does that mean?"

"It's hard to understand everything about God, especially when we are locked in time, space, and matter, but not God. To understand God is like containing the Atlantic Ocean in a small cup. The Bible only tells us enough that we can handle for now until we graduate from this life. But for now, it remains a mystery. The Bible tells us that there's the Father, the Son and the Holy Spirit. What the Father thinks, the Son told us and the Holy Spirit has been and still is acting upon. Rather than an analogy of adding units, one plus one plus one equals three, the Trinity could be explained as multiplying wholeness, one times one times one, equals one."

Jim seemed puzzled.

"OK, it's like an egg. It has three parts, the white, the yolk, and the shell. It's one egg, but it actually has three parts."

Jim responded to that one better, by nodding.

"Or like water, can be liquid, or ice, or steam…"

"OK. I get the picture," said Jim with a smile.

As they were talking, Gracie came over, looked at Jim and said, "Hi." Then she said to John, "Dad, Mom is waiting in the car."

"OK," John responded, then said to Jim, "this is my daughter, Gracie."

"Hi, nice to meet you." Jim smiled and said to John, "I'll see you at work then. Bye."

Controversial Lunch

Monday, John decided to go out for lunch instead of the company's cafeteria, to avoid any conflicts with his boss regarding his praying. He went to a local cafeteria, got his lunch, sat down, bowed his head to pray and asked for the blessing. After he finished saying grace, he noticed some people who saw him pray get a little embarrassed; they rubbed their eyebrows or forehead.

John thought, *they don't know what they're missing in Jesus' wonderful gift of Salvation. God sent His Son to die for us. He rose from the grave and ascended into heaven for us. He's coming again for us! I'm not going to be ashamed and will let my prayer of blessing turn into an evangelistic opportunity.*

While he was eating he overheard a voice say, "ASHTA SHAMA SHAKALAAM, in the name of Jesus, Heal…" then there was loud laughter. The voice came from several people sitting behind him, having a discussion. John was disturbed to hear that and wondered, *what synagogue of demons produced these Christian scoffers.* John could not help but listen to what they were saying.

"No seriously, speaking in tongues is one of the gifts of the Holy Spirit," the second person said.

John thought, *maybe I was wrong about this person. He's making sense now.*

"I don't believe in speaking in tongues," said the first person. "I think the first century Christians spoke different languages from other countries. How come we don't see tongues of fire over their heads when they speak in tongues today?"

The second person asked, "Which is easier to believe speaking in tongues or the stones talking?"

The first person asked, "Are you talking about the time when Jesus entered Jerusalem on a donkey, and the whole crowd of disciples began joyfully to praise God in loud voices for all the miracles they had seen? When some of the Pharisees in the crowd said to Jesus, 'Teacher, rebuke your disciples!' and Jesus said, 'If they keep quiet, the stones will cry out'. Well, that's different."

The second person asked, "What about the prophet who had a conversation with a donkey? Why should talking in tongues be more mysterious?"

By now it seemed to John as if there were three people having this conversation. John couldn't see the people who were having this conversation because they were sitting behind him with a barrier in between. Meanwhile, all the demons present in the cafeteria abandoned their subjects, who were gossiping and talking about the stock market, infidelity, and other worldly matters, and gathered around those believers to see what they were saying, because when believers talked, demons listened and would try to plot and strategize against them.

"OK, even if speaking in tongues is possible," continued the first person, "and it did happen to the first century Christians to complete the Bible, could they just please not push it on me?"

John thought, *no problem, it's only one of the gifts of the Holy Spirit and speaking in tongues is the last one mentioned.*

"What bothers me is that they tell other Christians that unless they speak in tongues, they don't have the Holy Spirit. Can you imagine the damage to other true and sincere Christians who don't have that particular gift? Don't they know that Christians who don't get the gift of speaking in tongues will have doubts in their salvation and reject Christianity? Are they trying to monopolize the Holy Spirit? And doesn't the Bible say that they should interpret when speaking in tongues? I didn't see anyone interpreting when I went one time for a visit.

"If they speak in tongues and can't speak English with others or have no love, they're just making noise. You know Dan; he's one of them. We had a double date, and his wife looked down at my wife because she was wearing pants. Now, what do pants, hair, or makeup have to do with salvation, and where is the love when they start judging others? As far as I know, when the command was given in the Old Testament, men didn't wear slacks they all wore flat gowns. Slacks weren't introduced until much later on. When God said that men shouldn't dress up like women, He was warning against the homosexuals, men shouldn't be effeminate by dressing up like women."

John thought, *if they're only following a human tradition of the world and only as a preference, then a dress code is OK to justify. If they do it to be accepted by God, then they're in danger of falling away from grace. Holiness isn't the way to Christ; Christ is the way to holiness. We don't work our way to Him – He is the way. I always say religion is nothing but a set of rules and traditions that make sinful people conduct themselves better. But it can't really change a person's heart and overcome a sinful nature.*

He wished that he could go over and tell them what he thought, but the seating arrangement was single tables with two chairs each. So he continued eating and thought, *I always tell my ladies 'If it isn't for sale, don't advertise.' So they've learned to look in the mirror before they go out of the house and check if the way they're dressed would make anyone stumble. Everything should be done in order, whether pants or skirts. It shouldn't be revealing or too tight, enticing men to lust.*

John thought that there were three voices at first, but later he could only recognize two.

One of the guys sounded like he was slurping his soup before asking the next question, "At least they don't follow the mother and son worship with their idols and repetitious prayers! If the Lord Jesus said, 'I'm the only way,' what is it they don't understand about that?"

"What I don't understand is how Easter eggs and bunnies got into the picture of the Lord's crucifixion and resurrection."

"I know how, and believe me, you don't want to know! But it seems like people want Easter without the cross of Calvary. I think that the church has failed to fulfill the Great Commission and ignored the teaching of God. There are many denominations that no longer hold the Bible as the inerrant teaching of God; they don't see the need for it because the public school is their religion. That's what's causing spiritual apostasy, falling away from the word of God, and rejection of the truth."

The Holy Spirit within John seemed to grieve and John lost his appetite when he heard Christians divided over issues that weren't the core or foundation of the Christian faith. He thought, *they were choking on bones instead of eating the meat.*

"So, are you buying a Christmas tree this year?"

"Um—, um—" there was a delay as the person swallowed his food. "There goes another pagan holiday, which the Old Testament warned about. No, I'm not going to do that, tradition or not! We all know that the Lord wasn't born in December, so what's the point? They turned Christmas from a holy day to a holiday filled with booze and commercialism. They don't even call it Christmas anymore, it's Xmas now or happy holidays. The church is in a spiritual famine and Christians are anemic, lacking the word of God in their lives. Satan's has increased the ways of pleasure and entertainment to keep the Christians from reading the Bible."

"If parents would spend the same time and effort with their children convincing them that there is a Santa Claus, and tell their children about Jesus instead, a lot of souls would be saved."

John thought, *we don't worship the Christmas tree, but this Son who was nailed on the tree.* And then he remembered the scripture that said 'Don't let anyone judge you by what you eat or drink, or with regard to a religious festival, a new moon celebration or a Sabbath day.'

Then the same man continued, "Some churches are putting gold and silver on the doorposts instead of applying the blood of the lamb, Jesus, to cover their sins. Today, false religion says blood is gory....And what about these men of God that molest children? Don't they know that the Bible says if a person is in heat, it is better to get married than to sin? And that if someone offends a child, it would be better to put a millstone around their neck and throw them in the river?"

The other man said, "There is one holiday I'll never participate in, and that's Halloween. That's a no-no!"

The two men said, "Amen."

John thought, *Amen,* and was glad that the two men agreed on one thing.

Then one person said, "Hey, you know, we're members of the only two denominations that actually go door to door to witness, yet we're the most rejected among denominations!"

The other person answered, "The Bible does say that we will be hated for His name's sake."

"I'm just going to keep doing what the Lord tells me to do in His word. Why don't you join us? We'll give you a bike, a white shirt and tie and a helmet, no more nonsense about being one of the one hundred and forty four thousand elect. I hear you have exceeded that number!"

It started to get noisy at the restaurant, and John leaned backwards so he could hear the reply, as it was harder to hear the two men.

"Well, I don't want to be a god after I die, either, there is only one God. And thank you, but I can only afford one wife for now. What is it called... polygamy?"

"Hey, we don't do that anymore!" There was a pause. "At least you and I don't believe in the rapture. They really think that they are going to fly in the air!"

"Yeah, really. We'd better get going or we'll be late. What about Saturday worship, and the Sabbath, what's that all about?"

As they both stood up to leave, the other man said, "Yeah right, what about prophesying? The Bible is complete, and you cannot add anything to it. And if all anyone is going to say is something that is from the Bible, how is it prophesying? I think if Jesus said..." The voices grew faint after that, as they left.

Then John looked back out of curiosity and he saw four guys walking away, two dressed up casually and two dressed up in suits. He wasn't sure which two were sitting behind him.

When John turned around, a handsome, well-dressed man was standing at the other end of his table with a smile on his face. He politely asked, "May I share this table with you? The cafeteria is packed and there is no room to sit anywhere."

John looked back at the table where the two had just left from and sure enough, it was already occupied and the restaurant was indeed full. The place was known for its good soup, and that packed the place.

John replied, "Yes, sure!" for the man asked in a polite way and had a peaceful smile on his face.

The man sat at John's table. He looked like an executive, and only had a bowl of soup and a small salad. He said, "I just overheard two guys argue about baptism, whether it is required or not, and whether to submerge or sprinkle."

John replied with a smile, "Yes, I think I know who you're talking about. Those two guys were sitting behind me and they were bashing other denominations. Very sad. I think if it can be arranged and water is available, then submerge. If not, then God understands the circumstances. Jesus' message and instructions are simple; man tries to complicate them."

Then the man bowed his head and prayed first. John was very impressed. The man took a sip of soup and said, "I don't know why Christians criticize each other about this or that. When the denominations are divided, the world says look at them, they can't even get along between themselves. But when Christians are united, we have a greater opportunity to reach our world. And a church united can make a better impression on the world. Knowledge has greatly increased in the church, but there's a lack of genuine love."

"Yes, I noticed that, too," said John. "These days, it seems like most religious Christians say that they follow Christ, but want to pick and chose what they want to believe in, what is right, and what is wrong. Churches have become consumer centers where everyone wants his or her own style of worship or programs. People want a 'make me feel good' church, send me home feeling good, don't stir anything, and don't confront or convict me. They want to have some theology that promotes attaining material things, but don't bring up the cross or the blood of the Lamb."

The man said, "When denominations fight against each other, it only hurts the little flock. Satan and his workers are organized and undivided. If only believers could be united in their defense and their warfare, Satan would not win so many victories. The Lord Jesus said 'a house divided will fall,' Sad to say, Christians too often are so busy fighting one another that they have no time for fighting the devil."

"I agree," said John as he finished off the food on his plate. "Even the leaders of the church are fighting among themselves, calling others cotton candy preachers and criticizing others for having a bodyguard, or comparing the size of the congregation or the size of the worship building. Many polished preachers, with high style of leadership and padded pews, are preaching prosperity and expect every Christian to be as prosperous as they are."

The man nodded his head in agreement and said, "Meanwhile, there is a preacher in Africa who lives in a hut and preaches to naked people. Spiritual leaders are not supposed to be above the people or higher than the people. The ground is level at the cross. We're all made priests, and we can all go to God ourselves. The church isn't built on preachers but on Jesus Christ, the only perfect pastor," said the man. "God is very capable of raising workers for the harvest. He'll find a way to deliver His message to the little flock. Jesus Christ is the master Teacher, and His message is very simple and there is no need to add anything to it. The pastors are not the chefs, they are the waiters. A preacher doesn't prepare the meal, the meal is already cooked. All they have to do is deliver it and serve it to the people."

John finished off his drink and said, "That's very true. It's like giving someone the Mona Lisa as a gift, and they turn around and modify the picture, thinking they can make it better, only to make a priceless item worthless. But I'm concerned also about the church splits and denomination squabbles. They should be part of the same body. The mouth doesn't bite the hands off its body, nor does the eye say 'I don't like this face' and slap it."

The man said with passion, "Yes, the Lord also said that the gates of hell will not prevail against His church. He knows how to take care of His bride. The church is the bride and body of Christ and Christ is the head and the foundation of the church. People of God are the church. The church isn't a religious physical building made with bricks, but is supposed to be an embassy of heaven. When Jesus set up the church, He didn't want it to be a religious club, but a place where His sheep could receive help, training in the laws of His kingdom. And be provided the spiritual food they need for effective life on earth."

John was captivated by what the man said, but couldn't help looking at his watch to see if it was time for him to go back to work.

"He loves the church even though the church isn't perfect and has no perfect people. The blood of Jesus provides the righteousness for sewing the wedding dress on the inside, while on the outside; the righteous acts of the saints sew the dress. Men are not saved by works, but are saved unto works. Faith without works is dead, and the saints work in response to faith in Jesus.

"The Groom is absent now in heaven; you haven't seen Him yet. You love Him as the deer pants for streams of water, and so your souls pant for Him, your souls thirst for God, for the living God. The church is supposed to be united in intimacy with union and communion so that it would stand before Him with joy in that day. Christians should contribute to the beauty of the bride and work together. However, the liberal church is denying and refusing the Bible, the love letters from Jesus. The engagement vows are broken. The night is coming when no one can work."

By now, John felt chills going down his back after hearing all this because this person spoke as a theologian with authority.

Then the stranger said, "You see, John, you should trust God and believe that He's in control. Only God, who knows all your work, can judge. Don't judge anyone."

John said, "But you know..."and he paused for a second, wondering how this man knew his name. He felt his badge, which was tucked inside his pocket, which he usually does as soon as he leaves the office. So the stranger couldn't have known his name by looking at the badge. And just when he tried to ask the stranger how he knew his name, he felt something fall at his feet. He looked down and it was a lady's purse. He looked back up and there stood a woman who had a neck brace on.

She said, "Oh, I'm so sorry."

He leaned down to pick it up for her. He gave her the purse and said, "No problem, ma'am."

She thanked him and walked away.

When he looked back, the stranger had already disappeared. His tray was still on the table and on it was a napkin that had something scribbled on it. John became fidgety now, wondering how the stranger knew his name. He couldn't have left without saying goodbye first; he was too gracious for that. John couldn't wait anymore. He picked up the napkin and looked at it, and on it was written - Prov 29:25.

John went to the restroom to look for the man, but no one was there. He went back to his table, the trays were gone, and new customers were already sitting there. He thought of asking the woman with the neck brace if she saw where the man went, but it was getting late and he had to go back to work.

He rushed to his car to see what the verse said. He got into his car, opened his pocket Bible and quickly turned to the book of Proverbs. The pages stuck together as he hastily flipped through them. Finally he got the verse out and read it, then looked at the napkin again and read the verse again, and it said, 'The fear of man brings a snare, but whoever leans on and puts his confidence in the Lord is safe and set on high.'

John felt as if a ton of bricks hit him, followed by a bucket of ice-cold water. His heart skipped a beat or two as he realized what this all meant.

He thought, *the stranger was as wise as Solomon, and as confident as the Lord Jesus. He knew my name and read my mind. Was he the Lord Jesus Himself or a messenger?* He wondered, as he was sure that it was a divine encounter, *who am I, for God to send me a special message this way?*

A devil said, *You blew it, buddy. You refused to pray at work for the fear of men.* But the Holy Spirit rebutted, *Your belt of truth is dragging, tighten it up.* John did by confessing his sin.

He put his head on the steering wheel and started crying and prayed, "Oh Lord God almighty, you're all-knowing; forgive me, I'll never be ashamed of You again. I'll pray before my meals at work and everywhere I go. Give me the strength of Daniel in the lion's den. Forgive me by your mercy. I worship You right now in Jesus' name, oh Lord—"

At that moment, he heard a horn beep, coming from the car parked next to him. He lifted his head up and a lady in the next car had already rolled down her windows and gestured for him to roll his window down. And as he wiped the remaining tears, he rolled down his window. She then asked him, "Are you all right? Should I call someone?"

"No thanks."

"If you are going through a divorce, things will get better. I was devastated by my first divorce. Now, it doesn't scare me anymore after I have gone through a couple of them."

"Thanks, ma'am, have a good day," said John as he started his car to go back to work.

John was very happy, as something supernatural had happened to him. He couldn't wait to tell his family and church friends. When he got to the parking attendant he said, "Praise the Lord."

The attendant looked at him with a straight face, as if John was from another planet, and said, "Just pay the fee, man, and get the hell out of here, freak." John, still cheerful, said, "Yes sir." He paid the fee and exited the parking structure.

He was driving cheerfully, saying, "Hallelujah," and praising the Lord. As he merged into the traffic outside the parking structure, a truck cut him off and then the traffic stopped at the traffic light immediately. On the back window of the truck that cut him off were written the words 'F— YOU.'

John became angry and thought, *why would anyone put these words on the back of their car? If I would report the driver, the liberals for the freedom of speech will probably protect him.* John also wondered what would happen if he were to put the word 'Hallelujah' on the back of his car, if there would be a freedom of speech then or if his car would be subjected to attacks from heathens. The Holy Spirit said, *Keep your cool, John, and don't let the enemy steal your joy. Remember, a minute ago you touched the heart of God and were praising Him. You should know the enemy's tactics by now.* John took a deep breath and calmed himself down.

Raphael, who was in the front passenger seat, looked at the offending truck's back window through the dark glass and saw a demon with a smirk on his face.

The traffic light turned green and moved forward and shortly after, John saw another bumper sticker on a car that said, 'In case of rapture this vehicle will be unmanned.' John smiled and the Holy Spirit said, *There are many people just like you out there who are obeying the word of God and waiting for His coming. You're not alone, son.*

Born Again

Tuesday, Jim phoned John at work and asked him if he would like to join him for lunch in the cafeteria at work. They met at the cafeteria, picked out their lunch, and sat down to eat. John remembered his vow to God from the day before and bowed his head to say grace before he started to eat.

When he finished praying Jim asked, "Why do you have to pray before eating?"

John answered after taking a bite, "When I was a kid, we had a dog who loved to eat all day. I mean, if there was food, whatever kind, it would eat it. I never saw it refuse food, and the minute you put that plate down, its head was in the bowl, digging in. See, that's an animal that wasn't created in the image of God. On the other hand, God gave us the ability to pray and praise Him and thank Him for what He has given us—"

Jim's expression started to change as he put together where John was going with this.

The Holy Spirit said, *Slow down, John, he's just a babe in the truth and he might get offended by this.*

John was in the middle of his sentence and had no idea how to get out of this subject now. Suddenly, a man stopped by their table and said, "Hey Jim, I read your report and am looking forward to the next milestone to be completed, so please keep me in the loop on that one." John was thankful for the sudden interruption by Jim's colleague.

Jim answered the man, "Yes, sure, no problem."

When the man left, Jim turned his attention to John and asked, "Where were we?"

John replied, "This soup is really good today. Did you try it yet?"

Jim tried the soup and they moved on to another subject.

* * * * * *

Later on that afternoon, Jim was invited into his manager's office. His manager told him that they were downsizing staff and that his name came up on the list. The manager was very sorry to let him go and wasn't sure why his name was on the list. Nevertheless, Friday would be his last day at work. Jim was shocked at hearing the news.

Sheila heard about Jim's layoff. She sent him an e-mail saying that she wasn't interested in the relationship and wished him good luck.

Daemon met with Sheila's demon and asked, "Why did she break up with Jim?"

The demon said, "She was only interested in his position in the company, and his ability to make a lot of money. She was hoping that he would promote her one-day. She is only interested in successful people. She felt that she had no future with Jim if he was out of the company."

Jim couldn't believe how his day had turned out. He was really crushed; so far, within a matter of days, he had lost his two girl-friends and his job.

He went home feeling very depressed. Daemon called for backup. At this point, there were three demons around Jim: Daemon, loneliness demon, and suicide demon.

The suicide demon said, "I just assisted three souls to end their lives and there is one more that is close to it. I can't stay for long, this better be good. There are seven billion souls and not enough of us to cover them all."

He started working on Jim; he searched the whole house looking for any drugs, medications, alcohol, a gun, or anything that would help with a suicide.

Damon said, "He doesn't keep any drugs here. Pat usually provides them."

Jim called his father and he received a recording from his answering machine saying, "I'm not available to take your call, I'll be out of the country for a couple of days, please leave a message."

Then the suicide demon said to Daemon, "I better use plan B, isolation," and whispered to Jim, *You're all alone and nobody loves you. No one in your family wants to talk to you. The two girlfriends you used to fill your time are gone like vapor. The job you didn't like, but did anyway to pay the bills, is gone. The friends you thought you had have turned against you. And the house and car are on a payment plan. When you think about it, your life is empty and you really have nothing.*

Jim was at the end of himself and the thought of suicide crossed his mind. But then he remembered John and decided to call him for help, first. When he tried to use his cell phone to call John, Daemon said, 'Oh no, not him!' and caused interference on the phone line to stop him from contacting John. However, Jim used the landline and was able to get a hold of John. He told John everything that had happened, so John invited him to his home and discouraged him from doing anything stupid.

Jim left his house, and before he got in the car to drive to John's house, he noticed a flat tire. He called the auto club for roadside emergency service. Then Daemon asked the suicide demon to cause a delay or prevent emergency service from arriving. The demon accepted the assignment and said as he disappeared, "Some road service truck somewhere is going to have trouble of its own."

While Jim was waiting for the road service truck outside his house, a taxi unexpectedly drove by and Jim stopped it. Jim got into the taxi in the back seat, and so did Daemon. The loneliness demon, L sat in the front seat.

The taxi driver said, "Hey man, how are you today! I don't know why I drove by here. I was supposed to go somewhere else and all of a sudden I found myself driving here. It's crazy, I tell you."

Daemon said, *Look, Jim, you don't want to do this. If you become one of them, you would have to go to church every Sunday, they will brainwash you. You have to wear a special dress code to go to church. There will be new people to meet. You don't have to go.*

Demon L said, *The Bible is a fairy tale and a bunch of lies. Contrary to what Christians think, Jesus didn't get resurrected.*

Daemon continued, *And you have to give up sex and drugs. God is a killjoy, a judge with rules. Believe me, you don't want him! Moreover, you have so many unforgiven sins, what makes you think he'll take you? Believe me, this is not for you!*

Then Daemon looked at demon L and said, "Try to turn the traffic light to red."

"Why?"

"Just do it!"

Demon L did. The taxi stopped and a very attractive woman with high heels and long hair crossed the street.

Daemon said to demon L, "I thought he was going to kill himself, now he's doing this! I hate it when our slaves make a hundred and eighty and completely turn around." Then said to Jim, *Look Jim, if you want, I'll find you another girlfriend. Look at this sexy woman; you can't give up all this. C'mon, don't be silly; tell the cabbie you want to go back home.*

Finally, the taxi arrived at John's house. Jim paid the driver and got out. The two demons got out and looked at each other.

Daemon said, "Hey, how did the cab driver know to come here? Jim didn't give the address." The other demon looked shocked too and said, "I smell the enemy's presence."

"Yeah, me too." They both looked at the taxi as it drove away. Then they both looked at the house and demon L said, "This place is possessed."

"C'mon, let's go."

"End of the line for me, brother, my work is done here. He's your assignment, and he's all yours. However, if you want my opinion, I think you lost him. Good luck explaining that to the leader." Then demon L disappeared.

Daemon followed Jim. When Jim got to John's house, John was there to greet him and welcome him. Then John hugged him. When Jim went inside, so did Daemon.

After they sat down, Jim said, "I have done a lot of bad things in the past, and I'm not sure if God will forgive me, and take in someone like me!"

John replied, "Guilt is an unclean wound that never heals until confessed. Jesus' blood is thicker than any sin you have committed. When God looks at our scarlet sins through the red blood of Jesus, we look as white as snow. Jesus sat down with tax collectors and prostitutes. Healthy people don't need doctors, but sick people do. Let me tell you a couple of stories; the first one is about Peter, the disciple who denied the Lord Jesus the night before He was crucified. Peter, the rock, turned into sand after he denied the Lord our God, but he repented and God reinstated him. Our God is a God of second chances. Second, is the story of the prodigal son—"

Jim interrupted and asked, "What do I have to do to be saved?"

John answered, "Just believe in Jesus Christ and have faith, and receive the great gift of salvation through His blood. God loves you very much, but sin separates us from God. Jesus came to take our sin away and He will never leave us or let us down. Sin causes the mind to go dark and the heart to go hard. Only the Master can fill the human heart and make the darkness go away. If you make the right choice, you go to the cross and get born again and get a pardon, a 'get out of hell card'. The body is physical, the soul is mind, emotions, and feelings; the spirit, however, is in darkness until it's born again. Either you take the judgment of sin, or Jesus takes it for you. God is a good, loving God with absolute justice, and He holds us accountable for sin. Sinners can't go to heaven; they have to be cleansed and washed with the blood of Jesus."

Daemon said to Jim, *That sounds too simple, it can't be that simple.*

John continued, "So, to answer your question, you're saved when you tell God that you are sorry for your sins, and then turn from them in humble repentance. Then you'll have renewal of spirit and mind and become a new man, righteous and holy. Of course, the devil will try to make you resist getting rid of sin. But we're more than conquerors in the Lord Jesus. To dislodge the devil, repent, confess, and clean house."

Jim said, "Ok, I'm ready. I haven't prayed in a while. I'm a little bit rusty."

"Just pour your heart out to Him. It's your heart, not the words that really matter. Then put your faith in Jesus as your Lord and

Savior. Pray something like this: 'Dear Lord, I know that I have done wrong, I want to turn from my sin. I believe Jesus Christ died for me. Please come into my life and forgive me. I receive you in my life as my Lord and Savior as best as I know how right now.' Then trust Him in the same way we would trust a pilot with our life when we fly on a plane. The pilot is but a mortal man, so how much more should we trust in God?"

Before they started saying the sinner's prayer, Daemon whispered, *If you want to be saved, don't do it today, you have plenty of time.*

As they started saying the sinner's prayer, another angel appeared and said to John's angel, "Greetings in the name of our Master. My name is Celestiel, can you brief me on the situation here?" The two angels protected Jim from Daemon's influence.

Then Jim prayed and asked for forgiveness for his sins and Damon said, *You don't deserve forgiveness.*

Jim thought, *thank you for reminding me, devil, this is all the more reason why I love God for His mercy and forgiveness.*

After the prayer, John was overjoyed and said, "Welcome to the ark of salvation. You have a ticket now, and your reservation has been confirmed."

Jim asked, "Where am I going?"

"To heaven. Today, your name is written in heaven's official registry as valid proof that you are now a citizen of heaven, even though you still live on Earth. So even though we're aliens physically away from heaven, we're still residents and citizens of the kingdom. You have been adopted into the family of God. Remember when we talked about the Trinity? Well, now you are next of kin to the Trinity. You are a child of the King! Since you are part of God's family, Jesus isn't only your Lord and Savior, but He is your friend and brother. God is our father and Jesus is our older brother. We have friends in high places. You have been transformed from death to life and from darkness to light. You have to be heaven-born to be heaven-bound. Your former life ended today. Starting now, you deny yourself and follow Jesus, carrying a cross. He is your Master and Lord; you are purchased by His blood. And what a Master He is, His rewards are eternal, His burden is light, and His lordship is perfect."

"I feel a heavy weight lifted from my shoulders, but I don't feel like Jesus yet," Jim stated.

"It takes time. When a baby is born, he only looks a little bit like daddy. As time goes by, he starts walking and looking like daddy. They say if a child doesn't look like his father, feed him. And that's what the church does; feed the Christians until they look like Jesus in characteristics. We become more like Jesus day by day, until we arrive at eternity. Think about a baby before it is born. It has eyes that can't see, ears that can't hear, nor use of the other senses. However, after it is born, it can see, hear, and has full use of all the senses. Adults also can see and hear, physically alive, but dead spiritually. After being born again, the person becomes a new creature spiritually discerning and mind regenerated. The physical birth is to physical life, but the spiritual birth is for a spiritual life and eternal life. So now, you have the Spirit of God in you, which will start to work a number on your conscience. You can't get away with wrong anymore."

"So this is it, as simple as that. An hour ago, I was destined to hell and now I have admission to heaven. It sounds too easy."

"Yes, it's a gift from God, and I don't know why people refuse to receive the gift of God. By grace, you are saved and salvaged. Law means that I must do something for God, but grace means that God does something for me. Grace cannot be deserved, grace cannot be earned, and grace can only be given. Today, you have deposited a large credit of grace in heaven that you can withdraw from any time you sin and break the law. The balance of this grace is greater than all one can sin, never ending. However, this doesn't give us a license to sin.

"Today, your life's file, with all of its good works, is deleted, then you go to Jesus' file with His sinless life and you copy it and then paste it over your file. This way, you gain His righteousness. Your name has been transferred into the white list, but Satan has just put your name on his blacklist," John explained.

"That doesn't sound too good."

"There are three kinds of people: those who are afraid, those who have no sense of fear, and those who know God. Don't be afraid or waver, stand firm with prayer, Jesus has conquered all and gave us power. Submit to God and resist the devil and he will flee. It's not bad; it's good to have the devil as my enemy. I wouldn't want God to be my enemy."

"Tell me more about the resist part!" Jim exclaimed.

"Either you submit to God and resist the devil, or submit to Satan and resist God. The Bible says we wrestle with the devil. Wrestling is a close contact sport, so he's going to be in your face, trying to discourage you."

"I don't like the sound of that."

"Believe me, he's been in your face for years now, teaching you his ways and leading you astray to keep you asleep until you die, to prevent you from going to heaven. But now you have become an enemy to him, and right now he is plotting his next move against you," John warned.

"What if he doesn't flee? Does that mean you are not submitting to God or not resisting the devil?"

"Most likely, but sometimes discipline comes from the Lord or from our past mistakes, which we have to suffer the consequences for. We don't want to mix the different categories. Trust God and ask for forgiveness of sin and protection from the evil one."

Daemon felt defeated and thought, *OK, I'll go now, but I'll be back to check on you later. Don't think I would leave you without a fight.* Then he started mumbling to himself, *I spent years grooming him, and then in a flash they think they can snatch him out of my hand? They'd better think again.*

Jim asked, "Where do I go from here?"

"The world is behind you and the cross is in front of you. One day you can go back to the burning building where you came out from, alive, and save someone trapped inside from eternal damnation. But for now, read the Bible daily, and obey what you read, and God will never fail you. We were saved by saying 'I will.' As we respond to God's gracious call, we grow and serve God by saying 'Thy Will.' It's not enough to say the sinner's prayer, as vital as that is. I'll teach and mentor you; it will take months to get you on the road to maturity, and victory over sin and habitual problems. Remember, salvation is the work that God does for us, sanctification is the work that God does in us next, and then service is the work that God does through us. After you repented, the wall between you and God went down, and now He listens to your prayers, so start praying."

Daemon waited outside the door of John's house. He was able to hear the cheering of the angels and the sounds of victory from the two men. Then when it was time for John to drive Jim back home, the two men came out of the house with two angels following them. The men got in the front seat of the car and the angels in the back seat. Daemon said, *OK, I'll just see you when you get home!*

Jim got home, waved good-bye to John, and went inside his house. Daemon tried to come in, but an angel blocked him and said, "Where do you think you're going?" Daemon had no answer. Celestiel continued, "The old Jim doesn't live here anymore, you're divorced. This new Jim doesn't cook for you, or do your dirty laundry or scheme for you, and you have no power over him anymore. His body is the temple of God and under the new management of the Holy Spirit. He is filled with the Holy Spirit now, and you have no home here. We can't have you and the Holy Spirit living in Jim's body at the same time. A fig tree will not produce thistles and a sweet fountain doesn't give bitter water."

Damon replied, "I know you; you're the angel that protected the Jews from the Egyptians when they were on the run. But you were leading at first, then you came to the back!"

"So you were one of the demons leading the Egyptians then," said Celestiel.

"Yes."

"I received instruction to watch and protect their back, and so I did with a cloud over them and we put darkness over your troops."

"I'm glad I ran into you again. Why didn't you just kill the Egyptians that night?"

"The psalmist said 'I will make a table and make you eat in front of his enemies.' God wanted the Egyptians to see the Jews across the river. He also wanted the Jews to see His power."

Daemon said, "So you must have been demoted, from watching over a whole nation to babysitting this insignificant one!"

"You're wrong; God loves him just as much. Moreover, you are not welcome here anymore," said Celestiel, and went back inside.

Daemon stayed outside for the first time in a long time.

Jim noticed a message on his answering machine, and when he played the message, it was from his father saying, "I'm sorry I missed your call, son; I'll call you back tomorrow. I love you."

Jim slept like a baby that night.

* * * * * *

After his defeat in losing Jim, Daemon went to report to his local leader. When he arrived there, the leader wasn't available, so he went up the hierarchy and ladder of command to his territory leader. He was assembled in the desert where thousands of demons were busy training and schooling.

When it was Daemon's turn, the leader, who seemed larger in size, asked, "How are things going?"

Daemon answered, "Things are going well, master. We win some, we lose some, but we're winning more than we're losing."

"You lost one, didn't you?" asked the leader. "Then the counter to eternity went up by one. Well, it's a good thing that he wasn't the one that completes the count that God has in mind for the fullness of the Gentiles. If he was, then we'd both be in trouble, trying to explain that to the big boss."

"No, the Holy Spirit is still with us. As a matter of fact, I'm here to report a mortal, a spiritual terrorist, armed with the Holy Spirit," Daemon replied.

"We should stay away from people who are indwelled by the Holy Spirit unless they invade our territories first, then we attack them. What you should do is go back to Jim and make him doubt his salvation, ask him 'are you really saved?' and then ask him 'How can you witness, pray, and serve God if you're not sure?'"

While they were talking, the leader was interrupted by three demons, who said, "Master, we found the answer to your question about the best way to deceive humans."

"OK. Let's hear it."

The first student came before the leader and said, "Master, I decided when I go to my assignment, to sow the seed of evil. I'll tell them that there's no God."

The leader said, "You cannot do that because the creation speaks of God everywhere you look and in their hearts they know there is a Creator. You'll lose all credibility and no one will believe you. You'll be totally unsuccessful."

The second student came along and said, "I'm going to go down there and tell them that there is no hell or judgment."

The leader said, "Well, a lot of them would like to believe that, but in their hearts they know better. They will believe you for a little while, but then they will return to their senses because they really know there is a hell. You'll never accomplish your purpose."

Then the third student came along and said, "I think I've got it, Master. I will tell them that there is no hurry to get saved. This way they'll sleep at the wrong time with no oil, waiting for the groom."

And the leader said, "You got it! That is it. You'll consign more people into hell than anyone else could ever do. They won't be prepared when Jesus comes back. While you're at it, spread the phrase 'eat, drink, and be merry, for tomorrow we die.'"

As the recruits turned around and started to leave he continued, "And remember to tell your new subjects that there are no absolutes, but a sliding scale. If you can't get them to sin, try to get them to stop doing good. And all that is necessary for our evil to prevail is for good men to do nothing."

Then one of them stopped, looked back and said, "Master, we've read the Bible so we can misinterpret scriptures. But we're told not to read the book of Revelation!"

"These are the Father's own words, 'The day we read the book of Revelation, we shall surely die. So, don't do it."

Then after the recruits left, Daemon said, "We try to convince these dysfunctional creatures 'you only live once' but the enemy tells them 'you only die once.' What about telling them that Christ wasn't resurrected?"

The Leader answered, "Maybe, but the best way to get them is when you convince them that they are saved by works. You know, you could use a refresher course; you sound rusty."

"Maybe, but the harvest is big," Daemon reminded him.

"I hope that you still remember the basics of our mission! Our mission is to draw them away from God, to thwart God's purpose in their lives, to remove God's glory, and ultimately to destroy them."

"Yes, I remember, but what can we use against a strong believer who has the biblical blueprint?"

"The best weapon I recommend is to misinterpret the truth of the word of God. Lies that include some truths are the most effective of all. You might also want to try to redirect their attention from the spiritual to the material and from the invisible future to the visible present. Make them concentrate and narrow down on what they need now, so they forget the other blessings they have."

"This is a different culture, time, and society, you know."

The leader answered, "Use modern everyday terms. Tell them that the road to heaven is like a five-lane highway; you can get on or off whenever you want, and pick the lane you want. But keep them from finding the narrow road of faith in Jesus. Use the new culture strongholds against them; the empire of gambling, divorce, abortion industry, pornography, narcotics, and drugs. Tell them this is a different culture; these commandments don't apply for this time and this society. Use this reasoning to blind their eyes to the truth of the word of God and disobey Him. Throw in questions like: 'Is this really what that means in the Bible? What does God say? Maybe there is a different opinion.' Introduce doubt and unbelief to misinterpret the principles."

Then Daemon said, "I need a new assignment."

"You seem to have been through a lot. I'll give you this guy, Joe," as he handed out an ID file, "he's a bench-warming Christian who sits at church and won't fight you back, lethargic, halfhearted, tolerant, and consumed with entertainment and pleasure. When the heat of persecution is turned up, part-time Christians and weekend warriors in the reserves like him will abandon the faith."

Daemon looked at the ID file and said, "I'll still check on Jim to see if he changes his mind."

"Good. Don't be discouraged. I have agents, wolves in sheep's clothing, inside the church to cause divisions, denying the deity and divinity of Christ. The Creator is allowing the wheat and tares to stay mixed together. He doesn't want the tares removed, worried about His precious wheat. They can't tell who the tares are, anyway. Even the disciples didn't suspect or know that Judas was the betrayer, even after he dipped his hand in the dish after Jesus. Judas was our goat and he hid the truth from all the eleven disciples...Now go and good luck with your new assignment."

Bible Study

It was Wednesday, another day at work. Jack stopped by Jim's office. He wasn't aware that Jim had lost his two girlfriends and job or that he became a born again believer. So he invited him to a party after work to meet his new girlfriend from the fifth floor and asked him to bring one of his girlfriends for a double date. Jim declined. Jack was disappointed, but told him a new dirty joke he just heard. Jim smiled, but didn't join his buddy in laughing like he usually did. Jack lashed out at him, "What's happening to you lately, you used to be a fun guy? I see Jim on the outside, but I don't know who is on the inside," and left his office.

* * * * * *

In the evening, Jim showed up for his first Bible study at Bill's house. Bill opened the door and welcomed him and said, "Hi, I'm Bill, we've been expecting you. John told me that you were coming."

Jim replied, "Hi, thanks for inviting me."

Jim went inside the house followed by Daemon who trailed back from a distance.

John greeted Jim and introduced him to the group, and the group welcomed him as he sat down. One of the group ladies wanted to make an announcement and she excitedly said, "We'd like everyone to know that I'm about three months pregnant! Here is an ultrasound picture of the baby." Everybody congratulated her and looked at the picture.

Then Bill suggested that they play Bible charade, and asked the question, "When was the first ultrasound in the Bible, taken?"

Gracie said, "The Virgin Mary had to be the first one, she knew she was having a son, Jesus Emmanuel."

Another man said, "No, it was Elizabeth, the mother of John the Baptist."

Then Mary said, "No, it was Abraham, he knew he was going to have a son Isaac."

Another lady said, "I think it was Hagar. The Lord told her that she would have a son, Ishmael."

Bill said, "Technically, Hagar had the first son, but the Lord promised Abraham, a seed and a nation, way before that. So, Abraham had to be the first to know that he was going to have a son."

Later, Bill said to Jim, "Well, since you're new here, we'd like to know if you have any questions you'd like to ask."

Daemon whispered in Jim's ears, *Ask them about the End of times and prosperity, which is it?*

Jim hesitated at first, but then he asked, "When I attended church last Sunday, at one part of the sermon the preacher said that he can hear the footsteps of Jesus in the clouds ready to take His church to heaven, very soon. But later on, he encouraged people to buy his CD on prosperity. If he's getting them ready to go to heaven, why is he teaching them how to get rich?"

There was silence in the room. They thought he might ask a question about creation, Satan, the Bible, sin, suffering, etc. the usual new comer's questions.

Daemon thought, *I hit the jackpot. I opened a big can of worms. Let's see them get out of this one!* Then he got his darts out and shot in every way and direction at the group.

One lady said, "You read my mind…"

Daemon thought, *No, he didn't, but I did. I got a direct hit and greed is written all over your face.*

The lady continued, "I was wondering, why is it that I have been tithing for six months and nothing has happened. While the people in the church next block to our church, are prospering? Not to mention non-Christians who never tithe are also doing better."

At that time, Daemon was joined by another demon who said, "Hello, I'm an exchange brother. I was just promoted from the Far East. Christians are very hard to defeat and discourage down there. I'm going to do a good job here so I won't be demoted to that place again."

Daemon replied, "It is easier down here, this is the I-want-it-now culture, and the prosperity club, name it and claim it, blab it and grab it. Right now, they're talking about getting rich financially."

The exchange demon said, "Praise Lucifer, I'm going to like it here then. I specialize in this area, Greed. We give the money to those who work for us, the faithful ones God rewards anyway. Those who don't get blessed quickly, members of the bless me club, get disappointed and leave the faith, and say get behind me Jesus instead of get behind me Satan."

Daemon replied, "C'mon in, I have created a good atmosphere for you, the lack of knowledge will destroy them!"

Then John who said, "Prosperity doesn't mean riches only," started a discussion. "It could mean well-being in health, physically and mentally through peace of mind. Jesus said, 'Be friends with the Mammon of the world.'"

"Jesus also said 'You cannot serve God and Mammon, for either you'll hate the one and love the other, or you'll hold to the one and despise the other,'" Bill responded. "And He also said 'give us our daily bread.' He said to be friends with the mammon of the world only to supply our basic daily needs, not to make riches. After all, it is more difficult for a rich man to enter the heaven of God than a camel to enter the eye of a needle."

"Yes, but Job, Abraham, David, and Solomon...they were all rich men," John replied. "Adam was prosperous in the Garden of Eden, and that's how God wants us to be."

"Joseph of Arimathaea, a disciple of Jesus, was a rich man, but he craved Jesus' body and wanted to bury him in his tomb," Bill replied. "The apostle Paul was a tent maker and the apostle Peter was a fisherman. If prosperity teaching were true, then they would have been a bad example. The Lord Jesus said sell everything and follow Me. He also said foxes have holes, but the Son of man has no place to lay His head."

John nodded in agreement, and Bill continued his reasoning. "You know there are millions of poor Christians in the world who would love to get their hands on a copy of the Bible or go to church without getting shot. They're not thinking of prosperity at all, but more concerned about safety."

Demon G said, *Don't remind me of these people. They made me work overtime.*

Bill continued, "Again, if a person is seeking prosperity with the kingdom of God in mind ... a person who will help those persecuted Christians in other lands ... then God bless that person, and may he or she prosper. However, we need to pray about it and make sure that it isn't going to be a stumbling block. People these days are looking for preachers to tickle their ears with promises of prosperity — money, money, money — to keep them tithing and coming back to church."

Then Mary said, "To me, prosperity means no lack, but no gold either. And prosperity isn't a goal; it's a byproduct of righteousness in life. I also know that a borrower is a servant to the lender. That's why we paid our bills on time to be free from debt ... no bondage. I think it's okay to have money as long as one doesn't fall in love with it. We should not lust after the things that God gives, but rather love the Lord who gives these things. Lust takes and love gives. Lust runs out, but love lasts."

"To me prosperity means health, peace, and joy," another person said. "The Bible says 'I have never seen the righteous forsaken.' The apostle Paul said, 'I have learned to be content whatever the circumstances, whether well fed or hungry, whether living in plenty or in want. Someone wrote, 'A little is as much as a lot if it is enough.'"

"I think abundant life is when all of our needs are met," John said. "More than that, though, abundant life is when we have enough to bless others. Not only do we receive a blessing, but we are also a blessing. It isn't just life out yonder in the sweet by and by, but in the nasty now and now. God meets our needs, and He cares about our general welfare. He wants us to be fulfilled and to enjoy His blessings."

Someone then said, "Our God is a benevolent and generous Lord of infinite resources. It's better to have a father who owns a bakery than to have a warehouse full of bread."

And everyone said, "Amen."

Finally, for Jim's sake, Bill acknowledged the fact that the pastor shouldn't have mixed the two messages together.

"There is nothing wrong with checking on the pastor," Bill said. "The Bible says we should examine the scriptures. We should be careful who leads us and makes decision for our salvation. The Pharisees refused to believe Jesus because His teaching was bad for business, and they led the Jewish nation astray."

Bill looked at the lady to answer her question. "Believers who don't prosper sometimes think that they're doing something wrong or maybe not worshiping right or that God doesn't love them," he said. "That is not true. There could be two people sitting next to each other on the pew, both of whom tithe. One may be prosperous, and the other may not. God will supply all our needs according to His riches, not according to the person sitting next to you on the pew. We live in an age of fast food, fast marriage, fast divorce, and fast faith. People don't want to wait anymore; God is too slow for them. Abraham waited twenty years for Isaac to be born after God promised him a son.

"People who are doing better than us right now, may not be a couple of years into the future. Also, how do we know that it isn't Satan that has been blessing them, Christians or non-Christians?

"Being poor isn't a disease, folks. Even if we die poor like Lazarus, so be it. In heaven, there are upside-down standards where the rich gets tormented and the poor gets comforted. Not every poor person goes to heaven nor every rich person goes to hell."

Daemon whispered to Jim and said, *See? They're not sure about things, and their leader, the pastor, is wrong. C'mon, let's get out of here.*

Jim thought, *no, I'm not leaving yet.*

Daemon, astonished, said, *Who said that?* Then he looked deeper into Jim and found the Holy Spirit glowing but dim. He asked, "What are you doing here?"

The Holy Spirit answered, "I was always here. I just wasn't activated yet, and now I'm getting energized."

"Okay, here's the outline for today's meeting," Bill said. "Before Jesus, gentiles were considered like dogs eating crumbs falling from the tables of the Jews. When Jesus came, and when we opened the door for Him after He knocked on it, He lifted us up to the table, and He dined with us."

Did he just call you a dog? Daemon asked.

Jim was offended by that statement and left the Bible study. As he was walking away, Daemon shot him with a fiery dart - Pride of life.

John followed Jim and asked, "What's wrong, Jim?"

"This guy, the fat tub, needs to be more sensitive about referring to non-Jews as dogs."

"I'm sorry; we need to give you milk and not solid food at first," said John.

Daemon shot Jim with another fiery dart and said, *Pride of life*.

"Are you calling me an infant?" Jim asked John.

John realized that Jim had gone through a lot this week and was edgy. "No, I mean we should start with a Bible study with me, one-on-one from the beginning, step-by-step with the basics."

Jim accepted, and they walked to John's car, which was parked on the street in front of Bill's house. And they sat there.

"Don't let the devil trap you in the area of offense," John said. "Assumptions are also the work of the devil.'I thought he said this or that,' and 'I assumed you meant this or that.' Satan is the master thought manipulator and can take an unintentional remark from a friend or family member and twist it around in our mind until we believe his distortion. He is the author of pride, and he has unending supply of it."

"Okay, what's the story with this devil? Is he for real?" Jim asked.

"Satan is alive and well on planet Earth," John explained. "We're at battle with him in a spiritual war, and the battleground is in the mind. However, we have an advantage over him; we have a mouth and he doesn't. He only attacks through our thoughts with his fiery darts. We, on the other hand, can say, 'The Lord rebukes you.' He cannot reply to that, but only take it. Because he is constantly studying us and plotting against us, it only makes sense for us to study the enemy and find out how to break down his plan to confuse and intimidate us. We don't debate with the devil. He will distort and mix error with truth, and we can't win. He's a very crafty master debater, liar, and deceiver. He had plenty of practice and thousands of years of experience. We're not smart enough or powerful enough to outwit him. Eve learned that the hard way. Adam was so intelligent, he tended the whole Garden of Eden and named all the animals in the world, but he still was no match for the devil. God knows that we're weaker than Satan. That's why He gives us a back door of escape in every temptation."

"That's good to know. What else?"

John continued, "Satan has destructive powers and dangerous demonic forces at his command. He is the ruler of this world and we're rebellious aliens living in his territory because we're citizens of heaven and we obey heaven's laws and submit to heaven's Lord. Satan wants us to worship and serve him; he wants our will submitted to his will. But the devil is a defeated foe if we're saved in Jesus as a personal savior and have received the Lord in our heart. Since Satan controls humans' emotions, when we renew the mind, we then can pull down the thoughts of Satan and he can no longer control our emotions."

"What about the demons? How do they choose which person to attack?" Jim asked.

"Demons comprise a universal network that is led by an arch criminal mastermind. When someone starts thinking wicked thoughts, he or she attracts them like an antenna receives a TV broadcast signal. They don't hang around you unless the imagination starts thinking and generates wicked waves. So, guard your heart and take heed what you see and hear.

"There are certain things that attract evil spirits like a magnet: drugs, alcohol, sexual perversions, pornography, and idolatry. They also come against us when we have unforgiveness, strife, contention, and bitterness in our life. Once they find an open door, these tormenting evil and unclean spirits remove the peace of mind of their victims by fear, oppression, heaviness, hindering, and suicide."

Jim thought about the night before when he almost committed suicide. He listened attentively and was fascinated by this invisible army that never crossed his mind before.

"Satan chooses a time when we're most vulnerable and makes his move. He takes advantage of our time and energy limits. The best time for Satan to get out his quiver full of darts, and tempt us is first, when we're hungry and weak. He tempted Jesus to change stones into bread after He fasted forty days. Second, when we're angry, that's the worst time for us to make decisions. Third, when we're lonely, he makes us believe that nobody loves us.

"Fourth, when we're worn out and burned out physically. That's when Satan roars like a lion to magnify our problems and make them appear too big to deal with, and weakens our ability to think straight and fight back to solve them. A real lion uses the same tactic, when it roars to paralyze the animals in fear and causes them to not run as fast."

Then Jim asked, "Does Satan mess with us after we're born again?"

"Absolutely. After Jesus got baptized, He went into the wilderness to pray and fast for forty days. When the forty days were ended, Satan tested Him. If he tempted the Lord, he'll definitely tempt us. We're swimming in this ocean we call life, surrounded by sharks whose objective is to take us down. Relentlessly, they swim and circle around us and once in awhile they nibble on us. This vicious cycle continues until we reach land, our final destination in heaven." Then John sadly said, "And I have seen many of my brothers, while swimming with us, get bitten viciously many times and go down in the deep waters and backslide, never to be seen again. Jesus said, 'don't be afraid of those who kill the body and after that can do no more. But I will show you whom you should fear: Fear him who, after the killing of the body, has power to throw you into hell.'"

"If the devil is so powerful, how do we defeat him then?"

John got a picture out of his Bible and gave it to Jim. "A Roman soldier?" asked Jim, "What's that has to do with fighting the devil?"

"Well, it is a fight. Satan is our worst enemy and we need to prepare for the battle. And since our battle isn't against flesh and blood but spirits, we need different type of weapons. The enemy is invisible and very powerful and most people don't believe he exists which makes him dangerous. And those who believe that he exists, the devil makes them think that they are just too bright to be controlled by him."

"Yes, but these are not spiritual weapons, are they?" asked Jim as he looked at the picture again.

"Let me explain; these are provisions we need to outmaneuver Satan and have victory over him. We have no power against Satan by ourselves, only through Jesus and His power. His might and the armor of God is our only hope. We need to dress up spiritually, and each piece of the armor of the soldier you're looking at represents a spiritual weapon. Starting from the top, first we have the helmet of salvation; we need this to protect our mind from evil thoughts by reading the Bible and educating ourselves in the scriptures. It gives us the power of God we need to demolish strongholds and trenches of the devil like porn, drugs, and nudity."

Jim thought about his addictions and said, "I see."

"Next - the sword is the Bible, God's word. If we want to shut down the destructive mind games the enemy plays in our heads, there is one tactic guaranteed to win, the Bible. But we have to believe and obey the truth in the Bible as the word of God. We need to remember it and use it every day. Popeye eats spinach and the believers eat the word of God."

Jim smiled.

"Next – the breastplate of righteousness to protect the heart and guard our emotions, and trust in Jehovah-Tsidkenu. Jesus took our sins on Him on the cross and gave us His righteousness. It provides protection from the devil's accusations because God looks at us through Jesus' righteousness. Therefore, we're not afraid to go witness and spread the word even if we feel unrighteous because nobody is. What's important is that we love that which is righteous and refuse what is sinful, so that our neighbor would want to be a Christian.

"Next - the shoes of peace. We have confidence in the commander-in-chief and prince and author of peace, Jehovah-Shalom. Great peace have they that love His law and nothing shall offend them. This one protects against anxiety and fleshly temptations. The shoes of peace help us to be peacemakers and not troublemakers.

"Finally - the Shield of faith with which we can extinguish all the flaming arrows of the evil one. We have an enemy who throws at us fiery darts of doubt, worry, anxiety, and fear which all work against faith. Let's see what else..."

Jim pointed at the belt that the Roman was wearing in the illustration.

"Of course we can't forget the belt of truth, buckled around your waist. It holds the breastplate, the dagger, and the sword. Finally, notice the armor has nothing that covers and protects the back, which means retreat isn't an option; we have to stand firm. And this is the complete armory of the Christian. Our enemies are the world, wanting us to conform to it and squeezes us into its mold, the flesh, give me, give me, give me lusting all the time, and the devil who says 'believe me', and he's a liar from the beginning."

Celestiel, sitting in the backseat, looked at Raphael sitting next to him, smiled and said, "You've got a good man there. The Lord is pleased."

"You've got a good man in Jim, too, a diamond in the rough. John will mentor him and make him shine. When Jim was stuck in the elevator, he couldn't wait to get away from John. Look at what the Holy Spirit accomplished in him now."

Then the two angels looked outside the car where Daemon was standing with his wing drooped down with disappointment.

Jim curiously asked, "Who is working on the good side, then?"

"When you were born again, you received the Holy Spirit. Imagine your body without the white blood cells; every germ and microbe gets in without any resistance. With the Holy Spirit inside you, you're not going to allow every wicked thought to come into your mind He's the filter. When white cells battle a new germ, your body heats up with fever the first time. But after they win, they cross out that germ from the list because they know how to defeat it next time. The same thing with your mind; it will heat up at first, but then you'll train to the ways of the devil and his tactics and you'll be able to resist easier the next time. Sometimes the virus mutates and changes and the white cells have to start all over to fight it. The same thing with the devil. As soon as we train ourselves to a certain mature thinking, he repackages the idea and sprinkles some misquoted scriptures on it to make it sound biblical and resends the idea to see if we will bite. He's a slick customer, using the gifts God gave him against us."

There was a pause then Jim asked, "Not to change the subject, but I heard the word tithing from the other lady. Why do pastors have to repeat the subject of tithing all the time?"

John explained, "Some of them are greedy and some of them do it because they have a very strong and persistent adversary who tells us all the time that our money could be used for something better. When we were born again, we became a citizen of heaven with rules and regulations, and tithing is one of them. We pay taxes to the earthly government to build streets, schools that teach evolution and safe sex, and to support a government that votes against the Ten Commandments. In the kingdom of God, we tithe to build churches and Sunday schools that teach the gospel, creation, and print Bibles and spread the gospel. While the government offers retirement at age sixty-five, Jesus offers an eternal retirement."

Jim pondered on these thoughts and new concepts with mouth half open and speechless.

Then continued John, "Our righteous and generous Lord owns all the money in the world, and we're all made stewards to the portion of the money that He gives us. It is His will that we give ten percent back with our time, talent, and treasure. This way you'll position yourself to experience more of His blessings and more of His wisdom. It is more blessed to give than to receive."

Jim shifted gears and asked, "Is heaven real?"

"People say that this world is real and heaven isn't, but I say heaven is real and this world isn't. The world also says 'seeing is believing' but Jesus said 'believing is seeing'. The summation of our life on this earth will be less than two seconds in our eternal life. In reality, this short life here on earth is only a testing ground, a steppingstone to a more real life in the presence of God.

"If you tell a caterpillar that it will fly one day, it will say 'are you crazy?' We'll see heaven one day. Heaven is the place to be; it's where forgiven righteous saints go and be delighted."

Then Jim asked, "How do we get to heaven. I remember you telling me that I had a ticket last night?"

John explained, "When I witness to people, I present them with the ticket to heaven. Some people appreciate the offer, but never take it. Some will like the ticket and take it, but because of the rain and thunder they decide to get off at the next port. That's why I never promised you smooth sailing when I talked to you. Some will see a colorful titanic in a smooth sailing and exchange their tickets without realizing the consequences of getting off the ark and not knowing where the titanic is heading. So my advice to you is to stay on the ark through the rain and thunder."

Jim was still unsure about his salvation, so he asked, "How can I know for sure that I'm going to heaven?"

"You already embraced His death and resurrection as being for you and you accepted Christ as your sin bearer. The Bible assures us that we'll have eternal life. We'll be accepted by God not on the bases of our own imperfect performance, but on the bases of what Jesus did which was accepted by the Father when He died on the cross, rose again and was taken into heaven."

Jim asked, "Is Hell real?"

John replied, "Yes it is. Jesus spent more of His time warning His listeners of the impending judgment of hell than speaking of the joys of heaven because He wants us all to go to heaven. God doesn't send people to hell; they send themselves by rejecting the Savior. Hell wasn't created for humans, but for Satan and his demons. Hell is where forsaken sinners go and have retribution."

Jim came back with more questions and asked, "Why do you pray, if God knows everything?"

By now, John was very impressed with the interest that Jim showed in spiritual matters. John was used to new comers getting turned off by now. Not Jim; he was like a sponge thirsty for God's word and absorbing it quickly.

John answered, "Prayers give us instant access to the throne of God through the Holy Spirit. It invites God into our lives and binds us to Him. God opens the windows of heaven to bless you and me when we pray. God says 'pray to Me and I will answer you.'"

"How long should a prayer be?" Jim asked.

"Well, if you want to get a raise, you prepare a speech to talk to your boss. How much more time should we spend with God, the one who can change all circumstances on heaven and earth for us. But prayers should not be repetitive, but from the heart with confidence and no unbelief."

Jim was like a loaded gun, hungry for knowledge and asked, "Does God know the detours we take?"

"God said to be anxious for nothing because He already has our life mapped out. Under anxiety, from the devil, we make detours by our wrong decisions. God knows our weaknesses and He predicts how we react to situations. Before the creation was formed, God studied every scenario that man would take and try and God looked into the future and found out what we're going to try. So, He sent us a letter, the Bible, telling us what not to do and what will harm us."

"Is the Bible the word of God?"

"The Bible is breathed by God, written by man, inspired by the Holy Spirit and He's able to preserve His word. Satan tries to discredit the Bible, but Jesus supported it when He talked about Adam, Noah, Abraham, and other Old Testament characters. We have the original Dead Sea Scrolls and epistles to verify the Bible to be true. The Bible is basic instruction to operate on this earth before leaving it."

"Does God change the world events to fit His prophecies?"

"God didn't write a script and then manipulated men's actions throughout history into His preset plan. No, God who isn't limited by time as we are and already exists in the future as well as the past, told the prophets what He saw happen in the future. He does, however, have the authority to choose kings and presidents to fulfill His purpose. If you compare world events in the newspaper with Bible prophecies, you'll see that they match if you have spiritual eyes. The Bible is without a doubt, planet earth operating system disguised as a piece of literature."

John looked at Jim whose face expressions looked like an old computer having antivirus software installed in it. He was busy thinking and processing while deleting viruses and protecting from future infections and old programs were replaced by newer programs. Jim had a lot of new things to learn and a whole lot of old things to unlearn.

"Do we know when the rapture is going to happen?"

John yawned and said, "I'm sorry. I've had a long day… When you see Christmas decorations at the mall before Thanksgiving you know that Thanksgiving is getting close. When you see the signs of

Jesus' second coming and the rapture isn't here yet, you know that the rapture is coming soon. And we're seeing the signs."

Then Jim asked, "What makes your faith so strong? What do you see in God that empowers you like this?"

John ecstatically replied, "How do I describe God; He is.., He is.., He just is. My God, He is 'the I Am', the Almighty. He split the Red Sea in half and made water stand on its feet and salute the Jews while they crossed it without getting their feet wet. He made the sun stop in its tracks when the Jews finished off the heathen armies. My God made a city's fortified walls collapse just by having the Jewish men shout at it. He shone a star, from heaven to earth to lead shepherds to His newly born Son. And this is how big God is."

Jim was enjoying the Bible study, like a good night story, but he asked, "Tomorrow I go to my last week at work and face the reality of the hustle and bustle of the world. What would I do with the stuff you told me tonight?"

John answered, "Just know that God is good and in control and watch out for the evil devil traps."

Just then, Bill's house door opened and people started coming out. "I guess the Bible study is over," continued Jim, "how embarrassing, I acted like an idiot earlier storming out of there like that."

"Don't worry, they'll understand. We're a little bit different than the world. Here is my wife and daughter," said John, then he introduced them to Jim and everyone went home.

Tragedy

It was Thursday afternoon when Mary called John at work and franticly told him that Gracie collapsed at school and was rushed to the local hospital. She asked him to meet her at the hospital as soon as possible. John informed his colleagues about the emergency and left work and headed out towards the hospital.

When he got there, Mary met him at the waiting room and told him that they took brain scans and other tests to find out where the problem was.

Mary asked with tears in her eyes, "How could this happen to us, John?" she thought, *how would God allow this to happen* but she didn't say it.

John, trying to be the strong one, replied," It's not over yet, honey. We need to have God on our side and ask the Lord for a royal favor."

There were a couple of people in the waiting room that were reading magazines and talking. John held Mary's hand and prayed softly and said, "I first rebuke you, devil, for causing Gracie's sickness. Heavenly Father, we approach Your throne with praise and thanksgiving. We're washed by the blood of the Lamb Jesus. Lord, if this is a test, then Thy will be done. But I ask that You would hold our hands while we go through the fire. Our heavenly Father, if we're out of Your will, forgive us our sins. Amen."

Mary added on, "Please, dear Lord Jesus, heal our daughter Gracie."

There was a demon in the waiting room who said to John, *This is happening because you denied your God in front of men and wouldn't pray in the cafeteria in public.*

The Holy Spirit rebutted that and said, *That's not true. You already confessed that one and repented and I covered it by the blood of the Lamb on the cross. Don't let the devil exploit that!*

The Holy Spirit requested help from above and for an angel to be sent to heal Gracie. Immediately, an angel was assigned to the task and was dispatched to the hospital. But on the way to the hospital, demons blocked the angel above the hospital and delayed his arrival.

Gracie was transferred to a room and the parents went to see her. She laid there motionless with tubes all over her. Mary wept and said, "My baby. I can't believe this is happening. Oh Lord, help us."

The demon thought, *You want to go to heaven, well, I'll make your life on this earth a living hell. Where is your God now?*

Meanwhile, the dispatched angel was prevented from coming to the room where the little girl was. There were demons forming a bubble around him and every time he tried to move, the demons prevented him from getting out.

John and Mary spent the rest of the afternoon praying and sending praises out to their heavenly Father for a breakthrough. John knew that the more praises went up, the more blessings came down. The same relationship between water vapor going up producing rain coming down.

* * * * * *

Later, John went to a soda vending machine to get a drink. He noticed a child, about three years old, having a spat with his father at the snack bar vending machine next to the soda machine. The child was upset because he couldn't get his candy bar.

The father said, "See that red light? It means that they have run out. But if we go to the first floor, there are more vending machines and a huge cafeteria," the father continued, "I can get you any kind of candy bar you want." But the child insisted on staying there, fussing while putting those coins again and again only for them to come out again.

John got his soda and stayed there for a minute, reading a bulletin board on the wall while listening to the conversation between the father and his son. John received a phone call on his cell phone, which he answered. It was Mary's sister, Martha.

She sounded very excited and said, "I want to thank you both because I didn't go on that ski trip as you advised me. And I'm so glad that I didn't because the resort I was going to had a major accident. There was so much snowfall that it collapsed and about ten people died. So I'm very excited and happy and wanted to thank you for advising me not to take that trip. But of course, I feel bad for those who died—"

While she was talking, there was an announcement over the PA system in the hospital asking for doctors so and so to report to the operating room.

Martha asked, "Where are you right now?"

"We're at the hospital. Didn't Mary leave you a message on your answering machine earlier, telling about the situation?"

"I never received the message. What's going on?"

"We had to bring Gracie to the hospital. She is in a coma and not doing well."

Martha, terrified, said, "I'm taking the next flight out to be with you. Please tell Mary that I didn't receive the message. I'll call her cell phone right now. Bye. I'm very sorry, John."

John hung up with Martha and looked back at the father and his son. They were still standing there with the son bickering and the father was still pleading with the boy. The child still didn't want to move and still tried to put coins and they came out. The father even tried to get him a different candy bar from the same machine, but the child refused and cried louder. By now, twenty minutes since John first got there, the father was finally fed up, spanked the boy and said, "No candy bars for you today!" and the two walked away.

After the drama ended, John walked back to Gracie's room and thought, *Our heavenly Father deals with us the same way and we miss out on God's blessings when we don't listen to Him by being stubborn. The Lord knows where the blessings are; we just need to trust Him and when we insist on doing things our way, we lose out in the end.*

* * * * * * *

Later that evening, Jim visited John in the hospital. He first went into Gracie's room and greeted both John and Mary who were sitting there. Then the two men left the room and walked to the waiting room.

Jim said, "Do you mind if I just sit here with you?"

"Not at all. Job's friends sat with him for three days without saying anything."

Three minutes later, Jim asked, "How is she doing?"

"All is well, my friend."

"What do you mean 'all is well'? She's got tubes all over. Is she in a coma or something?" Jim asked.

"We're believing God to take care of us."

Daemon said to Jim, *Where is his God now? Where are His promises to the believers?*

Jim said, "Everyone in the office knows that you are a Christian by the way you lived out your faith. But when they heard that you're going through some difficulties in life, I feel that everyone must be thinking, 'where is God now? We thought God promised to take care of the Christians.' And I myself can't help but think that if your faith is so strong, why isn't God helping you with this problem? Why is God allowing this to happen in the first place?"

"We can't figure out the consequences of a life event. So when we go through a painful situation, we don't know how it is affecting others, or how demons are involved in the situation, only God does. God also has the benefit of knowing how the situation is going to turn out. Sometimes I tell God, 'Lord, I thought about all the angles of this situation and I don't see how it serves You and brings You glory. Why don't You change the situation already?' But the problem is, we don't know all the angles. Jesus waited four days to raise Lazarus; why not two or three. Because He knew that the demonic operated Sadducees would say that the dead man's spirit was still in him even on the third day; that's what they believed anyway. They would have used that to discredit Jesus' miracle. So, God needs to be comfortable with His sheep that He can use them to His Glory without them questioning Him every step of the way."

"When you say 'use', that sounds like taking advantage of someone," Jim stated.

"Well, when you think that He made us and owns us, and the fact that we have already been granted entrance into His heaven, it shouldn't matter much what happens here, the short time on earth." John took a deep breath and said, "My daughter is a soldier for Jesus Christ, wounded in battle."

Daemon said, *No way, she's going to die. Her fate is sealed.*

Jim got frustrated and said, "Are you telling me that your heart isn't ripping apart right now?"

John, with teary eyes replied, "Of course, but the same God who brought me through in the past will bring me through again. Don't get me wrong, I don't like pain either. But God knows all about our sufferings and He also knows how much we can take and what our limits are. He has promised us His presence in the midst of our trials, and He'd never leave us or forsake us. Jesus also said in this world we'd have trouble, but to be of good cheer; He has conquered the world. What makes Christians different is the way we handle these challenges. Some Christians are less likely to follow the leading of the Spirit of God and respond emotionally or intellectually to the challenges they face."

Daemon said, *C'mon, let's go now. Ask him these same questions tomorrow, and let's see if he feels the same way then.*

Jim said, "If you are a faithful believer and love God and this happens to you, I need to know what kind of God we're serving and what to expect from Him."

John replied, "Jesus said 'if you lose your life you'll find it and if you find your life you'll lose it.' It's like a sergeant telling his soldiers 'this next mission is a deadly one, chances of getting injured or killed is high, but it's a voluntary mission. If you make it back, you'll get awarded medals on your chest.' There is no reward higher than spending eternity in heaven with a crown on our head. So there will be some volunteers and some will chicken out. They'll die anyway, on a different regular mission, where there will be no special rewards whatsoever. The choice is ours."

"What kind of God, who is all powerful, doesn't protect His own, the people that He loves?"

"He does protect them, but not all the time. Remember He let His Son die on the cross to accomplish a goal."

"I can see that, but what would our suffering accomplish?" Jim asked.

"God gets glory out of every one of us, somehow."

"Wasn't it cruel for God to send Satan Job's way?"

"How did the story end? Job got everything back that he lost and the devil was proven wrong. God taught both Job and Satan a lesson about His sovereign will in our lives."

"Who is behind all the bad things, God or Satan?" Jim asked.

"Everybody has been trained to blame God while Satan gets away with murder, literally. We have to be careful not to blame God for our struggles because they come from our adversary, the devil. Instead of blaming God for the storms, we need to turn to Him for the strength to resist the devil. Our world wants to blame God for evil, but we know who is really to blame. God isn't to blame for human evil and suffering. We brought these things on ourselves by our own selfishness and rebellious spirit. God would like to help, but won't intervene unless we invite Him to do so through prayer."

"Yes, but we live in the info age. And people want to be in the know. They ask why a powerful God allows bad things to happen," Jim stated.

"It's amazing, how insurance companies call natural disasters, 'Acts of God' on their forms as if they know for sure they are acts of God. No one asks why there are so many good things in this world. God is God and He doesn't have to explain Himself to anybody. God sometimes brings about good from evil. This race and place fell into futility when Adam and Eve sinned against God and our world has become fallen and broken. Pain is a gift from God because it makes us realize that we need God's help. God whispers to us in pleasure, speaks to our conscience, and shouts in our pain. Pain is God's megaphone to a deaf world. Some of these storms are to perfect the character of the saints or to put the saints on the right track. Satan wanted to kill Apostle Paul, but Paul said to die is gain; Satan said OK, I'll keep you alive then. But then Paul said to live is Christ. Satan put Paul in prison where he wrote many letters to the churches. Satan didn't know how to defeat a person with this kind of outlook on life and death."

"Do you think that God is testing us?" Jim wanted to know.

"I don't think God is testing us to see for Himself if we pass or not or to see how much faith we have. Remember He is all knowing. Before we were born, He knew everything about us. I think He wants us to know how much faith we have for ourselves. When the Lord does test us, He doesn't torture us but makes us better. Satan may have questioned Noah, 'you're building what, a boat? For what, a flood! It never happened before.' Satan may have said to Moses, 'why don't you stay in your palace and enjoy the good life, help your people from the inside.' But Moses wanted to be with his people. Satan will try anything to stop us from obeying the Lord's commands."

Jim replied, "I admire your courage. If I were in your shoes, I may have broken into pieces."

"I just don't know how atheistic people go through a crisis alone; it must be very scary. I draw a lot of power and encouragement from my God who stands right beside me and holds my hand and even carries me. He gives me hope that whatever the outcome is, He is in control and I will still be a conqueror. God expresses His love towards the saved believer by offering daily comfort, joy, inner peace, patience, self-control, and safe harbor in times of trouble. He doesn't offer these benefits to the unbeliever. You know, the Bible says that we should consider it all joy when we go through severe testing."

Jim snapped and said, "Are you serious? Where am I supposed to get this joy from, when we're in pain? Your daughter is in bed in the next room and you don't know if she is coming out of here alive!"

"I may not have happiness because of what's happening in my life right now, but I have joy that comes from the Lord." John was under a lot of pressure that day and didn't have the patience he had the day before. He said, "You know, the Bible also says that we're supposed to encourage each other and you're not doing a good job at that."

Jim raised his voice and said, "How can I encourage you when I myself am discouraged?" People in the waiting room started looking at Jim so he lowered his voice and continued, "I miss the sex, the drugs, my job, and my mom won't talk to me. Look, I told you before, this stuff isn't for me. I have only been born again a few days and already am discouraged."

John calmly said, "We all get discouraged at one time or another, whether after a few days or a few years, as long as the devil is out there. Spiritual growth isn't dependent on time or learning, but is dependent on obedience. The drugs will take some time for you to get over and overcome, because you did it for a while. I drank four cups of coffee for a long time and when I had to give it up, it wasn't easy, so I sympathize with you. Bill, the brother from the Bible study, can't pass by a refrigerator without snacking and he had to get that under control. Some brothers and sisters struggle with smoking. All of these are hard habits to kick, but we do it anyway. It's hard to resist sin the first time, but afterwards, it gets easier. And once you have victory over all these issues you're having, you won't have to fight against them again. Satan will continue to test you in these areas of weaknesses, but once he figures out that you're over it, he won't test you again."

"What about my job? How am I gonna find another one in this economy?"

John looked at his watch and asked the Lord to give him strength and patience to carry on this conversation to encourage Jim and said, "It would be easy to get scared and stressed out because you have bills to pay and no money coming in. But remember that you are now a citizen in God's kingdom. You can be confident and try to rejoice in the hope of a bright future because you have a source of supply that those outside the will of God can't even conceive. So, go and have a prosperity party! The Lord is preparing to bless you from an unexpected source. There is another job on the horizon, a better one. As for sex, you'll find a nice spouse from church and stop living in sin…and as for your mom, I wouldn't worry too much; she might change her mind one day and call you. When my wife gets mad at Gracie, I tell them to both look at their belly buttons and point out that they were attached together for nine months, and that usually brings them together and closer."

Jim smiled and asked, "What if Gracie was mad at you and vice versa?"

"I'd tell her to look at her wrist and at her veins, and remind her that my blood is running in them. Your mom will come around; be patient. When you obey the Spirit of God, you'll not carry out the desires of the people you know and they will be offended by you. Don't allow their unpleasant reaction to discourage you from what you know in your heart is true. As a result, you'll suffer in the flesh. Just remember, now you have a big Christian family that loves you. You also have the Holy Spirit to lift you up."

"Tell me something I can understand and help me now," said Jim impatiently.

"What helps me when I'm down is the thought of Christians out there in the world giving up their lives for their beliefs. Compare that to our problems!" There was a silence for one minute.

"You mean people actually die in this day and age, for being Christians?"

"Of course. Now persecution is coming to our doorsteps. Bill was put in jail last week for being a witness. And you already know about my employer threatening my job for praying in public," John replied.

Jim was shocked and said, "I didn't know that Bill was put in Jail!"

"Jesus said that He conquered death and hell, and all things work for good for those who believe. God will get the glory out of this experience."

"When I pray and talk to God, I still hear those ugly voices in my head."

"The phone line to God is being tapped into by a spy, the devil. He can listen and talk through the tap. Ignore him. This is a good sign that you have a red siren for carnal thinking now, compliments of the Holy Spirit."

Jim looked down and shamefully said, "You know, I still get bad thoughts, sometimes."

"Whenever they come, don't dwell on them, refuse to let him bring them inside your mind, shred them like confetti, over and over again and occupy your mind with the word of God. Those images, habits, and thoughts were in your head for a long time. It will take a while to get rid of them, so be persistent. And pray for God to help you with that, too. Don't let failure cripple you. Be like Peter; admit your mistakes to God. Ask for forgiveness and let Him restore you. Since you asked the Lord to come into your life, you had peace because you and God are reconciled together. Before, you were running away from Him, but now you run to Him for help. If you allow Him, He can use even your mistakes for His Glory."

There was a short pause, and then Jim asked, "When I pray for guidance in a situation or matter and I get an answer, how do I know if the answer came from God or the devil? They both know what I'm thinking."

"One thing I know is that time works against the devil and works for God. The devil will lead us to instant gratification, 'the now solution', and leave the future consequences alone. If you are in doubt and want to make sure, then wait a while and continue to pray, and God will reveal more signs and ideas to you. Another suggestion is to deny yourself and love your neighbor. You'll see a better picture that way. Because the devil will always put you first, the 'what's good for me' solution, which sometimes leads to a trap. You also ask yourself, am I doing this for the glory of God or just to please myself, am I rushing ahead impulsively or am I willing to wait? Sometimes I didn't know what's good for me so I just simply prayed for God to do what's best for me. After all, He is the best adviser anyone can have."

"Amen," Jim said.

"But be prepared because sometimes God's ways may surprise you at first. But if you follow through His plan, you'll get a clear picture when it's all said and done, in this life or the one after. And always remember, conviction of the Holy Spirit brings you closer to God and condemnation of the devil sets you apart from God. Guilt is good in the first case. Of course, in the future after you have read the Bible so often, you'll get acquainted with hearing the voice of God and recognize a stranger's voice instantly. Governments make their agents memorize real dollar patterns by studying it over and over. Then, when a counterfeit is put in front of them, they identify it instantly because it doesn't fit the pattern their eyes have trained on. So, spend more time learning the voice of God." John looked at his watch again and said, "I'd better go back with my wife in case she needs me. Thanks for stopping by." Then he stood up.

Jim stood up also and said, "I don't think I'll be going to church this Sunday if you're not going to be there."

"I don't know what tomorrow holds, but I know who holds tomorrow. Remember, you're not going to church just for yourself. There are people there who could be encouraged by seeing you. I already know one person whom I told about your quitting drugs cold turkey, and he was encouraged because he is struggling with that addiction too. It's not enough to go to church once a week, for the devil works all week long and you'll need spiritual food and rein-forcement during the week. This is an evil world we live in and we need God to protect us, and we have to ask Him for it to get it."

"Thanks for talking to me and I hope and pray that your daughter gets better."

After Jim left, John took a deep breath and prayed, *Lord, reveal yourself to him in a great way. Bless him with your presence and let him know you more intimately. May he be pleasing to you and bring glory to your name.*

Spiritual Warfare

A day went by and it was now Friday. John and Mary's prayers hadn't been answered. They were in Gracie's hospital room still praising and worshiping while waiting for the results of the new tests the doctors conducted early in the morning. Finally, the doctor informed them that they found a tumor in the brain. She was in a coma right now and a serious surgery was the only option. After the doctor left, Mary, out of her grief, said to Satan, "She's only a child, how could you be so cruel? You have no mercy; the Lord rebukes you, devil!"

A demon present in the room thought, *I have no problem hurting children, women, or old people. I'll do anything to discourage and destroy you mortals.*

Meanwhile, the Holy Spirit requested a rescue dispatch to release the restrained angel who had been detained and delayed by demons.

Bill came in to visit with John and console him in the late morning. He stepped into Gracie's room and found John sitting there.

After exchanging greetings, John sadly said, "I never had a day of trouble out of my daughter; she is so heavenly minded and earthly good. It just doesn't make any sense."

Bill replied, "We may not understand it because we're not God. His ways are higher than our ways, and His thoughts are higher than our thoughts. You can't make logic out of a fallen world, a world that gives this kind of tragedy, misery, and headache. But we know that there is a God in heaven. We know that in the midst of our trials, while we don't understand His hands, we trust His heart. And when answers aren't enough, there is Jesus. He's a God who will hold us in the midst of our storms. He is a God of providence, a God who lifts us. We're not alone in this life. We have a God who gives us grace through every storm in our lives. Whatever suffering may come to our lives, God has ordained it and is in complete control."

John listened attentively, looking for encouragement in what could become a frightening day.

Bill continued, "Don't be discouraged when trouble comes your way; it is the road that our Savior has walked before us. It is the way of the cross, and He has won the victory. We have pushed in the spiritual realm and we're being pushed back into the furnace of adversities. This world system is under the control of Satan and we have been spreading the Gospel into his domain. This is the kingdom of darkness' response to our efforts: strong resistance. Jesus told us that we'd be resisted just as He was."

Bill had no pat answers or solutions; he didn't hand out tiny theological packages. But he spoke courageously even though it wasn't easy. So he tried to give John a message of hope in a time of despair and said, "When God permits Satan to light the furnace, He always keeps His own hand on the thermostat. The devil isn't running anything; God has all power and control. Satan can plan plots for destruction, but he has no control over the outcome. God can intervene and change the course of the events depending on our reaction to the attack. When Abraham obeyed God and went up the mountain to sacrifice his son, a goat sacrifice went up the other side of the mountain at the same time. God provides provisions that we may not see, but they're there. Our God is still on the throne. He is the same yesterday, today, tomorrow."

Bill's heart was ripping apart every time he looked at the girl lying in bed being tormented like this and her parents with her, too. Yet he kept his calm and kept counseling his best friend and brother in the faith, the only way he knew how to combat evil. So he pulled out as many scriptures from the Bible as he could and went to battle.

Bill continued, "I know exactly what you're going through because I had a horrible experience last year. I decided to start a Bible study in my home and my health just went downhill after that."

"Yes I remember you lost a lot of weight last year."

"The doctors couldn't explain it, but I knew who was behind the attack. I thought I knew the devil well, but when I decided to serve God, he showed his true colors and took off his gloves. I persevered for a whole year of bleeding and excruciating pain. Because of my condition, I was forced into fasting for a whole year. It turned out that fasting is not as difficult as I thought. So, I trusted the Lord Jehovah-Rapha to heal me, and He delivered me. Praise God. Now, my Bible study group is the largest in the church. Satan knows the potential we're carrying and our importance to the kingdom of God, so he does everything he can to keep our gifts and talents from thriving and our dreams from being accomplished. He was trying to get me to be in disagreement with God and I have to admit that at my weakest point I did have my doubts. But I was rooted and grounded in Christ, thanks to the Holy Spirit. Satan has robbed the world of spiritual wealth by attacking the bodies of believers and their health.

"Another lesson I learned from the experience was that, when I went through that intense trial, I became rude and unkind to my wife. Trials in this life expose what's in our hearts. These bad traits were there, but I never knew they were there until the trial made them surface. I repented and received forgiveness and the Lord has removed those impurities from my life. God gets in the midst of the storm, takes a tragedy and pulls triumph out of it. A test is only a test and when it is conquered, there's a testimony and glorifying of God."

"That's a great testimony. I'm getting comfort just by listening to you."

"Praise the Lord. See, Job's friends accused him of sin because they probably didn't have any tragedy or experience of suffering in their lives, so they weren't comforting him, but only accusing him. When someone goes through a tragedy and suffers, the experience will either build character or causes the person to be bitter and sulk. If a character is built, the next time tragedy hits, the person can lean on the previous experience and believe that God will deliver them from this one, too. And when someone else is suffering, they'll be a good comforter. Trees endure the hot sun and rainstorms by driving their roots down deeper into the ground. The harsh conditions they face eventually become the source of great stability."

John nodded his head in agreement, then Bill continued, "Again, Job didn't know what was going on behind the scenes. He had no idea that God had moved His protecting hand for a season and allowed him to suffer, so that Satan may be proven wrong. The real battle was in the heavenly places. Job's home and body were all made the arena in which God and Satan were wrestling against each other. Satan used Job's body, family, and friends to cause him to curse God and God used them to prove Satan wrong. God tests to develop while Satan tempts to destroy. Job had trouble in chapter one and two; he got his blessings in chapter forty-two. If he had given up in chapter forty, he would have lost his blessings and Satan would have won. God gives a season for rewards. The devil tries to hold us back from reaching our God-promised blessings, and from passing his time limit; he tries to get us to quit early.

"The attacks of the devil sometimes look like they never end, but they have a time limit and they expire as they lose their potency after they reach that time limit. Satan has a season to hold us back. We just have to outlast the devil to get to our God-promised blessings and defeat the devil. Satan has no patience; our patience must outlast him because we have the fruits of the spirit. Impatience is a mark of unbelief. Faith and patience go together. The only way we can learn patience is by going through the trials that God assigns to us. So, pain may endure for a night, but relief is coming in the morning. After a few months, you won't even remember the details. God will bring it to a close; don't doubt God that He is going to bless you. After all, we're not better than Paul, who had a thorn in his flesh. His grace is sufficient," Bill encouraged.

"You know, Peter and the other apostles did the same miracles. They didn't have thorns!"

"Maybe, it's not mentioned in the Bible. But everyone has a different nature and God knows who to give the thorns to, for He knows our nature better than we do! The blacksmith looks at gold until he can see a reflection of himself, then he turns off the heat. When the Lord looks at us and can see His son Jesus, He turns off the heat. God sometimes permits His children to suffer that He might discipline them. God's purpose isn't to persecute us, but to perfect us. Discipline isn't the work of an angry judge who punishes a criminal. God is a loving Father who perfects His children. God will not be tempted neither will He tempt anyone. There is a difference between temptations and trials. Trials are sent by God to cause us to stand, and is intended for our maturity. Temptation to sin is sent by the devil to cause us to stumble and be miserable."

John knew all these facts, but being discouraged, said, "A trial like this can come with such a force that it blows you off course. What a temptation! It can strike at the backside and almost give you whiplash."

Bill sensed fear in John's tone of voice and he knew that faith comes by hearing the word of God, while fear comes by hearing the word of the devil. So he kept on injecting faith in John's spirit and continued, "My brother, count it all joy when you fall into divers temptations. The gift of suffering is the most misunderstood gift. Sometimes I have to admit that it's hard to 'count it all joy', we complain rather than being humbly grateful and try to be like the saints that have gone before us. In due season, we'll reap the harvest so don't give up, but be patient. When trouble comes, you either get bitter or better."

"I have to say, if I pretend to be cheerful right now, I would be lying to myself."

"No, no, that's not the reason God tells us to go through trouble with joy. It's because the devil is watching every move you make and every thought you think, and if he thinks that he's succeeding, then he'll keep doing it to break you. The sooner we follow instructions, the sooner we can stop him." Then Bill took a deep breath and continued the battle, "Jesus cannot put us in a zip lock bag in a Holy Spirit freezer to keep us from trouble. The Bible says, 'Beloved, think it not strange concerning the fiery trial which is to try you, as though some strange thing happened unto you.' Pray and seek help always and listen to the Holy Spirit."

"I just wish I could hear from the Lord. He seems to be silent and one can't help but wonder if He has forsaken us," John said desperately.

"The teacher is always silent during the test. When problems get over your head and you feel like you're in a sea of trouble, remember they are under His feet. Jesus might be sleeping in the back of your boat through your personal tidal wave, but He is on board. And as long as He is on board, your boat will never sink." Bill pointed up and continued, "God is on the throne and in total control, so have no fear. Everything will be all right.

"Don't let tough times stop you; keep running, and fight a good fight for Jesus. Tough times never last. God will strengthen you during this trial and persecution. God brings good out of tough times. Strengthen the faith and be like Christ. Continue lifting up the cross. If God is before us, who is against us for we're more than conquerors. We're not going to rejoice only when things are going well." Bill's tone of voice became stronger and felt like he was going to preach as he continued, "Praise Him in the good times and don't stop rejoicing in the bad times. Shall we receive good at the hand of God, and shall we not receive evil? Look who are cheering us from the bleachers; Abel, Joseph, Abraham, Moses, Samson, David, and a lot more."

"You know Jim, you met him last Wednesday. He was here yesterday; it's always hard to explain to a new Christian why God allows these trials," John told him.

Bill admonished, "Don't let the thought enter your mind that this is happening because you have done something wrong. Before you know it, you'll fall into a pity party, taking yourself apart to see where you went wrong and get discouraged. What if God is simply testing your faith? We cannot control the origin or the operation of suffering but we can, with God's help, control the outcome. Jesus had to go through all the injustices of His arrest, trial, and crucifixion and when He was hanging on the cross, He embraced what He knew instead of reacting to what His mockers didn't know. You shouldn't feel that you have to apologize for what God hasn't done; remember all the things He has done for you in the past. God's timing and His decisions don't always meet our expectations. But that didn't keep Jesus from trusting Him that day on Calvary."

"I know that there is going to be trouble in this life. So what do you do when you praise and worship and things get worse?" John asked.

"Some of the trouble is on assignment, not because you sinned, or because you're being tested. God allows it to prove a point to the devil. There are no spiritual maneuvers one can do to get out of it. So prayer and fasting, altar call, speaking in tongues, and agreeing with a prayer partner might not work. You still do all that, not to get out of trouble, but to help you endure and go through the storm. We shouldn't try to change God's mind; faith accepts God's will. He knows better than we do what's good for us. You know that He can heal her, but would He? It is His prerogative to do it. We also have to go through close encounters of the third kind. The first kind is when the devil presses on us. The second kind is when God tests us. And the third kind is when God and Satan fight over our loyalty. Remember, temptations come from Satan, tests come from God, and trials come from man."

"Thanks, Bill, for the encouragement. I really appreciate your coming here today."

"I'm sure if I were going through the same trouble, you'd encourage me, too. And make sure you thank God; Satan hates it when believers thank God in their trials. Remember, don't be anxious about anything, but in everything by prayer and supplication with thanksgiving let your requests be made known to God. And the peace of God, which surpasses all understanding, will guard your heart and your mind in Christ Jesus."

"There is a group of Christians, who are against blood transfusion, and they have some good reasons; the Bible says that life is in the blood. There is also the safety factor, whether we can depend on the Red Cross to prevent disease from getting into the blood supply. So let's pray and ask guidance whether I should accept blood transfusion for Gracie or not if it comes to that."

"No brother, we'll pray that she won't need blood transfusion at all and that she would have a complete healing and get out of here. Don't let fear get to you. Let me remind you that God is the Prince of peace, and to remain calm even in the middle of the storm. I saw a picture of a furious storm on the sea with the winds blowing and the waves crashing on a big rock that stands alone in the middle of the ocean. And when I looked closer, I saw a little bird snuggled safely in that rock peacefully! Only believers understand this kind of peace that surpasses all human understanding while going through severe trials and tests, it is God's safeguarding presence in the midst of the raging storm," Bill responded.

"Well, should I do what the doctors say or stay firm on what God promised?"

"Do both pray to God and follow the doctors' instructions, and you'll be fine. Sometimes the Lord doesn't prevent surgery, but He holds our hands during the surgery and the recovery process. By His stripes we're healed," said Bill as he stood up.

"Amen. Thanks again, Bill. Where are you going now?" asked John.

"Back to the mall and the Bible tracks. We're going to keep on sailing, serving, and loving Him. We will run the race with endurance, looking unto Jesus."

"Again! You'd better find someone to bail you out."

"Oh, don't worry. I'm covered. I hope Gracie gets well soon. But before I leave, I brought some oil with me, the balm of Gilead. I'm going to rub it on Gracie's forehead and we'll pray for healing. Just like God is a jealous God over us, if we love something or someone more than Him, we also have rights and privileges in this relationship. He promised that he'd never leave us, so if we get sick we remind Him about His promises. But we're not going to be obnoxious when we remind Him."

Then, they prayed after Bill put the oil on Gracie. Bill left afterwards, leaving John with enough spirituality to face his trying day.

* * * * * *

Later that afternoon, while John and Mary were waiting for an answer to their prayers, strange noises came from the room adjacent to their room. Mary asked the nurse about it and the nurses said that they just brought a teen-age girl into the room next door. The girl tried to commit suicide and the nurse who looked after her said that the doctor diagnosed her as being psychologically disturbed with multiple personalities, but her parents claimed that she was possessed with demons. John and Mary included the disturbed girl in their prayers.

The suicidal girl's parents requested the local hospital chaplain to come into her room to exorcise and cast the demons out of her. When the chaplain arrived outside the girl's room, the parents greeted him and asked him to help their daughter. He replied, "I haven't exorcised anyone before. I have no experience."

The mother begged, "Please you're the only hope we have to help our girl, Stephanie."

The chaplain reluctantly agreed to try.

He went into the room by himself gripped with fear; he broke out in a sweat and felt his hands trembling. He looked at the beautiful girl strapped down in her bed peacefully. He gained a measure of confidence, as the situation didn't appear to be as out of control as the nurse had described to him when she called him on the phone.

He spoke, as he got closer to the bed, "Hello Stephanie, I'm the chaplain in this hospital and…"

The girl looked at him, interrupted with a horrible and evil voice, and said, "What the hell do you want!"

He spoke with weakness and fear and said, "I'm speaking to the demons inside Stephanie. I come in the name of Jesus," said the man with much trembling.

The demons said, "Jesus we know, but who are you?"

The man replied, "I'm a man of God …I'm a servant of God. I'm a good man and help the community…"

Meanwhile, the chaplain had a demon following him, who gave the possessing demons an update on the chaplain's weaknesses.

After they got the update, the demons then interrupted the chaplain and said, "But you hate what you're doing here, don't you? And your boss denied your transfer request. You want your own congregation, don't you?"

The chaplain was shocked at their knowing his life's details and started to sweat even more. He made things worse by lying about it, saying, "That's not true."

"You're a liar, too! Do you like the naked girls in those magazines you keep at home?" said the demons with a condemning voice.

"I don't have to listen to this. I'm leaving," said the man as he walked towards the door. "No, wait," said the demons with a soft voice this time, "if you cast us out and save this girl, you might get your request approved after all and get your transfer. This is a good opportunity for you."

The chaplain stopped and looked back. The demons continued, "But you'll have to do something for us."

"What?" asked the man.

"Come closer and we'll tell you."

The next thing, the room door opened and the parents saw the chaplain leaving the room with only one shoe on. He also lost his jacket and his shirt was untucked and had green stains of what looked like vomit. He had bruises on his face that he tried to cover with his hand. The parents looked at him and wondered what happened to him.

The chaplain's demon followed and said, *Look, I'm sorry but you came in the room using the 'J' word, you ruffled our feathers. You're really not too bad; we have clergymen who are pedophiles and molesters. Actually, you can expand your horizon and get on the Internet, get online and watch live porn with young girls. If you're worried about your credit card being traced or you being exposed, use a check card or prepaid credit card, no one will know.*

The man continued walking towards the nurses' station and wasn't listening to the demon at this time out of shock over what just happened. He was in pain and stunned that a thirteen-year-old girl could have wrestled him down like a professional wrestler and jabbed him like a professional boxer with both power and accuracy.

The demon continued, *I told you many times to change your clothes, drive a couple of hours to the next town, and go to the local bar and pick up girls and have sex. And no one has to know about it.*

When he got to the nurses' station, one of the nurses giggled at his appearance and condition. Feeling embarrassed he said, "The girl in room 203 C is loose and she could hurt herself. Send out the orderly there please ...on the double." As he was leaving the station, he heard more giggles. The man's pride was dragged through the mud, so he took off the only shoe he had left and walked without shoes.

The demon sensed that the man was sinking deeper in disappointment and discouragement. So he said, *Hey, who needs this? You should quit and find another profession. You can be anything you want. And then you can have sex with as many woman and girls as you want.*

The man was in despair; people were looking at him as he walked down the hospital hallway with embarrassment. The man became conscious to the fact that God had shaken and awakened him to his true sinful condition, to bring him closer to his true foundation. He realized his faith was weak and decided to fight back and give up his secret addictions. All of a sudden he started to walk with confidence and resolved to improve his ministry in Christ and said, "Help me Jesus."

The demon found himself three steps behind and said, *Hey, wait for me.* Again, the man said, "Help me, Lord Jesus." Now the demon was six steps behind and said, *Hey, where are you going?* Again he said, "Help me, Jesus." The demon had to vanish but before he left him, he thought, *OK priest, I'll see you in a couple of days.*

Then the demon grabbed another demon and said, "See this man here, he has been just convicted by the Holy Spirit and he is hard to reach right now. But in a day or two, if he loses that determination and becomes undecided, then we grab a couple of our brothers and go down on him like a ton of bricks and make him worse than before."

Stephanie's parents were disappointed that the man of God had failed his mission and their daughter's condition hadn't changed. Then they overheard John and Mary praying in the room next door. The mother whispered to her husband, "We don't pray like that!"

"Yes we do! On Sundays."

"Not like this prayer, with faith. We have ignored our daughter; that is why is she is in trouble."

"Well, their daughter is in trouble too. Maybe they don't have enough faith either!" the man said.

Then they went into Gracie's room and explained to John and Mary what had happened to their daughter. The mother said, "My daughter is a good girl, but she hung around the wrong crowd. She likes all kinds of witch and sorcery movies and plays violent video games, some dungeons and dragons or something. I don't know how she got interested in witchcraft and horoscopes. And when she started hearing things in her head and even saw some shadows and things move around her, I got worried. She said she was touched once by an unknown being or spirit and saw a hideous face. I think that's what drove her to suicide." She took a deep breath and continued as her husband put his arm around her, "I admit that we have neglected her by working too many long hours. Now she's in the next room tied down to the bed because she slit her wrist a few hours ago and they brought her to the hospital." She cried and appealed with tears to Mary, "From one mother to another, I beg you, if you can do something to help."

John looked at Mary to see how she felt about this and he was hoping that she would say no because they had too much on their plate. In addition, what those parents were requesting wasn't a small favor or something that he had done before. He didn't feel like he had enough energy to tackle this one. Surprisingly, Mary nodded her head with an approval.

Stephanie's mother excitedly said, "Thank you. Thank you so much."

John looked at Mary with a smile and thought, *I didn't expect that*. He followed the parents to Stephanie's room where they waited outside and he went inside by himself. He had never done anything like this before and didn't know what to expect. He felt a chill as he went in, as the room temperature was unexpectedly low. He knelt in the room as he closed the door behind him and said, "Holy Father, in the name of Your Son I approach Your throne. My Lord, I know that this is the work of the devil; I know that You have defeated the devil and all his demons on Calvary, and I know that You have given us the power to defeat him. So, I pray now in the name of Your Son Jesus, to evict any evil spirits that are at work here. I need to exercise my faith in the name of the Lord Jesus who teaches us that 'He that is within us is stronger than the one in the world'. Without the Holy Spirit, I'm nothing but a shell of flesh and blood. I thank You, Lord for hearing my prayer. Amen." Then, he stood up and cautiously got closer to her bed.

"What do you want?" the demons asked in an evil voice like thunder mixed with waterfall noises.

John answered, "Get out of this child of God."

The voices said, "You must watch too much TV. Once we get in, we don't leave. We're here to stay."

"I'll tell you a story, not from TV. When Jesus told your brothers, called Legion, to get out—" The demons started groaning. John continued, "And by the same power of the Holy Spirit that Jesus gave me, I command you to leave. The name of Jesus sets the captives free." The demons started growling louder.

John started out shaky when he first confronted the evil forces, but now he felt filled by the Holy Spirit and confident. Even his body felt stronger after he prayed and felt like Popeye after eating a can of spinach. He was feeling so strong, that if these demons would take on a body and come out, he would shred them to pieces. But this was a spiritual war, so he continued his spiritual offensive, "I rebuke you demons in the name of God Almighty and Jesus Christ and upon the basis of Calvary's victory, I command you to be bound and cast into the abyss. Pack up your bags and go to the dry places, demons."

There were three demons present in the room. All three of them shrieked with evil voices and shook the bed up and down, and the teen-age girl convulsed in spasms.

John shouted, "Be quiet!" and continued firmly, "I speak the blood of Jesus over this place; you demons can't cross the bloodline of Jesus. The Lord Jesus gave me power to tread on serpents and scorpions, and over all the power of the enemy, and nothing shall by any means hurt us. I come at you by the name and authority of the Lord Jesus Christ and by the cross and His resurrection."

The demons trembled in fear of the name Jesus and immediately scattered away. Some of them joined their brother demons above the hospital, and created a tight sphere around the angel so he couldn't move in any direction.

Finally, Stephanie was in peace, she now seemed calm, and John saw peace in her face. She was changed by the power of Jesus. John took a moment to reflect on what just happened. He usually got a thrill when he witnessed to others and felt the presence of the Holy Spirit speaking through him, but nothing like the feeling he just had. This experience with the demons felt like multiple shots of Holy Spirit adrenalin. When he was filled with the Holy Spirit, his body never felt as strong as that. It came to his mind that Jesus said if we had faith we could move mountains.

John approached the girl slowly. She seemed tired and scared, and asked for her parents. John said, "Don't be afraid, I'm a friend, and Jesus loves you."

Sounding weak she asked, "Jesus?"

He kindly said, "Yes, Jesus. He saved you today. Keep Him in your heart," as he was untying her hands first then her feet. Then he said, "And now I want you to denounce Satan and all his work, so he won't be back. If you don't, he will come back even stronger and destroy you." So she did willingly as he instructed her. Then John said, "I declare the blood of Jesus on you."

John walked towards the door and said, "I'll be right back with your parents." He went out of the room and signaled the parents to come in to the room.

The mother asked, "How is she?" as she went into the room and saw the daughter who seemed relaxed and her arms extending towards her. The mother ran towards Stephanie, hugged her, and said, "Darling." The father followed and feeling relieved, said, "Pumpkin!"

Stephanie said, "I was so scared!"

The mother said, "We're here for you, baby. We won't let anything bad happen to you."

"I'm hungry," said Stephanie.

"No problem," said the father as he pressed the nurse's button.

A voice came from the intercom, "Can I help you?"

"Please send some food," said the mother. She was overjoyed to hear her daughter asking for food because she was a fussy eater.

"Ok, I'll be right there," replied the voice.

The mother then turned and hugged John and said, "May God bless you. If there is anything we can do to help you and your family..." The father turned around and got something out of his pocket; he seemed like he was writing something.

John said, "That's quite all right. Just pray for my daughter."

The father turned around, and gave John a check for ten thousand dollars and proudly said, "Just write down your name on it."

John said, "No thank you, that's not necessary."

Meanwhile, a nurse showed up with lots of enthusiasm and a tray of food in her hand. John was surprised at the speed she responded to the call. The nurse put the food on a transportable tray and positioned it in front of the girl. And sure enough, her dad reached into his pocket and got out a bill for a hundred dollars and gave it to the nurse.

"Thank you sir, call me if you need anything," said the nurse with a big smile and left. John thought, *no wonder, the rich man was handing out a hundred dollar bill to anyone who entered the room.* The girl started eating and gobbled the food fast for she hadn't had a decent meal in days."

While Stephanie ate, John asked the parents, "Can I speak to you privately outside?" They moved closer to the door and John continued, "Mom and Dad, now I cleaned house of all evil spirits. The next step is up to you."

The father asked, "What do you mean, next step. Aren't we done?"

"Well, these demons will come back and believe me, they will be bringing with them more of their cousin demons and the outcome will be worse than before," he whispered, "Maybe suicide. If she jumps off the roof, there is no cure for that!"

The mother grieved, "Oh my God, what must we do?"

"Remove the reasons that brought the demons in the first place. Remove all movies about witchcraft and material such as tarot cards, wee-gee boards, or crystal balls. You know, anyone who consults astrology is an abomination to the Lord. Make sure that she doesn't associate with anyone who communicates with the dead, a fortune-teller or palm reader. And most importantly, repent of your sins and get baptized in the name of Jesus. If you are a human and don't have God in you, there is a spiritual vacuum, which invites the devil in."

The father said, "That's a tall order prescription. I don't mind the first part, but the second part; um…can't we just make a contribution to the church? I know the priest would like that unlike you—"

The Mother stopped him and said, "We'll do it; if you could please help us follow your direction. Here is my phone number."

"I'll be glad to help," replied John.

While John was defeating demons in one room, there was a nurse in the next room visiting with Mary. The nurse looked at Gracie's chart and said, "Look, I have seen you pray earlier and that's good, but you really need to come down to reality and face the fact that your daughter is in serious trouble, and you need to let the doctors do what they do best. I'm looking at her chart, and maybe it's none of my business, but I think if prayer hasn't worked, you should let the doctors take over."

Mary politely said, "Thank you for your concern and your help."

Yes, I'm trying to help you stop praying, lady, thought the nurse's devil, Zebub. Then Zebub thanked the nurse for opening the door for him and thought, *they must be important people to send me personally to handle this case,* as he looked at Mary and Gracie. Then one of the demons that were scattering from the room next door accidentally stumbled into Gracie's room and Zebub said, "Stop, why are you running, boy?"

The demon who was trembling said, "There is a mortal next door, armed with the Holy Spirit and dangerous."

Zebub said, "A man. You never let them see you run, boy."

"Oh, no sir, this man is anointed by the Holy Spirit. We recognized that the minute he entered the room. We thought maybe we could shake him, but he is as solid as a rock in his faith. He's on a higher level and requires another skilled devil."

"Why was I sent to this room then if my assignment is next door? Am I in the wrong room?"

"I think these two here are related to him, sir."

"Why wasn't I informed then?"

"They don't have any demons assigned to them, sir."

"We'll see about that. I guess I'll start here with these two then," said Zebub as he looked at Mary and Gracie and continued, "And use them against him. But you stay here. I might assign you to them while I take care of the man."

Then Zebub went to work and whispered to Mary, *what if she dies?* Mary shook and fear gripped her heart as the thought entered her mind. Zebub triumphantly said, "I have an open door now. I feel a slow burn coming over her."

The Holy Spirit said to Mary, *Daughter, concentrate. You're going to be tempted.*

Mary's angel said to the Holy Spirit, "My Lord, her fear is weakening her faith."

Mary rushed out of the room and walked to the room next door. She peaked in to see what was taking John so long. The teen-age girl smiled at her and waved. Mary smiled and waved back and it was obvious to her that the girl was made well. She then lost the smile when the devil said to her, *He helped other people, but he couldn't heal his own dying daughter.*

John looked at Mary, and she seemed upset as she stormed out of the room. John excused himself and followed her into the visiting room in the hospital where she said with frustration, "How come you can't help your own daughter?"

Zebub said to the demon, "Here comes bitterness, followed by anger. Works like a charm every time."

Then she stormed out of the waiting room and said, "I'm going to pick up my sister from the airport and get some fresh air." John was baffled and stood there in confusion and hurt.

Zebub said, "And there goes clamor and hostility; just look at that red face." Then he said to Mary, *Hey, come back here, we're not done here. Tell him that if Gracie dies you'll divorce him, and tell him that you hate him and you wish you never married him and you wish that he were dead—. Hey, come back, slap him a little—. Oh... You're no fun.* Zebub was surprised that Mary didn't bite anymore. Zebub thought at first that Mary was an unstable person, easily moved and swayed by the storms of persecution and trials. But he realized now that she wasn't that easy. He looked at the demon who said, "I told you they're not easy."

Then Zebub looked at John who was crushed by an onslaught of words launched in hurt and frustration and said to the demon, "You go ahead and follow the woman. I don't need her any more. I have a bigger fish to fry here, and I got him right where I want him. She's opened the door for me. This is working better than expected."

The demon left after Mary, even though he didn't want to because of the whipping he received at John's hand. But Zebub outranked him, so he had to follow his orders. He trusted his superior's ways, especially after he saw John crushed which made him feel vindicated.

Then Zebub reached for his quiver and took out a dart and said, *Here we go mortal. Let's rock.*

Raphael said to Zebub, "You're the mortal. This soul," pointing at John," is an immortal."

"We'll see about that."

The Holy Spirit said, *John, I want you to concentrate; you are going to be tempted. Get your walkie-talkie out, and connect with the commander in chief, pray.*

John was bewildered, frustrated, and numb after what just happened. John had just defeated demons in their own territory and gave the kingdom of Satan a big blow, yet he lost the war on the home front. Mary was so angry that John saw something in her eyes for a split second that he never seen before, the devil. These were the same beautiful eyes that he fell in love with, filled with passion and sweetness. She was the love of his life and the mother of his child. He considered his wife not only his lover and best friend, but also the person he confided in more than in any other person. John loved Mary with his heart unconditionally, with his soul passionately, and with his strength continually. She was a prudent godly woman, an excellent wife, trustworthy, a hard worker, financially responsible and compassionate to the poor and sick, without looking for a reward back. She had fear of the Lord in her heart in reverence, worship, and awe, respectful, sensible and on top of things. Mary had so much joy in the Lord that she never depended on John to make her happy even though she loved him very much and he loved her very much. In fact, she had so much joy that it overflowed to him and he felt that joy.

John, now in turmoil, wondered if he should call Mary on the phone to talk this over as they usually do.

The Holy Spirit said, *Let me take care of it.*

John called her anyway, but he couldn't get a signal through.

Zebub said, *I won't let you contact her unless you call to tell her that she was wrong to disrespect you. That she is a weak Christian and God will judge her. And tell her that maybe her attitude is the reason Gracie isn't getting better and blocking God's favor.*

There was a silence in the room. These thoughts could not penetrate John's shield of faith. Zebub was surprised and realized what he was dealing with. He remembered what the other demon told him earlier and said, *So, you're going to give me the silent treatment. I know that you had a glimpse of me a minute ago and our eyes locked. I'll surely break you before the day ends. Maybe you've won one round with the three imbeciles. But by the end of the day, I'll have you chained, branded, and doing my will. We can do this the easy way or we can do this the hard way.*

* * * * * *

Meanwhile, Mary left the hospital and drove her car to the airport. While she was driving and listening to her gospel station, she heard one of her favorite songs and she started crying. She realized what the devil had done. She got angry and thought, *ok devil, I know you can read my mind, you have won round one and I won't let you win another one. But let me tell you this, I'm washed by the blood of Christ, I have repented and I'm back into His will. But you might like to see the lake of fire that the Lord has prepared for you. I imagine a fire like the sun, burning forever, and you're in it.*

The demon screeched and screamed in pain the words, *Forget this, the whole family is messed up,* as he fled.

Mary continued driving to the airport.

* * * * * *

Back at the hospital, John started to get upset because of the fact that his daughter wasn't healing but instead was getting worse. He found himself all alone in the waiting room. He started praying and asking, "Lord, why hasn't my prayer been answered? Why the delay in Gracie's healing, Lord?" Still, the presence of the Lord seemed nowhere to be found.

The Holy Spirit brought to His attention the couple of times when the angels were delayed in answering the saints' prayers. When Daniel prayed, the demon of Persia held the angel back twenty-one days. Also, there was the time the apostle Paul prayed and his request was delayed because of resisting demons.

Then the Holy Spirit said, *When Lazarus was sick, Jesus was with him the whole time and He knew that Lazarus was going to die, but the disciples didn't. Lazarus' sisters said," if you were here, he wouldn't have died," but Jesus was there! He knew he was going to raise him from the dead. He did it so the disciples would believe.*

Soon, a bunch of people came into the waiting room weeping for someone who just died. One of the men asked John, "Excuse me, is this the third floor?"

John answered, "No, this is the second floor."

The man looked at another man who accompanied the group and said, "I pushed the third floor button. How did we end up here?"

"I have no idea; let's go back to the elevator." And they escorted the women too towards the elevator.

One of the grieving women said, "She was so young; how could she die like that?"

Fear entered John's heart as he heard that statement from the wailing woman.

The angel looked at Zebub who was reaching for his quiver for a dart and realized that it was the demon behind the nasty move of bringing this grieving party this way.

John weakened and thought, *my soul is grieving.* At that point, the demon was outside the waiting room blocked by Raphael who stood at the entrance of the room and prevented him from entering. Still the demon was able to sneak in a fiery dart at John, shot it and thought. *Here is a fear dart.* The dart reached John, made a hole in the shield, and penetrated it.

The demon was surprised and excited at his success and thought, *My Lucifer, there is a door open. Gotcha!* Then said, *Where is your God now? It seems as if God had turned his back on you. I thought He was going to give you wings like eagles to soar; you look like a chicken to me.*

Getting encouraged, the demon got his quiver out, full of darts, and sent out a slew of fiery arrows towards John with attacks of doubt, discouragement, loneliness, mistrust, etc. There were so many of them it was hard to count. One dart the demon couldn't use was unforgiveness, because he forgave Mary right away.

However, Raphael slowed down the fiery darts so that the Holy Spirit could get a chance to retaliate and reinforce John with scriptures. Some of the scriptures that came to John's mind were in Isaiah that say, 'God will hold your right hand, Fear not; I'll help you.'

And as soon as the other darts came in, the Holy Spirit battled against them with scriptures. For the Worry dart, the Holy Spirit brought to John's remembrance, *Cast your burden on the Lord, and He shall sustain you; He shall never permit the righteous to be moved.* For the Anxiety dart: *Don't be anxious about anything, but in everything, by prayer and petition, with thanksgiving, present your requests to God. And the peace of God, which transcends all understanding, will guard your hearts and your minds in Christ Jesus.*

John still sadly thought the presence of God seemed to have eluded him. He asked, "Where are you? You said you would be my comforter, yet I have no comfort!" He needed someone to talk to, so he called his friend Bill, but his line was busy.

The Holy Spirit said, *The Lord is with you; He will never leave you or forsake you, even to the end of the age. But, Satan has desired to have you that he may sift you as wheat; but I prayed for you so that your faith fails not.* The Holy Spirit also reminded John that King David encouraged himself one time when he was blamed for something that he didn't do and his followers were going to stone him.

He also said, *Remember the last time you were in trouble, how God helped bring you through it? Trust the Lord; the same God that was with you yesterday, He is the same yesterday, today, and tomorrow. Then approach the throne of grace with confidence, so that you may receive mercy and find grace to help you again in your time of need.*

John thanked the Holy Spirit for the advice and encouraged himself in the Lord. The Holy Spirit comforted John and peace entered his heart in the midst of his grief. Joy started to enter his heart in the midst of the trial; the Holy Spirit was flowing through his life. John remembered that the Holy Spirit could never forget him.

John thought, *I wish I could hug you, Lord.*

The Holy Spirit said, *I'm a spirit and I'm talking to your inner spirit, from one spirit to another. I dwell inside your physical body, so one can't get any closer than that.*

John's fellowship with the Holy Spirit had never been as sweet as it was now. At that time, the darts reached John, but the shield that was protecting him quenched them and the hole was closed.

Zebub said to John, *Who do you think you are, full of yourself like you're somebody. You're nothing but a sinner; you don't deserve any mercy or grace. God doesn't love you; you're a sinner.*

John thought, *I'm a son of God Almighty; you're right about one thing, I sin everyday and the blood of Jesus Christ cleanses me when I confess my sin. But you, on the other hand, sinned just once and you got kicked out of heaven, you lost your job and position. Thanks for reminding me of the goodness and mercy of my savior.*

Zebub roared like a lion out of fury. Raphael took a step backward, looked back to make sure the Holy Spirit was there, than he stepped forward and held his position. John continued, *You tell me who he loves more, you or me?*

Then Raphael said, "Every time John, the prodigal son, sins and confesses his sin, I do what the Lord tells me and cover him with the robe of righteousness. The only reason you had a foothold, for a short time, is because you used Mary against him. Otherwise, you wouldn't have gotten a chance with him."

Zebub got frustrated and said to John, *You're giving me a nervous breakdown, what are you?*

However, John surprisingly replied, "I'm a spirit trapped in this body and guided by the Holy Spirit."

Raphael was surprised and looked at the Holy Spirit and asked, "How did John hear the devil's question?"

The Holy Spirit replied, "He has reached such a spiritual high, that I allowed him to hear the question and enjoy his victory."

Raphael asked, "Can you make him see me, like you did to Elijah's servant?"

"If you would have asked me an hour ago, maybe I would have. However, right now he doesn't need any help; He will get to see you very soon, sooner than you think."

Then John walked back to Gracie's room where she was still lying there in coma with tubes all over and no change in her condition. John was discouraged again and said, "God, I wish I knew what you're thinking and see through your eyes." Then he asked the Holy Spirit to intercede for him.

The Holy Spirit prayed to the Father with groaning on John's behalf and said, "Holy Father, protect him by the power of Your name from the evil one. I, the Spirit of truth, came into John's life and guided him into all truth. I didn't speak on my own; I spoke only what I heard and I told him what is yet to come. I bring glory to the

Lord Jesus by taking from what is His and making it known to John. All that belongs to the Father is the Lord Jesus'. That is why the Lord Jesus said He would take from what is His and make it known to John."

John got a terrible headache after going through the emotional roller coaster. He had his left hand on his forehead and lifted up the other hand like a spiritual antenna and said, "Jesus." repeatedly. He was sending out an SOS distress signal to his Heavenly Father, only instead of an SOS they were G-SUS. He prayed, "Lord, I'm your son, I'm in trouble, please have mercy on Your servant, and if it glorifies Your name, Your will be done, not mine. Amen and hallelujah."

John was completely isolated and couldn't reach anyone over the phone so he stretched out his hand and asked his angel to hold it and comfort him. Raphael was amazed at John's grief and uncontrollable crying. Raphael had been with John for a while now and he is very close to him. John's prayers were a sweet smelling aroma to God, and the angel collected his tears and special delivered them to the Lord. John felt wonderful when the angel touched him.

John was exhausted and started to drift into sleep. As he was drifting into sleep, he said the names of God; Jehovah, Jesus, Emmanuelle and went to sleep.

Zebub said, *I'll follow you into your dreams and give you nightmares. You won't get rid of me that easy. I'll break you.*

The Holy Spirit gave the order for Raphael to pull out his sword.

Zebub said, "What's the matter, has he reached his limits on testing, does he need a backdoor to escape?" When the sword was completely out of its sheath, Zebub vanished.

* * * * * *

By now, Mary had picked up her sister at the airport and tried to call John several times with no luck.

She said to Martha, "Give me your cell phone. I need to call John; my phone isn't connecting."

"Still no luck?" asked Martha.

Mary explained what happened and said, "I fell into the devil's trap in a moment of weakness. I blew up and left John vulnerable to demons' attacks. The devil has isolated John and I have to hurry back and help him. I'm so ashamed of what I did. But I repented and God is so merciful, He is still talking to me – not mad at me."

Martha said, "You're the one who always said 'when the devil attacks, gather and circle the wagons. Don't run away from each other.'"

"I know. I just can't believe I did that to John. He has been a wonderful and loving husband, a hard worker, and a provider. He's a good husband and father, I couldn't have asked for anyone better. Very loyal, he never gave me a reason to be mad at him. I can always go to him for sound advice and counsel. He's a good spiritual leader and I have never seen him drunk, smoking, or gambling with his money or soul. He's honest, God-fearing, sincere, and not too many wives can say that their husband is a demon slayer."

"Praise the Lord, sister. You should see yourself; you're on fire with God's zeal."

"I have a righteous anger towards Satan and his evil ways, the way that he gets us when we're tired, weak and our guard is down. An evil character who delights in our destruction and enjoys torturing us. I told God to take me instead of her," Mary replied.

"God doesn't work that way. When He lived on earth, He healed everyone; His only command after healing people was to go and sin no more or go and make an offering. Of course, the person being healed would have to have accepted the offer to be healed and had faith that Jesus could heal him. Your case isn't about sin. What you have here is a Job situation. God and Satan are betting on your case. Job was rewarded for his faithfulness. As for us, we should consider it an honor to suffer for God. All the angels know about our sufferings and are glad to see us wear crowns in heaven. This is just a test to see if we pass. Abraham was tested."

"I'm sorry; I didn't ask you how you're doing in school," Mary said.

"I'm doing all right, thank you," Martha said. "In my philosophy class the professor asked, 'Who is stupid enough to believe the Bible?' I raised my hand and said, 'I do.' I was the only one raising a hand. He asked me, 'You mean to tell me that you believe the story of the fish that swallowed the man for three days and then he survived afterwards. It doesn't make sense!' I said, 'A lot of these things don't make sense. Walking on water doesn't make sense and neither does stopping the winds or raising the dead nor feeding thousands with two loaves of bread and a fish. God is God. God doesn't have to make sense or logic; He created them.' Then he asked, 'How can you believe that?' I said, 'If God said it, then I believe it to be true.' He asked, 'How could God do something like that with Jonah's fish?' I said, 'I don't know, but when I get to heaven I'll ask Jonah.' He asked, 'What if Jonah isn't in heaven?' I replied, 'Then you ask him.'"

Mary started laughing and said, "Oh it feels good to laugh. The last twenty-four hours were very hard. I admire your standing up to your teachers and professors and debate the Bible."

"Are you kidding? I admire your witnessing to strangers and making cold calls. May God bless you."

"That's why the body of Christ consists of many parts and each one has a different gift," Mary replied.

"We work as missionaries to unbelieving friends and students in a dark and decaying society and school system. They say we've got to go along to get along. I tell you, fathers need to prepare their children spiritually before they send them to the university, where professors attack the scriptures. They should build themselves strong, and hold true in the word of God. And only through Christ can we live as people of purity in a twisted world."

"Amen," agreed Mary.

"It's not always easy to shine in this dark world, but we may be the light that God has sent for a soul in need of a Savior. I had another professor who didn't believe in God. My Christian student friend hesitated to mention her belief in God for fear of sacrificing her grade. While I knew God called me to write my final paper on how to become a Christian, despite putting my grade at risk. At the end of the semester, my friend walked away with an A grade, while I barely passed the class with a C grade on my paper. Then one day, I ran into the same professor and during our conversation, she confessed to giving me a C because she didn't appreciate sharing the gospel with her in my paper. She also thanked me for taking that chance because my C paper led her to accept Christ as her Savior."

Finally, they arrived at the hospital and rushed to Gracie's room.

John was still sleeping and in his weary mind dreamt a conversation with God.

What is it son, I'm listening. I will shake heaven and earth for you. You are the apple of my eyes.

"Abba, why haven't you answered my call, request, and prayers?"

Do you consider me a FedEx service? Am I a genie in a bottle you rub twice to summon me?

"No, Lord, may you forbid. Forgive my ignorance. Mary pressured me into this."

Yes, that's what Adam told Me about Eve, too. Tell Me if you have a more thought out plan than My plan and show Me how it glorifies My name. Just remember that in the past, out of ten times you asked Me for a favor, you only kept your promises to Me half the time after I granted your wishes. I did what you wanted Me to do and you forgot about Me afterwards.

"O Lord, forgive me. I present my body a living sacrifice to You."

Did you see what they did to my beloved Son, pure precious blood, perfect in every way? I allowed it so that your sins can be forgiven.

"Thank you, Lord."

Do you love your daughter Gracie more than you love Me?

"I would give my life for You, Lord."

I know that, Johnny, but do you love Me more than your daughter?

"Yes, Lord, I do I love you more than anyone and anything."

You answered like Abraham did. Your daughter will be fine. Gracie was healed yesterday when you first prayed, even though you don't see it yet.

"Do you hear me John,... John,... John."

John woke up and saw Mary standing by his chair and calling his name. They hugged and kissed.

John said, "Gracie will be fine. God told me so. No operation is necessary."

"Okay, Honey, I believe you. You're the head of the household and I submit to your decision."

* * * * * *

Meanwhile, a doctor that treated Stephanie earlier came into her room and informed the parents that he gave her a relaxing medication a few hours ago and that's why she is relaxing right now. He had his personal demon standing behind him.

The father said, "I thought that the girl was possessed by demons. There was this guy here earlier, who said he was able to get rid of them."

The doctor laughed and said, "Don't make me laugh. I don't believe in demons. They are a myth, something you read in fairy tales." Then he continued mocking, "And Satan, the scaly monster with red horns and a pitchfork wearing red long underwear, a comical character and a fictional villain. I don't know what your religious background is, but I don't believe in the devil. The only devil I know is in deviled ham, deviled cake, and deviled eggs. I think you've been duped into believing in a medieval superstition that doesn't exist. God doesn't exist either. All religions are based on a superstition and mythical deities. Not one deity can be proven to exist. The Bible is a myth; Man created God not the other way around."

The demon behind him grinned and said, *That's it, buddy, I don't exist. Good job ruining John's testimony and a successful discredit of his miracle, by saying that the medication is working in her system.*

The father said, "And I was going to give the man a check for ten thousand dollars! I almost got conned by some foolish story about demons, devils, and spirits."

The mother said, "O Harold, you know there has been an increase in demon possessions. It's all over the news."

The doctor's eyes flashed dollar signs and said to the father, "Well, you know if you want, you can contribute it to the hospital, and they will put your name on a plaque and put it on the wall for everyone to see."

The father turned around, took out a pen and said, "Who do I make the check to?"

The doctor happily said, "Springfield Memorial Hospital."

Holy & Unholy Assembly

After midnight, a very bright light appeared. The demons, who were surrounding the angel and restraining him, screamed and said, "The Lord is coming, run!"

The sphere of demons broke apart and the demons started scurrying and scattering. They ran just like foul things, bugs and slimy insects, do when a rock is removed and the light hits them; they seek darkness and shade under another rock.

At that time, the restrained angel was freed; he descended down towards the hospital and to Gracie's room. Mary and John were sleeping on chairs beside the bed. Raphael and Mary's angel said in excitement, "The Lord Himself is coming, He's here!" Jesus appeared in the middle of room where everyone was sleeping. The two angels in the room got on their knees and worshiped the Lord.

Raphael said to the other angel, "Look how much He loves this one. He didn't have to come down here Himself. He is a respecter of no person, but He sure has more intimacy with some of them. Remember King David?"

"Yes, I don't know what the Lord saw in him," replied the other angel.

"He kept repenting."

"What about the apostle John? He wouldn't let him die until he saw the end of the drama."

Raphael said, "All demons abandoned their posts in the hospital and every demon within miles has scurried. They felt His presence."

"A lot of saints are getting healed in this building. The Lord Jesus MD is in the house."

Then the third angel who was restrained, arrived in the room and knelt and said, "Sorry, Lord; I was delayed."

Jesus answered, "I know." The angel stood by her bed where she was laying.

Then another angel appeared, knelt down at Jesus' feet and worshiped, then said, "Lord, there are plans to attack Your beloved city."

The Lord answered, "I know. I have given instructions to the Archangel Michael. He knows what to do." Then the Lord said, "Talitha, Gracie koum!" In the middle of the night, Gracie was healed immediately.

Raphael said, "If He hadn't said Gracie, all the dead in the basement morgue would have got up and walked."

Suddenly, Gracie made some moaning noises and everyone woke up. They were happy to see her awake and hugged her. Mary went and got Martha who was sleeping in the waiting room. When they got to Gracie's room, they found John on his knees.

"What is it?" asked Mary.

"I feel a strong sense of the presence of the Lord, Jehovah-Shammah, right here. It's the most wonderful feeling."

Mary and Martha rushed to where he was kneeling and fell on their knees next to him and were overwhelmed and awed by the Presence.

"Hallelujah, thank you, Jesus. We love you," worshipped Mary.

Gracie stayed in bed, as she still had tubes attached to her. She said, "Hallelujah!"

The family continued to worship and enjoy the presence of the Lord.

Later, Gracie said, "I'm hungry."

* * * * * * *

In the early morning, the doctors were amazed by the unexplained recovery.

After removing her from a respirator and a feeding tube, Gracie's doctor said to John, "I'm amazed at your daughter's recovery. This is the most incredible recuperation I've ever seen in my career. It's as if she never had the disease to begin with. This was completely unexpected, and all the different ailments that she was experiencing were starting to improve. She has won a verdict for life."

The doctor already found out from a nurse that John was the one who helped the possessed girl. He said, "I have seen Christians come and go under my care. They whine and plead with their God, and I have seen many of them get disappointed. But you, I have noticed strength and confidence! Where do you get your power from?"

"By the power of Jesus Christ. An unsaved person trusts himself and other humans; the Christian trusts God."

"When I was younger," the doctor said, "I used to think that I was God, the way I held other people's life and death in my hands. I'm in my sixties now, and my body is disintegrating. I don't feel like a god anymore. My only son doesn't even call me. What is this life all about, I wonder? I guess I'm trying to get what you have."

"You need to go to a local Bible based church and invite the Lord Jesus into your life."

"Which church do you go to?" the doctor asked.

"I go to the church where Jesus Christ is Lord."

The doctor thanked John for the experience of knowing him and showing him a different vantage point on Christianity.

The Holy Spirit said to John, *This is the reason we came here, son. You helped so many people in the last two days that I needed to reach. If you had crumbled sooner, we would have lost our testimony. I told you all things work for good to those who believe.*

As they were talking, there was a dead person completely covered with a white sheet being rolled away by an orderly.

John wondered, *what about this one, they didn't make it?*

The Holy Spirit answered, *God deals with each individual on a one by one basis. He is in control. If I want this person to go and be with the Lord Jesus, what is it to you? Follow me.*

John thought, *thank you Lord, I will follow you anywhere, any time and forever.*

Then John looked back and saw Mary finishing packing and getting ready to go home. Then he heard a voice from behind, saying, "Excuse me sir."

John looked back and saw the chaplain standing with a smile and continued, "Hi, I'm the parishioner for this hospital. I heard that you delivered that girl from her demons. And I just wanted to stop by and thank you for doing that; it encouraged me. For, now I know what faith can do. I admit that I was a disgrace to Grace and became a source of mockery for demons. I have cheated myself by not discovering and deploying kingdom authority in my life and ministry. I'm determined to strengthen my faith to a higher level. Even the disciples themselves couldn't heal and cast the devil from an epileptic boy because they had lacked faith. So, I realized that in order to be in authority, I must be under authority, and He will not put things under me until I conquer the things He put over me. I will make my life honorable and constantly say, 'yet not I, but Christ.' God bless you my brother."

John was stunned and said, "God bless you" as the man left.

* * * * * * *

Later, as they were leaving the hospital, Mary stopped by the nurses' station and said to their nurse, "Thank you for your help yesterday. I just wanted to tell you that my daughter has been healed by the power of God almighty and not by a physician this time. Prayers do get answered according to God's timing. We believe in God and prayer. If you're interested in knowing the truth, here is my phone number; contact me if you like. Have a blessed day." The nurse didn't seem interested, so Mary left after she gave the nurse her card.

* * * * * *

While Zebub was reporting to his lieutenant regarding his defeat with John, the lieutenant himself was called in for a meeting with the big guy himself.

When the lieutenant arrived at the meeting place, an uninhabited desert island, he hovered above and saw Satan and the other lieutenants were already assembled. Satan had called in all his main agents from all the corners of the world to give a report. Satan, the devil himself, was standing in the middle, bigger in size than the lieutenants and his wings were multicolored like the colors of precious stones, but the colors had faded away. He walked with a proud look, nose in the air and chest puffed up. He was leading the meeting surrounded by his ten lieutenants, the unholy Mafia, who represented their territories.

Beelzebub, the ruler of demons started the meeting by saying, "Welcome to the state of my kingdom for this century. This is my world. Adam gave me the keys of the kingdom when he sinned and now I own the kingdoms of the world. He dropped the ball; I got it and am running with it, and soon will score a touchdown."

All the lieutenants said, "Hail, Lucifer."

He continued, "We hold this meeting once in a while as you know, and I appreciate you all coming. I myself just came from the presence of God on His throne where I accused the saints; those whose names you gave me last time we met. After this meeting is over, make sure you give me a new list of saints so that I can go back to God and accuse them, and make sure that you provide me with evidence of their sins. They don't call me the ultimate critic for nothing.

"I know that you are all very busy and I appreciate your coming. We've been busy from the beginning of time, except for the time of the flood. There was no one for us to test except those eight people on the ark, but they were sealed unfortunately. We had no one around to deceive; that year was our longest vacation."

Satan Continued, "I didn't mind fellowshipping with you guys at the time of the flood, but the real thrill is to mislead these mortals using their vulnerable emotions and deceive them all the way to hell. If the Creator loves these miserable and insignificant creatures, then let's inflict pain on them and then destroyed them."

One of the lieutenants said, "I'm surprised we haven't wiped them out yet. They seem to be multiplying at a fast pace."

Satan replied, "I tried to thwart God's plan by influencing Cain to kill Abel to destroy the righteous seed, but God raised up Seth and the seed continued. Then we witnessed the birth of the Jewish nation, the mother of the Christ, which I hate with a passion because they gave the world the Messiah. God also promised to leave a remnant of them at the end of time, but I don't want to see that happen, and that's why I've been trying to annihilate them. God promised Jacob-Israel that on the fourth generation, a deliverer would be born of the Jews to save His people. So we marked our calendar, and at the appointed time, we had a pharaoh kill the babies born to eliminate Moses, but that didn't work. When Gabriel told Mary about the birth of Jesus, we marked our calendar and used King Herod to kill the babies of Jesus' generation to destroy the savior, and amazingly, that didn't work either. We don't know the future, but we can spy on the humans and angels to thwart God's plan.

"I then attacked Jesus' ministry; I tried to kill Him first by pushing Him off a cliff, and then tried to drown Him in a boat at the Sea of Galilee. I tried to have Him stoned at the temple mount in Jerusalem but Jesus always managed to escape. When I couldn't defeat the leader, I got inside His ministry and was successful with Judas Iscariot. I was surprised when Jesus gave me a green light to indwell this man and use him to deliver Jesus to the enemy. Before Jesus went to the cross, I realized the error in judgment I made and used His disciple Peter to get Jesus to change His mind about going to the cross and get crucified. I did that to counteract what the Holy Spirit revealed to Peter that Jesus was the Son of God. I couldn't fool Jesus; He saw me through Peter and told me to get behind Him. I sent the Pharisees to get Him off the cross by double daring Him 'if you're the Son of God, save yourself! Come down from the cross' and that didn't work either.

"So while we had to worry about the Jews the first couple of thousands of years, now we have to worry about a new bread, the gentile Christians, too, and we have a church to deal with. We tried to use persecution, martyrdom, and poverty and couldn't defeat the early church. I tried to forge letters with Paul's signature to throw a curve at the early church. Then we crept into it, started divisions, and had people teach false doctrines and ideas with the help of seducing spirits that entered the church and brought in sorcery, occult, and counterfeits. What persecution didn't accomplish, the church marriage to the world did. Remember, a cancer cell is a bad cell that tells other cells to follow it and destroy the whole body.

"So, anyway, our mission for the last two thousand years was to destroy the works of Jesus Christ and His church. We've had some success and good results in the last century: two world wars, a holocaust, and an evolution concept that is widely spread. However, and most importantly, most of the Jews of the world are in one place, which makes it an excellent opportunity to annihilate them once and for all. But it is a race against time for if we don't move in fast, then the Creator," looking up into the sky he continued loudly, "would win and we cannot allow that."

Satan furiously said, "As for these Christians I have been destroying them since Jesus left earth. Anyone that didn't worship me, I threw some to the lions, burned some at the stake, dipped some in oil, cut them in half, and hung them. I don't mind the false Christians, but the ones that built their house on a rock we need to destroy.

"With that, let's start with your reports," directing his attention towards the Jewish Lieutenant, he said, "Tell us about the center of the earth, Israel." The devil then looked at the map of the world, pointed at a dot and said, "If it wasn't for Calvary, I would have had the world."

The Israeli lieutenant said, "We don't have to do too much in that area. The Jews have been blinded for the last two thousand years. God knows their pain, and I'm trying to blind them from the fact that He is full of compassion and rich in mercy to prevent them from calling upon Him. The Jews misunderstood the Lord Jesus and saw Him as a radical teacher, a misfit, and a fanatic.

"Israel is a secular humanistic nation. They are no different from the old Israel, who, throughout the ages, kept straying from God's commandments into lawlessness. The Zionist Jews are committed to their country and are mostly atheists and agnostics; they are not the Jews of the Bible. They don't have prophets that bring fire from the sky like old times. I'm talking about that day our prophets took a bull and called on the name of Baal from morning until noon, but no one answered. And they limped about the altar they had made."

Satan interrupted with frustration, "You don't have to tell me. I was there all day watching and I hated to disappoint our followers, but my hands were tied."

One lieutenant said, "We'd like to hear the rest of the story, boss." Satan nodded for the lieutenant to continue.

"At noon Elijah mocked us, saying, cry aloud, for he is a god; deep in thought, or busy, or traveling. Maybe he is sleeping and must be awakened. And our slaves cried aloud and cut themselves after their custom with knives until the blood gushed out upon them. Midday passed; there was no voice and no one paid attention. Then Elijah took twelve stones, and built an altar in the name of his Lord. He put the wood in order, laid the bull on the wood and said, 'Fill four jars with water and pour it on the burnt offering and the wood'. And he said, 'Do it a second time and a third time'. The water ran around about the altar, and he filled the trench he made about the altar also with water. At the time of the evening sacrifice, Elijah prayed, then the fire of the Lord fell and consumed the burnt sacrifice, the wood, the stones, the dust, and also licked up the water that was in the trench. And Elijah slew our prophets of Baal, all four hundred and fifty of them."

The Middle East lieutenant laughed and mocked him, but the Jewish lieutenant said, "I wouldn't laugh if I were you; it's easy to criticize, but I heard what Moses did with his rod to Pharaoh's magicians. He turned his stick to a snake and it ate the magicians' snakes."

Then, as the lieutenants started blaming each other for failures, Satan screamed, "Enough. Don't argue between yourselves. The church is divided, not my kingdom. Let the enemy have their fun, when the Antichrist comes, he will bring fire from heaven very soon. We will dazzle them and the tables will be turned around that time." Then he looked at the Jewish lieutenant and asked, "Anything else?"

"These Jews don't sacrifice today; therefore, they have no atonement. And even if they did sacrifice, it wouldn't do them any good. The old covenant has been replaced by the new covenant through Jesus' shed blood. They say that they will bring their promised messiah with a gun, a tank, or bullets, reacting to the tragedy of the holocaust. They boast in their nukes and not God, unlike King David who took five stones and faced the giant of life, Goliath, totally depending on God. I'm trying to bring back the Anti-semantic attacks on them and drive them into the sea. I know you hate them because they wrote the Bible and the Son of God is one of their descendents.

"I've been able to present tombs that were excavated in Israel with the name Jesus written on the outside and some bones on the inside, to discredit the faith and introduce doubt to the fact that Jesus was resurrected. Doubt worked with Adam and Eve and I know that it works today, too. I hid those tombs centuries ago and I knew that I would need them in a day like this."

Satan said, "Didn't the Agnostics lieutenant try the devious idea of Jesus marrying Mary Magdalene and bringing a child? It didn't work, did it?"

The Agnostics lieutenant said, "No, master, it didn't. But you taught us if we don't succeed we should try and try again."

"Ok then. What about the Middle East lieutenant!"

He answered, "Yes, lord, we're doing good. Islam is the new giant of the world using the spirits of deception. The creator made a mistake blessing Ishmael, Isaac's half brother. They have discovered oil under their feet and have become wealthy, and now they have become bolder than ever before and will control the world. The Muslim world thinks that Jesus was simply another prophet who was a great teacher and a good man. Yet, we're losing a thousand Muslims a day to the Christian faith due to the success of Christian TV, Internet, and satellite propaganda to propagate the gospel and fulfill the great commission."

The devil said, "Well, we'll have to destroy these tools!"

"But we can't, because we're using these tools ourselves to spread porn, sex, and lies. But our white enemies are using it to spread Christ's message, too."

One lieutenant asked the Arabs lieutenant, "How come you didn't push evolution in your territory?"

"I didn't have to; their religion tells them that the Jews are descendants of monkeys. A reverse evolution, if you will. Moreover, the Muslims think that they will make the Jews into monkeys."

"How do they turn into monkeys?"

"I don't know, but they hate the Jews with a vengeance and call Israel the small Satan. The word of Allah teaches Muslims to kill non-believers and that believers of any other religion must become second class citizens."

The European Union lieutenant said, "Darwin never had a clue where his theory would lead to in America and Europe. If we were to bring him back to the present time, he would be amazed at the consequences of teaching his theory in the last century. It caused a decay of their society by abandoning God and His teachings in the Bible, and by abandoning creation and believing in evolution."

"Ok, ok. What about the giant red dragon? Let's hear from the Buddha and Confucius lieutenant?"

The Chinese lieutenant said, "The majority has superstitious beliefs and thinks that Christianity is an import from the western world. They have no idea what repentance is; it's a revolutionary idea to them. There is a decline of morality and personal values, but materialism is high. The more pressure I put on the church, the more they resist. We're killing the Christians and the missionaries by slicing and dicing them and still they grow stronger in faith; their faith comes with a price. The Creator must be giving them the strength to survive. They hold secret meetings despite the persecution by the Red Guard and the militia and we put them in jails.

"The communist government controls the church. Christians are on the wanted list and the persecuted church is a way of life. We have decreased the chapels, but the Christians are increasing. They conduct house churches, meet in caves, orchards, and barns and even cornfields. The Apostle Paul used the horse and donkey to spread the gospel; they are using bikes between cities, and preach bare footed in the mud, traveling on boats. It's a good thing that the western world has not awakened to the atrocities committed against those Christians."

The EU lieutenant said, "They're so busy making money that they forget about the spiritual battle and the countless souls in our grip."

Satan said to the Buddha lieutenant, "Just make sure that they don't come up with the two hundred million troops that they will use at Armageddon."

Then he said, "Good, now let's hear from the Hindu lieutenant?"

The Indian lieutenant said, "I have created millions of gods in my territory. The Hindus, those who heard of Jesus, think that He was a good teacher, a good man, and just another divine being to add to their list of gods. They think that Christianity is a poor man's religion, a foreign religion and a colonial imposition. Christians comprise only three percent. We prevent Christian literature distribution, but they walk for days to obtain and distribute Bibles. Several provinces have passed anti-conversion laws, making it a crime to publicly become a Christian. Converts lose citizenship, become second-class citizens and are ostracized from their families. Anyone who confesses Christ is considered to be a stability threat, so they are hunted down all over the country and face the death penalty. Hindu extremists are burning or demolishing Churches and Christians have gone underground and refuse to give up meeting. Pastors and church leaders are being forced to renounce their faith or get martyred during torture. And their wives and daughters are harassed and raped. As for our followers, they enslave children at age five by the millions.

"In our fanatical neighboring Pakistan, we made the apostasy act into a law, under which any man who leaves Islam for another religion would be killed and women would be imprisoned for life. The two rivals have their nuclear warhead pointed at each other, a total annihilation waiting to happen, when the time is right."

Then Satan looked at the American lieutenant and said, "Everyone, welcome the new American lieutenant. I demoted the other one because he lost two world wars. Even though it wasn't his fault, the Creator intervened, but still. This devil here has a good resume. He was responsible for breaking the back of the Roman Empire by breaking down the family unit. How is the giant of giants doing, brother?"

The lieutenant replied, "Your Lordship, three words - going to sleep."

The devil said, "Just a minute, son, hold that thought!"

The devil started to clear his throat and sang a very beautiful melody while spreading his wings, after which all the ten lieutenants fluffed their wings and said, "Hail Lucifer."

His voice wasn't up to par, so he said, "Excuse me, I've been out of practice for about six thousand years. These lousy creatures have taken over my position in heaven. I hate them."

One of the lieutenants said, "Your voice is still good, boss."

Then Satan said, "I just made myself happy. I think after the meeting I'll take a quick spin around the world and deceive at least a million souls to worship me through the worship of animals, nature, idols, or money, just to tick off the Creator." He looked up at the heavens and continued, "I cannot get to you right now, and so I'm going to hurt those you love and break your heart."

The lieutenant was encouraged and continued, "Yes, sir, the giant has fallen asleep behind the wheel. The Roman Empire was degenerated then disintegrated over time because of the moral degeneration, spiritual apostasy, and political anarchy. No nation ever survived the collapse of the family; neither will this one. One out of two marriages end up in divorce, and many are not marrying. Millions of children every year are affected by divorce and single parent homes. We also have agencies helping us abort children, and unions fighting born-again Christians. Just like there's no smoking on the streets, we're promoting no Jesus or Bible on the streets.

"America the beautiful is no longer beautiful; violence and sin has made her ugly. The thought that they have somehow offended God doesn't even enter their mind. The society has lost its soul because of growing materialistic attitude and the decline of religion. Many people have become obsessed with work, sex, and eating in an attempt to ignore their misery. And the pursuit of financial success has led to a rise in depression and emotional need."

Satan took a deep breath with a grin of satisfaction on his face.

The lieutenant continued, "As you know, America fought twentieth century fascism and communism. They ruined our plans at world war two because they were protected back then with a hedge. This century they're fighting terrorism, militant jihad, radical extremist Muslims, fanatics, the most brutal enemy they ever faced. They call America the great Satan.

"But now they have practically kicked God out of the country and society. I taught them to praise our father in Washington. Jesus knocks on the door of the church and they have locked him up outside. They've abandoned God and He's abandoned them. This mighty nation is committing a slow suicide. God is removing the hedge just as He did with Israel. They have cursed themselves and will bring the wrath of the Creator on themselves. Our Evil is invading the country and overtaking it and no one is putting up a fight of faith. We're making big headway towards their destruction, unless the Creator steps in and causes a miraculous revival. So the only thing left is to make sure that the conditions for a revival don't occur."

One lieutenant asked, "What are the conditions?"

"First, I keep them from humbling themselves and confessing their sins. God gives grace to the humble and resists the proud. Second, we stop prayers completely and strip them from all the power that can come from above. Third, we keep them from seeking God's face; they are after His hand to see what He'll give them and do for them. This way they'll never experience the face-to-face love of God and draw near to Him. Fourth, we keep them practicing their wicked ways. So you see, there's no way that they will have a revival."

The Middle East lieutenant said, "Don't get cocky, let me warn you. The Holy one might give a final slap on their face to wake them up, as a favor to their forefathers who built the country on a Judo-Christian foundation. Back in the days when I was responsible for Nineveh, present day Iraq, I had the whole city doing my will and was hoping for the Creator to destroy it, like Sodom and Gomorrah. The Lord gave them a second chance by dispatching the prophet Jonah to warn them. I sent out troops to intercept Jonah and put a little bit of hate in his heart towards the people of Nineveh. We succeeded initially and he refused the assignment. We ran him out of town, but the sea got wild and they threw him overboard. We thought he was finished, but we were all shocked at what happened next. God exercised His veto powers again and had a big fish swallow the prophet for three days. He slept on the wrong boat and ended up in a blubber mattress.

"I haven't even seen a fish like that before, and I have been around all over the world. I think the Creator created it on the spot at the right place to provide Jonah with a two night and three day fish motel accommodations, sleeping with the fish and eating seaweed. The Creator had the advantage of creating…"

Satan was displeased with that comment and began to growl.

The lieutenant realized the slip of the tongue and backed off immediately and continued, "The fish released him afterwards at the right place to resume his assignment. To our amazement, the city repented and was saved from total annihilation. It seems that we would have been better off not interfering with Jonah; it was possible that Nineveh people would have laughed at him if he just went in and warned them. But they were scared when they heard the story of the fish and everyone believed him and the plan backfired on us."

Satan, still sore over the previous comment, asked, "Didn't I demote you for that?"

"Yes sir, your Lordship, but I won so many battles afterwards, that you promoted me again."

Satan said, "OK, so let's keep an eye on Jonahs of today, and work together to outsmart and trick them in new ways to prevent revivals in the future. Let's not wake up the big giant and make him have a righteous resolve to fight us back. We can't have the Christians stop America's ship from sinking and make her ship-shape again. This is the good side's last stand and I want the giant destroyed. So how do you plan to cripple them completely?"

"I have a few options; I could use terrorists to decimate them with a nuclear attack, or isolate them for lack of leadership, or bring a judgment from God on them. Actually, Earth Lieutenant can help by erupting the Yellow Stone Park's volcano."

Earth Lieutenant commented, "I'll see what I can do!"

The American lieutenant continued, "Any of these options will bring the country to its knees. Of course, eventually, the rapture, which fulfills the Creator's promise to the believers, will also be judgment on those left behind. It will make the US a second rate country."

Planet Earth lieutenant represented his territory and said, "Sir, we have turned the Garden of Eden into a cesspool. We know that you have a vengeance against the creation of God. So I have good news; Earth is being plagued with killer earthquakes, killer hurricanes, devastating tornadoes, calamitous floods, terrible droughts, and new incurable diseases. We have introduced killer bugs and viruses, mysterious infections, flesh eating bacteria, and multi drug resistant germs that will cause biological havoc and severe pandemics. We're hoping to generate a global medical catastrophe, an apocalyptic scenario where this world would be on the edge of oblivion. What helped me accomplish this are the changing trends in morality, ethics, medicine, lifestyle and politics. There has also been an increase in pestilences, ozone depletion, and Global warming. Earth's temperature is rising. The melting of the North Pole is causing the water to rise in the oceans, and by the time we finish this meeting, this island will disappear."

Satan asked, "How are they handling the global warming?"

"I'm telling them to drink more beer to solve the problem, if they can afford it. I'm trying to get them to start drinking at a young age. I scare them with either a runaway heat or a new ice age. If we can confuse, upset and frighten the masses, we can control them. I'm also training them to care for the environments more than human life, against God's teaching that human life is more valuable to God than the rest of the creation. Modern environmental movement says that man is the enemy of nature and the best environment is one untouched by human hands. Earth is better off without humans, which is contrary to what God told Adam, to subdue and rule the earth.

"I have mortal scientists working on the development of a devastating military destructive force to be used against each other. These new cutting edge weapon systems utilize radiological, chemical and biological weapons of mass destruction warheads. The man-engineered biological killer viruses, advanced bio-war viruses, and super killer mutant viruses can spread throughout the world and cause billions to die. By the way, I'm increasing the pot and marijuana output around the world."

"Good, we'll need a lot of that in the tribulation period. What about the bird flu, how is that going?" Satan asked.

"I have scientists working on putting the death poison in a bottle and using it as a weapon. Chicken flu can wipe out half the population and nuclear bombs can take care of the rest."

"I need that formula in my possession soon." Then Satan looked at the lieutenant for the Special Forces and said, "Here is a brother who previously commanded our daring brothers that are locked up in Tartarus now. Those are our brothers who lusted after the daughters of men, and had intercourse with them four thousand years ago.

They brought up a demonized giants breed, and God destroyed them with the flood. We miss those brothers and soon I'll get the key to their jail cell. Do you have any new plans for this century?"

"I have been conditioning these immortals to the existence of life on other planets, and that these aliens, little green men, come to earth using UFOs. We did this by flashing lights in the sky combined with other illusions and, of course, the godless imagination. They think that these aliens abduct people on their ships and have sex with them. When the time is right, and with your approval, I can unleash my demons for the invasion."

"Great, and good work with the flashing objects in the sky. If that caused so much stimulation now, then they will worship the Antichrist when he brings real fire from heaven."

"Lately, I've been throwing in other signs like, cattle mutilations, crop circles, and big foot just to add to the confusion."

"Ok, let's hear from you, the revived Roman Empire," Satan moved on.

The EU Lieutenant said, "This union is going to be the new strength and force in the world, as far as economy and military power. We're ahead of the American lieutenant and were successful in inflicting a moral collapse of the western culture. Society has lost its moral anchor and the church has lost its confidence in the word of God because of our attacks on the Bible. Islam is on the rise in these nations and gaining power and influence."

Satan looked at another lieutenant and said, "Christendom lieutenant. How is false Christianity doing?"

"They think that if they live a good life and do good works and give money to church, they're guaranteed to go to heaven. Jesus' teachings have become nothing more than a plan to get to heaven and a fire insurance policy for escaping the tormenting hell. They go to church and worship one hour a week and two days a year at Christmas and Easter. There is no renewing of mind or becoming a new creature and no relationship with their God. So they conform to the world and behave like the atheists do. They have sex without marriage, and have sex after marriage with other people; infidelity is normal. Their children take illegal drugs, and think that nudity is acceptable and sin is normal. They think God is a Santa Claus or an old man waving them in through the pearly gates. If grandpa were that nice, he would have spared us.

"And I have Christendom convinced that Jesus came to earth to abolish Judaism and start Christianity and not for everyone to have life. In cooperation with the Middle East and Jews lieutenants, I'm going to merge religions into one world religion. The Pope will be praying in the mosque and the Molalla, which is the Muslim preacher, will sing in the church."

"I want the church crushed and out of my way. We need to rock church, brothers."

At that point, a huge bright light came down from heaven. The devils wondered if the sun had changed direction and turned night into day. However, it was the Archangel Michael. He appeared in the middle of the assembly in a surprise visit. The devil was shocked and said,

"What are you doing here?"

"You show up unannounced at our meetings. Remember Job?"

"Yes, I remember that loser. That was just one man that I lost. Big deal. I have been winning millions and billions of souls since then."

"I just came to tell you that the gates of hell will never be able to destroy the church," Michael announced.

"Yes, sure, your master loves those precious mortals He created. What about us? Don't we deserve a fair chance just like He gives them in forgiveness," Satan asked.

"Adam and Eve were enticed and deceived by you, and so they have an excuse. But you, you don't have any excuse; you rebelled against God by your own will."

"Well, we don't have to have this harsh of a sentence."

"The universal law of murder says if you kill innocent blood then you'll have to be destroyed. You know very well that when you forced our Lord Jesus Christ to the cross, you spilled innocent blood and you sentenced yourself to death. And in due time your execution will take place."

"Is the Holy Spirit going to be taken out of the way soon?" asked Satan anxiously.

"Only our God knows when."

"He isn't my God. I'll be worshipped by all mortals." Satan changed the tone of his voice and tenderly said, "Are you still upset about the argument we had over the body of Moses, I let you have his body, didn't I? Obviously, God wanted to retain it for a future purpose. Look, it's not too late to jump sides; I'll give you a high position and leadership in my kingdom."

"The LORD our God, the LORD is one. I serve him only." The Archangel Michael, out of residual dignity towards Lucifer's old position in heaven, didn't dare to bring a slanderous accusation against him but continued, "The Lord rebuke you." And disappeared quickly and darkness set on the island again.

Satan said, "Then, tell your boss, it's His move now in this chess game. Tell Him to take out of the way the Holy Spirit."

The Devil turned around to speak to his lieutenants who were silent, motionless, and gripped with fear the whole time the arch-angel Michael was present. They knew that one day they would have to go to battle against him and his angels. They also knew that the Lord doesn't send him on a mission to have a tea party and cookies. His objective has always been to execute the plan and will of God, with emphasis on the word execute.

Some of them had personal experiences with him. The Persian lieutenant remembered a long time ago when he prevented an angel from responding to the Prophet Daniel's prayer until Michael showed up. The lieutenant lost a few feathers that day. Also, the Asian and African lieutenants were anxious as they remembered recent encounters with him and losses in the years 1973, 1967, and 1948.

Satan said, "You heard Michael, our time is short, " Then he directed his attention to the EU lieutenant and said, "How is my special assignment to you doing?"

"He's doing great. He's much better than the previous ones you picked. It seems each coming generation produces a more devious Antichrist than the previous one. This one is, again, charismatic, mesmerizing, and brilliant with the characteristics of Hitler, Napoleon, Alexander the great, and Nebuchadnezzar put together. He has a devilish spirit that could be encouraged. He's a liar and a deceiver, a smooth talker and a diplomat all in one. Right now, he's very confident of himself and proud. He is getting what he wants with the women and men, officials, politicians, and he feels good about it. He also has influence on his local church and religious people. He's getting the training he needs for the big task ahead. I thought Hitler was your final choice!"

"Yeah, that's what I thought, too, but Israel wasn't born yet. I didn't realize that the Creator really meant it when He said thousands of years ago, that the Jews would have a country again in Israel. Also, the restrainer, the Holy Spirit, wasn't taken out of the way yet. The Antichrist is a sleeper cell who won't be activated until the Holy Spirit is taken out of the way with His church. Keep an eye on him and groom him to be my right hand man on earth."

"What about the Antichrists present right now, the ones who claim they are Jesus?"

Satan replied, "They will get on their knees and worship the coming Antichrist."

Now the American lieutenant felt close to Satan at this point since he received praise from him earlier. So he asked the question that was on the mind of all the lieutenants, but no one dared to ask. He asked, "Master, how are we going to beat the enemy if there is twice as much of them as there are us?"

"Well, I have a two-phase plan. After the Holy Spirit is taken out of the way, we'll strengthen our kingdom down here on earth by rallying all mortals behind my Antichrist. Once we're secure on earth, we'll wage a war against God and His angels on His turf in heaven, that's plan A. If we lose there, which I doubt, then we implement contingency plan B. We'll go down to earth and destroy the Jews so that His plan cannot be fulfilled."

"Why not kill the Jews right away after the rapture?" the American lieutenant asked.

"I want to give my Antichrist credibility in a desperate world looking for peace. If he attacks right away, the world won't trust him after that."

Then the American lieutenant built enough courage to ask the unspoken question and said, "Sir, what if God decides to come down to earth to defend the Jews and battle with us down here?"

Satan answered with frustration, "Then we'll battle Him on earth, on our turf, with the help of the Antichrist and his human armies. At that time, we're guaranteed victory and that is plan Armageddon. If all fails, then we'll inspire rogue nations with demonic inspired leaders to destroy the world and themselves."

"Master, I hate to tell you this, but there is a wave of writers, defenders of their faith, who have put your plan in writing and explained it in a way that everyone can understand. While things were vague and complicated in the Bible, they are making it simple and easy to understand with their new writings."

"We have to stop all those Pauls of today and bring in more writers to promote weakness to the faith. You'll have to discredit these faith writers, kill them if you have to, if you can. Put pressure on them, give them health problems, and if they still persist, hurt their family, their wife, and especially the little ones."

"We tried that, but it only made their families stronger and love each other even more."

"I hate them, instead of fiery darts, send them blazing missiles. I want them crushed, do you hear me?" Satan became so furious, that the plantation around him withered and died.

"Yes, boss," they all answered.

"We cannot afford to have a lot of people understanding this plan. It will make it harder for my Antichrist to establish the trust of the nations in the tribulation. Fortunately, they will be deluded by our lies after the rapture."

Then he said, "If you can't hurt the writers, give them pride; that will do it. Pride defies God and defiles man. I want to strike them out and pack hell with souls, souls, souls." Then he directed his attention to another lieutenant, "Ok, we don't want to close the meeting without hearing from the Russian Lieutenant, the king of the north and giant of nations, Gog, I have a lot hanging on your territory."

"I'm resurrecting the climate of the Cold War using this super-power. Unfortunately, the economy collapsed under the communist controlled government. The government is the only true god, the provider of blessings, the solver of problems, the basis of civilization's progress, and the distributor of justice and mercy. We have a strong alliance with the Arabs and are getting ready for the Ezekiel war games. As for our next secret move, you don't think Michael knows about it, do you? Only you and I know about it!"

"We have our spies, and they have their sources. I'm not sure if he knows our plan, but you go ahead and proceed with it as planned," said the devil, then addressed all his lieutenants and said, "OK, boys, spread out there, and continue to do a good job. And boys, keep them from praying, we'll beat them every time; otherwise, they will beat us." Then Satan looked down to earth and said, "Let the gates of Hell open up wide, for my great harvest is coming."

The Holy Spirit

Today, Jim went to church again. He saw John standing outside the church auditorium, and said, "I'm very happy for Gracie's healing and your victory over disease."

"Thanks. I'm going to give a testimony for the whole church and give more details about yesterday's great miracle."

Then Jim noticed that somebody brought two cats in a cage to church and asked John about it.

John said, "I guess they want the pastor to bless the cats. When will people ever stop this nonsense?" Jim shook his head and smiled.

Then when the service started, Jim went to sit down by himself because John was up on stage giving a testimony for what happened to Gracie and how the Lord had delivered her from death. Daemon was still following Jim from a distance and arranged for him to sit in a certain chair. When Jim got to the empty seat, he noticed pot on it, as he was about to sit down. Daemon knew that Jim had an addiction with drugs so he asked another devil earlier for assistant to put the pot on that chair. The other devil made his subject stand up and leave the chair and drop his pot by accident, which landed on the chair where Jim was to sit down.

Jim picked it up and sat down. Jim held the pot in his hand, shook his head and thought, *I prayed the sinner's prayer, I'm saved, and I have the Holy Spirit who will help me in this situation.*

Daemon was unable to get too close to Jim because Celestiel was guarding and protecting him.

Daemon was standing at the end of the row where Jim was sitting and said, *You didn't think you could get rid of me this easily, did you? Why don't you get out of this dump and light up that pot, you know you want to!*

Jim remembered what John told him about Satan finding a foothold and he keeps coming back to it just like boxing. When one boxer notices the weakness in the other boxer, he keeps hitting that area of weakness until defeat.

Daemon shot a fiery dart in Jim's direction and said, *Lust of the flesh.*

Jim found himself with a dilemma in his hand, literally. The Holy Spirit said, *Your body is the temple of God, you shouldn't defile my dwelling place. It doesn't belong to you. God wants you to use your body to glorify Him; Satan wants to use your body to disgrace the Lord. And remember, you gave Jesus the keys to all of your house closets. You had a renewal; you put off the old man and his habits, and put on a new man. When you were born again you started your own warfare with the flesh and the demons. Give not the devil a place. You should resist the urge and nail the flesh to the cross.*

Jim was still resisting the urge on his own, but with the pot in his hand, he was craving it and the fiery darts kept coming. Meanwhile, Jim's new angel, Celestiel was standing by, waiting for Jim to ask for help to defeat Daemon.

Daemon said, *Last call for pot lighting. Remember how good it felt and how nice it tasted and smelled.*

The Holy Spirit, on the other hand, said, *Son, he who grieves over and detests sin is a saint, but he who boasts in sin and jumps into it is the devil. You're a Christian now, and when you sin you feel dirty and defiled. The conscience of the sinner doesn't bother him; he sins and forgets it. I won't allow you to forget through your cleansed subconscious. I have to deal with my children and put pressure on them. When you face temptation like this, remember it isn't a sin to be tempted. Temptation to sin isn't sin. If temptation is a sin, then Jesus is a sinner. Jesus felt what you feel. He was just as much a man as though He were not God at all, and He was as much God as though He were not man at all. He was the God-Man, and Jesus never sinned though He knew those temptations.*

Evil is real, son, and Satan is the author of every bit of it. That's why he showed up when he saw an opportunity to trip you up. Satan makes sin appealing and tells you to do what feels good to you. Pleasure in sin is for a season, a blast that doesn't last. I wish you could only see where a wrong decision will take you in the future. When you use drugs, they alter your mind. You can't renew an altered mind. If you smoke pot, you could go to jail. And after a while, you'll no longer be satisfied with that and start looking for something stronger like marijuana and then fry your brain. My child, God honors obedience. Your obedience will bring you trust and peace, order and stability, wisdom and favor. You belong to Me and I want to position you to experience more of His blessing. I have plans for you, and I have something better for you.

Then the Holy Spirit told Jim a story of a boy pushing a big rock with all his strength and couldn't move it. The boy's father who was watching said "Are you using all your strength, son?" The boy said "yes." "Are you sure?" asked the father again. "Yes." answered the boy, but he never asked his dad for help. The Holy Spirit continued, *It is difficult for men to resist the urge for pot, but nothing is impossible with God. Just ask him.* And Jim said, "Lord, give me the strength to resist."

Jim gained power from the Holy Spirit and asked for Jesus to help him through this dilemma. He submitted to the Holy Spirit and resisted the devil.

Meanwhile, Daemon started to make a fuss with Celestiel and fought with him.

The Holy Spirit said to Jim, *It is finished. The old you is wrestled into submission by My power. Stand still and watch the fight between the Holy Spirit and the demon. He that is in you is greater than what is in the world.* The Holy Spirit appeared to Daemon and said, "Not now, not here, get behind me, demon, and stay away from this man, you evil spirit! You are only allowed to exist for a season."

When Daemon saw the Holy Spirit, he fell on his knees in front of Him. He shouted at the top of his voice, "What do you want with me, Holy Spirit? Swear to God that You won't torture me!"

Then the Holy Spirit asked him, "What is your name?"

"My name is Daemon," he replied, and he begged the Holy Spirit again and again not to send him out of the area. There were two cats in a cage outside nearby. Daemon begged the Holy Spirit, "Send me among the cats; allow me to go into one of them." He gave him permission, and Daemon went into one of the cats. The cats fought together and their meow was heard by the whole church and caused a disruption of the service. The cage fell off the table and the cage door opened. One of the cats ran away and was never seen again.

The Holy Spirit said to Jim, *Open your hand, son.*

When Jim opened his hand, he found out that the pot had been pulverized because he squeezed it so hard. Jim had no taste for pot after that, but instead acquired a new taste for the Holy Spirit. He was amazed at the power flowing through him that gave him the ability to resist the temptation.

Then the Holy Spirit said, *You haven't unwrapped your birthday gift yet, son. Every born again believer is a gifted child of God. Since you like to ask so many questions, I'm going to give you the gift of teaching.*

While John, Jim's mentor, was telling the church about his testimony and the victory over the demons in the hospital, Jim, his protégé, was having his own victory inside the church. That Sunday John was known as 'the demon Buster'.

* * * * * * * *

After church, John had to stop by a gas station to get some gas. While he was pumping gas, there was also a man across the aisle who was filling up his car with gas. He was dressed up, so John assumed that he had gone to church that day.

John said, "Praise the Lord Jehovah."

The man replied, "I'm sorry, I'm not a Jew."

"I'm not either; that's the name of our God."

"Then you must be one of those who knock on our doors."

"No, I'm a born again Christian. Have you been born again?" John asked.

"I'm fifty five years old and my mother has passed away, so how am I going to be born again?"

"Born again means when the old man dies and a new creature is born with Christ living inside."

"I thought born again meant you belong to some cult," the man said.

John wanted to discontinue the conversation with the man, but the Holy Spirit insisted that he continue. At that time, one of the car windows rolled down slightly. The windows were tinted so John was unable to see who was inside. John continued, "Jesus said unless you are born again you cannot enter heaven." By now, the man looked perplexed and disturbed, and said, "Look. I'm not going to change my religion."

"I'm not suggesting that one changes religion or denomination, only change the heart and mind. I myself stopped doing the religion thing and started enjoying a relationship and salvation, a vital relationship with Jesus Christ the Son of God."

"Jesus gave the keys to Peter and built the church on him."

"Yes, but God also commissioned the Apostle Paul to elaborate on Jesus' teaching and give instructions on what Christianity is for Gentiles," John replied.

"Who is Apostle Paul?"

"He wrote the majority of the New Testament by instructions from the Holy Spirit and without him, we'd all be circumcised now."

The man seemed to wiggle his legs a little bit at that time and said, "All I know is that Peter is the leader of the church."

"No sir, Jesus is the leader of the church and these good men were used to spread Christianity all over the world."

"None of the other denominations could be traced back to the original apostles except our church."

"But the Holy Spirit is the One who's doing the work, not men," John replied.

"It's Sunday, for God's sake; do you have to do this today? You should talk about Jesus to non-Christians. I'm already saved."

"If your car broke down on Sunday, wouldn't you call roadside assistance?"

"This car won't break down," said the man as he tapped on his brand new shiny car, "and if it does, then, of course, I would call."

Then his pump stopped pumping and he put the gas tank cap back and said, "Have a good day, sir," as he got into his car.

Then the other door opened and a fancy lady came out of the car dressed up elegantly and said, "Forgive my ignorant husband; your message was for me. I have been struggling with these questions lately and didn't know who to talk to about it, and now I know what to do. Thank you very much and have a blessed day." And the man said, "Darling, we're late for brunch." So the lady got into the car and drove off. When John finished filling up with gas, he went back into the car and said ecstatically, "Did you see that?"

Mary answered, "Yes, dear, I did."

"God works in mysterious ways. The Holy Spirit told me to speak, and I didn't know why because the man wasn't receptive, but my message was for her, not for him. I mean, he asked me why I was witnessing on Sunday!"

"The Pharisees told Jesus not to perform miracles on the Sabbath, too, and Jesus asked them if a donkey fell in the ditch on a Sabbath whether they would save the donkey. You did good, honey."

"Let's thank the Lord." As they started praising God, a car behind them started beeping so John started the engine and drove away and thanked God at the same time.

Good Bye for Now

The next day, John was driving his car out of the company parking lot to go home after a day at work had ended. As he reached an intersection, the light was green so he proceeded forward. There was a truck approaching the intersection from the left side. The truck driver had a demon sitting next to him. There were cans of beer on the floor of the truck, and the driver was smoking and listening to filthy music. The demon received instructions to destroy John. So the demon caused the driver to look directly at the direction of the bright sun and caused his eyes to be blinded momentarily. The driver didn't see the red light ahead and slammed into John's car, causing a head-on collision. John couldn't see what hit him; it was that quick. His body was thrown through the driver's side window. When he got ready to hit the ground, he knew he was going to die and said with fear, "Jesus, help me!" John felt death looming and his life slipping away. He died instantly. The Holy Spirit said, *Go ahead John, go to the Father's house. I'll catch up with you soon.*

Before John died, a bystander stopped by and looked outside John's mangled car and he heard John saying, "Here, here, here." The man asked John, "What are you saying?"

John answered in a weak voice, "There is a roll call in heaven and I want to make sure that they hear me."

John's soul hovered over his body that lay outside the wreck of a car. John said to his body, "You can rest now, my precious knee; I'm sorry I got you into that accident. No longer will I put my weight on you, especially when I prayed, and so you can rest now, rest, rest…"

Then the grim reaper suddenly appeared and out of surprise John asked, "What are you doing here, are you lost?" and before the grim reaper was able to answer, Raphael appeared and said to the grim reaper, "He is off limits", he escorted John away and both of them vanished.

"I think he's dead," said the bystander to the medics as they checked his pulse on the scene. Then he continued, "I've never seen a man in such peace while he's dying. Just look at his face!"

"Did he say anything?" asked one of the medics.

The man told the medics what John said before he died and said, "Most people say they're leaving home, but not this man. He said that he was going home."

"He was a Christian then," the medic said.

"I'm a Christian, too, and I don't want to think about dying. It scares the hell out of me. I don't have the slightest idea what happens after death."

"He was a born again Christian," the medic said.

"What in the world is born again?"

"Look, I'm on the job right now, but here is a church tract from where I go to church and if you come, I'll explain everything to you. There is even my phone number on the back, if you'd like to contact me. The card has on it the church schedule and meeting times. There is one meeting tonight if you'd like to come."

"You know, I've seen many accidents in my lifetime. I don't know why I decided to stop here and come to see this dying man. But I feel like I'm lost in this world and have been wondering what the meaning of it all is. And no one seems to have the answer. So, you can count on me being there tonight, thanks."

The medic pulled the sheet back off John's corpse and said, "Good work, brother, even while you were dying, you witnessed, and you may have saved a soul. See you in heaven."

The second medic driver looked back from the driver seat and said, "You know, you're talking to a dead man!"

"His soul isn't dead."

"Oh no, I see a sermon coming on. I told you I'm not interested."

The man muttered, "I'm not done with you yet."

A Slice of Heaven

The next time John opened his eyes, he was in Heaven, the abode of God and His angels, a realm of spirits, and the 'no time zone'. He looked around and couldn't see his body for the first time. When he looked around to examine the new environment, he saw what looked like an angel with wings. He looked with curiosity at the angel who seemed friendly and they admired each other for a Heavenly minute. The angel was as curious about John as John was curious about him.

"Hello, John," said Raphael, the angel.

John was overwhelmed and fell at the angel's feet out of shock, not to worship him, for he knew if that were Jesus, he would have the nail-scarred hands and feet and wouldn't have wings.

"Don't do it!" said Raphael, "I'm a fellow servant with you and your brothers, the prophets, and of all who keep the words of the Bible. Worship God."

John stood up feeling awkward. By now, he felt like he knew this angel's voice, but couldn't quite put his finger on it.

"I'm a ministering spirit that the Lord sent out in the service of God for the assistance of those who are to inherit salvation. My name is Raphael."

Even though John had no physical body, he found himself able to communicate and said, "I feel like I've known you for a long time."

"I'm an angel of the Lord, your guardian angel. I have encamped around those who fear the LORD and He delivered them," replied

Raphael. "I've been with you since the day you invited Jesus into your life."

Immediately, John went back into memory lane and remembered that day when he was in his early twenties when a friend invited him to church. It was as if a video recording played back in front of his eyes. It was in that church that he later on met Mary, his future wife, who changed his life. By now, John was starting to get excited for he realized that he made it to the third Heaven, not that he ever doubted it, but it was good to be finally there.

"Do you remember that skiing trip you took a few years after that?" asked Raphael.

"Yes, there was a severe snow storm followed by an avalanche and snow came down towards me at an incredible speed. I couldn't outrun it; that's when I tripped and injured my knee and passed out. When I came to, the rescuers told me that when they found me, I was in a six-foot deep hole surrounded by snow on all sides. But they said that there was no snow above my body and the hole I was in, had the shape of what looked like two wings. They said that it was a miracle."

The angel smiled the whole time John was speaking as if he knew about the details all along. John understood that this angel saved his life that day by blocking the flow of snow over his body.

Raphael replied, "I covered you with my feathers, and under my wings you found refuge; my faithfulness was your shield and defense. A thousand may have fallen at your side, ten thousand at your right hand, but it wouldn't have come near you."

At that, they joined in a Heavenly hug.

"Do you remember the restaurant incident when I took on a physical body to get a message to you?" asked Raphael.

"I knew it," said John excitedly, "that was so very clear to me, and the clue you gave me helped. That day, I remembered what the Apostle Peter said, 'Don't forget to entertain strangers, for by so doing, some people have entertained angels without knowing it.' Were you really beside me the whole time?" asked John with a smile.

"I wish I could have opened your eyes so many times when you were at a bottom low and scared, so you could see that I was there right beside you, standing on guard. That was a privilege which the Prophet Elisha bestowed on his servant, for when the servant saw an army with horses and chariots had surrounded the city, he asked, 'Oh, my Lord, what shall we do?'

'Don't be afraid', the Prophet Elisha answered. 'Those who are with us are more than those who are with them.' And Elisha prayed, 'O LORD, open the servant's eyes so he may see.' Then the LORD opened the servant's eyes, and he looked and saw the hills full of horses and chariots of fire all around Elisha."

"I thank the Lord for you," said John.

"Amen. As time went by, you strengthened yourself in the Holy Spirit and I found myself less and less needed. When you got in trouble, I wished you pray and call for backup. God dispatches angels that way, you know. There were times when I could have helped, but I waited for you to pick up the phone and start a prayer, but you didn't. You did much better, however, when it came to prayer than other saints I guarded in the past."

"So this is how it feels to live in the spirit. I mean I can see you and hear you, and obviously, I can think. My physical body is back on earth still?" John asked.

"Yes. When a man is born physically, he is born with a body, soul, and spirit. As the man grows, he has a decision to make. He either continues in the flesh, and worries about what he shall eat, drink, wear, and live in the flesh all his life, only to die twice. Or he has his spirit regenerated to see and hear the Holy Spirit and realize that he is really a spirit trapped inside that physical body. And then he will control the flesh and put it under subjection away from its worldly desires and live forever."

"Wonderful, I'm glad I chose the latter. Tell me a little about the creation and God's story of man's past, present, and future," asked John with excitement.

"Ah, a classical question. We angels were created on the second or third day of creation at the time when God was creating the foundation of the earth and we all worshiped the Lord. He created millions of us; we're God's secret servants, God's army doing His bidding on the earth for the saints. We were very excited to see God create the universe. God created the rest of the world by day six, and we shouted for joy."

"The world, so large and complicated with all the fascinating details and spectacular creatures, was created by God in such a short time. Were those six days, literal twenty-four hour days, or thousands of years?" John asked.

"Of, course twenty-four hour days! Elohim created plants on day three; the sun was created the following day, day four. I don't think that the plants would have survived without the sun for a thousand years. I mean, the Lord could have created everything in six minutes if He wanted to, but God wasn't in a hurry creating the world. He enjoyed and admired what He created and said 'It was good', which is something you guys forgot to do as you rushed through everything you did in life without enjoying it. He also wanted to make a model for man to work six days and rest on the seventh day. Now, on the sixth day, God created Adam and Eve, and that was the most exciting creation since the Lord created them in His image. What an awesome sight that was and we all glorified the Lord. Then the Lord saw everything was good and He rested on day seven," Raphael explained.

"Why do I have a feeling that things will go downhill from here?"

"Yes, God revealed to us that He was going to create mankind and that the creation of mankind would lead to the eventual purpose of all His creation. We were to share the joy of what He was creating through mankind. Now in our spiritual Heavenly realm we have an organized structure with some of the angels having a higher position. Three of these angels are Michael, Gabriel, and Lucifer, who were superior to the rest, in importance, authority, might, beauty, and power.

"Lucifer had the seal of perfection, full of wisdom and perfect in beauty. He was the anointed cherub that covers with overshadowing wings. He was upon the holy mountain of God; he walked up and down in the midst of the stones of fire like the paved work of gleaming sapphire stone upon which the God of Israel walked on Mount Sinai. He was in Eden, the garden of God; every precious colorful gemstone and dazzling jewels were his covering, and his settings and his sockets and engravings were wrought in gold; on the day that he was created, they were prepared. He was blameless in his ways from the day he was created until iniquity and guilt were found in him. His heart was proud and lifted up because of his beauty; he corrupted his wisdom for the sake of his splendor. He sinned; therefore, God cast him out as a profane thing from the mountain of God and the guardian cherub drove him out from the midst of the stones of fire."

"What was his problem?" John asked.

"He didn't think that God's way was best, but that his own way was better. He actually became deceived into believing that he could rise up against God and take over all reign of the physical and spiritual dominions, making himself God. Lucifer planned and plotted mutiny in Heaven, and began to con and convince other angels with his lies, promising them positions in his kingdom. He surprised two-thirds of us angels, when we learned that he had planned to ascend to God's throne and rule in God's stead. What's more shocking is that a third of the angels believed and sided with him in a rebellion against God, even though they all saw God create everything. Lucifer learned the hard way that he was no match for God Almighty, when God banished him and his followers from Heaven and gave him limited access. I saw Satan fall like lightning from Heaven, and from that point forward, Lucifer became known as Satan, a significant adversary and an archenemy of God. Michael and Lucifer became forever-mortal enemies."

"Here is an age old question; why did God allow him to do this?"

"God didn't choose to make us, the angels and humans, like robots to function as programmed. He could have forced man into automatic worship. However, removing our free will, would also have taken away our capacity to give our love to God freely. Love cannot be forced. Instead, God created us, angels and mankind with the capability of free, individual thought. Lucifer didn't like what God created and choose not to follow God."

"What happened next?" John inquired.

"After he rebelled, Satan went from living in a time eternal state to living in the time zone on earth where God slapped him with a watch and a time limit to end up in Hell. Lucifer and his angels lost their position in Heaven and have been creating havoc on earth ever since then. Satan was the worship leader in Heaven but after he fell, he no longer had his job. There was a vacancy in Heaven, but the rest of us angels still worship God. Satan hates mankind especially you saints who worship God, because you took over his job of worship. Then Satan planned to destroy the earth and unleashed his power on mankind because he so hated God's plan, which was to be fulfilled through man on earth. Therefore, there is cosmic conflict between the kingdom of God and the kingdom of darkness, putting mankind in a balancing act between good and evil with earth as the battleground. So, while the Lord rested on the seventh day, the enemy planted sin in God's created man. Satan planned to destroy the human race by introducing sin to the first couple which caused death and chaos."

"Poor Adam and Eve, what a mess they were getting into."

"Satan has been around Adam and Eve for a while and he figured that he would succeed more with Eve, so he attacked her first because he knew her weakness. So Satan, through the snake, questioned God, contradicted Him, accused Him of having no love towards the couple, and told Eve that she could be like God and she fell for the lie. So when Adam came home, he looked at Eve and realized the predicament she was in. He knew that she blew it, was deceived, and had partaken of the forbidden fruit. Now the world was split in half, the sinner side of Eve and the righteous half of Adam, who hadn't sinned yet. After all, there were only the two of them in the world. So, here is Adam looking at flesh of his flesh, and bone of his bone, offering him the forbidden fruit. He could have turned his back on her, and she'd have been lost forever by herself. Nevertheless, he loved her so much that when she gave him the fruit, displaying selfishness and being already in sin, the still pure-in-heart man took the fruit. He chose to join her in her predicament rather than be without her, 'For there is no better love than when you give yourself and your life for a friend'.

"When Adam sinned, Satan had a victory party, laughed loudly and said, 'You're mine, I own you and your world. I have the deed to the world kingdoms.' But his celebration didn't last long. God slapped a watch on him for six thousand years, and the promise of someone that will be coming to bruise his head. God also slapped a watch on Adam for nine hundred and sixty years. He went from 'no time-zone' to the 'time-zone' and the couple lost their position in the Garden. Before the fall, Adam and Eve were clothed with light eternal and had an eternal spirit that was able to respond to God, a privilege that no other creature on earth enjoyed. When they disobeyed God, that spirit died. This created a vacuum in the human spirit, which causes mankind to search for answers beyond his own realm. That's why Christ came so that whoever believes in Him has that dead spirit 'born again'," Raphael explained.

"What a sad story with a good ending!"

"Satan's kingdom is a sad one. The person I was guarding before I was assigned to you had somewhat of a strong faith and foundation in the Lord. However, he started flirting with sin and eventually got a divorce. I wish I could have shown him how much Adam loved Eve, and made it known to him that the devil was manipulating him into destruction. You know the feeling you get when you fall in love the first time, that's how much Adam loved his wife every day. However, after Adam died spiritually, he accused his wife saying, 'The woman whom You gave to be with me—she gave me fruit from the tree, and I ate.' We were amazed at this transformation and how contagious sin was."

"What happened next?" asked John, even though he knew the story by heart, but it was more exciting when the angel told it.

"After they sinned, they lost righteousness that day. They used fig leaves to cover themselves, and that represented their own works to cover their sin, which wasn't sufficient. Then they ran from God and hid. God asked Adam, 'Where are you, son?' God knew where Adam was. Then said, 'Hang in there, son. You can't come to Me by your works, but I'm coming to you in a rescue mission to show you the way, tell you the truth, and give you life eternal again.' God used animal skins to cover them up. A sacrifice had to be made and innocent blood had to be shed. No one died in the Garden before, not animals nor plants, the flowers blossomed forever, and there was no suffering there, until that day. The lion and the lamb were sitting next to each other, licking each other with the sun up and bright that day. After the sin, the lamb was so relaxed that it took a nap. When it woke up, the sun was darkened and the lamb noticed that it was bleeding. It seems that the lion had bitten his neck."

"The whole creation is suffering," said John sadly.

"God gave Adam the title deed of the earth and dominion over it when He created him. However, that day, sin had dominion over the one who had dominion over the earth and that title deed was lost. Satan was given the title deed to earth; he was the usurper and all the kingdoms of earth belonged to him since then. Adam and Eve were transferred from the Kingdom of God, of Life and Light into the kingdom of Satan, of Death and Darkness. Satan was hoping that Adam and Eve would eat of the tree of life after they sinned and become immortal sinners. But God removed them from the Garden to prevent such a disaster.

"Later, God cursed the earth so that Adam would be busy laboring because it was idleness that caused him to get in trouble in the first place. God also cursed the ground with thorns; ironically, He suffered from thorns, too. When He was crucified, they put a crown of thorns on His head. He said, 'cursed is the ground for your sake.' He didn't want the human race to live in a sinful condition in a perfect world environment. This isn't the way that God wanted a man to live, but man was marred by sin and scarred by rebellion. You, however, are here today because you have turned over the title deed of your life to the Lord."

"Thank you, Lord Jesus."

"After they were kicked out of the garden, the Holy Spirit started working and helping them on earth—"

"Did you miss the Holy Spirit when He left Heaven?"

"My brother, you are still thinking in the three dimensions of earth's matter, space and time. The Holy Spirit is omnipresent. He is here and on earth at the same time, the Comforter, Helper, Intercessor, Advocate, and Strengthener remains with you forever. The Spirit of truth, whom the world cannot receive or take to its heart, because it doesn't see Him or know and recognize Him, but you knew and recognized Him, for He lived with you constantly and is in you. The Holy Spirit, whom the Father sent in Jesus' name to represent Him and act on His behalf, taught you all things. Every time the saints gather and pray, especially on Sundays when millions and millions of Christians gather, they were sharpening the two edged sword of the Holy Spirit which He uses the rest of the week to go to battle to further their cause and restrain the evil forces.

"For the Lord Jesus said, 'If two of you on earth agree about anything and everything they may ask, it will come to pass and be done for them by My Father in Heaven.' And, 'For wherever two or three are gathered and drawn together as My followers in My name, there I AM in the midst of them.' If you think the world was in trouble when you left it, you have no idea what is going to happen when the Holy Spirit is taken out of the way."

"What about the Lord Jesus? Tell me about the hope of salvation; I can't wait to hear the good news. Did you miss Him when He came down to earth?" John asked.

"The Lord Jesus we did miss, up here, even though He was gone for a short period of time. However, we could not stay away from Him. When He was born, we delivered the good news to the shepherds. God sent His Son into the physical world with a message that the kingdom of Heaven is at hand. Then we told Joseph to move to Egypt when King Herod killed the little children in Bethlehem. Later, we would go down there on the earth, make Him a meal, and minister to Him. Even two of the humans up here, Moses and Elijah, went down there to earth to meet with Him on a mountain where the Lord was transfigured in front of His disciples. One of us encouraged Him in the garden of Gethsemane when He was agonizing the night before His crucifixion. The pressure of the sin of the whole world being distilled upon Him caused Him to sweat blood. If Jesus would have given up in the garden, no one could have been saved. But before that, in the garden, He and His disciples were singing hymns and Jesus was happy because He saw the salvation of mankind through His sacrifice. Adam lost dominion in the Garden next to a tree; Jesus gained it back in the garden of Gethsemane next to an olive tree. He got back the keys to death and Hell from His foe and adversary by virtue of His completed work on the cross."

John responded by saying, "Thank you, Lord Jesus."

"On the day of His crucifixion, some of the warrior angels, more than twelve legions of them, that's eighty four thousand angels, had their hands on their swords ready to draw at the first drop of blood that gushed out of His body. They looked at God and waited for His signal to go down to earth and slay every last sinner. That meant the wiping out the human race, just like God did in the flood when God was grieved that He had made man on the earth, and His heart was filled with pain. Again, when the Jews sinned after God bailed them out of Egypt, He said, 'The spirit shall not strive with man forever.' But Moses interceded and saved them from annihilation. And after annihilating mankind, the angels may have just turned around and finished off Satan and his demonic followers once and for all.

"On the cross, those angels had half their swords drawn out of the sheath and looked at God the Father and the Son waiting for a signal. Moreover, at one moment, we thought that God might give the signal when we heard the Lord Jesus say, 'My God, My God, why have You abandoned Me?' But later, we heard the Lord Jesus say from the cross, 'Forgive them their sins; they don't know what they are doing.' At that time, they put their swords back in their sheaths and took their hands off their swords. He loved them as they were killing Him!

"We didn't know exactly what was going on that day, neither did Satan. Nevertheless, we remembered that the Lord said, 'For God loved the world so much that He gave His only begotten Son', also, 'whoever believes in Him would have eternal life.' God, in His infinite love and holy hatred for sin, devised a plan by which sin would be punished and you would be forgiven. Jesus suffered the penalty for all the sin of the world for all of time upon the cross. He was treated upon that cross as you would have been treated if you were punished for your sin. He paid a debt He didn't owe and you couldn't pay."

John said, "Thank you, Lord Jesus. So many atheist people and believers too, ask, 'Why did God allow His only Son to be butchered like that?' They had better thank the Lord Jesus then, for if it weren't for Him interceding that day, none of them would exist."

"Yes. Satan, on the other hand, thought he had fully crushed the savior when Jesus died on the cross. But the truth is all he did was bruise His heel. Satan had no trophy to hang on his wall that day. Jesus didn't stay crushed! On the third day, one of us went down and removed the stone of the tomb. The stone wasn't rolled away to let

Jesus out, but to let others in. He rose from the dead in triumph; He was resurrected, and we were so glad when He came back up here. Christ stroked a fatal blow against Lucifer and his schemes and will ultimately crush Satan in the end. Jesus told Satan that He would see him at Armageddon. Therefore, you see, He died, so your sins would be covered, so that you would be able to come up here today."

"Well where is He? I want to thank Him personally. I'm absent from my body; shouldn't I be present with the Lord? This is all great, but I want to see Jesus. I have been waiting to see Him all my life, and I have so many questions for Him," John's excitement showed.

"Then why don't you ask Him yourself?" said the angel as he bowed down and fell on his knees.

A huge light, bright and shiny appeared from behind John, which made him feel warm inside; the warmth was coming from the light. John realized that it was the Lord Jesus Himself. John tried to turn around as fast as possible to see the Lord, but those few seconds felt like eternity. *This is the moment I have been waiting for all of my life,* He thought and then wondered, *Am I really going to be face to face with the Lord Jesus, will my heart take the excitement, what would I say and what would I do?*

At about a quarter of a turn, he wondered whether he should sing or dance out of excitement. At a half turn, the brightness increased and his heart started doing the flips inside and he thought, *maybe I should say hallelujah.*

Finally, they were face to face with the Lord Himself in front of him, the King of Kings and Lord of Lords. He couldn't help but fall on his face at Jesus' feet, and said, "Adoni." In the presence of God, John thought, *John the Revelator was right; Jesus' head and hair were white like wool, as white as snow, and His eyes were like blazing fire. His feet were like bronze glowing in a furnace and still have the scars on them; His face was like the sun shining in all its brilliance. He is dressed in a robe reaching down to His feet and with a golden sash around His chest.*

Then Jesus said in a resonating voice like the sound of rushing waters, "Johnny," while placing His right hand on him, "Don't be afraid. I'm the First and the Last. I'm the Living One; I was dead, and behold I'm alive forever and ever!" Only John's parents and

Mary, who were closest to him, called him Johnny. This showed how close the Lord was to him, and the kind gesture served as an icebreaker. Then John stood up and looked at Jesus who had a glow and a sweet smile radiating from His face. Before he knew it, Jesus hugged him and put His arms around him. John was now in the arms of royalty, and was thrilled in His presence.

I'm finally in the arms of the Lord, thought John, *the safest place in the universe. I might as well melt like an ice cube, for on the inside I feel like a piece of charcoal burning with fire. Heart, don't fail me now from the excitement. If they would have dipped me in hot oil, burned me at the stake, cut me in half, or thrown me to the lions, it would have been worth this moment.*

"Welcome to life eternal," said Jesus, "You are already in Heaven and your eternity is secure. You have overcome, and the second death will not hurt you at all; the sting of death is no more because I paid your debt in full."

Of course, you can read my thoughts, thought John, *I had forgotten in all the excitement. I might as well die right now and go to Heaven. Whoops, I'm in Heaven.* Then he said, "Thank you, Lord."

"I'm the resurrection and the way, and you shall live forever with Me. I will never blot out your name from the book of life, but will acknowledge your name before My Father and His angels."

Then Jesus said, "Welcome home, son. Well-done, good and faithful servant, enter the joy of the Lord. I tell you the truth, I prayed for you to be with Me to behold My glory. You were like a tree firmly planted and tended by the streams of water, ready to bring forth its fruit in its season; its leaf also didn't fade or wither; and everything you did prospered and came to maturity today. You are royalty; I will make you a king and a priest. You have put yourself under my authority and now I will put things under your authority. Just as I overcame and sat down with My Father on His throne, you overcame and I give you the right to sit with Me on My throne, and give you authority over the nations."

"Thank you, Lord," said John as he looked at the scars on Jesus' hands and continued, "Lord, I'm sorry that you had to go through the crucifixion for my sins."

"I tell you the truth, if you were the only one down there that needed salvation, I'd still have gone through it for your sake. When I was on the cross, I saw my blood cleanse your sins. And when I was resurrected, I saw this day, when you have been raised with Me to a new life, thus sharing My resurrection from the dead. I take care of all of My sheep. And neither death, nor life, nor angels, nor principalities, nor powers, nor things present, nor things to come, nor height, nor depth, nor any other creature, could have, or will separate you from My love."

"Thank you, my Lord and God."

Then they started walking together in Heaven like old friends and Raphael followed. John wanted to learn the mysteries of God and God told John everything.

John said, "I see now, Lord, that this is what was missing in our lives on earth! You made us in Your image so that we can fellowship together. Sin separated us and now we're united again."

"That is the truth. Now follow me, son," said Jesus as He signaled a distinguished angel to sound his trumpet.

"My Lord, I will follow you to the end of the world," said John.

"I know you will, my son, I know you will."

Then, John heard the Lord saying to the distinguished angel, "Son, get your horn ready, blow it and call My sons and daughters up here."

Jesus disappeared as the distinguished angel blew his horn. John thought that the distinguished angel was out of sight and scary at the same time. So he asked Raphael plainly and without offending him, "Who was that angel?"

"That's Gabriel," Raphael answered, "Do you hear that trumpet? The last person to accept the Lord Jesus, just did, the fullness of the Gentile is complete and the blessed hope that the church has been waiting for, is coming to earth."

"Where is my body then?"

"It's in the grave right now, and you're going to unite with it very soon. When the trumpet finishes shouting, your body will kick open the grave and move upwards towards Heaven. Then you'll reunite with it and meet Jesus in the clouds—" Raphael answered.

"How is my dead body going to be raised and get up here?"

"The Holy Spirit on earth takes care of that. He's like what you call a GPS, Global Positioning System that will guide your body up here. Then those saints who are alive will come up here in the Rapture and meet with you and the Lord in the air. Get ready to have your mind blown away by your new and upgraded body."

"How do you know that?" John asked.

"I've seen Adam and Eve in the Garden of Eden, remember. And let me tell you, they were a piece of art, having the image of God."

"What was I then, chopped liver?" asked John smiling.

"Indeed you were, if you show someone who has never seen a liver, a chopped liver and say there is a liver, they'd believe it to be liver when it is only a mess of a liver. You were never in the image of God, brother; you've never seen a man the way he was intended to be, not in the kingdom of Satan where sin had dominion over you. When God created Adam in His likeness with mind, will, and emotion he was invisible. But to function in a universe of matter and move through time in space, He gave him a body. You, however, were born in the image of fallen Adam, a faint echo of the image of God, tarnished and distorted. But the new resurrected body you're getting will be in the image of God. Then, and only then, you'll understand what being in the image of God means."

"So, then the invisible Son of God's image was put in a physical body and was called Jesus. Thank you heavenly Father for the Lord Jesus," replied John, then asked the angel, "Who is coming up here, out of earth?"

"The church age dead saints with their resurrected bodies, and the church age living saints with their transformed bodies. For the Lord said, 'This is the will of Him who sent Me, that I shall lose none of all that He has given Me, but raise them up at the last day. For my Father's will is that everyone who looks to the Son and believes in Him shall have eternal life, and He will raise him up at the last day.'"

"So, we were right then about the pre-tribulation rapture of the church?"

"Of course, the Lord Jesus loves His bride and she loves Him. Why should He subject the Christians to His wrath? The church is betrothed to Him with deep commitment and has a date with deity for a wedding in the sky. She is engaged to Jesus in a love story, and was selected by Jesus. He left glory and came down to earth to select the bride so that later on He could take the bride to His Father's house. The church was made ready for the wedding. The next seven-year period is God dealing with His people, the Jews. The four hundred and ninety year Jewish prophetic clock of God given to the prophet Daniel, stopped at the Cross. Then the church age started for the last two thousand years, and today the church is taken out of the way and the prophetic clock started ticking again for the Day of the Lord."

As John followed the angel to receive his resurrected body, he bumped into Adam and Eve.

"Speak of the federal heads of the human race," said Raphael, "we were just talking about you guys."

John marveled at the couple and said, "It is an honor to meet you here. I'm sorry for your loss in the garden."

"My loss was your gain in Jesus Christ, brother," replied Adam.

"How do you mean?" asked John with respect and awe.

"It's true that when I sinned in the Garden, I traded power and authority for spiritual weakness, for I no longer had the power to do what I ought to. I traded Godliness for ungodliness, for I was no longer in the image of God. I traded absolute perfection for sinfulness. I traded approval for wrath, which leads to condemnation and Hell, and traded peace for warfare. But you, my brother, you gained much more. When I was innocent and sinned, my sin was added to my account. You, however, were justified and reconciled after you sinned, and even better, not only were you forgiven; your sin was never imputed to your account. I walked with God in the Garden and you had the Holy Spirit within you—He came to your heart and gave you life regeneration. While I found life after my redemption came, you had it more abundantly. And finally, I had an earthly kingdom, and now we have a Heavenly Kingdom. So you see! He gave you much, much more than whatever you lost in me."

"When were you guys redeemed, and how did you get here?" asked John.

Adam answered, "After we died, our souls went into a place called Paradise. Then one time, while we were waiting there, the

Lord Jesus appeared and told us that He was the one, the Messiah we were waiting for, who crushed the head of the old serpent. He took us out of that place and brought us here to Heaven, and now we're going to go and get our resurrected bodies."

"It must have been awkward when Eve offered you the fruit; tough decision!"

"When I saw her that day, I looked in her eyes and I felt something different about her. Her eyes talked and said 'look, I ate the fruit and nothing happened'. I knew that something had happened on her inside though because she wasn't the same. Then she offered me the fruit in one hand while she was twirling her hair and covering her breast with her hair, in a new way, with the other hand. She had never done that before. I didn't have lust in my heart yet, and didn't know anything about flirting. Little did I know that the daughter of God just a little while ago, had now turned into the daughter of the devil. Her eyes spoke again and said, 'I ate the fruit, and I feel out of the ordinary, maybe the snake was right. Why don't you try, too?' Satan instructed Eve to get the fruit close to my mouth. So I took the fruit and looked at it, when I thought I heard a voice from the tree say, 'shove it in your mouth, you insignificant fool, don't ruin my plans.' I took a bite, and the same voice came from the tree again saying, 'checkmate, it is started.'"

"Satan perverted my perception of God's character," said Eve. "He persuaded me that God was keeping back a good thing from me. He made me think that God didn't love me as I thought. He stirred up a desire to sin in me because God's word no longer meant love, but law. We were kicked out of the Garden and life became really hard for us. We faced misery and death especially when we learned that our first-born child took the life of his brother Abel because of religion. Cain tried to impress God by offering the works of his hands. His worship to God was by his own strength and it was rejected. Abel, however, brought an offering, by God's grace, of the best first born of his flock, and was accepted. We realized the seriousness of sin and warned our other children about the devil. From that time on, we looked forward to the Messiah who would 'finish it' as we were told by Enoch our grandson."

At that time, John noticed two old men wearing robes, so he asked Raphael, "How come these two men already have bodies, and why are they old?"

"These two are the prophets Moses and Elijah and they are getting ready to go down to earth on a mission as the two witnesses, as soon as the Antichrist signs the seven year treaty."

"Heaven's super highway is busy these days," said John. "Some people are coming up and some people are going down. And who is that angel escorting them? Whoa!"

"That is the Archangel Michael; a mighty angel who does the Lord's bidding, and obeys His word. I report to him, and he takes his instructions from the Lord."

John couldn't help himself anymore and said, "Wow, that is some magnificent angel! No wonder when these guys appeared to humans they always said, 'have no fear'."

"We'd better get going now," said Raphael, "the trumpet has stopped blowing. The resurrection of saints is going to take place now, followed by the evacuation of believers."

"Wow...wow...wow," said John as he and Raphael went into a new dimension.

Funeral

Meanwhile on earth, Mary was mourning her husband's death. At the funeral, three days after John's death, Bill gave the eulogy. He said with sadness, "We're gathered today to be reminded again that sin has entered the world, and death is the penalty for sin. John is my friend and brother in the way and truth. And now he has graduated and is walking in Heaven and having a great time with Jesus right now. He doesn't have to worry about the rising prices of food or gas or cope with a failing body. So I'm not going to say to his family, 'sorry for your loss', because you don't lose someone if you know where they are. When a baby is born into a new environment, it cries. When a person dies people cry and they have every right to be sad. I don't sorrow for him, but for myself. I miss him; he was a very decent brother, fun to be with, exciting, and loved the Lord with all his heart."

Mary and Gracie wept quietly.

"You know, folks, John isn't where his body lies," pointing at John's body in the casket, continued Bill with teary eyes. "This was only the house that his spirit dwelled in." Then Bill took off his jacket, held it with his finger and said, "See the jacket is idle and motionless." Then he put the jacket back on, moved his arms and said, "See, it started moving again. I'm not the jacket and the jacket isn't me, it's just something I wear. We're triune beings just like our Creator. We're spirit beings with the same nature of God. We live in a body, which is our earthly suit that allows us to exist on earth, express ourselves, and communicate with others. We possess a soul, which is our mind, will, and emotions. We're perfectly suited for our physical environment the same way God is suited for Heaven. When the body is no longer able to sustain the spirit, God will release the spirit. That's a blessing to the saint. John's spirit is somewhere else, a much better place."

Jim was present at the memorial, listening and wondered who would guide him, now that John was gone.

Bill wiped his eyes and continued, "Suppose you had a friend, someone who lives in a dump, don't you feel sorry for them? One day, you hear that they got an inheritance and they moved into a big mansion. You're going to be happy for them, if you love them. Earth is a dump and Heaven is our big mansion. I'm amazed when people say that God took the deceased to plant him in His garden. God doesn't need flowers in His garden. Sometimes, He loves us so much He can't wait to hug us in Heaven like He did with Enoch. I'm sure Enoch's grandparents, Adam and Eve, wondered where he went and missed him, too. However, they saw him again in paradise and Heaven later.

"Now if you ask what if my wife were the one lying in the casket there, would I feel the same way? Yes, it will break my heart to million pieces, but I know and am certain that nothing happens if God didn't allow it. And if my wife weren't saved, then I would live in terror. That's why Christians shouldn't mix yoke and marry unbelievers. And if you came to the truth after marriage, then keep working on your partner and pray."

As the procession moved towards the cemetery, Jim rode in Bill's car and asked, "What is a yoke?"

"A yoke is a device farmers use to connect two animals together by the head to pull the plow and they usually use animals of the same kind, two oxen or two donkeys. But if an ox is sick and the farmer has to mix an ox and a donkey and connect them with a yoke, then it wouldn't work because the animals will go separate ways."

Jim, being a city dweller all his life, had to imagine the scene of two animals yoked together.

Bill continued, "I guess I'll take you under my wings, now that John is no longer with us. I should tell you that I have a different style. I don't baby-sit or spoon-feed anyone. Many converts have prayed the sinner's prayer, confessed Jesus with their mouths, studied the Bible, attended church, and became active. Unfortunately, it is without the revelation of who He really is, and without laying their lives down for Him. And when they went through a test or discipline, they got offended with God and wanted nothing to do with Him. And that's what happened to the last person I spent a lot of time and energy on, only to see him backslide. It would have been better for him not to have known the way of righteousness, than to have known it and then to turn his back on the sacred command that was passed on to him. He never truly repented and his flesh wasn't dead with Christ. Instead, he was still burning with unlawful desires and the latter was worse for him than the beginning. 'A dog returns to its vomit,' and, 'a sow that is washed goes back to her wallowing in the mud.' Time is short and I want to reach as many people as I can."

Jim, who could have easily been offended by this remark a week ago, replied, "I see. I thought about it and I'd like to be baptized soon."

Bill almost jumped out of his seat and happily responded, "All right, now you're talking. Either John did a good job showing you the truth or you have great soil or both. Let's do it then."

At the cemetery, the pastor prayed over the casket, "The Lord is my shepherd; I shall not want—"

Jim whispered and asked Bill, "I hear that prayer all the time on TV and at funerals. What does it exactly mean?"

Bill stepped aside and answered, "It means that the Lord Jesus is our Shepherd not the pastor, or parents, or friends, or the king, and we're His sheep. We're privileged to be His sheep and in His tender care. Sheep are defenseless, easy to get lost. They don't know what's good for them or what could hurt them. The only defense we have is the blood of Jesus.

"The first part, 'The LORD is my shepherd, I shall not be in want' means that I don't have any needs because God takes care of us and provides for all of our needs. He cared for us yesterday and He cares for us today, and He is making provisions for tomorrow. Another thing about sheep is that they don't carry anything on their backs, unlike donkeys and horses; the shepherd carries the stuff.

"Then the psalm continues and says 'He makes me lie down in green pastures.' The shepherd leads the sheep to green pastures. The sheep graze and the shepherd watches out for danger. Sheep are nervous and afraid of sounds. We also get discouraged and nervous at the first sign of adversity or trouble. When we worry, Jesus says 'don't worry; I'm watching over you', we say 'But...'" and He says 'don't you worry about these things.' This way we won't be concerned with the things that are going on around us because He's keeping guard and protecting us. That's why I'm not going to worry if the stock market crashes, or the global financial meltdown, or the unemployment rate goes high. I lay all of my burdens on Him and lean not on my understanding."

Jim said, "I saw a picture with a person walking on the beach at the worst time of his life. He saw only one set of footprints, so he asked the Lord 'where are you?' and the Lord responded 'those are my foot prints.' Jesus was carrying the man on His shoulder."

"That's beautiful. Then the psalmist David says, 'he leads me to still waters'. Sheep are afraid of rushing streams of water and would never drink of it. The shepherd creates a still pool by diverting the stream of water into a pile of rocks in a circle, and then they would safely drink.

"Then he says 'He restores my soul. He guides me in paths of righteousness for His name's sake' If the lamb wanders off, the shepherd goes after him and gets him back to the flock. The inexperienced lamb does it again and he brings it back again, and by the third time the shepherd brings it back, but this time he breaks its leg, makes a splint and puts it on its leg, binds it up then he picks the sheep up and carries it over his shoulder. God carries us on His shoulder and restores us this way. Some Christians say 'I love God, but I want to live the way I want and go where I want', and end up astray. Then God busts their spiritual leg and says 'I love you so much, but if you keep doing this, I'm going to break your bones'. This process leads to a steadfast faith, a willing spirit, and a humble heart."

"Would He break our bones, too?"

"If He has to, yes, He would. Because He loves us."

"How's that love?" Jim asked.

"The Apostle Paul had a thorn in the flesh. No one knows what it was, and it wasn't there because he strayed but so he wouldn't boast. He had a big mission and little time to do it in; God had no time to waste for Paul to go astray. When God writes our name in the book of life and we drift, what is He to do? Satan is persistent and so is God, He loves us so much; He doesn't want us to perish and go to Hell. Oh, He will remove our name from the book of life if He has to, but as a last resort. Do you see God's grace when He breaks our bones?"

"Yes, I do," then Jim lifted his arms and said, "Thank you, Lord, break all my bones if you have to. I don't want to go to Hell."

"Amen. Finally, he says 'though I walk through the valley of the shadow of death, I will fear no evil, for You are with me; Your rod and Your staff, they comfort me.' The shepherd uses his staff to protect the sheep from lions, wolves, and predators out in the field. Goodness and mercy are God's sheep dogs. So you see, Jehovah-Rohi provides all of our needs and protects us, and we, the sheep, hear His voice and follow Him, but we won't follow the thief who scatters us. And one day we will dwell in the house of the Lord forever."

"Speaking of shepherds, when I was a kid, I heard a Bible story of the man who had a hundred sheep and lost one of them. He left the ninety-nine in the desert! He left them and went after the one that was lost until he found it!"

Bill responded, "And when he has found it, he laid it on his shoulders, rejoiced and said to his friends; rejoice with me, because I have found my sheep which was lost. There is more joy in Heaven over one person who repents and despises his misdeeds and determines to enter upon a better course of life than over ninety-nine self-righteous persons who have no need of repentance. Jesus told this parable: Two men went up to the temple to pray, a Pharisee and a tax collector. The Pharisee prayed: 'God, I thank you that I'm not like other sinners—or even like this tax collector. I fast twice a week and give a tenth of all I get. But the tax collector would not even look up to Heaven, but beat his breast and said, 'God, have mercy on me, a sinner.' Jesus said that this man, rather than the other, went home justified before God. For everyone who exalts himself will be humbled, and he who humbles himself will be exalted."

Jim thanked Bill for being his new mentor and decided on a day for baptism.

* * * * * * * *

On the other side of the assembly, Gracie brought along her friend to talk to her Aunt Martha.

Gracie introduced her friend, who seemed distressed, to her aunt and said, "Auntie, can I talk to you for a minute? This is my friend Angela; we know each other from church."

Martha said, "Hi, Angela, how are you?" Gracie continued, "Angela is a couple of years older than me and we've been friends for years. She just found out that she is pregnant. She's thinking about abortion; can you give her some advice?"

"Yes, sure, who is the father and how did it happen?"

Angela answered, "It was a date rape; my boyfriend took advantage of me at a party that he invited me to. I had a drink or two, then we went for a drive and it happened. I only went there to dance and not to look for sex."

Martha asked, "Did you tell your parents?"

"Yes, they said that it's my body and I can do whatever I want. They are worried about taking care of a new baby. My boyfriend, who is no longer my boyfriend, said that he wanted nothing to do with this, and then he denied it ever happened. So I'm left on my own to make a decision. I was told by a counselor that if I have the abortion, I'd probably not be able to have children in the future, but I don't care right now; I just want to graduate from high school."

Gracie said, "Auntie, in her defense, you should know that her boyfriend also goes to church, although not the one we go to. So she... we, both thought he was someone that could be trusted."

Martha said to Angela, "Ok, well I'm shocked that your parents, who are church members, are encouraging you to go through with it. We can't break God's laws just because it is inconvenient. Not to mention that the Lord forbids it because it's murder. And you know research has shown that women who have abortion increase their risk of breast cancer, and are thirty percent more likely to develop ——— a mental illness. They are also three times more likely to develop a drug or alcohol addiction compared with other women. Why, because the post abortion psychological trauma of abortion will be more severe than the trauma of rape."

Angela said, "The lady from Planned Parenthood said that abortion is legal, and is every woman's right and it's my personal decision. She also said that it's just a blob of tissue and everyone is doing it. It's a very simple procedure."

Martha replied, "First of all, it's not a blob of tissue; it's already a living human being. Ask to see an ultrasound. Don't be deceived by a manipulative counselor and immoral health professionals into believing that your unborn baby isn't human. How would that person, who gave you that advice, feel if her parents decided to abort her when she was an embryo? If you go through with this, it will create a scar on your soul that you'll carry the rest of your life, unless the Lord frees you from that guilt. Moreover, the procedure isn't that easy; it's gruesome. They'll apply only a local anesthesia and you'll be aware of everything that's going on. You'll feel severe pain and hear the vacuum literally sucking your guts out. Then it will be too late, in the recovery room, when you find out that you ended the life of your own child."

The girl looking for a way to justify her decision said, "So what do you suggest for a fifteen year old girl, raise a baby all by myself?"

"Many parents want to adopt...I'll be finishing college next year. I'll move back here and help you raise the baby. And I'm not just saying that; I mean it."

"What if the baby turns out to be one of those who are mentally under-developed?"

"What do you mean?"

The girl frustrated said, "Don't you hear the news? One in thirty children are being born with this disease. And it can't be detected in the womb while you're pregnant like the other syndromes. It becomes apparent at age two; you have to wait two years after birth to see if the child has that condition. Having a baby these days is like a box of chocolate; you never know what you're going to get."

Martha, appalled by the information, said, "I do hear the news and last time I checked it was one in a hundred, just six months ago! Anyways, that doesn't change the rules about abortion."

The girl, still struggling to decide, thanked Martha and walked away with Gracie.

Martha, standing by a tree prayed, "Our country has sold its birthright. Satan is attacking this last generation before you come back, with abortion on demand, because he knows in these last days You'll pour out Your spirit upon all flesh and our sons and daughters will prophesy. Oh Lord, even our children are coming out deformed. When will you end this, and how long will you wait, Lord? The things that are happening in the world confound even the heathens. They know that something has gone wrong and they need to be bailed out. Let's get the show on the road, Lord...," then she said, "I'm sorry Lord I don't know much. You're all knowing, forgive me. Your will be done."

* * * * * *

Afterward, they all went to Mary's house. There, Mary overheard a lady from church whispering to another sister and said, "They must have sin in their lives; they have been through one tragedy after another. This must be God's judgment on them." Mary felt very sad and angry at the same time because she didn't believe that it was sin in their lives that killed John. But she kept her feelings to herself.

When the funeral had ended, Mary and Gracie were tired so they went to bed early. Gracie asked her mother that night if she could go to bed with her, and Mary welcomed her to her bed. She slept on the side where John used to sleep.

Mary turned the lights out and it was very dark in the room, so Gracie said, "It is so dark in here, Mom, and I can't see anything. Is your face towards me?"

"Yes, daughter, my face is towards you."

"Mom, I'm scared, can you hold me?"

Mary put her arms around Gracie and said, "Go to sleep, darling."

After Gracie went to sleep, Mary got out of bed and knelt beside her bed side and asked God the same questions, "Lord, it's very dark in here and I can't see anything. Is your face towards me?"

The Holy Spirit, who was always present, replied, *Yes, daughter, He's looking at you.*

"Lord, I'm scared. Can you hold me with your hands, please?"

The Holy Spirit answered and said, *You are in His hand and He's never letting you go; go to sleep my daughter.* Mary finished praying, got in bed and went to sleep.

Mary and Gracie couldn't see it, but there were two bright and mighty angels standing on each side of the bed. In the darkness and standing in the corner of the bedroom, there were also two demons. The demon that used the truck driver to kill John asked, "All I did was distract the driver. I was surprised that I succeeded and it actually worked. Do you think that we went too far on this one?"

The other demon replied, "Well, with these humans you never know. When you put pressure on them, some break down, crumble and backslide; yet others get emboldened and their faith gets elevated. But now that the head of the household is gone, we have a better chance with these two."

"Why are we whispering?"

"You see those two angles over there. Well, they're not carrying swords for no reason. They are special forces."

The other demon still whispered and asked, "What do you mean, special forces?"

"Well, the one on the left, I saw him kill a hundred and eighty five thousand human soldiers in an Assyrian camp. In a few minutes time there were dead bodies everywhere."

"When was that?"

"It happened about four thousand years ago, when the Jews were fighting my idol worshiping slave people. It wasn't a good day for my recruits."

The other demon trembled, gnashed his teeth and said, "Could we please go now?"

The demon started to shake and said, "I'm with you, brother." And they both disappeared.

Good Friday-Bad Friday

The next morning after the funeral, Mary's sister went back home because she had a final test. But before she left, she said to Mary as she usually did when they parted, "If I don't see you again, I'll see you in Heaven, Maranatha, [*which means Lord come*]" then she headed out towards the taxi.

Mary and Gracie, now alone, were hurting over John's death. They had breakfast without him and realized that he's not there anymore; he is gone. Mary looked at his picture and she realized that he wasn't coming back, and there would be no more phone calls from him. Later, Gracie went to school.

Mary was still upset over what the lady said the day before and thought angrily, *no Satan, you're not going to boil my blood with anger and keep me rehearsing the words that lady used to offend me, and hurt my feelings with. I rebuke you in the name of Jesus. I'll forgive her and forget it ever happened, in Jesus' name. I'm going to let the blood of Jesus cover that offense.*

Minutes later, she prayed, "Lord, I still can't get rid of this feeling. My heart hurts, help me please." The phone rang and she answered the phone. A voice on the phone said, "Hello, Mary, this is the pastor. I just had a feeling and an urge to call you."

"Thank God you called. I need some counseling. I overheard this lady, Lori, yesterday say that we have sin in our lives and in our home and that's why we've been having calamities lately. I can't shake the feeling of resentment off!"

The pastor confirmed that the lady was wrong and said, "If God punishes sin, we'd all be in trouble. And judging other people is dangerous because one may have to go through the same situation the other person they judged went through to see how they would handle it. Christians shouldn't try to figure out what happened to other Christians; we don't know why things happen. One church member had his tonsils taken out last week and another member told him that those were the tithes and offerings that the doctor got out of him. I say let the Judge do the judging when He appears.

"Mary, you cannot forgive her by your own human strength and ability. You must ask God for inspiration to love and forgive Lori for hurting you. It takes maturity and humility to bring reconciliation, and taking the first step is usually harder on the one who has been offended. Mary, we should keep an attitude of pursuing peace by putting our pride aside."

Then the pastor reluctantly said, "I'm not supposed to tell you this... and I'll have to ask God for forgiveness after I hang up with you. However, Lori has divorced her husband a few months ago even though he was a good and loving Christian. The man loved her even after she divorced him. God made marriage between a man and woman for life, but sin entered the world and because of the hardening of hearts, God allowed divorce. God never intended for marriage to be a torture of living in fear by either spouse. The evil spirit of divorce has deceived her. Now, she is just a bitter woman, even more than before. Her husband told me that he would rather live on the corner of the house roof, in an electric storm, than be with her in the same house. She is contentious and quarrelsome and deliberately lashes out at people. Did you know that snails have thousands of teeth on their tongues? The snail usually keeps his tongue rolled up like a ribbon but when it comes out, the teeth go to action. Her tongue is set on fire of Hell and she has no control over it and that's what ruined her marriage."

Mary was surprised and said, "I never knew any of that about her! She seemed OK to me until I heard her speak yesterday."

"We look at the outward appearance, but God looks at the heart. One shouldn't judge a book by its cover. She is a very pretty lady. When she walks down the aisle in church, all the men avoid looking at her so they wouldn't get in trouble with their wives. Her husband found out about her wicked ways before the wedding, but didn't want to disappoint the family; the invitations were sent out already.

"Look sister, Jesus said love your enemy, for who is our enemy, not flesh and blood, but evil devils. And our enemy that is released from the devil today will be a brother or sister tomorrow. After all, no one is guilty until proven guilty. Every man has until the last breath to receive Christ. But it isn't our job to figure out the sheep from the goats. We'll love our brothers and sisters and encourage each other as the day of His coming gets closer."

"What if the offending party is a Christian and makes it to Heaven?"

"No Christian will treat their spouse badly. It is against everything Jesus talked about. They may go to church and seem godly, but Jesus will say to them, 'get away from me, evil doers.'

"Then, they go to Hell and spend all eternity wishing a moment of love from that person they ignored and abused. They would say if they could have just listened, and how did they let the devil deceive them and so on.

"Plus, when you realize that Jesus delivered you from eternal death and torment, you'll release Lori unconditionally. We must take our lead from the Lord Jesus, as He has forgiven us and keeps forgiving us, so are we to forgive others. Unfortunately, unforgiveness is so rampant in our churches."

Then the pastor told her the story of Job and how he was tested by the devil and he then said, "And God blessed Job afterwards only when he forgave those three friends who accused him of sin in his life. I say you forgive her seventy seven times if you have to. What if we get raptured today? You don't want to go to Heaven with this on your mind. No, sister, I say shake off these feelings and go out and get some people saved. That will get your mind off things and renew your spirit."

Mary thanked the pastor for the encouraging words then called Lori. Lori was watching TV when her phone rang; she looked at her caller ID that displayed Mary's name. She thought, *oh no, I told her she could call if she needed anything; I hope she didn't take it literally! I better see what Miss Goody-Two shoes wants.* She muted the

TV and picked up the phone and heard Mary say, "Hello Lori, how are you? This is Mary."

"I'm fine; the world is going crazy though—"

"What do you mean, what happened?"

"Haven't you been watching the news? There was a nuclear attack in the Middle East. Some submarine fired a nuclear warhead at Israel, but something or someone changed its direction and it hit Damascus instead."

"Oh, my Lord, did you say a submarine—, a hook in the jaw!" Mary replied.

"What are you talking about?"

"Well, in Ezekiel, the prophecy says that God will put a hook in the jaw of Israel's enemies and bring them against Israel. A hook in the jaw, you know like a fish. I'm thinking maybe submarines will initiate this attack. Who fired?"

"They don't know yet—"

"Probably terrorists, trying to blow up the world - let them. Who needs it? There is a better world we're looking forward to. Only a believer can say that, secular people would say—"

"Are you insane?" Lori finished the sentence, "I love this world. Let them blow it up after I'm dead and gone. You're just saying that because your husband died. Anyway, they said that there were six Russian submarines positioned in the Mediterranean, the Black Sea, and the Gulf, and five of them are missing. The U.S. denied involvement and now the U.S. and the EU sent out their subs, too, to prevent another launch from that area. The U.S. has no stomach to engage in a war with Russia because of the economic woes on a national scale. So now every country is sending their submarines to investigate, a little mistake or a wrong move and we could have World War III.

"Not to mention the Arab nations who are on a state of alert after accusing Israel of diverting the warhead towards Damascus. I don't blame the Arabs for being angry. I mean, they showed the path of the warhead, which was picked up by satellite; it launched from the sea, headed towards Tel Aviv, which caught Israel by a total surprise, then the nuclear missile took a slight turn and proceeded towards

Damascus. All the military advisers on TV said that was impossible, but we all saw it happen in front of our eyes."

"Praise God. He protected them again. They can never wipe them out completely. Israel is there to stay. They can try to drive them to the sea or remove them from the map. It just won't happen." Mary responded.

"I don't know about all that; there are millions of people dead in Damascus. Is that God's will? Israel has turned the world upside down since they came into existence in 1948 and there has been nothing but conflicts in the region. They are messing up the world for us. Maybe it is time that these issues get resolved and send them back to where they came from for the sake of peace in the world. Doesn't the Bible say that it is better for one to die than a whole nation? One nuclear missile and they're gone forever."

Mary couldn't believe that this woman attended the same church she went to, yet she was ignorant of the Biblical facts, and said, "You see the Jews are God chosen people, people of destiny. And Israel was given by the Creator to the Jews in an everlasting covenant. Israel is a plot of ground that is the Biblical and spiritual center of the world and the center of the earth. It's where Jesus was born, lived, and died and will return to Jerusalem. Israel is the focal point of the future, and the final confrontation between good and evil. It is at the storm's center, where the final battle will take place at the plains of Megiddo. We prayed for the peace of Jerusalem; peace in Jerusalem meant peace for the whole world. But I guess it's too late for that, the stone of stumbling remains and real peace won't happen until the second coming of Christ."

"Well the future is here then. This must be the final confrontation. Israel is on its highest level of defense readiness condition and the Arab Leagues are holding an emergency meeting, probably to wage war and avenge their Syrian brothers. The Arabs are furious over Damascus. According to their Quran, Jesus is supposed to return to Damascus and slay the Antichrist, then The Hour, or Judgment day comes. Well, now that Damascus is obliterated, where is Jesus going to return? And Russia is searching for their vanished submarines. The EU has already dispatched their military forces, and the

Americans are just observing from a distance, too busy with their financial woes."

Mary realized that if hearing the pastor explain prophecy didn't reveal to her the significance of Israel in the Bible, then she wouldn't be able to, either. So she said, "Look, I just called to say that I'm sorry I had hard feelings towards you yesterday. I overheard you say that we were going through so many calamities lately because we have sin in our lives. Please forgive me."

Lori mocked and said, "Wait a second, I didn't know you had these feelings, so why bother confessing? You didn't have to tell me, and then apologize. This doesn't make sense!"

"It is important for me to do this because God knew that I had these thoughts. I care for what He thinks—"

"Now see, you guys take this to a fanatical level when you act and think like this. People like you discourage others from going to church; you hide your sins and act all holy on the outside. What good did that do to your husband? Ha—, Hello, Hello."

Lori got angry because Mary didn't answer her back, so she hung up the phone and said, "How dare you give me the silent treatment and not answer me? I'll never ever talk to you on the phone again."

After she hung up the phone, she started programming her phone to block any incoming calls from Mary's phone number. Next, she heard a knock on the door. She opened the door and it was her neighbor who seemed frantic and in tears.

"What's wrong with you?" asked Lori.

"My baby is gone!" said the neighbor.

"What do you mean it's gone? It's only five months old and in the womb; where can it go?" said Lori as she looked at the neighbor's belly.

"I'm telling you, it isn't there anymore. Do you want to feel my belly?"

"I don't want to feel nothing, girl. Get away from me!"

The neighbor started crying.

Lori said, "Wait a minute. I thought you said you wanted to abort the child, but your husband wouldn't let you. Maybe this is a blessing in the sky."

The neighbor stopped crying, "Yeah, it's true. But how will I explain this to my husband. He's going to think I aborted it."

"No, girl, just call him and tell him what happened!"

"But, but, I don't know what happened. I did drink now and then without my husband's knowledge. You don't think—"

"No, girl, you wished your baby away, that's what happened! You're the first woman that was able to do this. Go get a bottle of wine and celebrate. No stretch marks, no gaining weight, and no baby crying." Lori replied.

"I did call my husband but there was no answer even on his new pager which allows me to get to him even if he were on the moon. I wonder why he's not answering. It's not like him not to answer an emergency page; he'd have to be dead not to answer me back."

"Ok, you just go home and keep trying. Goodbye," Lori escorted her neighbor out and closed the door behind her. When she got back inside, the muted TV displayed a national alert system warning on TV. It read 'please stay indoors or take shelter immediately; the country is under attack.' She unmuted it and there was a buzzing noise associated with the message.

She flipped the channels and heard the news on another channel. The announcer said, "Enormous segment of the population, in the millions have vanished all of a sudden and preliminary reports indicate that this phenomenon is happening all over the world. Who or what is responsible for this act of evil? No news from the governments as for what caused a disappearance, but the military is on a full-scale alert. Our government has declared national state of emergency." The picture disappeared and Emergency Alert System (EAS) announcement came out again and said to stay off the phone, only officials and emergency crew should be using the phone. But she dialed anyway and got a busy signal. The EAS made another announcement to stay indoors and not to drive. Lori picked up her keys to leave the house, then the TV switched from EAS to the News channel again.

Lori received a call as she was baffled watching the news. She reluctantly picked up the phone and said, "Hello, who is it?"

A voice answered, "Hi it's me." Lori gave a sigh of relief as she recognized the voice of her friend from church on the other end of the line. Her friend said, "Hi, how are you? I'm watching the news; did you hear?"

"Yes."

"I thank my lucky stars that we were not abducted. Thank God you answered. Every church member I called didn't answer."

Lori anxiously asked, "What? What do you mean aliens? Is that what happened, an invasion from outer space? Did the laser beams zap those church people?"

"Yes. What channel are you watching? No, switch to the global channel."

Lori turned the channel and said, "I knew it. We were lied to and deceived. All that time and money we wasted on that church and it was an occult. Good riddance, the aliens got them now. Those bigots did the exact opposite of the message Jesus tried to spread. They are so simple-minded and impressionable sheep that can be so easily brainwashed by these evil humans who call themselves 'pastors'. They are probably more corrupt and far from what Jesus preached and yet those stupid sheep lacked the intelligence to see through them. I certainly didn't have to swallow the oral manure that these very low-level thinkers fed them at their services."

"I thought you only went because you wanted to hook Tony up."

Lori replied, "Yeah, that's true. I just called him and there was no answer. Hey, the news just said that it seemed that more women disappeared than men. Good, our chances of finding a good man have just increased."

"Amen."

"It just bothers me that the preacher tricked us, his followers, into making him money and fighting for his cause. I guess he knew about the aliens visit and tried to brainwash us about some snatching away rapture and flying in the air. The aliens are probably putting probes in their… you know where," they both laughed and she continued, "Did you know that the pastor's wife asked me if I could volunteer to clean the church women's toilets? How dare she ask me that? I wouldn't do that for a million dollars! I hope the aliens make her clean their toilets."

They both laughed, then her friend asked, "Hey, you don't think there is a chance that the rapture did happen, and we were left behind?"

"Girl, if there is a God, and He doesn't want me in His club, then the Hell with…Woo."

"What was that, Lori… Lori..?"

"Ah…Nothing, I thought I saw a shadow or something move. I hope it's not an alien. No, it's just the stupid cat. I got a call waiting; I have to go. Well, before I let you go, I'm going to ask you not to mention that we attended church to anyone else from now on. I don't want any trouble with the authorities putting my name on some occult list. After I hang up with you, I'm going to burn all the church materials I have in my house, Bible and all, and leave no traces and you should do the same, agreed?"

"Yes, of course. I cannot believe we bought into it either," Her friend replied.

"Okay. I have another line coming; I have to go now. I'll talk to you later. Goodbye."

Lori flashed her phone to the other line, but no one was there. So she started collecting her church study books and Bible, and went out to the porch and brought in a portable fireplace and put all the books in it as she closed the blinds and looked through the blinds to make sure nobody was watching. She finally dropped the Bible on top of the pile and the Bible opened up as it landed on the piled books. Lori noticed that there was a paragraph highlighted. So she bent down to see what it read: "Because they received not the love of the truth, that they might be saved. For this reason God shall send them strong delusion, that they should believe a lie" "Shut up," she said as she dropped the match on the pile and watched the whole thing burn.

Lori kept watching the news. "More news, ladies and gentlemen, preliminary reports from the air force indicate that strange activities are taking place in the upper atmosphere. It has not been confirmed yet if UFOs are present."

More news by another channel anchorman, "I have good news and bad new: the bad news is that it's been confirmed UFOs are present and they have probably abducted the vanished people. The good news is that the aliens are our friends as they have abducted only the type of people that are agitator, law-breakers, and rebellious persons who wouldn't be loyal to their government, so we're not going to miss them. Thank you, aliens, whoever you are, and wherever you're from."

Lori said, "Yes, they are agitators and aggravators all right, and I'll obey the leaders and do whatever they tell me."

A demon appeared behind her and whispered, *Good, they'll put a chip implant on your right hand, where your bracelet is. But for now, whatever feels good to you, do it anytime, anywhere. The restrainer is out of the way and anything goes. You can have as many men as you want at one time. You can experiment with other women, too, if you like, with no guilt; total freedom and no restriction whatsoever.*

Lori thought, *what if my neighbor felt like coming out to my house at night and raping me?*

Now, now; what is this rape business? If your neighbor feels like he wants to know you better, and you feel like you want to know him better, where is the harm in that? The word rape should be removed out of the dictionary. The demon said.

I see. What if someone likes my car and decides to steal it? Lori thought.

Then you steal someone else's car. The Bible says 'an eye for an eye, and a tooth for a tooth', right?

I sure hope things will work out the way I'm thinking. Lori thought.

Sure it will, trust me. Don't complicate things.

One channel commentator said, "We just got a bulletin from a high-ranking official in the government, a reliable source. He stated, 'Considering the difficulties that our economy and agriculture has been going through in the last year in food shortages and earth over population around the world, this event, or phenomena is a blessing as food will be more available for the rest of us with less people to feed. Unemployment will go down to zero percent and prosperity is on the way. All we need now is to come together and define a new world order, preferably controlled by one leadership to move our world forward. Peace is imperative and we have to help our neighbors and forget our differences. And we just heard that the nations are going to meet at the United Nations tomorrow to discuss what to do next."

The commentator was handed a paper and continued, "And we just received bulletin news. It seems that some of the Arab countries surrounding Israel were ready to invade Israel after the first nuclear attack has destroyed the Israeli infrastructure and defenses. But these plans were aborted when the first attempt was unsuccessful and the unexpected twist of events that happened later and continue to develop as I speak."

Another news channel had guests participating in a discussion panel. First was a professor from the University of Harvard who was an expert on aliens. The discussion moderator, Angie, asked, "Professor, tell us what you think happened today."

"Oh, I agree with what everyone else is saying, that aliens did abduct the citizens to study us and not to enslave them; they are trying to help us, not deceive us. And I do agree that they are selective by picking up the bad elements to show us that they are friendly and they come in peace and they don't mean the rest of us harm. And their ability to select like this shows their high intelligence. They are also far more superior than we are. They can blow up the earth in a second. I'm sure that they will reveal themselves to us at some point of time."

"Ok, professor, what about all these babies and children that have been abducted with them?"

"Oh that's very simple. I think they selected the children because they wanted clean specimens undefiled or uninfluenced by our world, easy to mold and train. I think that they will live in the alien world and grow up with the alien culture. They are going to show them their ways and mold them into their culture and when they're done training them, they will send them back to earth. That generation will tell us all about the aliens, their values, system of beliefs, and habits. This will be the aliens' way of communicating with us and sending us messages through our offspring. There will probably be a lot of secrets unveiled to us, like the pyramids in Egypt, for example. No one knows how they were built."

Angie said, "Well, this has been very educational. I can't wait to see the new breed."

"I wrote a book called 'Aliens and Humans together' about a year ago and it sold about a half million copies. I outlined all these facts before it happened."

Angie said, "Well that's just genius. I'm sure the book will sell even more now. Thank you very much, professor. Well ladies and gentlemen, the day started out bad but it's getting better and better by the minute as we start to understand why all this is happening and reach an understanding of what all this means. And as we get more information, we will pass it along to you."

Angie put her finger on her ear and said, "We just received news from the Middle East where these nations think that the Mahdi, their twelfth Imam who is supposed to come after chaos and war, has come and is punishing the Christian world for supporting Israel. But they can't explain why Israel is still here. They are holding off any attack on Israel for right now."

While Angie was conducting the interview with the panel, a young Jewish man appeared all of the sudden in the studio. He grabbed a chair and joined the panel. The stranger sat down looking puzzled.

"Excuse me, sir! This is a closed panel discussion. How did you get in here?" Angie noticed that he was wearing a skullcap and continued, "OK, maybe you can represent the Jewish people. Sir, what is your name and what do you think about what's been happening today?" After she mentioned that he was Jewish, he took off his skullcap and held it in his hand.

"My name is Eli. Today I saw my land get spared by God from a major disaster and destruction and my eyes were opened. But, no brothers and sisters, you have got things all backwards. The people who vanished were the aliens and didn't fit in this world." All of the discussion panel participants leaned forward to hear what he meant.

"All right, a new twist on the story. Do you mean that the aliens came down to earth, duplicated the human bodies and discarded the real humans and walked among us as if they were humans, just like the invasion of the body snatchers movie? And when their mission was over, they went home today?"

Eli replied with a perplexed look on his face, "What are you talking about? These people you call aliens, they were citizens of a far distant kingdom and they were all waiting for the king to call on them. He finally did and they all went home as their tour of duty has concluded. The king has called his ambassadors home and has declared an all out war on earth."

"So who is the king? Do we know him?" Angie asked.

"Yes I do, and you would too, if you read your Bible; He's none other than Jesus Christ the Son of God. I realized today that I have a Savior who died for me on the cross and His bloodshed cleanses me, and His resurrection saved me."

They all leaned back with disgust. Angie said, "He's one of those, a Jesus freak. You stupid, stupid man, how did you get in here anyway?"

One panelist said, "Don't be hasty; everyone is entitled to their opinion." Then he asked the Jew, "I'm just curious; so you're saying that the vanished people just up and away started beaming up themselves just like that? By what power, may I ask?"

"You have no idea what power the Holy Spirit has, but you'll know soon now that God has removed His hand of protection from the planet. He was the one that held this planet together and now that He is gone, this planet is going to come and go and literally blow up in the sinners' faces."

Angie said, "Here they go with the doomsday news and predictions. How come you're still here?"

"I was an unbeliever myself as of yesterday, but today I'm no longer blind. I felt like scales fell off my eyes and I can see the truth about our God and His Son and the Holy Spirit. God had a feast and He invited the Jews first. But they refused to go, so He invited the Gentiles later and blinded the Jews for a while. And the Christian nation's church age was born. But then they too started to refuse to come, so God took His saints who believed to Heaven and gave the spirit of delusion to those who were invited and didn't come. Praise the Lord."

The professor said, "Glory to man."

Angie asked the professor, "What did you just say?"

"I don't know why I just said that."

"No, I like the sound of that," Angie replied.

One of the panelists who was a representative of the world Christian council said to the Jew, "See, we don't talk like this now. You are wrong; all the roads lead to Heaven. We need peace in a hurting world, not strife. I would hate to be in your shoes because talking like this can get you in a lot of trouble in this new world order."

Eli looked at him with a smug look on his face and said, "I would hate to be in your shoes at the end, if I can only show you a glimpse of where you are going to spend eternity. You had your chance and you blew it. Repent everyone, before it's too late; get on your knees and worship the King. He is coming."

One of the panelists said, "Sir, you've been talking about this coming Messiah for thousands of years. I'd rather go to Hell than get on my knees and worship your God."

Eli said, "No problem, God will accommodate you, but believe me as sure as you can see me, every knee will bow down to Him one day. And you can mark your calendar, in exactly two thousand five hundred and twenty days from the next peace treaty; Jesus will come back to earth riding on a cloud. But between now and then, there is a beginning of sorrows and a great shaking coming up on the earth. The day of the Lord is here."

The Christian representative said, "Sir, I don't think the world can wait seven years for this Messiah. We need someone now, to bail us out of this mess!"

"You always wanted God to work by your timeline—"

Angie interrupted, "Call security. I want this man out of here."

Eli said, "Wait, there are thousands of people in China, India, and Africa who have just repented of their sins and accepted Jesus Christ into their lives." He looked at the camera and spoke in different languages and said, "Listen to me, saints, the kingdom is at hand and the good news of the kingdom of God will be preached."

Angie screamed, "Security, security—"

Eli said, "There is one like me on every other TV station in the world."

Angie said to her producer, "Check other TV stations to see if he's telling the truth."

Minutes later, the producer replied, "Yes, he is right. I checked a few international stations and there are peculiar persons saying the same thing."

Angie asked, "Sir, how many of you are there?"

"There are one hundred and forty four thousand people just like me all around the world; they will help people in their territories and reveal the end time deceptions. The majority of the world is in fear, chaos, and confusion, with anxiety building up right now. They are easy prey to believe a lie and be blinded by the world's explanations. With the Holy Spirit not restraining sin and evil, and the salt and the light of the world gone the next seven years, the world will get what it always wanted, unrestrained life without Ten Commandments or rules to keep. A war of worldviews and clash of civilizations; without salt for a preservative, everything will be rotten; without the light, there will be darkness. On the other hand, you'll have God's hand of judgment and His wrath mixed with the evil of Satan, a literal Hell on earth. One thing you haven't discovered yet is that some graves in every cemetery in the world has opened and their residents have also vanished."

Angie said to her producer, "Would you ask the copter to check on the local cemeteries?"

Then she looked at Eli and said, "If what you're saying is true, then this must be the first time ever that graves opened like this."

"Actually, it also happened about two thousand years ago when the Lord Jesus was resurrected. Many bodies of the saints, which slept, arose and came out of the graves after His resurrection, and went into the holy city Jerusalem and appeared to many."

Angie rolled her eyes and asked the producer, "Did you check?"

The producer said, "Copter one pilot has disappeared. Here is copter two pilot speaking." A voice came from the chopper with copter engine noise in the background saying, "Yes, some graves in the local cemeteries are open."

Angie was amazed and asked Eli, "Sir, what is your mission?"

Eli answered, "To tell the truth."

Angie asked, "What is truth?"

One of the camera operators left his position behind the camera and stepped forward towards Eli and said, "Sir, I want what you have."

Angie asked, "What are you doing? Get behind your camera!"

The camera operator said with an accent to Eli, "I was born in Russia and I came to this country just a couple of years ago. I have heard about Jesus Christ, but nobody explained this to me about Him. I want Jesus, please."

Eli said, "Open your heart, repent, and ask for forgiveness."

Then, four security men came in, looked around, but the stranger was nowhere to be found.

Angie asked, "Where is he? He was here a minute ago. OK, arrest the camera operator then."

As security personnel were escorting the camera operator out, he said, "Ma'am, did you notice that the stranger had no microphone on, yet his voice was on the air?"

Angie asked the producer, "Rodney, did the stranger's audio come through?"

The producer replied, "Yes, it did."

"Did he have a mic on?"

"I don't know. I didn't give him one."

Angie said to security, "OK, get him out of here." Then she looked at the other camera and said, "Ladies and gentlemen, please disregard the last comments you heard from the stranger who appeared from nowhere, then disappeared to nowhere." Then she turned back to the professor and asked, "OK professor, why was this man, Eli, spared by the aliens?"

"He wasn't spared! He said himself that he was converted after the disappearance took place, and as you noticed, they beamed him up right in front of our eyes. He was there a minute ago and then was gone."

The representative of the world Christian council said, "The aliens abducted the Christian fanatics. What you witnessed today is the cleansing of those crazy so-called Christian troublemakers who turned the world upside down disrupting our lives. They were biased, bigoted, and narrow-minded. The remnant Christians are peaceful, and will reunite with all the other religions and worship one God. We'll form a world unity in a global conglomerate church, one that will be loyal to the new world leadership."

Angie was handed a bulletin and she said in shock, "Ladies and gentlemen, while all the scientist of the world have had their eyes on the sky looking for UFOs, they found two asteroids on a collision course with earth. They haven't been able to determine how long before they will crash with earth because they're moving at variable speeds. But they are estimating the first and smaller one to collide with our planet in about three to three-and-a-half years. The second and larger one is of enough size to cause life on earth to go extinct. Preliminary reports estimate it to hit earth in about five to seven years. A Russian scientist, who called it Chernobyl, which means wormwood, discovered the second one... My God, is this day ever going to end? I wish I could go home, dip into the tub and go to sleep and when I wake up tomorrow none of this would have happened."

Lori's demon said, *I wouldn't say that; the show has just begun. Let the good times begin.*

Eli's voice echoed in the studio, "Good-bye, Heaven-bound saints, for now. As for earth, there's a global warming coming soon to a town near you, but it's not as described in yesterday's news. May God have mercy on the new believers in the next seven years and shorten the days of the last three-and-a-half years, for the sake of the elect. Amen."

Glorious Appearing

John found himself in another dimension, mingling with other believers' souls as they waited for their bodies and families to be raptured. Then John heard a man saying to his angel, "Are you sure I wasn't raptured? I was here in a blink of an eye. There was a brief pain, but I didn't mind it as long as I got here. I barely got a chance to talk to the Lord."

"What is he talking about?" John asked Raphael.

"Damascus was hit by a nuclear weapon. This brother was disintegrated instantly, and that's why he thinks he was raptured."

"Damascus in Syria, right! Who did it?"

"Yes, the attack was aimed at the holy land and the archangel Michael diverted it there."

John thought, *I have the best news network and source of information up here.* Then he asked, "But this man claims that his soul just got up here, while I died a while ago, yet it seems like we both arrived here at the same time. How is that possible?"

"You're still thinking in terms of earth's time and space. Some of these saints around you died two thousand years ago and they still think that their souls just got here. When you die in the Lord, you get raptured immediately; there is no waiting in the spirit. The meeting you had with the Lord, you were already raptured. How else could He have hugged you? Wait for your resurrected body and things will clear up for you."

The rapture occurred in a flash as they were speaking. John united with his newly resurrected body in the air with the Lord at his side. John's spirit entered the newly resurrected body as a hand enters the glove, and the new body started moving. Raphael escorted John back to Heaven where he examined his new body.

"Try it on for size, brother. What do you think?" asked Raphael excitedly.

"Wow! This is great! I feel like... like... superman."

"Check out your new knees."

"What? Oh yeah, they are just great. I used to walk with a limp, but I don't anymore. My whole body feels very well and healthy. I feel light on my feet as if there is no gravity here. I can't wait to explore the privileges and powers of the new body and the new brain that functions at full capacity, a hundred percent," said John excitedly.

John noticed the millions of saints gathering and having happy and joyful family reunions, celebrating their glorified bodies and final salvation. Heaven was having a happy hour without alcohol. The assembly looked like the largest Mega church ever and there were no sections for different Christian denominations, only blood bought Jesus followers. They weren't in Heaven because they went to church, but because they went to the cross. They all wore white robes and praised God.

John asked Raphael, "How am I going to recognize my family from these millions and millions of saints?"

Raphael smiled and replied, "Let me tell you about the penguins. See, the penguins' females leave their eggs with the males to sit on while they go have lunch that lasts for a couple of months. When they come back, the eggs would have hatched and the male had gone through a weight loss program. But the amazing thing is that the mother knows which baby belongs to her from thousands of newly hatched babies, even though it was inside the egg when she left. The father doesn't assist the mother in the search for her baby either; he just wonders where his late dinner is. She feeds the baby off her fat while the father leaves for a late dinner. If penguins can do that on earth, how much more can you do here in heaven, now that you have gained a hundred percent of your brain capacity?"

Then John heard a voice saying, "John..."

John, recognizing that voice, looked back with great joy and said, "Gracie, is that you? You look taller and older." They hugged.

"How long have I been gone?" asked John, then said, "Oh never mind, time doesn't matter here anymore."

"I'm so glad to see you," said Gracie.

"So am I. We made it. We're actually here in Heaven."

"I saw the Lord Jesus. He's so awesome," Gracie agreed.

"Yes, He is, and we'll see Him always and forever. Where is Mary?"

"Oh, she found Grandpa and Grandma. She said she'd be right over."

"Ok. So tell me, where were you when the Rapture happened?" John asked.

"Well I was sitting in class, and it was that time for us to present our paper about making a deal with the devil assignment, the one I told you about. I was really sweating it, as I was probably the only one that refused to participate in such a project. I didn't prepare for this presentation because it's against my belief. And I tried to get out of it; however, the teacher threatened to give a failing mark to anyone who didn't participate. Therefore, I showed up and I was praying to God for help. When it was almost my turn to deliver my presentation, I just vanished and found myself up here with the Lord. And that was just a blink of an eye ago, raptured, up, up and away. I wish I could see the look on my classmates' faces. The world viewed us as losers; captured, reviled, persecuted, and hated. Let them see us now, getting off an express shuttle service to Heaven!"

Gracie gave John a warm hug with a big smile.

"What was that for?" asked John.

"I'm very excited because I didn't taste death; we defeated death, which was swallowed up in victory. The Lord Jesus was the first one to defeat death by His resurrection and showed us also the way to conquer death. Thank you so much for encouraging me when I was on the earth and thank you for raising me a born again Christian. It was worth every effort to get here; this place makes all the trouble on the earth worthwhile."

"You make sure you thank Mary, too. We're all here today because we always prayed that we'd be counted worthy to escape the tribulation, be raptured, and to be standing before the Lord for reward."

At this point, the two heard a voice from the back saying, "Hello, Father!"

They both looked back and there stood a young man.

"I'm sorry, son, but there must be a mistake. I don't have any sons, only one daughter," said John as he looked at Raphael with a puzzled look on his face.

Raphael smiled and said, "Do you remember the first pregnancy that Mary had, when she lost the baby in a miscarriage?"

Suddenly, John went back into memory lane and rehashed what Raphael just said. At the same time, he was looking at this young man standing in front of him. A great feeling of happiness came upon him as he stepped towards the man and hugged him.

"This is my son and your brother," John said to Gracie, "Praise the Lord."

"Praise the Lord," said Gracie as she hugged her newly found brother.

"It is good to see you both," said the man, "and I was wondering if you could show me around the earth when the time comes, since I haven't seen it yet."

"Of course, son, when the Millennium starts, you're on!"

Then Mary appeared and hugged John in a happy and joyful reunion. All that they had dreamed, aspired, hoped, and prayed for, was celebrated in that wonderful moment.

"I missed you so much," said Mary. "Can you believe it, we're here, it's true we're really, really here and we're with Him."

"You look great! Here, I have a surprise for you. This is our son Hank, the son we never had," pointing at the young man.

Mary, feeling overjoyed, put her hand on her mouth with amazement at the beautiful specimen of a man who stood before her and gave him a big hug that lasted a while. There is no rush in Heaven. She said with tears in her eyes, "Hank, my son, I knew you'd be a boy, I even gave you a name. I thought about you all the time. I wondered what you'd look like and wondered what you were doing in heaven. I missed you, my son."

"I missed you too, Mother. I was in the presence of the Lord the whole time, surrounded by more love than anyone can ever give. I have so many friends who came up here as children, even more than adults. I'd like to know more about you and my family," he said.

"Of course, son, we have all eternity to do that. Praise God."

Then Mary's sister appeared and she said that she was on the airplane admiring the sky and praying when she was raptured.

"You should have gotten to the Lord before the rest of us since you were already in the sky," said Mary and both started laughing. "I'm just joking; the whole event of beaming up to the third Heaven happened in a split second. I don't think a couple of thousand feet in the sky would have made any difference," continued Mary.

"Hello, Johnny," a voice came from another direction. John looked around and saw his mother and father. John recognized his parents' voices and said, "Hi, Dad. You look different."

And his dad said, "You look different too."

"Mom, you look great."

"Hi son," said his mother, "it is so good to see you."

"I'm very sorry about your last years on earth," said John, "After you guys passed on, I've been wanting to tell you that I'm sorry I wasn't able to pitch in more in your final years living on social security, because my income was limited. It was my first job after getting married and we just had Gracie. I wished I could have helped you more financially."

"Don't worry, Son," said his father, "we managed all right. Jehovah-Jireh provided for us. The best gift in life you and Mary have ever given to us on earth was salvation, by introducing us to the Lord Jesus. I mean the real Jesus, not the religion thing we were doing all our lives. And any other social security or government program on earth can't match the eternal security we found here. We don't miss our failing and frail bodies on earth, or the worries and the anxieties, and time limitations. Here in Heaven we relaxed, nothing to worry about, just happy all the time."

Then Bill showed up, and knowing what good friends they were, everyone said to John, "We'll see you later and let you catch up with Bill; we have a whole eternity to catch up on things."

"OK guys," replied John.

After a hi-five and a Heavenly hug, John said to Bill, "Now we know why the Apostle Paul couldn't wait to get back to Heaven.

After he was caught up to the third Heaven and had a glimpse of it, he said, 'to live is Christ and to die is gain.'" They both laughed.

"Who would want to go back to that junkyard of a world after seeing this? He was anxious for the enemy to kill him after that," replied Bill.

Then John asked, "Tell me, brother, where were you when the rapture occurred?"

"I was in jail sitting in the same cell, talking to people about Jesus. I was waiting for my wife to bail me out and I wasn't in a real hurry."

"Not again! Why were you in jail?"

"They found out about the Bible study, and accused us of conspiring against the state. Can you believe it?"

"So, how did it end?" John asked.

"Well, I met this nice guy in the cell who was arrested for driving under the influence. After talking to him for a while, it turned out that he was a Christian who has drifted from the faith. He said that he used to believe but the Lord has tarried, and he didn't think that the rapture would happen in his lifetime. I said, 'You need to remember that He will come like a thief in the night to those who don't believe and are unprepared.' He said even the Apostle Paul thought that the rapture was going to happen in his lifetime!

"I said, 'yes but he didn't have access to the book of Revelation like we did, which was written after his lifetime.'

"He asked, 'do you mean to tell me, the man who wrote most of the New Testament and went to Heaven and came back, didn't know when the rapture was supposed to happen?'

"I said, 'No, only God Himself knows when, not even the angels know.'

"The man's continence changed and was cut to the heart. I asked him if he was OK.

"He said he was a faithful Christian and he had drifted away into Babylon's economic wealth and false religion. He said it was a gradual change over the years. He thanked me for giving him a wakeup call.

"I said 'that's what we're here for. When your car battery dies, my battery can jumpstart yours. The juice is there; it just needed to be energized.'

"Then he started to sincerely pray for forgiveness and promised to return to the sheepfold. And when we were done praying, I finished by saying in the name of the Lord Jesus, when we opened our eyes we found ourselves in the presence of the Lord Jesus. Talk about fast salvation."

John said with excitement, "My Lord, your witness, ended the age of the Gentiles. The full number of the Gentiles has come into completion at your hand! Look at how many crowns you've got, my dear brother."

"I'm just a servant of the Lord," said Bill with all modesty, "I have fought a good fight, I have finished my course, and I have kept the faith." However, a second later, he elbowed John and said,"I did get the crowns and I will lay them all down at the feet of the Lord when the time comes. Because He told me that, 'I have kept the word of His patience, He also has kept me from the hour of temptation, which came upon the entire world, to try them that dwell upon the earth.' Blessed be His name."

"Praise the Lord. I'm going to call you the fullness of the Gentiles bringer upper. Where is this man you saved?"

"He was no one special on earth and now he's walking with the Lord over there, and so is the thief that was crucified next to the Lord. I'm going to say hello to the other brothers and sisters and I'll see you later, " said Bill as he was leaving, then stopped, looked back and said, "You know, the last seven prophetic years of the Prophet Daniel have started clicking."

"Yes, I know," said John.

Best Seat in the Universe

At that same time, John saw Jim and said, "Congratulations, you made it."

"I thank our Lord Jesus and you for that."

"I told you Heaven is real. Check it out; it's not some vague and magical idea from the mind of man. Just because this realm of the creation has spiritual dimensions, doesn't make it less real!"

"Amen. Who were you just talking to?" Jim asked.

"That was the big fat tub you saw with your carnal eyes on earth. Look at him now, no pun intended."

"None taken. We have been given a new heart, free of self-centeredness, mean spirit, and frustration. There is no resentment, pride, or ego here. What are all these different crowns he has on his head?"

"He's already been to the Bema seat. Let's see; that one, with the most sparkling jewels, is a crown of righteousness for those who loved His appearing at the Rapture, those who were inspired by His imminent return. It's the easiest one to get of all crowns. The other one, with the cross on top, is a crown of life, which the Lord has promised to everyone who suffered for His sake, persevered under trial, and stood the test with a cheerful spirit.

"The crown incorruptible, the one with diamond like jewels, that will last forever, he got for beating his body and making it his slave so that after he had preached to others in the Bible study, he himself wasn't disqualified for the prize. He kept himself from the pleasures of the world in order to provide valuable service for the Lord. There is also the crown of glory, the shepherd's crown, the one with an arch on top, for feeding the flock in those Bible studies. Finally, there is the crown of rejoicing, for winning lost souls."

"Where and how did he get those crowns?" asked Jim.

"He got them at the Bema seat judgment from the Lord Jesus Himself; we're all in line to go to the judgment seat of Christ."

Jim felt uncomfortable at hearing the word 'Judgment' and asked, "What is the Bema seat?"

"When the Olympic runners finished a race, the winners usually get medals, some get gold, and some get silver depending on how they finished. At the time of the Roman Empire, they gave a laurel reef to the winner. We have just finished a spiritual race on earth and we're waiting for our reward just as the Lord has promised us. This isn't a judgment for salvation and isn't about sin, but about works, service, and stewardship of our lives. So, only the saved show up at this event for a review, reward, and evaluation of our life on earth. It is a time of revealing, and unconcealing all of our thoughts. Our works followed us to Heaven. Christ is the foundation; we build on it with works of wood, hay, stubble or gold, silver, and precious stones. He will reward each person according to what he has done. After all, He gave His life for us, and we have to put something in His nail-scarred hands to appreciate what He has done for us."

"What kind of works are we talking about; what will He be looking at?" asked Jim as he felt nervous.

"First; the Lord will examine how we spent our time, money, and spiritual gifts that He had given us through the Holy Spirit. We were to have laid treasures in Heaven, not on earth. Also the motives behind the giving would be considered; if we gave out of guilt or to gain, the reward is wood. However, if I gave out of generosity, joy, and thanksgiving to God, then the reward would be gold. Second, how a person controlled his or her body and put it into subjection, the way the Lord would have wanted, will be considered. Third, how much suffering did the saint go through for the Lord. Fourth, how nice he or she treated other believers in their circle of fellowship. Again, the motives are examined, if the person served others to be noticed or to impress men, the reward is wood. But if it was done to meet the needs of other people out of love, pleasing the Lord and living by His will, then the reward would be gold.

"And finally, how a person exercised his or her authority as a husband or wife, father or mother, and his or her position in the church and at work will be considered. The way a Christian lived and acted; either brought or repelled people to Christ. Trivial pursuits such as worldly success and material growth are stubble, but God's will pursuits are gold."

Jim was still nervous.

"Oh, don't get nervous. The Lord Jesus is our advocate and attorney in front of the Father. Don't worry; we abided in Him, so that we may have confidence, and not be ashamed before Him now. The athletes don't lose their citizenship if they break the rules; they only forfeit their reward."

At that time, Raphael appeared and said, "C'mon John, it is time to receive your eternal reward." Then he escorted John to the Bema Seat.

As they were walking to the courtroom, John noticed that Raphael had a book in his hand. He looked at it and realized that it was his book of works. It had a lot of red marks on the first half of the book.

Then John started going over his works in his mind and thought, *I sure hope that there would be more gold, silver, and precious stones than wood, hay, and stubble in the eyes of the Lord.*

"Don't worry, John," said Raphael, "Jesus has you covered before and after you came to the truth. It doesn't matter how you started, but how you finished. It's like someone taking a butterfly to court and suing her for eating the leaves on his yard tree when she was a caterpillar. What do you think the butterfly would say in her defense?"

"I think she would say, 'I'm sorry for what happened to your vine leaves, but that was the old me. I have been through a transformation, and right now I go from flower to flower and eat only the nectar. And at the same time, I carry pollen and spread it between them, which causes them to reproduce and bring about fruit.'"

"And that's exactly what happened to you when you were born again; you were transformed and began to spread the good news from one person to another. But I have to say, most saints worry about the Bema seat Judgment, but you are OK with it. You have read your Bible," Raphael assured him.

As John approached the Bema Seat thinking about all the things that Raphael talked about, he saw a brother getting out of the Bema Seat room who was as happy as can be. He had many crowns on his head and he was dancing a Heavenly dance. He was so light on his feet, it seemed as if he were flying in the air. Right away, John thought about the king of the Jews, David, at the time the ark of the LORD was entering the City of David for the first time. Israel celebrated and rejoiced with all their might before the LORD. King David, wearing a linen ephod, was leaping and dancing with all his might before the LORD just like this man was. The only difference was that David stripped himself of his kingly robe and uncovered himself. This brother, on the other hand, was holding on to his robe of righteousness that the Lord had given him. So John took a deep breath and straightened out himself and said, "This is silly, I shouldn't worry. Here I come, Lord."

Raphael said, "That's it, brother. This is a joyful day of triumph."

Jesus met John at the entrance, put His arms around him and said, "Well done, good and faithful servant! You've built your faith on the rock, the storms came in the form of atheists putting doubts in your mind about My deity, My life, miracles, and even existence, and they all bounced off your thick foundation. You have been faithful with a few things; I will put you in charge of many things. Come and receive your reward and share your master's happiness!"

"I still made mistakes, Lord," John said sadly.

"I know them all, and I have them all covered, and you're still getting your crowns. I tell you the truth. You have run to the end of the race and finished well. You ran a good race and have overcome and broken the barriers, a top-notch performance. You have overcome and I will make you a pillar in the temple. I came with a reward for the faithful."

Then John looked inside the Bema room and saw many angels waiting for the books to open.

When the events of the hospital incident were displayed, John thought, *I'll never know if my faith would have survived Gracie's death*. There was a freeze frame on the scene and a new scene started at the cemetery. John thought it was his funeral at first but then he saw himself standing next to Mary and weeping. He started wondering whose funeral it was. Then he was shocked when he saw the headstone which displayed Gracie's name on it. Then there was a fast forward showing John going to church and Bible study and still holding on to his faith. He realized that Jesus was proving to him that he'd still be faithful under any circumstance.

John looked at Jesus smiled and hugged him. Jesus said softly, "I tell you the truth. Nothing could have separated us."

When the proceedings ended, John received his crowns. It was the happiest day of his life and he gave all the glory to God.

* * * * * *

Later on, Jim came along to talk to John and said, "I just came from court. I didn't get many crowns on my head." Jim continued sadly, "After my case was over and settled, I stayed and watch my brother Steve's hearing. I was very surprised that he made it to Heaven at first. I mean I witnessed to him and told him what to do to be saved just as you told me, but didn't expect him to repent. I guess the Holy Spirit worked on him."

"I already know."

"How did you know?"

"When I was at my proceedings, I watched myself witnessing to you, and I saw how you helped your brother as a result of my helping you. That's how it generally works to try to get everyone here in Heaven," John explained.

"Well, we're both grateful to you. I wanted to see his proceedings to see how it happened. His book opened and I looked and saw Steve repenting just a couple of days before the rapture. I saw him crying and repenting sincerely and from the bottom of his heart."

John replied, "He's so forgiving and merciful, our Lord, isn't He? And if it wasn't for you, Steve wouldn't be here, so cheer up."

"My father was saved too, thank God. Unfortunately, my mother didn't make it, even though I tried to talk and witness to her many times. I regret the fact that I wasn't persuasive enough in the short time I had. I told the Lord that I felt remorse and a loss because I didn't save my mother whom I loved. Jesus said to me 'I tell you the truth, I chose you before the foundation of the world. I miss her too, son.' Then Jesus wiped my tears. I'll keep watching for her to come up, maybe she has a chance like the tribulation martyrs," Jim sighed.

"I'm sorry your mother didn't make it, yet," said John even though he thought it wasn't possible for her to live for Christ in the tribulation when she didn't live for Him before. But he also believed that nothing is impossible with the Lord and continued, "But we'll keep an eye out for her."

* * * * * *

In a different location in Heaven, Mary was walking around and recognized a member of her earthly congregation where she went to church, was being escorted by his angel to the Bema seat. On earth, this saint used to be a child in a wheelchair with some sort of physical and mental deficiency. She wasn't sure of what kind, but he didn't speak and seemed to be unaware of what was going on around him most of the time. So she decided to attend the hearing and listen in. As she got into the room, she saw his mother attending, too, and they had a joyful reunion.

"Look at my son Jacob now, walking and talking, no more speech or behavioral disorders, and no more eating or sensory problems," said the mother ecstatically.

"Praise the Lord," said Mary, "I'm so happy for the both of you."

"I so much looked forward to this blessed day." Continued the mother, "It was very hard especially after my husband left us, he couldn't take it anymore. The boy was restrained to a wheelchair with a horrible disease. I cried day and night, and I got so depressed. That was my new hobby besides praying. I never blamed God, but I rebuked the devil in the name of Jesus." Her eyes started getting teary. "I don't know how we managed to stay above water. God helped us with His Grace and Mercy."

As the records opened, the events of the book came alive and were shown like a video for everyone present to see. Then the records reached the moment that the Lord Jesus appeared to the little boy who was afflicted with darkness and confusion. The Lord whispered in his ear 'I love you my son and you'll live forever in my kingdom.'

At that time, Jacob spoke and said, "Lord—"

The Lord stopped the proceedings, and the record of his life came to a halt. "Yes my son," said the Lord Jesus.

Jacob said, "My Lord, your words touched my soul and encouraged me to go on. However, that creature, the devil over there, " pointing at Satan who was among the thousands and thousands of angels present, "he came to me afterwards in my despair, and said to me that you were a figment of my imagination, that I had made you up that night you talked to me, and that I would die in my darkness. I didn't like that creature and I chose to believe you and to live."

When the two women realized that Satan was present, they both hid their bodies quickly behind Jesus for protection.

Jesus continence changed and said, "I tell you the truth, the devil will continue a little while longer and then he will be no more, you'll never see him again."

"I was a big burden to my parents, they were fighting over my condition every day, and eventually my earthly father left my mother. And I've looked for him all around Heaven and can't find him," the young man went on.

Jesus said, "I tell you the truth, many had their eyes, that ensnared them and caused them to sin, and they didn't gouge it out and throw it away. When their hand caused them to sin, they didn't cut it off and throw it away. It was better for them to lose one part of their body than for their whole body to be thrown into Hell. You won't find those in my father's house." Jesus put His hand on Jacob and said, "I miss him too, my son."

"When I saw and heard my mother cry in agony every night after my father left, I thought that it would have been better if I was dead. But she still took me to church every Sunday, and I heard the preacher say that you love children. You said, 'Let the little children come to me, and don't hinder them, for the kingdom of God belongs to such as these.' and here, my mother prayed in faith for you to heal me, and I prayed for you to at least come and talk to me again."

"I tell you the truth, you were right in My hand the whole time," said Jesus, "may I also remind you of the time when you were in your mother's lap fussing and crying, and your mother felt so sad for you that she started crying too. Do you remember when I told you personally to wipe your mother's tears for Me?"

The mother said, "I couldn't believe my eyes when my son did that. For Jacob wasn't capable of comprehension like that. I thought it must have been You or an angel, thank you Lord. You took time out of your busy schedule to do that for me Lord!"

"If my eyes are on the sparrow, how much more I care for you, made in our image?" Jesus told the woman. Then He looked at Jacob and said, "Moreover, I left angels on your left side and on your right side, " as He pointed at the two guardian angels who were standing close by and participating in the proceedings.

"I wasn't aware that they were there Lord; all I saw was my mother's tears. Moreover, the other evil creature showed up every time I was at a low point and said that I was worthless and I didn't deserve to live. Sometimes, I thought maybe he was right; I should die. However, my mother said that she loved me all the time and you said that you loved me. Why did you take so long to fulfill your promise, Lord? Every day I said to myself, tomorrow you would come and deliver me out of my darkness, but you never showed up. You kept silent, you left me in my darkness, tormented and hurt." Jacob became emotional and his voice started to get shaky and finally broke down in tears and continued, "Didn't you see my heartbreak? Why didn't you do something Lord? Satan said that if you loved me you would have helped me and healed me. Where were you when I called on you? How did my condition glorify your name?" His tears flowed down as he spoke.

Jesus wept.

The three humans fell on their knees at Jesus' feet. When they saw the Creator of Heaven and earth in tears, not even their glorified knees were able to handle this and their legs gave way. As they were down on their faces, they thought:

Jacob's mother; *how dare you speak to the Lord our God like that? If I weren't in a glorified body I would have disowned you.*

Mary; *adult saints usually weep at the rewards ceremony, I can't believe the Lord is weeping!*

Jacob; *forgive me Lord. When I saw Satan, even my glorified body couldn't help the residual righteous anger from the past. Lord, forgive me for my weakness. I'm sorry if I offended you.*

The Lord touched their shoulders and they rose as He lifted them up. Jesus wiped their tears and said to them, "I'm glad that you held on." Then Jesus said to the mother, "You don't have to disown Jacob."

"Oh my Lord I forgot that you could read my thoughts."

Jesus said, "We created man in the beginning in our image and gave you, your will and spirit which was gentle, calm, and without fear. The devil changed man into a vicious, scared being; I know the devil's work."

Mary peaked from behind the Lord to see if Satan was still there; and she was relieved to see that he was gone.

Then Jesus looked at Jacob and said, "I'm not offended by your emotions, son. A long time ago another Jacob wrestled with me all night and wouldn't let me go unless I blessed him. He was a man who struggled with his own cunning and tricked others to get ahead, a schemer, and swindler. Until he came to utter helplessness as his enemies surrounded him. He had a change of heart, humbled himself and prayed. That's when I came in; to answer his prayer and he wrestled with me. I touched the socket of his hip so that his hip was wrenched, so he limped the rest of his life as a reminder to depend on Me and receive his commands from Me. He changed his personality that night and was born again, and I blessed him and changed his name to Israel, contender with God; for he had contended and had power with God and with men and had prevailed."

Then he said to Jacob, "I tell you the truth, your name was written in the book of life before the foundation of the earth was created. The gates of Hell could not prevail against you. Every time the enemy knocked you down, I helped you, picked you up, stood you up, and even put you on my shoulder when you could not keep going anymore. And the times when he knocked you out really hard, I was there crying for your pain.

"I didn't design my creation to go through these harsh temptations; the original design was for you to live in the Garden of Eden. Nevertheless, I chose you as I chose Job and the apostles who all died for my sake, and many others who presented their bodies a living sacrifice. Every day that went by when you kept the faith and didn't doubt, all these angels, " pointing at the thousands and thousands of angels watching over, "marveled and glorified My name. Especially in those days that you laughed and praised Me despite your pain.

"It is easy for a Christian with their health intact to serve Me, and I have different assignments for them too. Nevertheless, you didn't have to do anything for men to glorify My name but show up son. You are one of My best soldiers and now I will give you the victor's crown. However, let Me show you children your age throughout the ages who suffered just like you and even more for My sake."

Then a screen opened up and displayed various children from all nations who lost their lives by being eaten by lions, speared, beheaded, and thrown into the fire because of their testimony to God. At that, Jacob fell on his knees and said, "Forgive me Lord for thinking that I suffered more than others and that I was the most misfortunate."

"I told you the truth," the Lord replied, "everyone who has left houses or brothers or sisters or fathers or mothers or children or fields for My sake, is receiving a hundred times as much and will inherit eternal life. I have put your enemies under your feet."

Then the open screen showed the events of the Passion, from the time He was arrested at the garden of Gethsemane. When He was whipped and spat on, Mary and Jacob's mother, wept at the gruesome events. Then, Pilate's words resonated when he said, 'I'm not guilty of, nor responsible for this righteous Man's blood. I find no guilt or crime in him.' When the moment the Lord was crucified came with his face bruised beyond recognition, the two women saints felt their hearts rip apart and had no choice but fall down on their knees again. Jacob followed. They lifted their arms to the Lord while at His feet and shouted, "We're so sorry Lord and God, Thank you for saving us."

Then came the resurrection, and the three stood up and wiped their tears again. The Lord had risen with a beautiful and glorified body.

"Amen and hallelujah," said the three as their tears turned into joy.

Then Jacob's mother said, "Lord, I realize that you knew my son was going to be born with a disability even before the foundation of the earth. Yet you gave the stamp of approval on his disability knowing that I could handle the testing. I'm honored that you have chosen me as one of your sheep in the spiritual battle of the ages. I hope I didn't disappoint you Lord, many times I was weakened and asked you, 'why did I have to suffer like this, or why did this have to happen to Jacob and not someone else?'"

"I tell you the truth; you honored Me by your faithfulness. Neither Jacob nor you have sinned for this disability to happen, " replied the Lord Jesus, "but this happened so that My works might be displayed in Jacob's life. This wasn't about you; I own you and you are all My sheep. That is why I told you to manage your lives until I showed up and got the glory. Welcome to My Father's house."

At that point Mary looked at Jacob's mother and said, "It's true. Every time I was feeling low on life or mad at my daughter and saw Jacob in church, he made all my problems seem miniscule compared to his. And when I spiritually weakened and thought of skipping church, I saw your persistence in going to church and that encouraged me. Forgive me, sister, for not doing more for you. I should have helped you more with your needs, come to your home and served you and your son. I thought I was a good Christian holding onto my marriage and family in a wicked world, making ends meet. But now I see I haven't done enough." Then she started weeping.

"That's ok, sister," said the mother, "at least you stopped by once in a while and talked to me, and that encouraged me a lot. Most of the earthly brothers and sisters avoided us and treated us like lepers. Nevertheless, we're here now and it is over. Praise the Lord."

"Amen."

As Mary was leaving the celebration, she asked her angel, "I've never seen Satan here in Heaven before, and he wasn't at my proceedings. I know that the angels need to be at the proceedings to see the Lord's loyal subject's testimonies to prove to them that the devil was wrong. But what was he doing there?"

"Today the saints have come to present themselves before the LORD, and Satan also came with them," said her angel. "Satan, the morning star, was cast out of the presence of God as a permanent occupant. But he can come here only as a visitor once in a while until he will be cast out to earth first, and then to Hell permanently, when he will have no access to Heaven whatsoever forever."

* * * * * * *

At another location and time, John was walking with his angel when he saw a man whom he recognized from earth, so he ran towards him.

"Excuse me, sir, hold on," said John. The man turned around and said, "Yes." John ran towards him, hugged him, and said, "Pastor—"

"I'm sorry, do I know you?" asked the man.

"No, sir. I watched your program on TV for years and I enjoyed your preaching. It's good to see you here."

"Thank you, brother. You know, this has been happening a lot since I got here. I'll be walking around and saints I've never known or seen my entire life, suddenly hug me."

"You know, even after you went to Heaven, they still played your tapes. People got saved listening to a dead preacher's voice," John encouraged him.

"People get saved because Jesus died on the cross; I'm just the delivery boy, delivering His message and teachings," said the preacher with modesty.

"Of course. You probably have received all the crowns."

"Almost, but do you see that brother over there?" pointing at a distance.

"Yes."

"He received all the crowns. I didn't recognize him, so I figured that he must be from the era after my death. So I asked him, 'how many members do you have in your Mega church? And how many countries did your broadcast reach?' He said, 'twenty-five people and we didn't have any TV shows.

"I said, 'twenty-five! What country did you come from?'

"He said he was a missionary in the jungles of some country whose name I can't even pronounce. He said that his ministry ended when a neighboring village savages attacked his village where his mission was, and killed all of his church members. As for himself, they ate him because he had a lighter skin color and looked good to them. He said before they ate him, and as they were preparing him for dinner, he shared the gospel with his killers. And, to his amazement he saw some of these killer savages who ate him, here in Heaven. So, he asked them how they got here. They said that only one of the gang heard the preacher's message and received it. Later on, that man stumbled on the preacher's books and Bible, which were translated into their language. So, he studied the books and later on, he evangelized and told his villagers about Jesus. Some of the villagers converted, some didn't, and there was a war and the savages killed those who converted.

"After hearing the story, I gave the preacher a Heavenly salute and said, 'sir, you deserve every one of these crowns.'"

"Praise the Lord."

Revelation and Tribulation

At a designated time, the saints were invited to a worship meeting. By now they were all dressed up in white and had various crowns of gold on their heads. At the worship dimension, before the saints, was a throne with Someone sitting on it. The One who sat on the throne had the appearance of jasper, a reddish translucent gemstone. And a rainbow, resembling an emerald, encircled the throne. The saints also sat on thrones and surrounded the throne in the center. From the throne came flashes of lightning, rumblings and peals of thunder. Before the throne, the Holy Spirit was standing. Also before the throne, there was what looked like a sea of glass, clear as crystal.

In the center, around the throne, were four Cherubs. The first Cherub was like a lion, the second was like an ox, the third had a face like a man, and the fourth was like a flying eagle. Each of the four Cherubs had six wings and was covered with eyes all around, even under his wings. They said: "Holy, holy, holy is the Lord God Almighty, who was, and is, and is to come."

When the Cherubs gave glory, honor and thanks to Him who sits on the throne and who lives forever and ever, Bill looked at John and said, "This is the moment we've been waiting for." Then he laid down his crowns before the throne and so did all the saints. Then they all fell down before Him who sits on the throne, and worshiped Him and said, "You are worthy, our Lord and God, to receive glory and honor and power, for You created all things, and by Your will they were created and have their being."

Then the saints stood up. John looked at Bill and said, "This is the best and most amazing church service I have ever seen, a church service one can brag about. We're singing with angels in the presence of God. I can't wait for the next worship service."

While he was talking, John noticed an old man standing close by. So he walked towards him, and as he got closer he thought, *this must be the oldest man in Heaven that I have seen yet, except for the two witnesses. Could this be one of them?*

Then John noticed that the old man kept looking at the center of the tabernacle. So John also looked at the tabernacle to see what the old man was marveling at. John saw a scroll sealed with seven seals in the middle of the throne of God. And as John got closer to the old man, he looked and saw a mighty angel standing next to him who said in a loud voice, "Who is worthy to break the seals and open the scroll?"

At that, the old man started weeping in convulsion. Instantly, it clicked in John's mind that this was John the revelator visiting Heaven in a vision to write the book of Revelation.

John looked back at Raphael and said, "Is this John the revelator from 95 A.D.? How could that be?"

Raphael smiled and said, "I told you that you're no longer in the three dimensional matter, space, and time of earth."

"Well, if this is his vision, then this means that I'm taking part in the vision of John the revelator, I call him JR, as one of the characters in the book of revelation?"

"This is God's plan, for the saints participate in everything in His Kingdom."

"Praise the Lord," said John, "All my life I was intrigued by the book of Revelation and what it meant. It is beyond my wildest dreams that I would actually play a part in it. I knew some people who were afraid to even read this book because it was too scary for them. But how did I get the privilege to be a character in it?"

"Not just you, every believer who was resurrected or raptured. Look around you," as he pointed at the saints.

John looked and saw all the saint relatives and friends he knew, surrounding the throne of God. He was able to recognize Mary, Gracie, Hank, Jim, and Bill and many other relatives and friends, old and new. There were also millions of angels surrounding the throne and the saints.

John thought, *the last time the Lord Jesus appeared to His disciples, He said to Peter, "Follow me." Peter pointed at JR and said, "What about this man?" The Lord Jesus replied, "If I wanted him to live until I came back, what is it to you? Follow me." JR didn't die until he saw the Lord come back, in the spirit, when he received the revelation.*

While he was thinking that, Raphael said, "That sealed scroll is the deed to earth that Adam gave up to Satan, he forfeited it when he sinned. John, or JR, is sobbing because he thinks that no one in Heaven or on earth or under the earth has the credentials to open the scroll or even look inside it. So he has this horrible realization that if no one can open the seals, then the world will continue under Satan's control and power forever. That means the whole creation will continue to moan together in the pains of labor forever, and the saints will also continue to groan inwardly as they wait for the redemption of their bodies forever. All the cruelty, injustice, hatred, pain, and death that now prevail on the earth will go on forever, too. God doesn't want that and neither does man." Raphael cheered up and continued, "But what you are about to witness next is the biggest recorded escrow closing of the world."

"Praise the Lord," John said.

"See, the kingdom of Heaven is like treasure hidden in a field. When a man found it, he hid it again, and then in his joy went and sold all he had and bought that field. You were the treasure hidden in earth. The Lord Jesus was the man who bought the field. He bought the deed for earth on the cross and He is now taking possession of what He bought when He opens the last seal of the seven seals on the scroll. The escrow closing will be consummated at the Lord's second departure to Earth."

"I can't believe I'm looking at the deed of the whole earth!"

"This is the deed which the Lord has paid for with His bloodshed, the price to redeem the world back to God. However, He hasn't claimed, yet, what He had purchased. He made a down payment by the sealing of the saints with the Holy Spirit. He was your kinsmen redeemer. You were sinners and bankrupt and the Lord Jesus was willing to buy you. He is your blood relative; the Word became flesh. He was able to purchase you with His blood. He was willing and had the power to lay down His life."

"Thank you, Lord Jesus," John responded.

"Even though the Lord Jesus is the rightful King and Satan knows that, Satan refuses to give up his kingship and continues to rule over the world. 'Thy kingdom come, Thy will be done,' you pray. His kingdom hasn't come and His will isn't being done on the earth yet! But will be soon."

Then John turned to JR and said, "Don't weep! See, the Lion of the tribe of Judah, the Root of David, has triumphed. He is able to open the scroll and its seven seals," as he pointed at the Lord Jesus Christ.

JR didn't see a lion; he saw a lamb slain, carrying the mark of crucifixion on His hands and feet to remind everyone present, what He did for them to be able to get to Heaven. The Lamb of God had seven horns signifying power and omnipotence, had seven eyes signifying omniscience, and had seven spirits signifying omnipresence.

Raphael said, "JR has already seen the Son of man earlier in the vision in a way that caused him to flash back in time sixty years back, on the Mountain of Transfiguration when Jesus' face shone like the sun and his clothes became as white as the light. That same shining light caused Saul of Tarsus to go blind a few years after that event. He had to be born again to regain his sight back and was named Paul."

When The Lord Jesus took the title deed of earth from the hands of the Father, John and all the saints and angels fell down before the Lamb. Then they stood and sang a new song while playing the harp:

"You are worthy to take the scroll and to open its seals, because You were slain, and with Your blood You purchased men for God from every tribe and language and people and nation. You have made them to be a kingdom and priests to serve our God, and they will reign on the earth."

Then the angels started singing in a loud voice:

"Worthy is the Lamb, who was slain, to receive power and wealth and wisdom and strength and honor and glory and praise!"

And to that, replied in a loud voice, the saints that were raptured and those who were resurrected from under the earth and under the sea and sang:

"To Him who sits on the throne and to the Lamb be praise and honor and glory and power, forever and ever!"

To that, the angels replied, "Amen."

And the saints fell down and worshiped.

When the saints stood up, Mary said to John, who was standing next to her, "Look at the golden bowls full of incense in the angel's hand; all our prayers are in these bowls. The smoke of the incense, together with my prayers and yours and the prayers of all the saints, is going up before God. I never thought of our prayers as a sweet smelling aroma that God enjoys in Heaven. I'm so glad we prayed when we were on earth. Now that I know this, I only wish that I prayed even more. Did you know about all this?"

"My dear sister," said John, "I read the book of revelation a few times and I was so preoccupied by the mysterious creatures that I didn't see these details. I mean, we're playing the harp. How cool is that?"

Then, the pastor whom John talked to earlier asked John, "Who is that old man?" as he pointed at JR.

"It's John the revelator!" replied John.

"My Lord, I forgot all about aging and getting old, what a horrible thing to go through. Thank God it's something of the past! I feel like thanking the Lord right now for my new body."

"Yes, me too!"

Then, the Lord Jesus started opening the seals one at a time, while the revelator watched. Every time a seal was opened, the scrolled rolled open a little further and more was revealed. The first four seals were opened, one at a time, and they sent out what's known as the four horsemen of the apocalypse.

John said to the pastor, "Here starts the drama of the end of the age."

"I'm glad that we were always on the watch," said the preacher, "and prayed that we may be able to escape all that which is about to happen, that we may be able to stand before the Son of Man."

When the Lord Jesus opened the fifth seal, it appeared under the altar the souls of the martyrs of the tribulation period who had been beheaded because they refused to take the mark of the beast. They called out in a loud voice, "How long, Sovereign Lord, holy and true, until You judge the inhabitants of the earth and avenge our blood?"

Then each of them was given a white robe and they were told to wait a little longer, until the number of their fellow brothers who were to be killed as they had been, was completed.

Then John approached one of the martyrs under the altar and said, "Hello there, I'm your brother in the faith. My name is John."

"Hello, my name is Khalid," replied the soul.

"What's going on down there?"

"We, the martyrs, are crying out to the Lord to end the misery on earth. The enemy seems to be winning down there, and this angel," pointing at an angel who stood by the altar, "is telling me to chill for now, until the Lord Jesus takes matters into His hands. Praise the Lord, I don't understand it now, but He knows best. We're not seeking personal revenge, but only the vindication of God's holiness and the establishment of God's justice."

John replied, "This has been the cry of God's suffering people throughout the ages. We cried to the Lord for two thousand years too, and waited until the fullness of the Gentiles was complete. We all wanted the Lord Jesus, in the form of the Lion of Judah, but He came to us as the Lamb of God first and offered Himself a living sacrifice; otherwise, we wouldn't be here. Even John the Baptist when he heard, in prison, what Christ was doing, sent his disciples to ask the Lord Jesus, 'Are you the one who was to come, or should we expect someone else?' The Baptist was politely saying 'let's get the show on the road and bring in your kingdom already.' This is the man whom the Lord Jesus referred to as, 'Among those born of women, there hasn't risen anyone greater than John the Baptist.'"

John continued, "When I was on earth, I asked the same question 'how long, Lord' many times. And later on, I apologized to the Lord because I admitted that I didn't know anything except the prophecies in His book. For it is said that we have also a more sure word of prophecy. We did well to pay close attention to it as to a lamp shining in a dark place, until the day broke through the gloom and the Morning Star rose in our hearts. For back then I was looking in a mirror that gave only a dim and blurred reflection of reality as in a riddle or enigma—"

"That's how I feel right now. I wish I could understand better," interjected Khalid.

"But now, when perfection came, I can see in reality and face to face! All that I knew then was partial and incomplete, but now I know everything completely, just as God now knows me completely." John continued, "When I was on earth, I wasted time and energy on things that I look back at now and wonder, 'what was I thinking?' None of that mattered except what I did for God. I wish I had more of this Heavenly view when I was living on earth. It would have made my life more meaningful and even easier. You'll understand more when you get your resurrected body and all the mysteries will be unraveled in your mind."

"I can't wait! Hallelujah."

"Anyway, our deliverance came and here we are. Praise the Lord. The saints down on earth will have to wait, too, until their number is complete. The only comfort one can give them is what the Lord Jesus said, 'If those days will not be cut short, no one would survive, but for the sake of the elect those days will be shortened.' After the Lord Jesus had given the signs of the End of the Age, He said, 'This generation would certainly not pass away until all these things have happened.' Therefore, we're only talking about a few more years. Heaven and earth will pass away, but the Lord Jesus' words will never pass away. He said it; He has done it, and continues to do it."

"Amen. However, He also said, 'For then there will be great distress, unequaled from the beginning of the world until now— and never to be equaled again.' So I don't think that you have any idea how horrible things are down there. The saints are under fire, standing on the word of God. I'm talking about suffering that defies the imagination," Khalid explained.

"You're absolutely right in that, and I respect your loyalty to the Lord Jesus. But wait until you see the rewards. They will make it all worthwhile. So, again, can you tell me what's going on down there?"

Khalid answered, "I see! You must be from the rapture crowd."

"Actually, I'm from the New Testament crowd, but died only a couple of weeks before the rapture."

"Well, you saw when the Lord Jesus opened the first seal that a white horse came out! Its rider, the Antichrist, was a counterfeit who claimed to be the Messiah, but is a dark prince. He held a bow and was given a crown, and he rode out as a conqueror bent on conquest. Within days after the rapture, the world changed dramatically. The energy depleted, hungry, tired and sick world was looking for anyone that promised a way out of their misery. Then a charismatic man, who seemed to have the answers for the world devastating problems, made a dazzling debut on the world's political stage. This guy had experience and authority that enabled him to cut through the red tape and galvanize all governments into action. The charming and unusually articulate Antichrist was someone who promised to fix things. He is the ultimate leader and the final world dictator. Shortly after the rapture, the panic-stricken, war weary, famine ravished, disease ridden, plague infested world hailed and idolized him when he came on the scene. We had to accept the world's totalitarian government or die."

John said, "Well, we Christians decided before the rapture to put our faith and hope in the Lord Jesus, our Messiah. We came to Him with all of our cancers, tumors, pain, and all of our other disabilities. We, too, were all tired and hungry. We were discouraged at the unfairness of the world, but we held on. We trusted His words and promises. But let me tell you, I sure am glad that we did because look at us now. It can't get any better than this. And I don't mean it like the man in the beer commercial with a bottle in his hand who says, 'it can't get any better than this.' No, No! This is the best ever.

"We tried to inform these people before the rapture and for many, many years, we told them the truth and the good news about the Lord Jesus, and how the Lord can save their souls. But they rejected the message, ridiculed and persecuted us. It looked as if they were having it good back then. But look at them now, going through a downward spiral heading towards Hell."

Khalid said, "Where I came from, we were taught to hate and kill Jews and Christians. In addition, we saw what the Christian countries stood for and it wasn't pretty. But only Jesus was able to take someone like me, demon-possessed, and turn me into spirit-possessed person. And the Holy Spirit transformed a stone-throwing Satan disciple into living stones in His kingdom. Children of God, once enemies of Christ and of each other are being adopted into a family of living stones, built on the strong foundation of Christ."

"Praise the Lord. What else happened after the rapture?"

"People who were left behind looted the possessions that the raptured saints left behind. Everything was up for grabs. It was prosperity time, but the second three and a half years changed all that."

"So who is this Antichrist character, and what is his background? What made him so popular?" John asked.

"Nobody is sure of his background. They say his father was from Eastern Europe and his mother may have been a middle easterner. No one dares ask. However, one thing is for sure, he was raised an atheist. But he figured out what makes religious people tick and used it to his advantage. He speaks many fluent languages, including Arabic. The Bible has already mapped out the details on this guy. Many prophets, the disciples, and even the Lord Himself talked about him. By the way, I would like to thank you, saints of the pre-rapture era, for what you have done to keep the Bible alive for us."

"What do you mean?" John asked.

Khalid answered, "I'm talking about the Bible code that your engineers encrypted and hid on the Global Super Network. The Jesus Jews gave us the software key to decrypt the code and download the Bible on any digital device. That was the only way we could get to the Bible ..."

"I forgot about that. Yes, I remember contributing to that project."

"When the Antichrist came to power, he confiscated all the storehouses and print presses of the Christian ministries and burned all the literature, books, and digital media that talked about the Christian faith. He didn't make it a public thing, but slowly and behind the scenes, he destroyed them. He wanted to make sure that true

Christianity didn't spring up again. He also destroyed all symbols of Christianity, from cross-monuments to the Ten Commandments' monuments. He changed all the names of cities and streets that began with Saint or Santa and gave them new names. Moreover, with hail and fiery storms destroying one-third the trees, the press almost came to a halt and printed materials were scarce. So, thanks again for thinking of us."

"Well, I'm glad to see our plans to save the Bible came through for you," John said.

"Yeah, unfortunately, the code was discovered after the first three and half years mark, and was destroyed by the Global Intelligence Agency, GIA. I don't know how the saints will hear the good news after that!"

"God will find a way."

"Amen. Back to the Antichrist, he is a flamboyant and shrewd politician already known in the world of politics. After the rapture, he outlined remedies to the mounting problems lying ahead. The people elected him as a leader of the world because he seemed to be the most qualified for the job and his background is filled with examples of powerful organizing. You know, when they elected the Antichrist, Joseph came to my mind. I had a chance to read the Old Testament when I was in hiding, and I loved the story of Joseph. He interpreted Pharaoh's dream about the seven lean cows eating the seven fat cows. Joseph explained that there would be famine in seven years after seven years of plenty. The Pharaoh elected him VP after Joseph outlined a plan to save Egypt. While Joseph was a man of God and was given the gift of interpreting dreams to save his people, the Antichrist is a son of the devil and he has the gift of deceiving people to their doom.

"Oh, he spoke to the needs and insecurities of people and promised to save and secure the world through peace between the nations and through technological advances to destroy the two coming asteroids. His scientist tried to control the asteroids using space vehicles that presumably, would slowly divert the asteroid enough to miss planet earth. He did bring peace the first three and a half years, and the whole world was seduced by the utopian promises he made.

"Working by his side is the false prophet, who is a religious and spiritual leader, subtle in his approach. The false prophet has two horns like a lamb but spoke like a dragon; he looked religious but acted like the devil. He deceived the world with signs and wonders. The two worked together like a dynamic duo. They worked on the political and religion fronts simultaneously."

John said, "If the Antichrist is masquerading as the messiah, then the false prophet is pretending to be the Holy Spirit. This is the makeup of an unholy trinity, with Satan being the head."

Khalid replied, "Yes, with the born-again Christians out of the way, the Antichrist reinvented a new Christian faith without the Lord Jesus as the head. He dealt passively with the remaining religions in the world which he didn't mind that much, as long as they accepted any god but Christ. The Antichrist became a unifying religious guru and received the Nobel Prize for uniting the religions of the world. There was a truth vacuum and spiritual vulnerability in the world and the devil brought in his lies. The Antichrist declared that the various religions have poisoned humankind and divided people from the beginning. And religious people of diverse religions are close-minded, prejudice and intolerant. So, his solution was to put everybody's religious differences aside and start on working under one worldwide religion. His message was for everyone to be tolerant of each other, to love each other, to not judge others, and to do what-ever you want and whatever feels right as long as your actions don't hurt others and are within the law, which kind of sounded good at first. The media, with their spin-doctors, made the nations fall in line behind his schemes and agenda. Anyone who didn't follow the majority's common religion, lost privileges, was isolated, jailed, and even executed. New Christians went underground.

"Eventually, this new world religion exalted fallen man and mini-mized holy God. He eliminated any system of absolutes, no more black and white, everything is all relative. Full-scale Humanism and New Age beliefs that resembled Christianity flourished. He created a combo of every false religion, a melting pot of all world religions. It worked well for a while, but then things started going south because there are many gray areas when there are no abso-lutes! Moreover, there were no morals or values to uphold, and man made up his own rules, which led into perversion and sensual plea-sure. Uncontrolled and unrestrained evil moved across the earth and had its way on it."

John said, "The nations got what they wanted, a world without rule, without Christians, or commandments. And when they got what they wanted, they didn't want what they got. Demons must have felt at home in the continuing saga of Babylon the Great, the home of false religion. Babylon has been Satan's headquarters from the beginning, the fountainhead of false religions."

Then John looked at JR who was watching the events on earth with amazement. The revelator was so amazed to see a formal denominational church, not a pagan nation or king, attacking small Bible study groups, the same way that the Old Testament Jews killed their prophets and stoned those who were sent to them. John was less surprised than JR because he witnessed the church trans-form to apostasy and stray away from its original foundation just before the rapture.

John remembered that JR talked about the Antichrist in his two epistles and warned against him. He said in his letters, *many deceivers have gone out into the world, those who don't acknowl-edge the Lord Jesus Christ as coming in the flesh. This is the deceiver and the Antichrist.* Also said, *Children, it is the last hour; and just as you heard that Antichrist is coming, even now many Antichrists have appeared; from this we know that it is the last hour.* John thought, *I lived in that last hour.*

JR marveled when he saw a woman riding a seven-headed beast. Then an angel told, "The seven heads of the beast are seven hills on which the woman sits. They are also seven kings. Five have fallen, one is, the other hasn't yet come; but when he does come, he must remain for a little while. The beast, that once was, and now isn't, is an eighth king. He belongs to the seven and is going to his destruction."

Khalid asked John, "What are all these symbols?"

John answered, "Seven major world kingdoms ruled the earth: The Egyptians, Assyrians, Babylonian, Persians, Greeks, and Romans—"

"I counted only six!"

"Yes, well the last and seventh kingdom is the revived Roman Empire which is called the EU, European Union."

"I thought there was a mention of an eighth king!"

"The Antichrist is the eighth and he is a citizen of this revived Roman nation and the first dictator of the world."

Khalid asked, "But why is the Judgment occurring now, on this generation?"

"Evil has been permitted to increase until the world was ripe for judgment. God had never used His absolute power to bring about an end to evil, human rebellion, and the global injustice and suffering. The previous generations sowed the evil seed and God is visiting the iniquity of the fathers upon the children and the children's children, to the third and fourth generation. It's also happening now because of the number of people living on planet earth right now is the highest ever."

Khalid continued, "In the first three and a half years, the Antichrist gave people from all religious backgrounds a global holiday for the whole month of December, a worldwide pagan holiday. They celebrated earth, Mother Nature, the trees and rivers, and Darwin's day."

John said, "The kingdom of darkness is finished and Satan, the captain, knows that he's sailing a sinking ship. The passengers don't know that it is sinking, so the captain upgrades everyone to first class and offers free drinks from the wet bar and lets them do whatever they want to do. So everyone likes him and thinks he's a great guy who allows them to play any game they want and offers an all-you-can-eat buffet and a movie free of charge. But they don't know that they'll all be dead soon."

Khalid joined in, "Speaking of movies, we were watching movies about Armageddon and didn't realize that we were living in the tribulation and heading towards the Great Tribulation. When the Great Tribulation started, the mad man used the day of December the 25th to gather the saints in the arenas, whether football fields or soccer fields and beheaded them while the crowds watched and cheered. It became known as X-the Christians day."

John looked at Khalid and said, "Excuse me, sir, Do you see that real old man there," as he turned around and pointed at JR.

"Yes, I see him. Why is he still old?"

"That's the man who wrote the book of Revelation and he's just getting the vision right now."

"That's John the revelator himself! I was amazed at the fulfillment of every prophecy in that book, in front of my eyes. Of course, I didn't know anything about it until I became a believer and learned the truth," Khalid said excitedly.

"Yes, and please, whatever you do, don't tell him that we celebrated the Lord's birthday in December. He knows that the Lord wasn't born in the month of December, and even worse he knows what pagan holiday was celebrated on the 25th. He has seen enough horrible things for one day; so let's spare him," then John asked, "Who is working on God's side? I saw the two witnesses go down there!"

The martyr smiled. "We called them the untouchables. Yes, those two are amazing. They drove the world nuts. They had incredible power, the same power they had when they lived in the Old Testament, and they prophesied for three and a half years, clothed in sackcloth. They have power to shut up the sky and it didn't rain during the time they were prophesying and they had power to turn the waters into blood and to strike the earth with every kind of plague as often as they wanted. If anyone tried to harm them, fire would come from their mouths and devour their enemies.

"The false prophet, also an Israeli Jew, tried to match their powers by bringing fire from Heaven. But he wasn't able to bring down rain, which is what the people wanted in a severe drought that lasted for years. Nevertheless, the world was still amazed at the false prophet's fireworks and worshiped the satanic triune."

As they were talking, they saw an angel coming up from the east, having the seal of the living God. He called out in a loud voice to the four angels who had been given power to harm the land and the sea, "Don't harm the land or the sea or the trees until we put a seal on the foreheads of the servants of our God."

Khalid watched the Holy Spirit-filled men, being sealed, and pointed at one of them and said, "I know that man. I'm here because of him. I was lost in a world of chaos that didn't make any sense any more. Then this man came to me and told me about the Lord Jesus and I accepted. He is one of the 144,000 End time preachers. Thank God for those Jews for the Lord Jesus. They preached the good news to all who hadn't heard the gospel before. Just like John the Baptist, their message was: repent, for the kingdom of Heaven is at hand. The greatest revival and harvest of souls the world has ever seen throughout the history of mankind is taking place right now."

John said, "The message is clearly the last call; repent or die, turn or burn. It is mankind's last chance to receive Jesus as Messiah, Lord, and true God. We thought that we had a tough time witnessing in our time, but these guys have their work cut out for them. They're going to need that seal to make it through the horrible conditions of the tribulation time down there on earth. Just like Noah was sealed to go through the flood."

"They are the untouchables and no one can harm them. They are apostle Paul-like, powerful witnesses who spread the everlasting gospel to men on earth to every nation, kindred and people."

John said, "God never leaves Himself without a witness. Satan will try to copycat and seal his followers with the mark of the beast, but that mark won't protect them from the wrath to come."

Khalid asked, "I don't understand. I was executed about three and a half years after the rapture, and they're just getting sealed now for the beginning of tribulation! How is that possible?"

John looked back at Raphael, smiled, then looked back at Khalid and said, "Time doesn't work the same way up here. You'll understand when you get your resurrected body. So what else happened?"

"The Antichrist worked simultaneously to bring peace between the Jews and Arabs. He, being an intellectual genius, and the false prophet put together a peace treaty that everyone accepted to their liking. For the peace process to work, both Jews and the Arabs had to accept the terms of the treaty. Israel was to deliver all of its nuclear weapons codes to the Antichrist giving him total control…"

"Israel would never go for that!"

"In return, he promised to protect them from all their enemies so that they could live in peace with their neighbors for seven years. As an incentive for the Jews, he offered the land they needed to build their temple before the asteroids ended the world's existence. He disguised himself as a friend of Israel, initially. Israel, standing alone with no allies, and two asteroids heading towards earth, accepted the agreement. The Arabs agreed to it, too. The Jews built the temple on the temple mount in Jerusalem. They thought that the Antichrist was the messiah they had been awaiting for thousands of years and trusted him completely. The Antichrist received Nobel Prize for Peace, for bringing peace to the Middle East for the first time since the formation of Israel in 1948."

John said, "In Moses days, the Jews were misled by their leaders in the wilderness which caused the people to wander in the desert for forty years because the twelve spies gave a bad report about how big their enemies were. When the Lord Jesus came on the scene, again the Jewish leaders at the time misled their people by rejecting Him and lost out on salvation. When the Antichrist is finally here, the Jewish leaders have again mislead their people into believing that he was the messiah, just as the Lord Jesus had said. This fulfills another one of the Lord Jesus' prophecies when He said, 'I came in my Father's name and you rejected Me, but another one comes in his name and you'll accept him.'"

"Amen. After the success of the peace treaty, there was a new worldwide dominance and order. The nations became world citizens with the EU and its ten Prime Ministers leading. The world leader convinced the world to unite their efforts and strategize against the two asteroids heading towards earth. Technology advanced exponentially the first couple of years. There was also a flourishing global economic system, built on capitalism, commercialism, and indulgence. The Antichrist is a financial genius who controls the economy. He built this system even though the earth was coming apart with all kinds of calamities. Trade is still going on. There were a high-class people, who got richer and there was the very poor, which only got poorer. It wasn't just famine; there was rationing, too, and the world dictator decided who got what. Food is power, and the world tyrant used food to control behavior, the rich starved the poor. Luxury, lust, greed, and materialism are reserved for those loyal to the Antichrist. This gave an incentive for people to take the mark of the beasts to enjoy these luxuries. The world became prosperous and there was a sense of peace, initially.

"The city of Sodom was also prosperous and had a sense of peace, but wickedness continued in a downward spiral until the day it was destroyed by God. And so will Babylon the Great. That's when he broke the covenant with Jerusalem. And that's where my shift ended; I was beheaded a few minutes ago."

"Thank you, brother, for the update. Hang in there and wait for the resurrection of your body. We'll have supper together soon. Ok."

"Amen!"

Cosmic Battle

On another side of Heaven, Jim was walking with his guardian angel, Celestiel.

Jim asked, "Were you responsible for the strange events in my last days on earth?"

Celestiel answered, "When someone has his name written in the book of life, and the rapture gets so close while the person hasn't accepted Jesus, what are we to do? While Jesus doesn't push Himself on anyone, that doesn't mean we can't arrange the circumstances to hasten the decision; otherwise, a soul is at stake."

While they were talking, Jim suddenly heard fluttering of wings behind him and got an eerie feeling. So he looked behind him and saw a new kind of angel with pale colored wings. He looked at him and felt as if he knew this creature from somewhere, but couldn't quite put his finger on it. It felt like a Déjà vu. However, that wasn't possible because he had never seen a creature like this before.

"Hi, Jim, how are you, my boy?" said the demon.

Jim thought, *the voice of this strange angel sounded familiar and he said, 'my boy' which sounded very familiar.*

Jim wasn't too excited to be known by this creature, for he seemed like something coming out of the kingdom of darkness. Nevertheless, he's sure now that he knows this character from somewhere, but where?

Daemon replied to Jim's thoughts and said, "I have been with you since the time you rejected God. Remember when you got mad at God and didn't want anything to do with Him anymore?

That was my cue to come in. And ever since then, I have taught you how to get ahead in life, certain things to help you succeed and climb the corporate ladder by climbing on people, stepping on their hands, using them selfishly, scheming against them, betraying them, cheating, and whatever it takes to attain success and wealth. I taught you the different kinds of lies: white lies, black lies, fibs, half-truths and exaggerations. I taught you how to cheat on your tests in college and taught you all about lust and fornication. I arranged for you to have girlfriends and showed you how to cheat on them. I taught you how to steal—"

"I never stole," replied Jim, "Oh, wait yes, I did steal and I was forgiven."

"You stole time on your breaks," said Daemon, "on your lunches, leaving early from work. I was there with you the whole time giving you best ideas. You think this guy is your friend," pointing at Celestiel, "where was he when you needed to cheat on your exams? Or lie on your resume to get ahead at work and to prosper? Or lie to your girlfriends and have a good time? Or cheat on your taxes? I showed you all the short cuts. However, you betrayed me in the end by siding with my enemies."

"He could have also accomplished all that by being honest," said Celestiel. "And instead of every man for himself, one should show first regard to others; instead of getting, one should give; instead of grabbing, give up; instead of hating, love. If he would have taken the honest route, there wouldn't have been any guilt and horrible consequences."

"That would have taken forever," said Daemon, "and your methods caused him to blow his last job interview. All the interviewer asked him to do was to fudge a little on the numbers."

"He was raptured before the interview was over. He didn't lose anything."

Jim thought, *oh yeah, I wish I could have seen the look on the interviewer's face when my chair got empty all of a sudden.*

Celestiel continued, "You almost had him commit suicide and lose his soul," then he looked at Jim and said, "He used to come up here and accuse you to the Lord, after you became one of the believers."

Daemon said to Jim, "Remember when you started having thoughts of lust after your girlfriends broke up with you? I told on you because you became one of them."

"So what are you doing here?" asked Jim.

"After you decided to become one of them, I aligned myself with your mother's demon and I came up here to accuse your mother to God, so I can send her to Hell."

"Demon, you are a liar and your master is the father of lies," said Jim.

"If you had kept my teachings, I would have lost my teeth by now. They have brainwashed you well!"

"Vengeance is mine, says the Lord," replied Jim.

"So, you're starting to look, talk, and act just like your master, the holy one."

Jim said, "The Lord and I are one."

"Be gone, demon," said Celestiel with a commanding voice.

Daemon replied, "What a shame. We used to be best friends at the time of creation. Why can't we all get along?"

"You're either with the Lord or against Him, nothing in between. This is my best friend right now," pointing at Jim, "and that's a good trade off for me."

"Blah,... blah,... blah,... blah. You're so boring."

"You're spending eternity in Hell."

Daemon became furious and said to Jim, "Listen to me, son of Adam, don't get too comfortable here. Because my boss says that today he's taking over this place and it will be under new management, and you'll end up with me again. As for your mother, her soul is mine."

"What are you talking about?" asked Celestiel.

"What, you didn't get your angel-gram about the war in Heaven?" said Daemon as he started to take off, "I'll see you out there." And the demon vanished.

Jim looked at Celestiel who seemed preoccupied as if he were receiving a message, and said, "Why does he bother accusing the brothers?"

"He tells God that His people only love Him when He blesses them financially or gives them good health. He wants to prove God is wrong altogether, when He thinks that the saints love Him purely. And he thinks that the saints are fools if they are loyal to God without any ulterior motives. He was wrong so many times. That's why we, angels, rejoice every time someone makes the decision for the Lord Jesus because it proves to us that the devil was wrong and still is wrong."

"What about this business of war and Satan taking over Heaven?" Jim asked.

"Oh, I wouldn't worry about that. There are twice as many of us as there are of them. Actually, I do have to leave you for a short while to help my brother angels in this battle. I just received a message from the Archangel Michael. I'll be right back," said Celestiel as he disappeared, too.

Jim looked for John and found him walking with Raphael, so he went to join them. The minute he got there, Raphael excused himself and vanished, too. Gracie found John, too and joined the two saints.

"Where are our angels going?" asked Gracie.

"Look over there, sister," said John pointing at a new dimension," Do you see that commotion over there?"

Gracie looked and was amazed at what she saw.

"There is war in Heaven," said John, "It is the greatest cosmic battle ever fought. Michael and his angels are fighting against Satan, and Satan and his angels are fighting back. It has been exactly three and a half years to the day since the signing of the peace treaty."

"I can't believe we're witnessing angels fight," said Jim.

"I'm glad we have done our spiritual battle on earth and don't have to do anything here and now," said John.

"What's happening now?" asked Gracie.

"Satan, the serpent, wasn't strong enough, and they lost their place in Heaven. The great dragon Satan is being hurled down— that ancient serpent called the devil, or Satan, who leads the whole world astray. He is hurled to the earth, and his angels with him, on a one-way ticket, never to return here. God evicted Lucifer and his followers to ensure peace in Heaven."

"The war didn't last long!" said Gracie.

"Well, that's because they, the devil and his angels, were fighting a losing war," said John as they watched Satan and his demons fall down from Heaven to Earth.

Then John said, "There goes Satan. He said, 'I will ascend to Heaven; I will raise my throne above the stars of God; I will sit enthroned on the mount of assembly, on the utmost heights of the sacred mountain. I will ascend above the tops of the clouds; I will make myself like the Most High.' Look at him now!"

"Those demons are looking at us, and they look angry; they are scaring me," said Gracie, "Why are they so angry?"

"Because they just lost their home and natural habitat," answered John, "they were created to live here, and now they just realized that they can't anymore. It's like a navy jet fighter pilot flying over the ocean realizing that his mother battle ship was just sunk. So now, he knows that he can only stay in the air for as long as there is fuel in his tank. After that, he crashes into the sea because there's nowhere to land and so his final mission becomes suicidal. He will take out as many enemy planes and ships as he can before he runs out of gas. These guys also know that their time is limited so they will take as many souls as they can with them to Hell before their time is up. Satan is mad and we're glad. There goes the dragon disguised as the angel of lights. Don't be afraid of him, Gracie, he can't hurt us here in the third Heaven. However, people down there on earth should start to worry. Those who thought that the devil doesn't exist will surely have a rude awakening. The earth, sea, the first and second Heavens, and humanity are going to go through the greatest tribulation ever seen."

"What's the third Heaven?" asked Jim.

"The first Heaven is the atmosphere surrounding the earth; the second Heaven is where the stars are. The third Heaven is where the Lord and His angels dwell and now it's our temporary home and refuge for the seven years period of tribulation." Then John saw something that caught his attention and said, "Wait, Satan has a key in his hand; I think he stole some kind of a key from Heaven. Where is Raphael?"

Raphael had just returned from battle and didn't seem surprised at their victory.

"Raphael, look at Satan falling down; he has a key in his hand and I think he stole it."

"That's ok, John, it was given to him. It's part of God's plan," replied Raphael.

"Oh, ok, well that's different. What key is that?"

"It's the key to the bottomless pit."

"Oh, no. There is going to be real trouble down on earth," said John.

When the last demon had left Heaven, there was a real rejoicing in Heaven, and all Heaven's citizens were happy and sang with a loud voice: "Now have come the salvation and the power and the kingdom of our God, and the authority of His Christ. For the accuser of our brothers, who accuses them before our God day and night, has been hurled down. They overcame him by the blood of the Lamb and by the word of their testimony; they didn't love their lives so much as to shrink from death. Therefore, rejoice you Heavens and you who dwell in them! But woe to the earth and the sea because the devil has gone down to you! He is filled with fury because he knows that his time is short."

"Do you believe it; the devil was defeated by the blood of the Lamb and by our public profession and declaration of our Christian faith?" continued John, "Inhabitants of earth, here comes the devil, your way, that you don't believe exists."

It was another busy day for the Heavenly highway, for as Satan and his demons were going down, the two witnesses' souls were coming up.

"Welcome back, brothers," said John, "The Lord is with us."

"Amen," replied the two witnesses.

"What happened down there, brothers?" John asked them.

"Well, as soon as we got there in the holy land," said Elijah, "we started preaching the good news about the Lord Jesus. And within hours, we saw fifty men with the strange dress code coming at us with sticks that looked like made of metal; they didn't need any bows to shoot. The sticks started shooting small brimstones mixed with fire from its mouth and made a very loud noise; the small brimstones were able to pierce the wall! So we realized this wasn't a friendly act. They kept shooting and some of these small brimstones ricocheted off us and some missed us. We sent back to these men, fireballs of our own and they dropped dead, charbroiled style.

"When I lived on earth the first time, I usually asked God for fire to come down from Heaven and consume my enemies, and it did. This time, the fire came out of our mouths and devoured our enemies when anyone tried to harm us."

John said, "Those are guns; they come in different shapes and sophistication. They shoot faster and further than arrows."

"After that, we were in the narrow streets of the city Jerusalem prophesying," continued Elijah, "when we saw another group of fifty men riding strange metal horses that had two round black wheels rotating, and moving the men at a fast speed. They were making very loud noises we've never heard before and foul smell came out of the back."

"Those are called motorcycles," John informed them.

"They tried to do the same thing that the previous men did with their sticks or... guns, whatever you call them, " said Moses, "but they tried to outrun our fire. They were on to us and realized that we weren't helpless. Their speed didn't help them and they were charbroiled, too. They tried doing the shooting from the sky with what looked like a locust and had a tail as a scorpion, which was also made out of metal with sounded like thunder. It was able to fly around and stop in mid air just like a dragonfly. We thought it was a demon at first, but then we saw the face of a man inside it."

"We call it a helicopter," John explained.

"We sent them a fire ball and they exploded in the sky shortly after. Next, they sent fiery dragons when we were outside the city. Its breastplate was fiery red and yellow as sulfur. The head of the dragon resembled the head of a lion, and out of its mouth came fire and brimstone, smoke and sulfur. It crawled and moved forward and backward on its belly that slithered like a snake. Now I've seen dragons the first time around I lived on earth, but never seen anything like this. When we fellowshipped with our brother John the revelator in Heaven, he tried to describe to us the things he saw in his vision, but I had no idea how bizarre these things looked until I saw them with my own eyes. I wouldn't know how to describe these... these things, either. Bless his heart; it's not his fault. When we went to earth the second time, we tried to describe to men down there the colors we saw and the utterances we heard here in Heaven, but they were beyond the power of man to put into words, and a man isn't permitted to utter."

"John the revelator did try to describe the angels for us through his vision," said John, "and again, God bless his heart, he called them beasts. When I look at them now, they are awesome looking; they don't resemble beasts at all. Maybe it's because I have a resurrected body and I see them differently. I also think that the old English translation of some of the scriptures doesn't give the exact meaning of the original text.

"But I think what you're describing is an armored tank, a weapon used in warfare. See, science advanced exponentially in the last hundred years before the rapture. Some of the new technology was good for humanity in the beginning, but later the majority of it was used for evil purposes. So what happened next?"

"Well, this one was the easiest. I guess they were trying to match our firepower by bringing fire from the mouth of the tank; but our flames overcame their flames and devoured them. Just like my snakes devoured Pharaoh's magician's snakes," said Moses.

"They sent another fifty men in strange dress code that came at us with caution this time," said Elijah, "and this time the leader was wise and asked if we could please go with him peaceably to meet the king. So we did and we rode the horses they provided us. We didn't know whether they were lying to us or not, but we went with them anyway. They ended up putting us in jail and we shared the Lord with the people inside, but after a while, we got out of jail by opening the doors ourselves because that wasn't the place we needed to be. We wanted to spread the word to every man and woman we could get to.

"They didn't like the fact that we left the prison. So, when we were next to the sea talking to people about the kingdom of God, one of their chariots came out from beneath the water to shore and started walking on land, fired at us and went back under the water to avoid getting devoured by our fire. Just when we started getting used to chariots that moved on land without horses, they sent out something like this."

"Did you say it came from under the sea, walked on land and then went back under the water?" asked John.

"Yes," replied Elijah.

"At first I thought you were talking about what we call a submarine but you said it walked on land, too. I've been out of that world for just a couple of years and already they've come up with newer technology that I haven't seen."

"We turned the sea into blood and they had to come out because they couldn't see anymore and then we got them with our fire when they surfaced, " continued Elijah, "Since the blood thirsty people have shed the blood of the saints and prophets, we let the sea stay bloody for a while. And we gave them blood to drink, as they deserve. God is just in these judgments, He who is and who was, the Holy One."

"Blood was a symbol of salvation, but now became a symbol of condemnation. They will drink blood to satisfy their insatiable desire for blood," said John.

"Afterwards, we shut the sky so it wouldn't rain for a couple of years; there was a long and severe global drought."

"That is one bad weather report for the world."

"Yeah, I was known as the Rain man in a previous lifetime, but not for this period of time and these people. So, because of the drought, one summer a man who was girded with a strange belt around his body swollen with metallic ornaments wanted to kill us, the 'doom and gloom' preachers. So, he started running towards us, and the crowds scurried away, so we knew that wasn't a good sign. So we sent him a little fire wave and he exploded like a volcano and the fire that came out of him destroyed many surrounding buildings. That was unusual; he wasn't supposed to explode like that," Moses said.

"That sounds like a suicide bomber and those ornaments on his belt are called grenades."

"A short while later, again a flying iron bird flew over us. It had a flame coming out of its rear end and made what looked like a cloud in a straight line," said Moses, "We didn't see a man's face on this one; it flew by so fast and high in the sky. It made sounds like many thunders that hurt the ears and the glass of a nearby building shook. We wondered if that was a demon."

"No, these are airplanes. Towards the end of the age, people were traveling back and forth, not only on ground but they invented machines that fly in the air and transport people at a fast speed. And that's what you saw. And some of them do carry big brimstones," John explained.

"It dropped what looked like a star with flame coming out of its rear end. That thing was headed towards us, and fast, while it made a rumbling noise with a whistle," continued Moses. "When the star started falling down, the people that we were witnessing to, started running for shelter. So, we just sent it fire and it exploded and the iron bird blew up with it as well, and the sky was lit like the afternoon sun. After that, they left us alone for a while. We told everyone who listened, the meaning of the events that were going on, and what to expect in the next few years."

At this same time, a great angel flew by heading towards earth.

"My Lord, what a magnificent angel. Who is he?" asked Jim.

John replied, "That's the Archangel Michael."

"How do you know that?"

John replied, "I saw him before and the angel Raphael told me who he was. He must be heading towards Israel. Either the country or the Jews are threatened; there will be major bloodshed for the attackers. One almost feels sorry for the enemies of Israel."

Jim said, "I don't know; you'd think that they'd get it after a while. How many times have they tried to attack the Jews and have failed?"

John said, "When God puts a hook in their jaws, there is no escaping it. It's another busy day on the Heavenly highway. You know, this is just a happening place and I like it, never a dull moment. Not one long endless church service as some thought." Then he asked the two witnesses, "What else happened? We saw the four horsemen of the apocalypse and heard the first three trumpets up here."

Elijah answered, "Because we shut the Heaven so that it wouldn't rain the first three years, there was a drought and every plant on earth dried up. Then, there was hail and fire mixed with blood, which was hurled down upon the earth like fireballs from Heaven. And the fireballs caused a third of the earth to burn up, a third of the trees were burned up, and all the green grass was burned up, a Sodom and Gomorrah type of judgments. It rained a very heavy and dreadful fall of hail, the worst hailstorm. Everyone, who was in the open, was killed. However, the Antichrist told the nations that Mother Nature was renewing herself and everything was going to grow back. That wasn't true."

John said, "This sounds worse than the hail the Egyptians had to face. It must have created big holes in the ozone layer."

"Yes, but this was only a preview for things to come in the Great Tribulation. Also, because of the lack of rain and water, fires were erupting all over the world consuming vegetation and polluting the skies. The effects of the drought, and the trees and grass burning up were: locust and insect infestation followed by famine and incredible dust storms that blackened the sun. The dust storms were so devastating that people would wake up in the morning covered with dust as if they were buried alive. Later on, many people died of lung disease and smoke and dirt inhalation."

Jim said, "Severe drought and increased earth temperature isn't a good combination. One martyr told me that they tried to give nature a helping hand by blasting chemicals into the atmosphere to create precipitation. The clouds they were able to seed with chemicals produced hail to fall down that you two mixed with blood and fire. Then he said that the burning trees and grass caused the amount of carbon dioxide to skyrocket in the atmosphere. Talk about global warming on a scale never seen before, the kind that creates floods that put the world coastal cities under water. The skies must have seemed to be on fire as the ozone layer slowly got depleted."

Elijah continued, "Later on, something like a huge mountain, all ablaze, was thrown into the sea, a third of the sea turned into blood, a third of the living creatures in the sea died, and a third of the ships were destroyed. There was famine and disease because of the lack of fresh drinking water and adequate hygiene. People had to work all day to get a loaf of bread; the Antichrist had control of the world's wealth and there was no fairness in his leadership."

John said, "It sounds like the asteroid ignited as it slammed into the atmosphere. When it hit the sea, the heat wave from the explosion and the tsunamis destroyed the ships and sea life and turned the sea red."

Jim said, "I guess seafood supplies dwindled after that, and travel by sea became a scary thing to do."

John replied, "That's the least of their worries. This asteroid would cause the coastal cities to be obliterated and forest fires to erupt in the inland cities. A huge cloud of sulfur combined with the smoke of fires would darken the sky. This would alter the agriculture dramatically and civilization would start to break down."

"And all that was the beginning of sorrows; it was just getting earth dwellers used to the sight of blood. They could have avoided this entire gory scene by believing in the blood of the Lamb," continued Elijah. "Again, the Antichrist claimed that his scientists could purify any liquid and make it into water and that the nations shouldn't worry about this.

"Then another great star blazing like a torch fell from the sky on a third of the rivers and on the springs of water— they named the star, Wormwood. A third of the waters turned bitter, and many people died from the waters that had become bitter, bitter water for bitter people. That was another preview of things to come."

"The man of sin thinks that with technology he can control the weather, subdue earth and vegetation, and extend man's life. However, God will show him who has the ultimate control. In the Great Tribulation, God will trash the ecology; it's His creation, after all. As for the falling star, that must have been the second asteroid, which probably exploded into many pieces in the outer atmosphere before it reached earth. They have been known to contain cyanide, a poison, in their structure. With the drought already going on for a couple of years and now the water sources are contaminated, people are going to be thirsty. I bet the price of water skyrocketed. Hygiene practices will suffer, which usually is followed by disease, not to mention an ongoing drought; these things promote war. The combination of the three and half years of famine and plague, and the wild beasts of the earth; AIDS (monkey), Bird Flu, Mad Cow disease, SARS, Foot-and-mouth disease (domestic animals), West Nile virus (mosquitoes), rats, bacteria, and viruses must have been devastating.

The human condition seems to be deteriorating after all these disasters. What else happened?" John looked to Moses.

Moses said, "Finally, there were wars breaking out, for the Antichrist couldn't keep the peace too long. Moral values were low and greed was high, so nations fought against each other over water, food, and oil. The sweet-talking world leader had gathered governments and economies under his command to further his own evil agenda. He had control of the world's most powerful weapons, so he crushed those who opposed him. Men were killing each other based on whether they were with the Antichrist or against him.

"When sin abounds, people don't respect authority either. There was corruption, deceit, the buying and selling of justice, the adoration of money, the exaltation of lust, and the exploitation of the masses. A fourth of the earth's population was killed by the end of the first three and a half years. Even then, the Antichrist told the nations that it was good that the population was being reduced to lessen the demand on mother earth. He was reducing the population of earth and increasing the population of Hell. And the remaining blinded dwellers of earth bought every lie he dished out."

Elijah said, "After the Antichrist unfairly stripped the Jews of their Nukes and signed the peace agreement, which he never intended to keep, the enemies of Israel couldn't use conventional weapons against them. So they found a new way to squeeze the life out of Israel by boycotting the country out of oil supply. They also boycotted any other country that supplied Israel with oil, and nobody dared to come against the oil rich countries. The Antichrist agreement was to protect them from military aggression only so he stood by and did nothing about the boycott.

"So, we just moved the underground oil supply around from the neighboring countries to the Israeli side. The enemies were disappointed when oil was discovered in Israel and their oil supplies started dwindling in their lands. But they dared not carry a military offensive because of our presence in the land, which guarantees their failure in any attempt.

"The Jews burnt the oil as fuel for the next seven years; they didn't need to take any firewood out of the field or cut down any from the forests, for they made their fire of the oil weapon used against them."

John and Jim said, "Praise God," as they were fascinated by the unfolding events.

"Amen, now when we had finished our testimony, God allowed the Antichrist to attack us, overpower, and kill us. Our bodies are lying in the street of Jerusalem. For three and a half days men from every people, tribe, language, and nation had gazed on our bodies and refused us burial," continued Moses. "Did you know that they have this magic square box in every house where people sit and look at all day? I call it a magic box because it displays wonders and all kinds of things from animals and birds in the air, to all things on land and under the sea. What in the world is this thing? JR tried to tell us about this box and how it made images that get the breath of life into them and speak."

John answered, "That's called television and it's only been around for less than a hundred years."

Moses asked, "Well, how can all nations around the globe see our dead bodies at the same time on this box? Does the box have some sort of magic?"

"No, it's called satellite communications, also a fairly new invention, but the prophecy about this invention and this particular event of your death was recorded two thousand years ago in the book of Revelation."

Moses continued, "The inhabitants of the earth are gloating over our death and celebrating by sending each other gifts and sweets because we had tormented them. They are calling it the two dead witnesses' Day, and saying 'happy two dead witnesses day' to each other—"

Then the two witnesses heard a loud voice from Heaven saying to them, "Come up here."

Elijah said, "Now brothers, you have to excuse us, but we have to go get our bodies from down there; it's time."

As Moses and Elijah went back down to earth, John and Jim watched a breath of life from God entering their bodies. They stood on their feet and terror struck those who saw them on the earth.

When they got back to Heaven, they looked much younger as they came up with newly resurrected bodies.

"Welcome back, brothers," said John.

* * * * * *

Meanwhile, on earth, the devil called for an emergency meeting with his lieutenants. Once they gathered together, they started to go up to Heaven to have the meeting, but they couldn't do it as their wings were clipped to prevent them from going back up there. So Satan looked at Heaven and cursed God and cursed God's name.

"Let's meet in a desert then," said Satan.

They assemble in the desert and the devil, who seemed anxious, started speaking, "Remember plan B that we talked about before; we ask the Jews to worship me through the Antichrist. If they do worship me, then they won't call on the Son of God to come back, and we win. If the Jews don't worship the Antichrist, we go down and kill them all. We have to finish them before they say 'blessed is He that comes in the name of the Lord.' The Jews have to say that for the Christ to come down."

Then the Antichrist and the false prophet were summoned into the meeting. The unholy trinity was together in one place and Satan asked, "What in the Hell happened down there? What have you done? And who are all these dead people on the ground, all around the Holy Land?"

The Antichrist answered with shame, "Well sir, there was those two troublemakers in the Holy Land who worked against us by prophesying and spreading the message of God. We couldn't defeat them for they were protected supernaturally."

Satan said, "The two witnesses, Moses and Elijah, hah, they're back to their old tricks again!"

"The good news is that I was able to kill them just a couple of days ago. It was a great victory for your kingdom. We had people all over the world overjoyed to get rid of the two troublemakers." Then the Antichrist smiled with excitement and continued, "And I thought, what could be a greater gift to you than to annihilate the Jews once and for all, since you hate them so much. With the Israeli nukes out of the Israeli hands, and the two witnesses dead and out of the way, I thought it would be a perfect time to take over the land, rich with oil reserves.

"We were very confident in a victorious invasion and a total annihilation of the Jews. So I gave instructions to Israel's enemies led by the king of the North to launch a sneak attack on the holy land. I devised and conspired with them in secrecy, and I gave the green light for the attack. You should have seen it; they were flying like angry hornets, filled up the skies with the most sophisticated weaponry that the Air Force could come up with. They filled up their tanks with their last drops of oil. They were angry because their oil supplies were dwindling while Israel was enjoying an abundant supply of it. So they approached the land while the Jews were sleeping with their peace treaty under their pillows. I ended the peace that I started three and a half years earlier with them. It was a surprise attack. The enemies from the north with their allies gathered their forces and attacked Israel."

The Antichrist's voice changed and with disappointment said, "The forces of the attacking enemy were surprisingly decimated by the biggest case of friendly fire in history. The fools, our forces, ended up using the weapons against each other."

Satan was showing signs of irritation, as this defeat reminded him of the disappointing defeat in Heaven where he just came from.

The Antichrist continued sadly, "Our fighter jets fought each other and dropped their bombs on their ground troops, annihilating them. Their artillery weapons just came apart in the middle of the battle, and their tanks had their chains come apart. Violent rain, great hailstones, fire and brimstone came down on them from Heaven and killed them. The Jews were sitting ducks and had no way to defend themselves, yet they were miraculously delivered. There are many dead bodies around Israel from the war, and the Jews would probably have to pick up their bodies for the next seven months to clean the land. The vultures and prey birds are already helping them clean up by eating the flesh of the dead. There are so many dead that the travel routes between the east and west outside Israel are blocked. They called the place where they buried the dead the Valley of Hamon-gog. Not only five out of six of the invading forces were annihilated, but we heard that fire came down from the sky on the cities of Gog also."

Then Satan said, "There is one thing I should have asked you to do earlier, and that is to read the Bible. If you had read the Old Testament you would have known that the Jews used the bones of the dead prophet Elisha to win a war against their enemies. You jumped the gun, son. You started a war when the two witnesses' bodies were still on the ground!"

"You know, I did this for you and you weren't around to consult with—"

"I was only gone for a minute," Satan replied.

"Well, maybe it was a minute for you, but I couldn't get in touch with you for days. So anyway, you saw the outcome of the attack."

"Where are the two witnesses now?"

"Well, there is more bad news," said the Antichrist while rubbing his forehead to cover his eyes. "See, a couple of hours ago I had a victory celebration in Jerusalem over the death of the two witnesses. This party was planned before the decimation of the invading armies and a no-fly zone protected the party area during the attack. I had seven thousand dignitaries invited and gathered around and close to the dead witnesses. The event was broadcasted all over the world as part of the celebration. Another miracle happened today, these two dead witnesses rose up and they went up to Heaven in a cloud, while everyone looked on. At that very hour, there was a severe earthquake and a tenth of the city of Jerusalem collapsed. Seven thousand of my people were killed in the earthquake. I thank the stars that I wasn't present yet in the festivities. Now, how would I know that these two would be resurrected? I've never seen a resurrection before."

"You'll be soon, son, you'll be soon."

"I hope you're not leaving for an extended period again."

"No, son, I'll be so close to you that..." Satan didn't finish the sentence but said, "Never mind, give me a status on earth events and conditions."

The Antichrist spoke, "We had peace the first couple of years except for some unusual number of natural disasters like fires, bloody rivers and water, drought, mass starvation, and objects falling from the sky. We blamed it all on God and His two witnesses."

"I don't care about that. May all mortals die and go to Hell. The last three and a half years have been only a preview of coming attractions; next is a preview of Hell. By the time I'm done terrorizing this world, they will all be looking for the exit sign. What I really need to know is who or what the nations are worshiping right now."

"We made sure that true Christianity is discouraged and all other false religions are flourishing. We allowed the Jews their temple worship. We did have some obstacles, though. There is a multitude of preachers running around all over the world and preaching the gospel of the other God. They are also protected supernaturally and we haven't been able to destroy them yet."

"What did you do with the powers I had given you?" asked Satan, looking at the false prophet.

"My Lord, I brought fire from Heaven and performed many wonders which magnified the Antichrist. I became the head of the world church and introduced a self-indoctrinated religion."

"Is that it? What about the Jews?"

"Some of them still worship Jehovah their God, but the majority considers the Antichrist the messiah they've been waiting for."

"I want to up the ante now." Satan directed his speech towards the Antichrist, "You're going to go into the temple in Jerusalem, in the middle of the holy place, stop the daily sacrifice, and declare yourself as God and require that everyone worships you. I'm giving you an opportunity that many great leaders like Hitler, Alexander the Great, and others dreamed of and died trying to attain, and that's to be worshiped by the whole world. If the Jews don't worship you, then we'll annihilate them. Let's pick up where Hitler left off."

"Yes sir," said the Antichrist with excitement, "But—"

"There are no buts; this is my world and this is my next move. And as for you," looking at the false prophet, "I want you to construct an idol, a statue for everyone to worship just like Nebuchadnezzar, king of Babylon, did for us in his time. Only this time be creative and make it able to speak so that every human will worship it in awe and amazement. Also, I want you to come up with a mark and put it on the right hand of the forehead of every human and without it no one should be able to sell or buy. I want you to make worldwide broadcasts every day on TV in honor of the Antichrist. And I want you to implement the plan I gave to you before, regarding TV so that all who refuse to worship at the time of the broadcast will be killed."

"Yes sir," said the two hooligans with excitement.

"Ok, you two can leave now and do what I told you," continued Satan. "Oh, by the way, the world is going to see some really horrific things in the next few years. We'll blame it all on the Jews and Christians as a convenient scapegoat and rally the world against them. Annihilate them."

Satan waited for the Antichrist and false prophet to leave, then he looked back at his lieutenants and said," I'll possess the Antichrist's body, just like I did with Judas. When the Antichrist gets in the temple, I'll be declaring myself as God. If you want anything done right, you have to do it yourself. Inform all your subordinates and be ready. So, after that point you know where to find me. I'll be confined inside the Antichrist body so I need you to report to me there.

"As for now, I'm taking this key and heading down to the bottomless pit to release our imprisoned brothers there. Also, the river Euphrates will release its demons. I'm going to mobilize the forces of Hell and get some extra forces to help us down here." Then Satan proudly said, "Brothers, we're going to have the biggest world-wide invasion of body snatchers ever. Let's take Halloween to a new dimension; there will be tricks but no treats." Then Satan looked down to the center of earth and said with a loud voice, "Gates of Hell, open wide and receive my new harvest of souls." Then he went down the shaft leading to the center of the earth.

The Underworld

Meanwhile, down at the center of the earth and in a very dark place, in the land of gloom and deep shadows, another group of people, who had a terrible fellowship, existed in the underworld. These are the wicked, the disobedient who lived without God. They were like the chaff - worthless, dead, and without substance, which the wind blew this way to this place of shame and eternal contempt.

Tom, the electrician who died earlier from a heart attack before the rapture took place, was a member of this group and was having this kind of encounter with his soul. He came to conscience in this place of the regions of the dead, and found himself in complete darkness. His soul was fully aware of everything that was around him and he had all his senses and feelings intact. He walked around to explore his new environment and found many souls like him in the same situation.

Tom ran into another soul who was weeping loudly. So he asked someone who was standing close by, "Why is this man sobbing like that?"

The man answered, "I just asked him the same question. It turns out that he's worried about what will happen to him in Hell when he encounters those demons he cast out of men and women when he lived on earth."

Tom asked the man again, "Oh good, so we're not in Hell then. But if this isn't Hell, where are we?"

"We're in Hades, in the bowels of the earth, waiting for judgment day."

"What is Hades, and why are we in it, man?" Tom inquired.

"You and I are part of a group of people who throughout history chose not to believe in God and His Son. After we died, our souls departed from our bodies and our names were erased from the Book of Life. Our spirits are in layover in Hades, in an isolation place waiting God's judgment. Later on, our spirits will re-unite with our bodies for Judgment."

"Well, that's not too bad, man. So what if my name isn't in the Book of Life, as long as I do all right here."

"You don't know what you're talking about," said the man arrogantly and thought, *this is an ignorant man,* and walked away from him.

Tom followed him and said, "Look, I just want to know if I'm going to do all right here. And why is it so hot in here, man?"

"Because our names are not found in the Book of Life, we'll have some trouble with the judge, and eventually we'll be charged to the Lake of Fire. At least that's what the Bible says, if you want to believe that."

"This God doesn't sound like a good sport, man. Why can't we be judged right after we died and get it over with?"

"Because the results of our actions continue to affect those people who came in contact with us even after our death. The people who we affected, they in turn will affect other people as a result of our influence on them. Sometimes these effects continue for many generations. So the books continue to record all the events until it's all said and done. And when all things have come to an end, then the book of life and the book of works will be opened and judgment begins," the man, who seemed familiar with the facts of death, explained.

"Are you trying to pull my chain here, man? You could be making all this up for all I know. I've been to church and I haven't heard any of this mumbo jumbo. Who are you anyway?"

"I told you; this is all in the Bible. And, yes, you're right, I could be lying. Who can verify what I'm saying up here. However, the books will be opened soon and all will be revealed, even the hidden thoughts of man. And I'm sorry, I should have introduced myself, but I don't remember what my name was. Do you know what your name is?"

"Ah, ah…You know I don't remember either. But I was an electrician on earth."

While they were walking and talking, they passed by a man who was weeping nonstop in a bitter way. The two looked at each other, "It's your turn to ask," said the man to Tom.

Tom asked the weeping man, "What's your story, man?"

"I was the one who betrayed the innocent blood of the Master and delivered Him to the enemy, " said the weeping man, taking a little break from his sobbing, "and I have been in this awful place, Sheol, since then, instead of being with the Master."

Tom looked at his new intelligent companion and said, "I thought you said we're in Hades."

"Hades and Sheol are one and the same. This man is Jewish, so he calls it Sheol in Hebrew. It's also called Hades in Greek. I know this character from the Bible, but I don't remember his name. I know that he was referred to as the son of perdition by His master."

"A very short while after I got here, I saw the Lord go to that Paradise over there," continued the son of perdition pointing at a place across a huge gap, "where He took all the good saints and prophets of ancient time like Noah, Moses, and David, up with Him to heaven."

The two looked at the place where he pointed. "I always wondered what that empty place across the big gulf was," said the educated man, "so what was the point of bringing these people to Paradise first and then taking them up to Heaven later on?"

"The good Old Testament people died believing in God and trusting Him," said the wailer, "but their sins were only covered by the blood of animals, which wasn't adequate to cover their sins permanently. So, while these saints were obedient in sacrificing animals to God, they trusted by faith that one day God would provide a permanent cleansing through the sacrifice of His Son. I even saw a thief, a sinner who repented at the last minute, being carried by angels to that place of comfort, right in the bosom of Abraham." The man continued as he gasped, "Shortly after, the Lord took them all with Him that day; and I tell you, it was so awkward to see the Lord from back here, a place of eternal misery."

"You think that was weird; wait until you see Him on judgment day," said the intellectual.

"It would've been better if you were never born, man," said Tom, mocking him.

"Excuse me, sir," said another man to the wailer, "I couldn't help overhear what you were saying. I'm one of the men of Nineveh and I repented, for a short time, at the preaching of Jonah. And look, someone more and greater than Jonah, the Son of God Himself, was with you and you still ended up here. I must condemn you, then."

Then, Judas Iscariot started weeping again and the two men continued walking leaving him behind.

"So really, what is this guy saying?" asked Tom.

"Very simple," said the informed person, "the people God loved, He sent to Paradise before Jesus was crucified. After the crucifixion, Jesus emptied paradise and took those people to Heaven with Him. After that point, the people God loves went directly to Heaven. That's why we see Paradise continually empty."

"What about this place here, man?"

"This is the temporary place that God sent the people he didn't like and continues to do so until judgment day. And here is the kicker, He put a great gap between the two realms so that the miserable people here can see the comforted people there and talk to them, but can't cross over, a humorous design by the Creator."

"Well that's just great, man. He has a great sense of humor, a God of love, my—"

Suddenly, they ran into a conversation between two other men. They stopped because they recognized one of the men.

"Hey, I know this guy. He was on TV all the time making news. What was his name?" asked Tom.

"I don't remember his name either; let's see who he's talking to. I don't know who the other guy is. Let's listen in and maybe we'll figure him out."

"My Lord, king of the Babylonians, I'm your grand, grand, grandson," said the famous man, "I tried to build Babylon the way your father did. I even put my name on the bricks of the walls of the city."

"Did you build the hanging gardens like my father, what's his name, did?" asked the king.

"No, sir. I couldn't finish the project because it required a lot of resources and I was stopped by the enemies."

"Whatever happened to my empire after I died? Daniel, the Jew prophet told my grandfather that other empires would conquer and defeat Babylon. Did his prophecy come true?"

"Well, sir, remember when you gave that great banquet for your nobles and drank wine with them? While you were drinking your wine, you gave orders to bring in the gold and silver goblets that your father had taken from the Jewish temple of God in Jerusalem, so that you and your nobles, wives and concubines might drink from them. You all drank from the gold goblets and praised the gods of gold and silver, of bronze, iron, wood, and stone, which cannot see, hear, or understand.

"Suddenly the fingers of a human hand appeared and wrote on the plaster of the wall of the royal palace. You watched the hand as it wrote. Your face turned pale and you were so frightened that your knees knocked together and your legs gave way ..."

"You fool, I know all this, I was there. What happened after that?" said the frustrated king.

Tom quickly asked, "Is this where we got the saying 'read the writing on the wall'?"

"Yes, yes, now be quiet and let me hear what they're saying," said the companion.

"God gave your grandfather sovereignty, greatness, glory, and splendor. Because of the high position He gave him, all the peoples and nations and men of every language dreaded and feared him. So, when his heart became arrogant and hardened with pride, he was deposed from his royal throne and stripped of his glory. He was driven away from people and given the mind of an animal; he lived with the wild donkeys and ate grass like cattle, until he acknowledged that the Most High God is sovereign over the kingdoms of men and set over them anyone He wishes. However, you didn't honor the God who holds in His hand your life and all your ways. Therefore, He sent the hand that wrote the inscription, which basically said that your number was up. Your kingdom was divided and given to the Medes and Persians. That very night, you were slain, and Darius the Mede took over the kingdom."

"The Persians! I knew it, Damn you, Cyrus. I hate them Persians. Did the Greeks conquer the Persians afterwards?"

"Yes, that's right. By Alexander the Great; how did you know?"

"Yeah," said the king happily, "my grandfather had a dream and the prophet Daniel told him that according to the dream, these kingdoms would come one after the other. Did the Romans conquer the Greeks afterward?"

"Yes again. And after Alexander the Great, the Romans took over. And when I died, the Americans were controlling what used to be the city of Babylon, now is called Iraq."

"Who are the Americans?"

"They are Christians; their prophet descended from the line of Abraham, Isaac, and Jacob."

"Well, these three are the ancestors of the prophet Daniel, and they serve the same God. As long as it isn't the Jews that have possession of the city my grandfather built, it's ok," the king said.

"I wouldn't allow that on my watch. Unfortunately, I have no control over that anymore, when I'm in here," said the famous man.

"Why did you rebuild Babylon?"

"It was written in the Hebrew books that Babylon was destroyed and was never to be rebuilt again. So, I wanted to prove that the Jews were wrong."

"You fool; you don't come against and defy the God of the Jews. My grandfather did, and you know what happened to him; he turned into an animal for seven years."

The famous man thought, *then, why did you use goblets from the Jewish temple to drink, you drunken fool.* Then he said, "Well, I didn't believe their writings. Therefore, I started to rebuild it to prove to them that their Torah and Bible were incorrect. However, that got me overthrown from my presidency, and I turned into an animal myself for about seven months, hiding in caves and holes beneath the earth, just as your grandfather did. After they found me, they killed me."

The ancient king asked, "The man of God, Daniel, was very knowledgeable in astronomy. He was preparing and grooming some of the magi, to anticipate in the coming of the Son of man who would have a special star appear at His birth. He gave those magi his wealth of gold to give to that child when he was born. Did that happen?"

"Well, according to the Christian book, when the prophet named Jesus was born, a star did appear, and Kings and magi did bring him gold!"

"Who or what do you worship?"

"I had people worship me. However, in public, I pretended to worship the one greater God, Allah. Our prophet came from the line of Abraham through Ishmael."

The king Belshazzar, grandson of Nebuchadnezzar said, "My grandfather had respect for the God of the Jews because he saw His power. However, I was the king of the greatest nation on earth and the center of the universe, and I wasn't going to worship the God of my slaves. We had our own gods that we could see and touch. We had power and we had wealth, but the people became evil and sinful; there were no wrongs or rights. What happens to Babylon now, do you know?"

Saddam Hussein shrugged his shoulder and said, "I don't know, my Lord."

"Do you know, man?" Tom asked his companion.

"What happened in Babylon didn't stay in Babylon; it spread all over the world. Babylon the Great in the book of Revelation becomes symbolic of a state of false religion, which started in the first physical Babylon that this king's grandfather built and it is going to be destroyed forever, " said the well-informed man. "I think that there will also be a great city, Mystery Babylon, in the end times that will resemble Babylon, in idolatry, moral decay, and corruption and that city will be destroyed forever, too. I have my bets on the cities of New York, Los Angeles, San Francisco, or even maybe London or Paris, or ironically enough could be the same capital of old Babylon itself, which is current day Baghdad. Let's go ask one of the tribulation victims—, hey, duck…get down!"

They both ducked, as a mysterious object flew over them with a rushing noise.

Tom asked with shock, "What in the Hell is that? Is it a UFO?"

"No, it looks like an angel of some sort."

"Wow, man, I like that thing. It's so cool."

"Yeah, I like him, too. Magnificent," said the companion.

"Hey, what's that in his hand?"

"That looks like a key. Oh, no!"

"What? What is he doing? It looks like he's unlocking a door of some compartment."

The man said, "If I'm not mistaken, that angel there is Satan himself!"

"Righteous, dude. He's awesome. Is this where he lives?"

"No, actually this is his first visit here."

"Why do Christians give him such a bad rap? He doesn't seem so bad."

"I don't know, he is brilliant, though. He seems indestructible. But, let's wait and see what happens when he opens the door of that compartment."

Then when Satan opened the door of the bottomless pit, locusts came out of it. They looked like horses prepared for battle. On their heads, they wore something like crowns of gold, and their faces resembled human faces. Their hair was like women's hair, and their teeth were like lions' teeth. They had breastplates like breastplates of iron, and the sound of their wings was like the thundering of many horses and chariots rushing into battle. They had tails and stings like scorpions.

Tom said, "Splendid, man. This place isn't so bad after all."

Then the creatures followed their leader, Satan, out of the shaft that leads to the bottomless pit on their way to the surface of the earth. When the creatures got closer to the two men and hovered over their heads, the creatures' horrific inside character was revealed to the two men.

"Fudge, man; get these freaky vampire things away from me. God help me...," said Tom as he scrunched down and tried to cover his head with his hands.

The other man froze out of fear, closed his eyes, and couldn't say a word. When the demons and their king the angel of the Abyss, the destroyer, had completely disappeared, the two men took a very deep sigh of relief.

"If I had a body, I would have had an accident in my pants," said the man. "Did you see how fast they went out? They can't wait to begin their acts of evil."

"It's like letting every inmate out of every penitentiary prison to go out into the world to do their evil works. Satan was the fastest getting out; I would too, if I could, man."

"This is the last place he wants to be in; he'd rather be up there doing what he does best. Plus, he's their king so he has to lead them out."

"That's just great, man. He is the reason we're here, but he himself doesn't want to be here. Hey, by the way, was it just me or did Satan look like he was worried or nervous?" asked Tom.

The man said, "You're right, I noticed that too; he is on the defensive. He's been trying to hold on to the gates of this infernal region of the world, Hades, for two thousand years and it's finally crumbling down."

Tom asked, "Whom has he been holding out against?"

"The Church of Jesus Christ has been on the offensive, standing firm like a rock in his face and has been very detrimental to his powers and I can see that they've got him on the run."

"I don't like this existence, and I don't like this place, man. We're doomed to destruction. I want to get the Hell out of here."

"I don't know. As bad as it feels to be here, I'm not sure if I want to go up there and discover what these creatures would do to me if I had a physical body."

"This must be a nightmare, man. I know I'll wake up any minute now, any minute now, this is too much torment, man. And I'd sell my soul to the devil if I could have a fix."

"A fix?" asked the man.

"You know, drugs. Where have you been, man?"

"You already sold your soul to the devil and will end up in the smoking section anyway," mumbled the man under his breath.

"What was that?" Tom was bothered by the comment he heard.

"Oh, nothing. I'm actually very hot and thirsty and would like to get some water, but none is available."

"You think that you're better than me, Mr. 'knows it all'. Who the Hell are you, and how come you know a lot about the Bible and you're here?"

That's a very good question. See, I was a professor in a very prominent university and my expertise was in world religions. Someone gave me a grant, pretty much a blank check, to study the Bible and conduct research to try to find contradictions or inconsistencies in it. I did that for a number of years and made a career of it."

"And what did you come up with?"

"I found a few conflicting contradictions, but these Christians always come up with a logical explanation. Like for an example somewhere in the Bible there was a mention of angels at the four corners of the world, which indicated that maybe God didn't know that the world He created was round."

"And?"

"Well, the Christian community said that it was a figure of speech and the verse actually meant north, south, east, and west."

"Well, that makes sense. What else?"

"I found a discrepancy between two books that gave different numbers of soldiers for the same battle. And again, the Christians gave a logical explanation. I found another discrepancy where a king was mentioned in the Bible at an era where his father was supposed to be ruling according to the history books. This king was actually the one we were listening to earlier."

"How did that one go?"

"It turns out that both the father and son were ruling at the same time, in different cities. I have dozens of these. Noah used pitch to cover his Ark, even before pitch developed in the earth according to the Christians' theory. They say the flood caused the dead animals to fossilize and over time, the fossils turned into oil. So where did Noah get his pitch from, which is a byproduct of oil? Again, the Christians explained that the word 'tree-sap' in the original Hebrew book was translated to pitch. Tree sap produces the same effects as pitch, on building structures. So, it was a translation issue."

"Have you ever considered the fact that the Bible may have been inspired by God and not men? And is it possible that if you read the

Bible intellectually to find errors and faults in it, then God would close the eyes of your mind to understanding the spiritual things?"

"I don't believe that, electrician, man!"

Tom replied, "No wonder you're here, like that old saying goes; it's not what you know, it's who you know. Well, are there any more surprises and compartments in this God-forsaken place?"

"Actually, there is one more part called Tartarus. It has the fallen angels locked up there. They didn't keep and hold to their own first place of power, but abandoned their proper dwelling place in Heaven. These, God has reserved in custody in eternal chains under the thick gloom of utter darkness until the judgment and doom of the great day. We probably won't be able to see it, since it is supposed to be the deepest abyss in here."

"OK, just don't tell me anymore, man. This is like watching a horror fiction movie. I'm hot and thirsty. Just let me sit here in this gloomy dungeon to wallow in my sorrows."

"I sure wish I could take a look and see what's happening up there on the surface of earth, just a little peak."

Tom thought, *the dead are streaming here by the millions, nonstop, and he wants to go up there to see the bloodbath - idiot!*

Tougher Times

B ack in Heaven, a new wave of martyrs arrived at the altar and joined their brothers and sisters under the altar. John approached one of the new martyrs and said, "Welcome to Heaven, brother, my name is John."

"Hello brother, my name is Juan."

"What's going on down there? I saw the Lord Jesus open the second seal and another horse came out, a fiery red one. This time, its rider, the Antichrist was given power to take peace from the earth and to make men slay each other. To him was given a large sword. And the black horse is to come next with famine. What happened next?"

"Yes sir. Shortly after that, and right in the middle of the seven-year tribulation period, the Antichrist designated a day as a global holiday for everyone. That day marked the three and a half years since the signing of the peace treaty. He asked that everyone stay home and tune in to their TV sets at a designated hour of that day for an important global broadcast. Those who weren't able to be at home were to make every effort to get to a TV set at that hour because he was going to make a major announcement that would affect every man and woman on planet earth. He designated an hour when most people around the globe would be awake to be able to see the broadcast.

"When that day came, which happened to be on a Thursday, everyone on the planet was talking about the night before. The moon had a lunar eclipse and it, with all the stars, disappeared from the skies all over the world. And the third of the night was pitch black and all the earth dwellers marveled at the sign in the skies.

"When the appointed hour came that day, there was a live broadcast of the Antichrist entering the newly built temple of the Jews. He then stopped the daily sacrifice, and walked into the Holy of Holies where cameras were set up and a statue of him was already erected in the background. He said, 'Greetings, men and women of my world. Today I declare to you that I'm the king of the earth and God. And all those who dwell on the earth shall worship me.'

"There was a pause.

"The Antichrist continued by giving a list of his accomplishments to save humanity from the brink of disaster and save the world from total destruction. He said that the world religion, that has been running the last three and a half years, has been unsuccessful in uniting the nations, that it was the reason for all the natural disasters, wars, famine, and disease. So, he ordered that all religious activities halt and abolished all forms of worship, except for his worship. And from that point on he was the only one to be worshiped."

"He was trying to persuade mankind not to attribute their happiness to God, but to think that his own superiority and brilliance were the source of it," said John. "This was his way to wean men from the fear of God, by making them rely upon his own power. However, later on, he will change things into a dictatorship. The Son of Perdition fulfilled the prophecy of the abomination desolate in the temple that the Lord Jesus and the prophet Daniel talked about in the scriptures, this day."

"As he was speaking, a thick darkness took over the whole world for a third of the day," continued Juan, "even artificial light didn't work. It was as if the world blew a fuse. People could not see one another nor did anyone rise from his place for a third of the day."

While Juan was talking, the temple in Heaven, that is, the tabernacle of the Testimony was opened. Out of the temple came the seven angels with the seven plagues. The angels were dressed in clean, shining linen and wore golden sashes around their chests. Then one of the four breathtaking Cherubs who were in front of the throne, gave to the seven angels seven golden bowls filled with the wrath of God. And the temple was filled with smoke from the glory of God and from His power, and no one could enter the temple until the seven plagues of the seven angels were completed.

John looked at the altar in amazement at the anger of God and thought; *this is the ultimate blasphemy, the last straw of rebellion against God. God's throne is shut to the public and no one can approach the mercy seat in the Great Tribulation. It started and God will move now. Only forty-two months left before the Lord Jesus goes back to earth. Hang in there, saints.*

Bill came over and said, "You know God's anger isn't dispassionate; He is neither temperamental nor unpredictable. However, God definitely hates sin and loves righteousness and justice. The only time I know of, that the Lord got angry when He was on earth, was when Jesus went into the temple and having made a whip of cords, drove out all who bought and sold in the sacred place, spilling and scattering the brokers' money and tossing around their tables. He said, 'take these things out of here! Make not My Father's house a house of merchandise!' It is written in the Holy Scriptures, 'Zeal for Your house will eat Me up. I'll be consumed with jealousy for the honor of Your house.' Now this idiot declares himself to be God inside the temple of Jerusalem. If the Lord was angered for the house of the Father, how much more, when His Father is challenged?"

John replied, "If you ask me, I think God is weeping inside His sanctuary for what is about to happen on planet earth. He never wanted His children to go through a tribulation like this. The battle for the souls of men continues. These people down there are God's children whom He loves so much that He sent His only begotten Son to show them the way out, yet they choose the mess they're in. What a heavy sorrow on the heart of God. The devil is a liar. You know, I just don't get it; the devil just lost a revolt up here, now he's trying to make trouble down there. What is he thinking? He must be grasping his last straw," then he turned and asked Juan, "Then what happened?"

"Things didn't add up that day with the resurrection of the two witnesses, just days before, then the signs in the sky, and then the shocking darkness that fell upon the whole earth when the Gentile Antichrist defiled their temple by declaring himself god. And while the whole world couldn't see in the darkness, one third of the world

Jews thought this over, connected the dots between these events, and their eyes were opened. They realized that they didn't survive the massive attack they encountered a few days ago because the Antichrist protected them, but because Jehovah God intervened. And they started doubting that this Antichrist was the long awaited messiah they had hoped for, let alone was God. So they decided to refuse to worship the Antichrist.

"When the darkness lifted, the humiliated Antichrist sensed the rejection of the world to the idea of his deity. So he appeared again in public and in front of cameras outside the temple and he opened his mouth to blaspheme God and slander His name and His dwelling place and those who live in Heaven for ruining his moment of glory. And at that same hour, the Antichrist was shot in the head and fell dead on the ground. The whole world watched this unfold in front of their eyes via a live broadcast."

"This just wasn't his day, was it?" said Bill. "His parade got rained on. He was god for just a few minutes and didn't get to enjoy it."

"No, sir, there was a great commotion and confusion as everyone was shocked that the messiah had been shot. An ambulance was rushed to the scene and picked up the Antichrist and took him to a local hospital. The Antichrist's secret police, which didn't do a good job protecting their leader, captured the hit man, who turned out to be a zealous Jew. The press questioned the Jew as the police were taking him away.

"They asked him, 'Why did you shoot God?' and he said, 'When I heard this uncircumcised pig blaspheme the real God of Heaven, Jehovah, I felt that I was the man who should kill him and remove this disgrace from Israel. Who is this man, that he should defy the living God? He is no God. Did you see him bleed as he dropped dead? I felt upon myself the same duty that the boy shepherd David felt when he slew Goliath the giant. I aimed my sniper gun at the same spot right between the eyes.'

"Later on, the reporters claimed that the Jew was an insane man, a fanatic and mentally disturbed. While the police were taking the man away, their car got into an accident and the Jew fled the scene, blended into the crowd, and disappeared.

"Now the remnant one-third of the Jews looked into the Bible and heeded the warning of Jesus, now their Lord, to flee into the mountains. They also heeded the Lord's warning not to spend any time packing up their stuff or take their clothes, for the time must be short; otherwise, Jesus wouldn't have said so. Some of the Jews didn't understand why the rush, since the Antichrist had just been assassinated. However, those who read the book of Revelation knew that this wasn't the end of the Antichrist, and that somehow he was coming back."

Bill said," Good, the Jews remembered what happened to Jerusalem in 70 A.D. and didn't want to repeat the same mistake twice. For in 70 A.D., the Roman armies circled Jerusalem and besieged it. The Christians living inside the city took heed of Jesus' words for that specific time, recorded in the gospels. They fled the city and were spared. Their escape was possible because, for a short time, the Roman armies miraculously loosened the siege on the city, as there was political trouble in the capital of Rome. The Jews, however, stayed in the city and were slaughtered, over a million of them, and the rest were taken as slaves to the Roman cities and scattered throughout the world."

"Praise the Lord," said John, "The Lord Jesus told us about the events of the future; he didn't leave us in the dark."

"Thank you Lord," continued Juan. "It must have been very difficult to leave everything behind all of a sudden and go into some wilderness they've never seen before. But just like God took care of the Jews in the wilderness for forty years after they left Egypt, these Jews trusted Him to take care of them the next three and half years in the desert. I actually had a chance to talk to one of the fleeing Jews before I knew the truth. I asked him where he was taking his family in such a rush. And he said, 'to the rocky city of Petra, Jordan in the middle of nowhere'. I said, 'I don't think they have pizza delivery down there,' and he said that he was expecting food delivery from Heaven. Hot biscuits, I think he said. I didn't understand what he was talking about then, but I do now."

"Praise the Lord, only our God can rain manna from Heaven," said Bill," and now we feed on Him, our bread, and will live forever because of Him."

"So they started the largest and fastest air lift in history," continued Juan. "They wanted to expedite the process for whatever time was left of that Friday, before the Sabbath starts when everything is shut down and no one works. Commercial and other military aircraft were lifting the Jews to Petra and were parachuting them into the area. Helicopters were also used to transport people to Petra and to bring back the parachutes for more people to use. Buses were also used for those who couldn't be airlifted and this group of people drove all night."

Bill, intrigued by these events, asked, "How did the world take the news of the Antichrist's death?"

"While that was going on, the news of the Antichrist's death traveled around the world. Chaos started to form in different parts of the world within hours, for he was the glue that held the world together. People wondered who was going to take care of them now, for they put all their faith in him. However, the false prophet appeared Saturday and made a TV announcement.

"He told the world that the Antichrist wasn't dead and that he was recovering. This was shocking news and even though everyone saw the Antichrist on TV getting shot with a bullet in his head, the world gave the false prophet a chance to prove it, on an account that he had performed amazing miracles before, but never a resurrection."

"Only God can perform a resurrection," said John.

"Amen. On Sunday, the Antichrist came out on TV to show the whole world that he had recovered from the deadly blow. And all they that dwell on the earth, whose names were not written in the book of life from the foundation of the world, wondered when they beheld the Antichrist who was dead, but now was alive. The whole world marveled and worshiped him. He became the Mahdi for the Muslims, the Krishna for Hindus, the Idealist for the humanist, the Mantra for the eastern mystics, and the Messiah for the apostate Christendom and Jews. But only two-thirds of the Jews, left behind, believed in him. The Antichrist received a new category of a Nobel Prize first of its kind, the Life Nobel prize, for resurrecting himself and finding a way to extend life."

Bill said, "What a fake! This comeback is going to have a bad ending."

"He was a very persuasive orator. That day, he gave his infamous and most impressive speech. It went something like this, 'my children of the world, greetings to you in the name of my father the god of this world and prince of the air.' Then he continued, 'Blessed are those who have my spirit, for theirs is the kingdom of earth. Blessed are they that are loyal to me, for they shall be comforted. Blessed are they that obey me, for they shall inherit the earth forever. Blessed are they that take my mark, for they shall be filled. Blessed are the repenting enemies of the state, for they shall obtain mercy. Blessed are they that are after my heart, for they shall see my father.'"

John said, "In Hell, that is."

"Yes," said Juan, "then he continued to say, 'Blessed are the GIA, for they shall be called the children of my father. Blessed are they that persecute my enemies, for theirs is the kingdom of earth. Blessed are ye when you revile and persecute those who shall say all manner of evil against me falsely. Rejoice, and be exceeding glad, for great is your reward in my kingdom.' He continued by saying, 'Ask not, what your old God didn't do for you; ask what your new god can do for you. I have found the tree of life with its golden apples and the lost Holy Grail. I'm god and I shall live forever. I have the power to give all who follow me eternal life. My children, I'll give you the secret to the tree of life and the Holy Grail. I promise you, all those who believe in me shall not perish, but have eternal life. I'm here to make that dream a reality.'"

"What a bunch of bologna," said John.

Juan replied, "No, really. Those who did take the mark of the beast didn't die. It was hard for us saints to grasp why the heathens didn't die even if they wanted to, while we saints were being killed at their hands. We were discouraged."

Bill said, "This is why the Lord said that 'This calls for patience and endurance on the part of the tribulation saints who obey God's commandments and remain faithful to the Lord Jesus.' He told us to carry our cross and follow Him; in this world, we'll have tribulation, he who kills by the sword, dies by the sword. God always has a witness."

Juan continued, "But later on we found out that death took a holiday for only five months. And what the Antichrist didn't tell his followers was, even though they didn't die, during these five months they lived in pain and torment.

"After the speech, he brought a person out who at first bowed down and worshiped the Antichrist. Then to prove that the man would live forever, they hung him from the gallows that was already prepared. The man was hanging and his eyes were still open and blinking. When they took him off the noose, he got up and walked around. The Antichrist said, 'I'm the tree of life; worship me and live forever. And now the false prophet will tell you what you need to do to live forever.'

"Next, the false prophet took the stand and said, 'To worship the new god, you would have to go to the registration centers in the next following weeks, and the secret of life eternal would be revealed to you. Registration centers will open throughout the world very shortly.' While the Antichrist posed as god, the false prophet promoted him. Now, don't ask me how these demonized people were able to keep that man alive, but I saw it on TV with my own eyes. And this did stumble some of the saints."

John looked back at Raphael and asked, "How could they have done that?"

"Remember the time Satan had a key in his hand when he was kicked out from Heaven after his defeat?"

"Yes, the key to the bottomless pit!"

"Satan unlocked it and smoke like the smoke of a huge furnace puffed out of the long shaft, so that the sun and the atmosphere were darkened by the smoke from the long shaft. Then out of the smoke, demons came forth on the earth. They were incarcerated there for a long time, they're vicious, most diabolic, and the worst of their kind, and such power was granted them as the power the earth's scorpions have. They were told not to injure the herbage of the earth nor any green thing nor any tree, but only to attack such human beings that don't have the seal of God on their foreheads. Only the 144,000 Jews had that seal. These demons are evil spirits; they always seek embodiment and they will possess men that allow them to do that. They were not permitted to kill the people they possessed, but to torment and distress them for five months. The pain they inflicted on humans was like the torture of a scorpion when it stings a person."

"Satan was releasing more demons, like there aren't enough of them down there already," said Juan.

Raphael continued, "Both the Antichrist and the false prophet worshiped the devil. The false prophet was the first fruit of this plague of released demons, the first one to be possessed by one of these demons. The Antichrist, however, was possessed by Satan himself, thus it was said about him, he once was, now isn't, when he got shot in the head, and will come up out of the Abyss. Satan, that possessed him, came out of the abyss after releasing the demons there, and will eventually take the Antichrist to his destruction in Hell.

"Therefore, anyone who worships the Antichrist and takes his mark will be destroyed. After they took the Antichrist to the hospital with a hole in his head, they didn't know why he was still alive. He should have died, but the satanic spirit wouldn't depart from his body. So they spent three days patching up his head with plastic surgery to make him presentable."

John said, "The Lord Jesus was slain and resurrected to save the world. The Antichrist was slain and recovered to deceive the world. So you're saying that men couldn't die, once they were possessed; sounds like a horror movie where a person is shot several times and keeps going as if nothing happened."

Raphael answered, "Yes, in those days people will seek death and will not find it; and they will yearn to die, but death evades and flees from them. Satan is at large."

"Death is a blessing to the saint. I'm glad I'm out of there," said Juan.

John replied, "I'm glad that you're here too, brother. What else happened that day?"

"That same day, after the infamous speech, the Satan-possessed Antichrist heard that some Jews had fled to Petra. He was furious. And being the forceful military leader that he is, with unlimited weapons at his command, he ordered his forces to go to Petra and annihilate the place, so much for peace! He broke the seven-year covenant with the Jews by allowing their enemies to attack them first and this day he himself attacked them. His motto was, 'Worship me as your new god or die.' The Antichrist forces captured some of the Jews who lingered in their escape, those with children and babies, who didn't make it to Petra in time.

"He sat at the command and control center and observed ten fighter jets approach Petra. When they arrived there and Petra was within sight, he ordered them to commence operation Jewish extermination. That was the last communication he had with them as they mysteriously disappeared and were never heard from again. So he sent another ten fighter planes and the same thing happened to them. Then he ordered the army to move in. He sent 30 tanks and 30,000 soldiers to the area. They arrived to the area and within five miles from Petra, waited for a signal to attack. The Antichrist ordered the attack to commence. The forces moved in but they lost communications with them, too. So he ordered more troops to go in, and that's when the commanders of his army begged him not to do that. 'It's hopeless,' they said."

John said, "The Egyptian army was swallowed by the Red Sea. These people are being swallowed by earth itself."

"Then, outraged, he sent out nuclear missiles to the area and again they disappeared inside that area. They called that area 'the Petra triangle' because it was comparable to the Bermuda triangle in its mysteriously making anything that goes into it disappear. And from that day on, the Antichrist had been sending out a nuclear missile every month to test the area and see if God's protection had been removed."

"Not this time. The Jews in Petra will reign and rule with us in the Millennium," said John.

"So now, the Antichrist began a war against the remaining Jews and saints around the world and killed them wherever he could find them. That was another holocaust; the biggest Anti-Semitism ever and anyone who helped or harbored these Jews was to be killed. While the Christians and Jews were declared outlaws and ran to the countryside and lived off the land, the heathens traveled from the countryside to the nearest registration centers in town like a magnet. A few days after that speech, registration centers opened throughout the world and people flocked to them to receive their mark. When the word got around that the Antichrist had the secret to immortality, everyone wanted a piece of the action. Everyone who wanted to live forever was to be tagged and marked.

"The false prophet instituted a new religion where the Antichrist was to be worshiped as god and ultimately his father, the devil. The false prophet was also the one who promoted the means of worship, and planned all the preparations and regulations for the implementation of the mark of the beast. To worship the new god, a person would have to go to the registration centers and follow three steps to become immortal."

"What three steps?" asked John.

"The first step was to have a chip implanted under the skin on the back of the right hand or on the forehead. This was necessary to do any electronic transactions whether buying or selling. They said that the intention of the chip was to be used to pinpoint where missing people were, by the GIA. But it was actually designed to starve those who didn't take the mark and force them to take it. Most people got the implant on the back of their hand, but some paralyzed and maimed people got them on their forehead. The implants communicated with most other electronic devices and especially the newly modified TV sets."

"It's a scary thing when one person has total control of global economy and power, but that's what the world was craving before the rapture. What was step two?" asked John.

"Step two was a tattoo of what looked like the pharmacy emblem, Caduceus, which has a snake wrapped around a cup. Again, it was tattooed on the back of the right hand or on the forehead to identify a person from a distance and to spot unmarked people who automatically would be assumed to not have the chip inserted in the body. The chip and the mark went together. These people were considered enemies of the state and were executed if they were captured."

Bill said, "The snake was the tool used in the first deception and now it has become the emblem of the last deception. Satan deceived Eve when he tricked her into eating the forbidden fruit; now the forbidden fruit has taken a different shape. The Christians identified themselves with a sign of the fish and the heathens identified themselves with the sign of the snake. While most of the people who dwell on the earth would receive the mark of the beast, the 144,000

Jews received the mark of the Father in Heaven. What's the third part of the ritual?"

"I should mention that the Antichrist has been pushing recreational drugs in the streets and legalized their use for the last few years. So people were going around like zombies anyway. After being tagged and marked, the person had to make the pledge of allegiance to the new god, the Antichrist and his father the devil. They had a new salute where the new zombie would bend the right arm and make a fist with the hand and position it over the hearts, displaying the emblem of the snake. Then, they pledged allegiance to Satan and their new god, the Antichrist, and then bowed down."

John said, "There was a demonic dictator called Hitler, who lived in the last century; he had a special salute where his followers raised their arms and said 'Hail Hitler'. But what you're describing definitely resembles what the Roman soldiers did when they saluted their commanders, by folding the arm and making a fist that they then put on the heart."

"Once a person had gone through the three steps of taking the implant, the mark, and pledging of allegiance to the Antichrist, the person became a portal for demon spirits to enter and salvation was no longer an option. Salvation became impossible since the person's body and temple became occupied and possessed by demon(s). The entire world worshiped Satan, which gave power unto the Antichrist: and they worshiped the Antichrist, saying, 'Who is like unto the Antichrist? Who is able to make war with him?'"

John said, "God could and He will. Only God can destroy the destroyer."

"Anyone who doesn't worship the new God was to be killed. Once a day, the Antichrist came out on TV and everyone stopped whatever they were doing and worshiped his image that talked. The Antichrist would fold his arm showing his mark and everyone watching would also fold their arms, if they're able, and salute him that way and then say, 'Hail Satan'.

"This salute helped the implanted chip to communicate with the 3X6 chip inside the newly modified TV sets or other electronic devices. If a person wasn't in front of a TV, then any hand held device did the same thing. For those who were in the open, at that same designated moment when the Antichrist appeared on TV, people saluted and satellites scanned them to register their worship. This procedure posed a threat to the saints, as they had to take cover that moment so that they wouldn't register with the satellites as non-marked persons. If they missed the opportunity to hide and got scanned as non-marked persons, they had to start running because the satellite would then inform the GIA of their location.

"One time, I saw a strange and fading image of the Antichrist that got out of the TV set like a spirit or ghost; he walked around and talked to the people in the room. I have no idea what he said to these people or what the purpose of his coming out of the TV set was. Those who didn't have the mark, the authorities broke the door of their homes and arrested them."

"Again, it's only been a couple of years since I've been away from that world, and already what you're describing amazes me. I knew that they were working on a technology called Tele-presence, where a three dimensional image of a person could be brought to any place at any time. But they were years away from doing it, a distant future dream. I guess knowledge increased exponentially these last couple of years since I've been gone. You mentioned a TV new chip, what's that all about?" asked John.

The martyr replied, "I see, you must be a pre-rapture saint. You must be because you're not under the altar with me. See, the first three and half years, there were demonically inspired technological advances that increased exponentially in all electronic devices. A couple of years after the rapture and before the start of the Great Tribulation, the global leadership made a requirement for all new TV sets to be outfitted with the 3X6 chip which they claimed would improve global signaling and reception and make emergency global broadcasts possible. Devices such as TV sets, cell phones, and all other electronic devices, had transmitters outfitted inside them in preparation for the second half of the tribulation. It seemed harmless at the time and old TV sets were phased out gradually. They offered great rebates to exchange the old TV sets with new ones. When the Great Tribulation started, old TV sets stopped working completely. So it became necessary to get the new TV sets."

"So where was the problem?" asked John.

"Well, when a bunch of us saints refused to accept the mark of the beast, taking heed of the angel's broadcast in the sky, we were getting arrested left and right while sitting at home. We didn't understand how they located us. Saint engineers studied the 3X6 new chip and found out that it scanned its surrounding with a hundred feet radius for humans or any heat source that weighed fifty pounds or over. It did that using thermal sensors just like a snake would to find its prey."

"Here is that snake thing again," said Bill.

"When the heat scanner finds the heat source, it sends a signal to that human and if a person has the implanted chip, the 3X6 chip would send an ok signal back to the transmitting device in the TV set and all was well. However, if the 3X6 chip didn't receive a signal back, indicating that the person didn't have the implant, it sent a signal back to the GIA, informing them of the location where an arrest was to take place. And that's when they rushed to the building or home and made the arrest. Many tagged people had unexpected visits from GIA because they had large dogs weighing over fifty pounds."

"Is that how you were captured?" asked John.

"That's how I got arrested last week and got executed a few minutes ago. Fortunately, the word got around and when I was in prison I heard that the saints were either removing the chip from the TV sets which rendered them useless or got rid of their TV sets altogether. The saints have avoided all electronic devices. We tried to find old TV sets, but they didn't work with the new broadcast transmission systems. TV was also used to control a person's thoughts through subliminal messages suggesting worship and loyalty to the beast after the five months of torture were over. The new church no longer had a building; whoever took the mark could have fellowship with other spirits at anytime. Sometimes, a bunch of people would get together and let the spirits control the meeting."

"Satan built his church on the gates of Hell with false religion, a true synagogue of demons. Jesus built His church on the rock, Himself," said John.

"At the same time the Antichrist started implementing the mark, the angels in the sky were telling everyone not to take the mark of the beast and were preaching the good news. Angels shared the gospel with the tribulation saints just like the angel Gabriel did with the shepherds when Jesus was born. An angel flew in midair and over the long lines of people lined up outside the registration centers all over the world. He had the eternal gospel to proclaim to those who live on the earth—to every nation, tribe, language, and people. The angel said in a loud voice, 'Fear God and give Him glory, because the hour of His judgment has come. Worship Him who made the Heavens, the earth, the sea, and the springs of water'."

"The final call: This one is 'good news' for God's people, but bad news for the rebellious 'earth dwellers'," said John.

Juan continued, "Another angel followed and said in a loud voice: 'If anyone worships the Antichrist and his image and receives his mark on the forehead or on the hand, he, too, will drink of the wine of God's fury, which has been poured full strength into the cup of His wrath. He will be tormented with burning sulfur in the presence of the holy angels and of the Lamb. And the smoke of their torment rises forever and ever. There is no rest day or night for them.'

"I, myself, was standing in one of these registration lines, and when I saw the angels, something told me to get out of the line even though no one else paid attention to them. As I was getting out of the line, one woman standing in line said to me, 'Don't pay attention to these creatures; they were the reason those miserable people suddenly disappeared from the face of the earth a few years ago, remember that? And to think, I almost believed in them. You don't want to disappear too, do you?' Another man standing in the same line said to me, 'Listen, son, these are the enemies that the Antichrist was talking about. Stay with us so you can have eternal life, too; you saw it on TV that day, didn't you? Put your hope in our leader.' They almost sounded convincing, but I got out of the line anyway and walked aimlessly through the streets.

"That's when a Jew for Jesus ran into me and said that my name is already in the book of life, and that I'll be living forever with the Lord Jesus and not where the devil wants me to end up. I said, 'Who is this Lord Jesus that the angels above and you are talking about?' I only heard the name of the Lord Jesus probably a couple of times in my entire life. And even then, I was told that He was just a good man and a prophet.

"So, the Jew told me who Jesus really was and that's when I invited the Lord into my heart and was redeemed. I wish I knew more about the Lord before; I wouldn't have had to go through this horrible ordeal. However, I sure am glad that I heard the good news before I took the mark of the beast and before I died. Then the Jew told me what was up ahead and said, 'Blessed are the dead who die in the Lord from now on, for they will rest from their labor and their deeds will follow them.'"

John said, "The gospel is to be preached in all the world by angels and then the end will come. Only angels can accomplish the task of preaching the gospel throughout the entire world. It is a final attempt before the seven bowls of the wrath of God commence. See these seven angels carrying the seven bowls over there? They are waiting for a trumpet to sound, last chance to repent, no more chances after this. All the previous three and a half year events were for them to repent and change their mind, but the delusion was also strong."

Then, the martyrs held harps given them by God and sang the song of Moses, the servant of God and the song of the Lamb, and they started singing.

"Excuse me, brother, I'd like to join my martyred brothers and sing," said Juan.

"Sure, go ahead."

And the song went like this:

"Great and marvelous are Your deeds, Lord God Almighty. Just and true are Your ways, King of the ages. Who will not fear You, O Lord, and bring glory to Your name? For You alone are holy. All nations will come and worship before You, for Your righteous acts have been revealed."

"That felt good," said Juan, "Praise the Lord."

"Yes indeed. Amen. What happened to the other religions when the Antichrist declared himself as God? We heard the angel up here say, 'Fallen! Fallen is Babylon the Great, which made all the nations drink the maddening wine of her adulteries. She has become a dwelling place for demons, a dungeon haunted by every loathsome spirit. The kings of the earth, who committed adultery with her and shared her luxury, saw the smoke of her burning and wept and mourned over her. Terrified at her torment, they stood far off and cried'," continued John, "Then we heard another voice from Heaven say, 'Come out of her, my people.' God has been telling mankind to get out of false religion since the first Babylonian empire. Then the angel said, 'Woe! Woe, O great city, O Babylon, city of power! In one hour your doom has come!'"

Bill said, "God is merciful, even though they rolled their fists at Him, He still warned them to get out of false religion before its destruction by sending the angel to warn them. He did the same thing before destroying Sodom and Gomorrah, He sent two angels to warn Lot and his family. Only three made it out, the mother looked back and turned into a pillar of salt. Her heart was in the world and what the world offered."

"Amen," said Juan, "A day after the possessed Antichrist became a self-proclaimed god and the devil in human skin, he debunked Babylon the Great entirely. The son of perdition supported her the first three and a half years, but she became obsessed with power and used every type of corruption imaginable, to promote herself into prominence. False religion became a nuisance to him and he finally got her off his back. Satan had deviated humanity from the worship of the real God. And those same religious people who bowed to his image and followed him, he turned on and destroyed, later on. The Antichrist was a wolf in sheep's clothing and after the three and half years he took off the mask. The false prophet declared a holy war against all other religions; the unholy trinity took 'holy war' into a new direction here. It's a war where people who carried the mark of the beast exterminated the unmarked people. Their god ordered them to war and they carried out his commands. Every false religious leader hung their hat either peacefully or by force.

"The wicked one had at his disposal an army of fierce agents across the world, called GIA. They are the most elite force and very loyal to their leader. They're demons possessed and numbered two hundred million. The Antichrist used this elite force to crush all resisting religious people and hunted down all unmarked people with a brutal crushing force never seen before. They used the most advanced weapons of mass destruction. And with that, Babylon the Great of false religion was no more."

Bill said, "It sounds like Babylon the Great sat on a wall, Babylon the Great had a great fall, all the king's horses and all the king's men couldn't put Babylon the Great together again. This is the first phase of Babylon falling; a new false religion, the new mystery Babylon, masterminded by the false prophet will be established in the second three and a half years which is even more abominable than the previous one, the worst of all."

"The Lord Jesus tried to warn by saying, 'Why is my language not clear to you? Because you are unable to hear what I say. You belong to your father, the devil, and you want to carry out your father's desire. He was a murderer from the beginning, not holding to the truth, for there is no truth in him. When he lies, he speaks his native language, for he is a liar and the father of lies. Yet because I tell the truth, you don't believe me!" said John.

"And the rest of the men which were not killed by this holy war now worshipped the Antichrist and didn't repent of the works of their hands, that they should not worship devils, and idols, neither repented they of their murders, nor of their sorceries, nor of their fornication, nor of their thefts. The false prophet enticed them to build an image for the new god in the Jewish temple.

"It was amazing to see how much commerce thrived from false religion. The religious system was so fine with its gold and color, rich and elegant in every way. Even the saints could have been fooled by its beauty and glamour. However, they preached doctrine of demons; they had spies in the worship place to make sure of that. When it was destroyed, there was a big dip in the stock market as many people were laid off from whatever they did to manufacture products that false religions shoved down the throat of its consumers. At the end of this system, business was over and they lost their customers, followed by a worldwide inflation and hunger.

"Three of the Antichrist Prime Ministers rejected his deity and they were killed mysteriously. One was found drowned in his bathtub with a plugged in radio in the water, the other one crashed in a car accident, and the other one just disappeared with no sign of her whereabouts. And that, my brothers, is where my shift ended and here I am."

John said, "Thank you, brother, for filling us in. Rest forever in the Lord."

Juan replied, "Amen."

After that, there were large waves of martyrs ascending to Heaven every day. John talked to a martyr who was so glad to be in Heaven, resting from the trouble on the earth and said, "They drove the saints to the local stadiums like sheep to the slaughter, just like they did to our Lord. Moreover, they executed us before the games started, whether football or baseball or soccer. And the crowds cheered and called us enemies of the state. They hated us with a vengeance."

"How were you caught, brother?" asked John.

The martyr whose name was Vladimir replied, "In the country where I lived, there were some Jews, but not too many. When the persecution started against them, I took in a family of Jews and hid them in our basement. Later on, when the government imposed the mark of the beast on their citizens, we didn't participate and our rations started to dwindle because we couldn't buy anything without the mark. The rations didn't last more than a few weeks after that. It was hard enough to sustain ourselves, let alone a whole extra family. We did this because we obeyed God's command, for He said, 'Whoever gives a cup of water to My brothers, it's like giving it to Me.' We were caught after that and here we are."

Another batch of martyred saints arrived, so John listened in as one of the saints named Vu spoke. "Things are getting bizarre down there. Satan released his demons and now they have hurt both the saints and his followers. He is grasping on to last straws.

"As I was being beheaded, the executor said, 'lucky you' and I said, 'Yeah.' Then I looked at the executor in amazement and asked him, 'What did you mean by that; after all, I'm the one being executed?'

"'Look at me,' the executor replied, 'I have been tortured day and night for the last five months now, and the agony I suffer is like that of the sting of a scorpion when it strikes a man. I sought death, but didn't find it; I longed to die, but death eluded me and the spirit refuses to leave my body.'" The martyr continued, "There was a disease that hit those who dwelled on earth; their bodies swelled like a water bed flooded with fluids as if they were stung by some sort of insects, they seemed to be in great pain and suffered agony. The doctors advised them to stay away from the scorching sun that made the condition worse so they came out in the darkness of the night only. The man had horrible looking sores on his body; only the people who had the mark of the beast got these sores. I think it's possible that the chip inserted in the body was sensitive to sunlight and that is why they had sores. The inserted chips might have had bad batteries that leaked concentrated lithium and caused the sores.

"'I tried to kill myself yesterday,' continued the executor, 'I tried everything. I tried to shoot myself; I put my finger on the trigger and it seemed jammed, it wouldn't click. I tried to throw myself from the top of a building, but I stopped on the ledge and my legs just wouldn't move forward, as if some force were stopping me. A knife wouldn't touch my skin; I can't swallow more than one pill at a time. I can't stand living in this mess; I want out of here. When I watch TV, our messiah says that things will get better, that we should hang in there, he needs every one of us.'"

Yes, he's also sending you subliminal messages through the TV and radio airwaves brainwashing you so that you can't kill yourself, I thought, *He wants to use you to execute me and the saints, and he's using you and others to man his armies for wars.* Vu continued, "New TV sets were equipped with the 3X6 chip, it transmitted subliminal messages to control the viewers and make suggestions that they'd have to follow. At that instant, a Jew commando appeared and the executor said, 'Well, isn't that special, here is a man who no one can kill and we don't know if he wants to live or die. All we know is that he talks about this Jesus, day and night. I want to die and I can't, as for this man,' pointing at me, 'do you want to die?'

"I said, 'to live is Christ and to die is gain. If I die, I go to Heaven and I can't wait. If I live, I'll support my brothers and sisters and take care of my wife and son.'

"At that moment, the Jew interrupted, 'Your wife and son have preceded you to Heaven just an hour ago, my brother, you'll be seeing them soon. Your troubles are over - take courage.'

"I was overjoyed and wanted to tell the executer the good news of Jesus Christ, but the Jew brought to my attention the mark of the beasts on his right hand, the same hand he was going to use to push the button to sever my head. He already signed his death warrant, not his physical death, the second death warrant, his eternal separation from God. I started to feel sorry for the man, but then all of a sudden he had a pain attack and started agonizing and blasphemed God. That's when I thought, *God is in control; He knows what He's doing. Let me get out of here.* And that was just a few minutes ago."

"You know, TV was an innocent invention," said John, "who knew that the Antichrist would use it to control people all the way to Hell? God bless you, brother, enter to His rest," said John.

Bill said, "They said we were escapist to want to be raptured. Here is the Lord proving to the whole world, natural and super-natural, that His followers will follow Him whatever the cost, even if it means having their heads severed. And if our church would have had to go through the tribulation, most of the Christian saints would have done the same thing."

Another batch of martyred saints yet arrived and one of them, whose name was Wong, said, "It has been six years since the rapture and towards the end of the Great Tribulation, the situation has become unbearable. The Antichrist wanted to capture as many of us as he could, so he announced on TV and radio stations all around the world that Jesus Christ has appeared at certain places in the world. Some of the brothers fell for the lie and went to those locations and they were captured. Their lack of knowledge got them killed, not that there is anything wrong with being killed. I wish I were captured earlier. It was horrible down there.

"The trap was so successful that they repeated the process all over the world. I told my brothers that the Lord Jesus had warned and said, 'If they shall say unto you, behold, he is in the desert; go not forth. Behold, he is in the secret chambers, believe it not. If anyone says to you, 'Look, here is the Christ!' or, 'Look, there he is!' don't believe it. False Christs and false prophets will appear and perform signs and miracles to deceive the elect—if that were possible. So be on your guard; I have told you everything ahead of time. For as the lightning cometh out of the east, and shines even unto the west; so shall also the coming of the Son of man be.' ," continued the martyr, "The brothers were so exhausted, weary, and discouraged that they wanted to believe the lie. I almost wanted to believe it myself, but I was determined not to come out of my foxhole until I saw that lightening that Jesus talked about."

"How were you captured then?" asked John.

"My son called me today over the phone for help. When I went to see him, the authorities were waiting for me there. It was a trap; he gave up and took the mark of the beast and betrayed us all, myself and a couple of other brothers," said Wong sadly, "yet all is well, praise God."

"Praise God, I'm very sorry about your son, brother," said John sadly.

Other martyred saints were talking about their experiences on earth and John listened in.

"I was being pursued by GIA, when a pillar of cloud came behind my car and I was able to escape. Then I ran out of gas, so I left the car and wandered. At night, fireflies came out and helped me see in the dark. After a few days, I almost died of hunger, thirst, and exhaustion. That's when a white horse appeared out of nowhere and I was able to mount it using whatever energy was left in my body and passed out. When I came to, I was next to a brook, in an oasis. The ravens brought me bread and meat in the morning and bread and meat in the evening, and I drank from the brook. Later, I found my GIA pursuers, devastated, hungry, and thirsty, and I fed them. And they still turned me in."

Another martyr said, "Also, fruit trees appeared everywhere we went and birds fell at our feet. And the bees moved over when the saints wanted some honey from the honeycomb, even though bees have disappeared and have been extinct for a couple of years now."

Another martyr said, "A pillar of fire guided me at night as it lighted the way and kept me warm. An angel baked bread for me and after I ate, I didn't need to eat for forty days. Fish were easy to catch for the earthly saints, and sometimes there was a message inside the fish with instructions on where to go next."

Another martyr said, "When I was in hiding, a donkey spoke to me with instructions on what to do next and where to go to find plenty of manna."

John thought, *just like the Antichrist had signs and wonders, our God overmatched them.*

World War III

John, Moses and Aaron looked down, from the balcony of Heaven, at the events that were taking place on earth in the last days of the Great Tribulation. Satan had intensified his efforts to defend his evil realm, as time got shorter. The Antichrist had thrusted planet earth into a political and military chaos, which led to a series of wars that were to end shortly with the battle of Armageddon. People fought over what was left from the destruction and everyone was looking for himself. They killed each other in order to survive and no one obeyed the law. Darkness set on planet earth with clouds of nuclear dust hovering above and blocking the sun. There were blasts appearing through the thick clouds surrounding the earth, indicating that warfare was still going on. God removed His hand of protection and let man do his will and destroy himself, and earth, with nuclear weapons. Man was pushed right into the edge of destruction and extinction.

"What do you think," Moses sadly asked Aaron, "does this remind you of anything?"

"This sure reminds me of the ten plagues before we left Egypt. Only this time, the whole world is experiencing it and more intensely. Humanity has reached its worst point and condition in history, ever."

"Also, when the ten plagues fell on the Egyptians, they cried like never before or ever after. The Lord hardened the heart of Pharaoh, making it strong and obstinate, but the Egyptians changed their mind because the power of God was so strong. Afterwards, even Pharaoh said to me, 'I have sinned against the LORD your God and against you. Now forgive my sin once more and pray to the LORD your God to take the deadly plagues away from me.' However, look at these people, instead of crying to God for help they are blaspheming Him. What kind of people are these?"

John replied, "Demon possessed."

While they were speaking, fireballs fell from the sky and descended towards earth and disappeared inside the thick dark clouds as they penetrated it. Even though they couldn't see what happened once the fireballs reached earth, there was a glow of fire flames coming from behind the clouds as if earth were on fire.

John sadly said, "Hide, brother saints and sister saints. Hide well."

"During the ten plagues we, the Jews, didn't worry about a thing; the plagues didn't affect us, it only hurt the Egyptians until the tenth plague when we had to put blood on our doorposts as a mark for protection, so the spirit would pass over us. I wouldn't worry about the saints down there; they can only be killed by beheading, I thought!" Aaron said, looking at Moses. "I know that the 144,000 Jews are sealed, but I'm not sure about the saints. The heathens, however, have the mark of the beast on them, doomed to destruction."

Moses replied, "Throughout the tribulation, it was shown that men clinched their fists in the face of God and didn't repent. The nations were angry because they wanted to have their own way; they wanted to cast off all restraint. God permitted them to do so; the result of their anger is leading to Armageddon."

John said, "God didn't expect to convert the world through judgment. His plan was to save them through His grace. It's the goodness of God that brought us to repentance. It melted our pride, silenced our excuses, and prepared our hearts to humbly receive His grace. Of course, there was pain in change and suffering in true obedience, but the impending judgment of God caused us saints to listen and to think seriously about getting here. The same sun that melts the butter hardens the clay."

Aaron asked, "Our drama ended with the Egyptians drowning in the Red Sea. Do you know how this ends?"

Moses replied, "A couple of months ago, the four angels who were bound at the great river Euphrates were released, when the sixth angel sounded the trumpet. They had been kept ready for this very hour and day and month and year. They were released to kill a third of mankind."

John said, "The four angels were prepared up to the hour with such precision. God is never late; we're usually early."

"The number of the mounted troops was two hundred million. The horses and riders looked like this: Their breastplates were fiery red, dark blue, and yellow as sulfur. The heads of the horses resembled the heads of lions, and out of their mouths came fire, smoke, and sulfur. A third of mankind was killed by the three plagues of fire, smoke and sulfur that came out of their mouths. The power of the horses was in their mouths and in their tails; for their tails were like snakes, having heads with which they inflict injury."

John said, "It sounds as if every volcano on the planet is erupting and the skies are filled with ash so thick that the sun's rays can't filter through. Other parts of the world have the skies covered with flying demonic locusts, so thick that it creates darkness during the day. Add to that, all the stockpiled nuclear weapons the GIA unleashed on the planet causing deadly fallouts, no wonder their sores wouldn't heal. Not to mention meteor showers causing fires and earthquakes every hour, but the biggest earthquake is yet to come. When the angels orbit earth and say, 'woe, woe, woe,' you know that things are going to get really bad."

"Things started escalating," continued Moses. "The second angel poured out his bowl on the sea, and it turned into blood like that of a dead man, and every living thing in the sea died. Then, the third angel poured out his bowl on the rivers and springs of water and they became blood. So, pretty much the seas and rivers turned to blood and there was no fresh water to drink. They thought maybe if they dug into the ground, fresh water would come out. But what came out was blood. God was one step ahead of them. Even the angel in charge of the waters said, 'You are just in these judgments, you who are and who were, the Holy One, because you have so judged; for they have shed the blood of your saints and prophets, and you have given them blood to drink as they deserve.' And we heard the altar respond: 'Yes, Lord God Almighty, true and just are Your judgments.'"

"The angels agree with every step God takes," said John.

"Soon, the fifth angel poured out his bowl on the throne of the beast, and his kingdom was plunged into darkness. Men gnawed their tongues in agony and cursed the God of Heaven because of their pains and their sores, but they refused to repent of what they had done. The sores came when the first angel went and poured out his vial upon the earth; and a malignant, noisome and grievous sore fell upon the men which had the mark of the beast and upon them which worshipped his image."

"Can you imagine these people almost chewing their tongue in agony?" said John, "This must be the worst time and heartache in human history and a preview of Hell. I mean there is no water to drink and with the scorching sun above, these conditions create a global sauna. The second asteroid knocked earth out of orbit and she wobbles like a drunken man and sways back and forth like a hammock, which explains the bizarre weather. These people are in darkness with sores all over their bodies. With this kind of mental horror, their nervous system must be on fire. This is a little direct fellowship with their future cohabitation in Hell. No wonder they are asking for death. Everyone who blasphemed God in the Great Tribulation period will either have their tongue dissolve as a result of a Nitrogen Bomb explosion or they will chew their own tongue themselves out of agony. No one blasphemes the Almighty and gets away with it," continued John as chills went down their resurrected bodies at the power of that statement, for it was easy to say, but down on earth, the view of its fulfillment was sickening. The saints were holding on for dear life to the garments that Jesus gave to them for protection from the horrific scene on earth.

Moses took a deep breath, and then said, "You must be talking about the explosions responsible for those amazing mushroom like clouds rising from the earth, which vaporized men, plants, and beast for miles around them. They were popping up all over the globe."

John said, "The Lord Jesus created everything with the atoms glued together. Mankind found a way to unglue and split these atoms, releasing tremendous energy that in the hands of evil men could cause major destruction."

"I heard that this mushroom cloud would cause a person to have his tongue dissolved in his mouth and his eyes dissolved in their sockets before the dead body would hit the ground! What a horrible death; must be a demonic force. The Prophet Zechariah had told about this thousands of years ago."

John replied, "Yes. Then at the judgment and after their resurrection, they will be given a new tongue that will confess Jesus Christ is Lord."

"By the end of the seven-year tribulation period, half of earth population was destroyed as they were divided into two groups. The one-half that followed the beast and took his mark escaped some of the wrath of Satan, but were killed by the wrath of God and went to Hades. They were subject to sores, scorching heat waves with the sun going out of control, and other plagues. They were thirsty for they had blood for water and they were hungry for there was nothing to eat and food was expensive. And the other half that believed in the Lord and didn't take the mark of the beast, escaped the wrath of God but fell into the wrath of Satan and were starved, hunted down and if captured were beheaded, but they are eternally saved. A large portion of the beheaded martyrs is in Heaven with the Lord and us. There are still a good number of those saints down on earth hiding from the wrath of the beast. We'll just have to wait and see what happens next," said Moses as he summoned the prophets Zechariah, Ezekiel, Jeremiah, and Daniel to share what they prophesied regarding the tribulation period with him. When they appeared, John was ecstatic to see the Hall of Prophecy assembled together in one place at one time.

* * * * * *

At another time and dimension in Heaven, John and Jim noticed that the martyrs were no longer under the altar but were resurrected and had entered the Heavenly scene. There was a great multitude of the resurrected martyrs that no one could count, from every nation, tribe, people and language, standing before the throne and in front of the Lamb. They were wearing white robes and were holding palm branches in their hands. And they cried out in a loud voice, "Salvation belongs to our God, who sits on the throne, and to the Lamb."

All the angels who were standing around the throne and around the saints fell down on their faces before the throne and worshiped God, saying: "Amen! Praise and glory and wisdom and thanks and honor and power and strength be to our God forever and ever. Amen!"

John said to Jim, "Another awesome worship service."

"Amen."

John continued, "Their numbers must be complete, the souls of those who had been beheaded because of their testimony for Jesus and because of the word of God. They had not worshiped the beast or his image and had not received his mark on their foreheads or their hands. They're finally resurrected; this is the first resurrection. Blessed and holy are those who have part in the first resurrection. The second death has no power over them, but they will be priests of God and of Christ and will reign with Him for a thousand years."

Then John noticed that JR was watching all this so he asked him, "Do you know who these people in white robes are and where they came from?"

JR answered, "Sir, you know."

Obviously, JR didn't recognize who they were. He already saw the raptured church earlier, but this new earthly group seemed to be distinguished from the raptured church because they were saved during the tribulation.

John then said, "These are the martyrs who have come out of the Great Tribulation; they have washed their robes and made them white in the blood of the Lamb. Therefore, they are before the throne of God and will serve Him day and night in His temple; and He who sits on the throne will spread His tent over them. Never again will they hunger; never again will they thirst. The sun will not beat upon them, nor any scorching heat. For the Lamb at the center of the throne will be their Shepherd. He will lead them to springs of living water. And God will wipe away every tear from their eyes."

Jim asked, "Excuse me John; you mentioned the first resurrection and the second death; what are those?"

"The first resurrection is everyone you see up here that is getting ready to accompany the Lord at His second coming. As for the second death, there are souls of unbelievers out there somewhere in the center of the earth that are waiting for judgment day after which they will be sent to Hell."

"But why should they be tormented forever?"

"Nobody will be tormenting them there in Hell, I don't think. It will be hot with no water though. When these people will be judged and see the face of the Lord, the one they didn't believe existed, that's when the agony comes in. They will realize that they'll be missing out on the most important thing they could have had - fellowship with Him and His saints in a beautiful place prepared for us. I mean look at Him," pointing at the Lord, "If I were to go for an hour without seeing Him, I think my soul would wither and be in need of resuscitation. I want to be wherever He is, and go wherever He goes. He's very exciting, good, and loving."

Mary, who was present, looked at her earthly husband and smiled as he was already showing the traits of a righteous priest, a royalty King, and a ruler. She praised the Lord.

Then the angels came and said, "Calling all saints. Calling all saints. Your presence has been requested at the Marriage of the Lamb. The King says 'Behold, I have prepared my banquet, and everything is prepared; come to the wedding feast.' Suppertime, everyone, you're all invited. Make sure you have your wedding garments."

John said to Bill, who rushed to the scene with excitement when he heard the word supper, "The wedding garments are made of fine linen especially tailored by our righteous acts and deeds on earth."

"My Lord, Heaven is a happening place; there is something going on all the time. What a place to be. Let's also worship the Lord for bringing us here," replied Bill.

"Amen."

Then a sound was heard that sounded like a great multitude, like the roar of rushing waters and like loud peals of thunder, shouting: "Hallelujah! For our Lord God Almighty reigns. Let us rejoice and be glad and give Him glory! For the wedding of the Lamb has come, and His bride has made herself ready. Fine linen, bright and clean, was given her to wear."

After they received the wedding garments, Bill said to John, "Would you look at this beautiful garment? What colors and feel. Who said there is no fashion in Heaven? I wonder how the banquet hall is going to be. Do you think they'll have crystal glass, precious stones, banners, jewels, and wedding music with the Lord leading the band?"

Then John heard the angel say to JR, "Write: 'Blessed are those who are invited to the wedding supper of the Lamb!'" And he added, "These are the true words of God." At this, JR fell at his feet to worship the angel.

John said to Bill "Here goes JR again, making the same mistake I made. He's worshipping that angel the second time. No hard feelings, JR, but the angel doesn't want to be ensnared the same way Lucifer did."

The angel said to JR, "Don't do it! I'm a fellow servant with you and with your brothers who hold to the testimony of Jesus. Worship God! For the testimony of Jesus is the spirit of prophecy."

As the saints headed out towards the big reception, the place in which the wedding feast was held, it was filled with saints. They were engaged to Christ on earth and now the marriage is taking place in heaven.

"My Lord, would you look at this 'all you can eat buffet'. Luscious banquet of food to enjoy; this is my kind of God, Thank you, Lord," said Bill.

John happily said, "At the rapture we were caught up, at the judgment seat of Christ we cleaned up, at the marriage wedding supper of the lamb we're cheered up."

Next to John was sitting his wife Mary, his son, daughter Gracie, and across from the table was sitting his mother, father, and his grandparents and loved ones and friends and other people he hadn't met yet. Some were tribulation martyrs and Old Testament saints and some were the miraculously raptured 144,000 Jews.

Then the king who gave the wedding banquet appeared to view the guests. With everyone having put on the appropriate wedding garments, they all bowed down and worshiped. And the Lord served the supper while the music played and the angels' chorus sang,

"Hallelujah. Joyful, joyful we adore thee." The saints thanked the Lord for the eternal food.

"Can you believe it? We're eating in Heaven; how exciting!" Bill said.

"This is the largest communion in Heaven," John said.

"Everything the Lord told us would happen is happening," Mary said.

While Jesus was feeding and serving them, John thought, *Jesus fed the four thousand and the five thousand men, not counting women and children, with fish and bread when He was on earth. He commanded the multitude to sit down on the grass, and took the five loaves, and the two fishes, and looking up to Heaven, He blessed, and broke, and gave the loaves to His disciples, and the disciples gave to the multitude. And they did all eat and were filled. This time He is in Heaven feeding His sheep.*

John remembered what Jesus said, "He who feeds on My flesh and drinks My blood has eternal life, and I will raise him up from the dead on the last day. Just as the living Father sent Me and I live because of the Father, even so, whoever takes Me for his food and is nourished by Me shall in his turn live through and because of Me." The Bread that came down from Heaven is serving the saints who took that Bread for their food on earth and now live-forever.

He also overheard Gracie asking Mary, "What kind of food are we eating? I've never tasted anything like it." At the same time, John examined the texture of food in his mouth. Also, while his brain processed this, he listened to singing angels and heard them say, "Hallelujah, praise the Lord, the Lamb conquered." John thought, *if I had this gift of a resurrected-body brain-multitasking capability when I lived on earth, I wouldn't have gotten in trouble so many times when Mary talked to me while I was watching TV or reading the newspaper and then she checked to see if I was listening.* Then he wondered if this was the same brain he had in his physical body but without sin, and thought, *maybe sin was limiting our brain's functionality. No wonder God hates sin, and so do I.*

Mary said, "There is the Apostle Peter. He refused when the Lord wanted to wash his feet at the Last Supper on earth. Let's see what he does now when the Lord tries to serve him food."

"Oh, he'll take the food," said Bill, "he had two upgrades since that incident."

"Two upgrades?" asked Jim.

"Yes, the first one was when the Holy Spirit fell on him like a tongue of fire at Pentecost, and the second one was when he received his resurrected body."

"Yes, you're right; he's taking the food," said Mary.

"Check this out," said Bill, "Zacchaeus isn't so short anymore. Praise the Lord."

"There is the Apostle Paul," said John, "and he doesn't look like he has a thorn in his flesh anymore. I sure would like to talk to him."

"Look at JR. It is good to see him wearing a younger body," said John.

"How come the Lord isn't eating or drinking anything yet?" asked Jim.

"The Lord said, 'I will not drink of this fruit of the vine from now on until the kingdom of God shall come, that day when I drink it anew with you in my Father's kingdom.' He also said, 'I will not eat the Passover again until it finds fulfillment in the kingdom of God.' He will probably be the last one to eat after He feeds all of us and just before He goes back to earth to claim His Kingdom," Bill said.

Then Jim stood up and left the banquet.

"Where is he going, John?" asked Bill.

"He's probably going to go look for his mother again; I'll be right back," said John as he stood up and followed Jim.

"Where are you going? Wouldn't you rather stay here and enjoy the supper?"

"Believe me I would, but I have to help Jim out."

As John was leaving the banquet to catch up with Jim, he saw the old JR again. John was astonished and thought, *Buddy, I just saw you at the banquet and you looked great. Oh my, you looked so good. I wish you could see yourself. Maybe you already have.*

Then he saw an angel who was standing on the sea and on the land, give JR a book. John thought, *I only know two people that stood on water, the Lord and His disciple Peter. I wonder if I could do that, stand on water. I think I'll try that when I get to earth in the*

Millennium kingdom. Then he saw JR eat the book and it was sweet in his mouth and bitter in his tummy.

Oh JR, thought John, *I remember those days when I heard the word of God and was exceedingly glad to eat it by reading the Bible, for it was like honey in my mouth. Then there were times when I deviated from the word of God because of my sinful nature and the Holy Spirit disciplined me for my own good. That part didn't feel too good. Moreover, it made me feel bad because I disobeyed and grieved the Holy Spirit. But guess what JR; those days are long gone now. You should see yourself in this banquet here, everything is sweet and delicious, no more bitterness, sin no longer abounds. We're free from the bondage. Hallelujah.*

Then the angel that stood on the sea and on the land raised his right hand to Heaven, and he swore by Him who lives forever and ever, who created the Heavens and all that's in them, the earth and the sea and all that's in them, and said, "There will be no more delay! But in the days when the seventh angel is about to sound his trumpet, the mystery of God will be accomplished, just as He announced to His servants the prophets and said, 'There will be no more delay!'"

God has been delaying His judgments so that lost sinners will have time to repent. Time is up. The prayers of the pre-rapture saints and tribulation-martyred saints are about to be answered. All right, finally we're getting the show on the road, thought John.

Then the seven thunders uttered their voices. JR was about to write and he heard a voice from Heaven saying unto him, "Seal up those things which the seven thunders uttered, and write them not."

John heard what the seven thunders had said, and thought, *this would have never entered my earthly mind or imagination. No wonder the Apostle Paul said that he heard unspeakable words, which it isn't lawful for a man to utter, when he was caught up into Heaven. Also, Jesus said to the Pharisee, named Nicodemus, "If I have told you of things that happen right here on the earth and yet none of you believe Me, how can you believe Me if I tell you of Heavenly things?"*

* * * * * *

Back at the Hall of prophecy and as the final days of the Great Tribulation were winding up, the prophets saw the sixth angel pour out his bowl on the great river Euphrates, and its water was dried up to prepare the way for the kings from the East. Moses said, "The kings thought that the river had dried up in their favor, but it was a trap. Just like the Egyptians went through the parted Red Sea to lead them to the fleeing Jews, but it was a trap and they all drowned." The spirits of demons went out to the kings of the whole world, to gather them for the battle on the great day of God Almighty. Then they gathered the kings together to the place that in Hebrew is called, Armageddon.

Daniel said, "On the days preceding Armageddon, the Antichrist was moving his forces of the west from the holy land through Egypt to conquer and invade Africa and the world. When he heard news from the east and the north, China and Russia, gathering their forces to fight against him, he turned back in anger to meet these forces in Megiddo and that's where the war of Armageddon will take place. All the armies of the world are gathering in the plains of Megiddo and the valleys surrounding Jerusalem for the final battle - Armageddon."

Then the seventh and final bowl and judgment was poured out into the air, and out of the temple came a loud voice from the throne, saying, "It is done!" Then there came flashes of lightning, rumblings, peals of thunder and a severe earthquake. No earthquake like it had ever occurred since man had been on earth, so tremendous was the quake. The great city Jerusalem split into three parts and the cities of the nations collapsed. God remembered Babylon the Great and gave her the cup filled with the wine of the fury of His wrath. Every island fled away and the mountains could not be found.

John, who was watching these events unravel, said, "New York, Japan, Hawaii, Greece, and other islands no longer exist. The face of earth has changed." From the sky, huge hailstones of about a hundred pounds each fell upon men annihilating them by the hundreds of millions. And they cursed God on account of the plague of hail, because the plague was so terrible.

John thought, *this is phase two of Babylon the Great annihilation. There shouldn't be any false religions from now on. I mean, look at this hail; it pulverized everything in sight, and brought an end to civilization, as we knew it. This is the last judgment ever; hail stoning for their blasphemy.*

Meanwhile, the earthly saints were encouraged to see the judgments of God falling on the seat of the Antichrist.

After this, there was a sound like the roar of a great multitude in Heaven shouting: "Hallelujah! Salvation, glory, and power belong to our God, for true and just are His judgments. He has condemned the great prostitute, Babylon, who corrupted the earth by her adulteries. He has avenged on her the blood of His servants."

And again they shouted, "Hallelujah! The smoke from her goes up forever and ever."

The saints and the four special angels fell down and worshiped God, who was seated on the throne. And they cried: "Amen, Hallelujah!"

Then a voice came from the throne, saying: "Praise our God, all you His servants, you who fear Him, both small and great!"

After a while, Jesus stood up and was ready to ride a white horse, but this time He turned into a warrior ready for battle. The saints and angels in Heaven saw the warrior Jesus, but Satan on earth wasn't expecting it.

John, thought, *the prayers of the saints and martyrs are going to be answered. This was an ecstatic moment of prophecy being fulfilled, the second coming of the Messiah to planet earth.*

Then, the Lord Jesus, faithful and true, rode the white horse. With justice, He judged and made war. His eyes were like blazing fire, and on His head were many crowns. He had a name written on Him that no one knew but He himself. He was dressed in a robe sprinkled in blood, and His name was the Word of God. Out of His mouth came a sharp sword with which to strike down the nations. He would rule them with an iron scepter. He would tread the winepress of the fury of the wrath of God Almighty. On His robe and on His thigh He had this name written: KING OF KINGS AND LORD OF LORDS.

The sixth seal was opened and there was a great earthquake. The sun turned black like sackcloth made of goat hair; the whole moon turned blood red, and the stars in the sky fell to earth, as late figs drop from a fig tree when shaken by a strong wind.

The seventh trumpet sounded, and there were loud voices in Heaven, which said in a celestial cheer, "The kingdom of the world has become the kingdom of our Lord and of His Christ, and He will reign forever and ever."

And the saints, who were seated on their thrones before God, fell on their faces and worshiped God in a most momentous and climatic hour in Heaven, saying: "We give thanks to you, Lord God Almighty, the One who is and who was, because you have taken your great power and have begun to reign. The nations were angry; and your wrath has come. The time has come for judging the dead, and for rewarding your servants the prophets and your saints and those who reverence your name, both small and great— and for destroying those who destroy the earth."

After the worship was over, John looked and saw Raphael coming at him, quickly. "This is it, brother, that was the seventh and last trumpet; we're going to follow the Lord now because He is going to open the seventh seal. I have to join the rest of the angels for a small detail to collect and separate the wheat and tares on earth and get them ready for the judgment. This should take half an hour. The tares will be collected for judgment, and then burned in the Lake of Fire, while the wheat will be collected for further judgment of the sheep and goats. After that I'll come back to Heaven. You, however, will follow the Lord all the way to earth and spend the Millennium there. So, I'll see you after the Millennium and we'll have all eternity to fellowship together."

John was saddened by this and asked, "I won't see you for a thousand years?"

"Well, you won't need me anymore. Satan will be bound for a thousand years and the Lord Himself will be with you on earth. You'll be in good hands."

John still looked sad to part with his angel.

"When I come to earth from time to time to see the Lord," said Raphael, "or if the Lord sends me on a special assignment, I'll make sure I say Hello. Ok?"

"Ok," said John.

As they were talking, there were flashes of lightning, rumblings, and peals of thunder. John looked at the temple to see what was going on. An angel, who had a golden censer, came and stood at the altar. He was given much incense to offer, with the prayers of all the tribulation saints who were martyred, on the golden altar before the throne. The smoke of the incense, together with the prayers of these saints, went up before God from the angel's hand. Then the angel took the censer, filled it with fire from the altar, and hurled it on the earth; and there came an earthquake. Then God's temple was opened, and within the temple was seen the ark of His covenant.

"Wow, look, it's the Ark of the Covenant," said John excitedly.

"This is the 'original' Ark of the Covenant," said Raphael, "and it has always been here; the one on the earth was only a replica. It was merely a pattern and served as a copy and shadowing of what is in the Heavenly sanctuary. For when Moses was about to erect the tabernacle, he was warned by God, saying, 'See to it that you make it an exact copy according to the model which was shown to you on the mountain.' When Moses came down from the mountain, he not only had the Ten Commandments but also the blue prints for this ark."

Then Raphael rushed John and said, "Now you'd better mount your horse, for it is time. See you, brother." Then as he was leaving, he turned around smiled and said, "It has been an honor to be your guardian," and then he took off.

Then, amazingly, white stallions appeared all around the saints. John turned around and looked at the ark one more time and said, "Our Heavenly Father, Hallowed be Thy name, Thy kingdom is being established on earth, and I'll follow." Then he turned around and ran towards the horse closest to him. When he got closer to it, he noticed that the horse was no ordinary horse. It was just a cloud shaped like a horse. So, out of curiosity he stretched his arm to touch it, and the horse looked back at John with his big eyes, and John looked back at it and their eyes locked together for a second. John started feeling uncomfortable but didn't know what to think. Then the horse said, "Could you please hurry up and mount? We have to catch up with the Lord."

"Yes sir... horse," said John and thought, *I just heard a cloud that looks like a horse talk to me. Praise God, here I mount... by faith.* So he mounted, but prayed that this creature would support his body and not let him fall down right through him or it. To his amazement, he mounted just fine and the ride felt really good.

John chuckled and thought, *JR, my good brother, you sure have a good sense of humor. Every creature or character you described in the book of Revelation, whether on Heaven or earth, you said, 'and they looked like ... or were as a....' And then gave a thorough description of them. You could have given us a hint about the nature of horses we mount on here in Heaven, that they were as or like horses. I always wondered how horses would get to Heaven, but then again with God, nothing is impossible.*

As the horse moved forward, John felt closeness to it, so he petted the horse and stroked his hair. By that time, Jesus had already disappeared riding His horse towards earth. So John moved forward towards the balcony of Heaven with Gracie and Mary behind him on their horses. And when they looked down, the universe looked pitch black, for the sky rolled up like a scroll and vanished, the sun was darkened, and the moon didn't give its light, and the stars fell from the sky. But then there was a lightning, which flashed and lighted up the sky from one end to the other, from the east to the west.

"What was that?" asked Gracie.

John looked at her with a smile and said, "That's the Son."

Gracie had a puzzled look on her face because she thought he said 'that was the sun', but it didn't look like the sun that she knew. So John looked at her again and said, "He is the Son of God, Jesus."

"Wow, that's awesome."

Then John looked back and tried to locate Jim in the multitude of saints behind him and couldn't find him, so he summoned him in the spirit. Immediately, Jim appeared on his horse right behind him.

John, smiling, said, "Come here, Jim," and Jim moved forward by his side.

"Brother, do you remember that one time you asked me why I loved God so much and what was it I saw in Him?"

"Yes, I do remember that, in the car after the first Bible study. You always liked to brag on God."

"Yes, I did, I also liked the way God brags on Himself when He says 'I said this and I will do it' and He did and still does; just look down there."

John looked down at where Jesus was, pointed at Him and said, "There is our God, look at Him now. At His first coming He was a baby in a manger, His second coming He comes as King of Kings and Lord of Lords. He came along on a donkey last time, but now on a white stallion. He had a crown of thorns the first time on earth, and now He has crowns of Kings. He was the silent Lamb of God then and now He is the Lion of Judah."

Then Jim looked down and saw Jesus' glory turning the complete darkness of the universe into a staggering brightness, stretching from horizon to horizon, as He descended to earth. He said, "Glory to God, only God can do this."

"I wish all the people who said, throughout the ages, that He was just a good man and a prophet would see Him now. I'm sure that they won't say that about Him now. I'm sure the people down there right now don't think that either."

Jim said, "Do you know what the Lord asked me just before He went back to earth?"

"No, I can't say I do," said John as he kept his eyes fixed on the spectacular scene surrounding earth.

"He asked me if I wanted to participate in the judgment of Daemon, you know the demon that controlled my life for a number of years, and later on destroyed my mother's soul," said Jim with tears building up in his eyes.

"What did you say?"

With a broken voice, Jim replied, "I said, 'Of course, my Lord, I would like that.' Even thou He taught us 'vengeance is mine, I will repay', He still lets us in on His plan. Can you imagine me judging an angel, the one responsible for my mother's destruction?" Jim thought if his mother didn't make it to Heaven by now, it was too late for her.

John replied, "There is nothing I can't imagine if the Lord says it. Come on, let's follow our Jehovah-Nissi."

"What's a Nissi?"

"The banner, He's our leader and we follow His lead. In the old Calvary they always had someone carry the flag or banner and when that man charged forward all the soldiers followed."

Jim said, "Hallelujah," so did John and then Mary and Gracie and all the saints and the angels. And the catchy word echoed throughout Heaven.

Then John saw Heaven open and thought, *This is the second time I have seen heaven open, the first time it opened at the rapture, and now it opened again for the saints to follow Jesus in His return.*

The groups' leaders charged down first, and then everyone else followed. This was a ride that no amusement park can even come close to. The saints looked like an army sitting on a big white cloud from a distance.

John liked cowboy movies of the Midwest when he was a child. He liked the way the cavalry, who wore blue uniforms, charged and the dust flew in the air after the trumpet sounded. He looked at himself now, unarmed and without any military background, wearing a white linen robe, and charging on a Heavenly white stallion for a war, putting all his trust in and following his Commander. There was no ground dust as with cavalry charging but stardust or Heaven dust since all the stars had fallen out.

For those who were on earth, there appeared the sign of the Son of man in Heaven. They saw Jesus filling up the sky with His presence and brilliance after living in darkness for a while. Earth dwellers and tenants were wondering, at first, if this was another trick managed by the false prophet. Before Armageddon, they saw the northern lights of the North Pole and fire in the sky, all around the globe. But this sign was different, everyone saw His glory visible and every eye saw Him in the clouds. The king returned on a cloud just like He ascended to Heaven in a cloud after His resurrection.

Then all the tribes of the earth mourned when they saw the Son of man, the owner, coming in the clouds of Heaven with power and great glory. It wasn't a secret and it didn't have to be reported in the news. Jesus was looking down on earth as we would look into a fish bowl.

Then the kings of the earth, the great men, the rich men, the chief captains, the mighty men, every bondman, and every free man, hid themselves in the dens and in **the** rocks of the mountains. And said to the mountains and rocks, "**Fall** on us, and hide us from the face of Him that sits on the throne, **and from** the wrath of the Lamb: For the great day of His wrath is come; and who shall be able to stand?"

As the royal posse of saints got closer to earth, they were able to take a closer look at it. Earth looked very sick, brown, pale, reddish, instead of the healthy blue and white. The earth looked like it was screaming for help.

John said sadly, "Jesus will take care of our planet."

Jim said to John, "I think God allowed us to travel into space the last couple of decades and see the picture of earth from space so that we can compare that picture of healthy earth to this miserable earth condition, and see what happened when the devil took control of our planet."

"I think the angels, too, are unhappy when they compare the conditions of earth at creation with these conditions here," replied John.

Then the saints saw the Antichrist and the kings of the earth and their armies gathered to make war against the Landlord of earth, Jesus, and His army. This gathering was at Megiddo in Israel, a perfect battlefield and a place for war.

"This was the final assault on the kingdom of God," said John, "The devil's last stand and last ditch attempt at rebellion. This is World War III, the battle of the ages. World War II was only a dwarf compared to Armageddon. Right here, number 777 will run into number 666, the Lamb of God verses man of sin, God the Almighty vs. Satan the all nasty."

Then Bill said, "All the kingdoms of the world have come against Him, and He will conquer and take over all the kingdoms of the world. Satan offered these same kingdoms to Him when He was in the desert after forty days of fasting. But Jesus chose the hard way of Calvary to save billions of souls throughout the six thousand years of man's history, a perfect work in the eyes of the Father."

"The nerve of these people thinking that they could overthrow God from His throne!" commented Jim.

"Do you know what the Lord says to such people?" said John," 'Why do the nations assemble with commotion and confusion of voices, and why do the people imagine and meditate upon an empty scheme? The kings of the earth and the rulers take counsel together against the Lord and His Anointed One, the Messiah. They say, 'Let us break their bands asunder and cast their cords of control from us.' He who sits in the Heavens laughs; the Lord has them in supreme contempt He mocks them.'"

Then, Jesus spoke the words and the war on earth stopped; there were no more missiles or flashes. Then it seemed as if the earth was being scanned with a light going around it, ridding it of all demons and the Antichrist and the false prophet and sucking them up in the air.

Jesus destroyed the Antichrist with the brightness of His coming and consumed him with the spirit of His mouth. With a word of His mouth, Jesus destroyed the Antichrist, the false prophet and the demons. Then He sent His angels with a great sound of a trumpet, and they started gathering together His elect from the four winds, from one end of Heaven to the other.

John thought, *as the days of Noah were, they were eating and drinking, marrying and giving in marriage, until the day that Noah entered into the ark, and knew not until the flood came and took them all away; so shall also the coming of the Son of man be. Then shall two be in the field; the one shall be taken, and the other left. Two women shall be grinding at the mill; the one shall be taken, and the other left.*

Then the saints saw an angel coming down out of Heaven, having the key to the Abyss and holding in his hand a great chain. Then the angel seized the dragon, that ancient serpent, which is the devil, or Satan, and bound him.

John looked around to see if JR had been watching all the events that had transpired. And, there was JR with his angel companion.

Then Jim said, "Looks like Satan lost the key to the abyss; he only had it temporarily. Where is the angel taking him?"

John replied, "Satan's time is up, it's curtain time. He will be bound and locked away with a seal in a holding area for a thousand years. The angel will throw him into the Abyss, a layover to keep him from deceiving the nations anymore until the thousand years are ended, then, he must be set free for a short time. After that, he will be cast into Hell."

Then, a saint surprisingly came to the front and asked, "Excuse me, brothers, where is Satan? I want to see him."

"He's over there being taken away by an angel after he was tied down," answered Jim.

"Where is he? I still can't see him," asked the saint.

"Over there," pointed Jim.

The saint had to squint his eyes to be able to see Satan, and finally said, "That over there is Satan! I can't believe it. This is the angel, who deceived the whole world and caused all this trouble! This is the one who shook the earth and made kingdoms tremble! I just wanted to tell him that my ten children he killed back on earth are all here, and are accounted for," continued the man joyfully. "I even got ten more for a total of twenty. I just wanted him to know that I got double for my trouble."

"Brother Job,"said John happily, "it's an honor to meet you. I've read your story. The devil attacked you in chapter two and you held your ground until chapter forty-two. If you would have given up in chapter forty-one, you'd have lost the battle and we'd never have heard of you. You inspired many saints with your example of firmly standing against Satan's attacks. Thank you for that."

"You're welcome, brother. This character tried to make me renounce God, and used my dearest friends and even my wife against me. He caused a lot of pain and suffering to humanity, and when I look at him now, I'm just appalled by his insignificance." said Job.

"Yes, I know. The devil took advantage of being invisible to us on earth, and had mastered the power of suggestion and used it against us," continued John, "but Jesus and the Holy Spirit exposed him for us and that's how we managed to defeat him."

"Look at how he's being dragged away in front of everyone in humiliation, again," said Jim, "An unnamed angel, not Jesus or the archangel Michael or Gabriel, binds the devil with chains. A regular angel becomes his jailer; this is Satan's day of humbling."

The saints saw the Antichrist and the false prophet going in one direction, to the Lake of Fire, while Satan, himself, was being led by an angel in another direction towards the abyss. This was payday for the saints overlooking the events taking place on earth.

Then Jim's guardian angel, Celestiel, appeared. He was dragging Daemon behind him, in chains. Celestiel looked at Jim and said, "I motion that this demon should be thrown in the Lake of Fire. Would anyone like to second this motion?" Jim raised his hand and eagerly said, "I second that motion."

To that replied Celestiel with a smile, "Thank you brother." Then he dragged the demon away heading towards the Lake of Fire. But he stopped, looked back and said, "It was an honor guarding you, Jim, and I'll see you again in the new world."

Jim was lost for words.

"This angel seems very serious about what he is doing!" said John.

"He probably has mixed feelings right now. On the one hand, he doesn't particularly enjoy this assignment," said Jim sadly, "he and Daemon were close friends before the rebellion of Lucifer. On the other hand, he celebrates the fact that he didn't follow Lucifer as Daemon did and became eternally damned."

At that point of time, a black hole appeared with the Lake of Fire at the bottom.

"How is this possible?" said Jim with his eyes wide open in amazement.

"Eyes haven't seen, and ears haven't heard," said John in awe.

Then the captured demons, the false prophets, and the Antichrist were cast alive into the black hole, which contained the fiery lake of burning sulfur also called the Lake of Fire. After they were sucked into the Lake of Fire, the hole closed up, folded itself, and disappeared.

"Talk about a Black Hole," said Bill. "There goes the statue and image of Nebuchadnezzar's dream that was interpreted by the prophet Daniel, completely crushed by a Rock that was cut out, but not by human hands. The final world religion of Babylon the Great has ended and this marks the end of all false religion from the first Babylon to the end of the age. As for Babylon the Great's major players, they are in Hades waiting for judgment day."

"The Heavenly military won the first war ever," said John, "and the armies of Heaven didn't lift a finger, for the outcome was known."

Then an angel, that came out of the temple in Heaven, appeared with a sharp sickle. The angel swung his sickle on the clusters of grapes from the earth's vine because its grapes were ripe, gathered its grapes, and threw them into the great winepress of God's wrath. They were trampled in the winepress outside Jerusalem, and blood flowed out of the press, rising as high as the horses' bridles for a distance of two hundred miles.

"Look at the armies of the Antichrist; they're getting slaughtered. I've never seen so much blood. What a grisly scene," said John.

A nearby resurrected martyred saint said, "Adopt a horse program! In the tribulation, the Antichrist encouraged and later on, enforced every family to raise a horse. If you lived in the city, then you had to pay a horse tax. We saints living during that period wondered why. But now I see that the war of Armageddon was fought on horseback. The use of nuclear Electromagnetic Pulse (EMP) bombs on a global scale rendered all electronic war machinery useless and caused the Antichrist to use horses to advance to the plains of Megiddo. Donkeys became carriers for portable nuclear missile launchers. The rest of the troops were on foot."

John replied, "God is as mad as He gets. The heathens were decimated instantly with the sword, which is the word that came out of the mouth of the Lord Jesus. It was like a death ray from the sky, and Judgment of God on these people."

Then an angel standing in the sun appeared, who cried in a loud voice to all the birds flying in midair, "Come, gather together for the great supper of God, so that you may eat the flesh of kings, generals, and mighty men, of horses and their riders, and the flesh of all people, free and slave, small and great."

And all the birds gorged themselves on the flesh of the heathens; the two-thirds of the Jews population who accepted the Antichrist as God were destroyed also. Though the number of the sons of Israel be like the sand of the sea, only the remnant, one-third, would be saved from perdition, condemnation, and judgment! For the Lord had executed His sentence upon the earth, He had concluded and closed His account with men completely and without delay, rigorously cutting it short in His justice.

"They thought that they had us for lunch when we were raptured," said Bill who stood next to John, "but we were invited to the Lamb's Marriage Supper instead. Look at them now; the greatest blood bath in history. They are the supper, bird food special! No wonder there was an increase in the birth of vultures and birds of prey by leaps and bounds just before the tribulation."

"This place is for the birds," Gracie said. "Do I have to watch this gory scene?"

"Yes," replied John, "This carnival of blood shall pass. But we need to tell the children and grandchildren born during the Millennium what happened here today. Just like the Jews told their children and grandchildren how God dealt harshly with the Egyptians and how He performed His signs among them, that they might know that He is the LORD. The Jews saw the plagues in Egypt and the parting of the Red Sea, and while they crossed the Red Sea safely, Pharaoh's army perished in the sea." Then John thought, *I don't like what's happening on earth now, but am looking forward to the Millennium.*

Then he looked at Jim, as he had been quiet and noticed that tears were flowing down his cheeks. Jim knew that his mother wasn't fit for heaven the way she was, but hoped that she may had a chance of being born again. John remembered that Jim's mother was one of the devil's mislead victims. So he looked back at the brother and sister and signaled them to stop talking. Then he put his hand on Jim's shoulder and said, "I'm very sorry, Jim. Maybe there is a chance that she didn't accept the mark of the beast and survived the —"

"Excuse me, brother Jim!" said a saint who appeared from the crowds on his horse. Jim wiped his tears and looked at the man.

"You don't know me," continued the saint, "I'm one of the tribulation martyred brothers. And I just wanted to tell you that I was executed at the hand of your mother when I was on earth."

Everybody in the circle around Jim paid attention to hear the rest of the story, "What do you mean?" asked Jim.

"Your mother became an agent in the GIA force after she took the mark of the beast; she was no longer the mother you once knew.

These agents were possessed by demons and followed Satan's commands. She was the one who released the sharp blade that cut my head off. Before she executed me, she told me that before she took the mark, she mocked the Jew preacher who approached her to save her soul. She also rejected the angel that delivered a message of hope to her. The day she took the mark, grace ended for her as she sided with Satan in the hope to win in the final battle against God. I'm very sorry for your loss, and it would be my honor if you'd consider me one of your brothers."

Jim was lost for words and didn't know what to say.

"Excuse me, brother," said John, "first of all I want to thank you for encouraging our brother, Jim. But how did you know who Jim was and his relationship to your executor, and how did you know the right moment to come and talk to Jim?"

The saint replied, "The Lord Jesus told me to come here at exactly this time to talk to Jim."

"Praise the Lord. Jim lost a mother, but gained a brother," said John as he looked back at earth to see where Jesus was.

"This has been an incredibly emotional day, full of victory and sadness, and it's not over yet," said Bill. "A sweet-bitter day, never been anything like it before. But we'll probably see another day like this in a thousand years, in World War IV, Satan's final revolt."

John thought, *today feels the same way that JR felt when I saw him eat that book that the angel gave him to eat. Maybe that's what the sweet-bitter sensation in JR's mouth and belly meant, today's events!*

Then the surviving tribulation saints came out of their hiding places to meet the Lord, saying, "Hallelujah." They were jumping up and down, overjoyed at this momentous event and shouted, "The King has come." They were hungry, and the Lord came down as Manna from Heaven. They were thirsty, and the Lord was springs of water to them.

The remnant Jews asked the Lord if this was His first or second coming, and they had their answer when He showed them His wounds. Then they asked, "What are these wounds on your hands?" and He answered and said, "These wounds I was given at the house of my friends." Then He said, "Verily, verily, I say unto you, before Abraham was, I AM."

The Villain is captured

Meanwhile, down at the center of the earth and in the land of gloom and deep shadows.

"Hey, Professor, look who it is, man. Satan, the felon, is back but this time he's all in a chain of some sort of a force field. It looks like he's been arrested. The devil is inside a bubble," said Tom. "Who's that with him, tossing him in here? It looks like his jailer has the key now."

"Wow. Just like what the Bible said. That is one of the good angels acting as his jailer. See, he's locking up Satan in that compartment, the bottomless pit. Armageddon must have just taken place and ended," said the professor.

The angel locked up Satan and as the angel started to leave, Tom said, "Hey angel-man, come back here. Can you help me, please? I don't want to be here in the state of departed spirits. Wait, can you at least let me go back to earth, just so I can warn my brothers to do whatever they can to avoid ending up in this place of doom, like me?"

"He can't help you," said the professor.

"No," Tom replied, "if someone from the dead goes to them, they might repent."

"The angel will probably say, 'Let them listen to the two witnesses, the 144,000 Jews, and the angels; if they don't listen to those, they won't be convinced even if someone from the dead, like you, goes to them.' Besides, it's all over now; your brothers will join us shortly... and here they come," said the professor, as they saw an influx of souls by the millions stampeding into their space.

"Here comes who? Who are these guys?"

"Armageddon casualties; these billions of souls of people were just killed in the biggest battle on earth yet."

"They keep coming, man. Ever since I got here, I noticed that a lot of people are coming in here. When will it stop?"

"The tribulation period had a lot of casualties but they were spread out over the seven year period. Armageddon is a one-hour thrust of souls, after this thrust of souls ends, things will really quite down in here for a thousand years. There might be a trickle of souls occasionally, but nothing more, until the thousand years are over. I sure would like to talk to one of those new arrivals to hear what happened during the tribulation."

"Tribulation, Millennium, where do you come up with all this nonsense?" Tom asked.

"I told you, it's all in the Bible."

"This has got to be a horrible nightmare I'm in. Maybe I overdid the fix. You know, if I'm here because of this character, Satan or Devil, then I'm going to go ask him why he duped me. 'Do your own thing', he said. I want to know why he did this to me."

"Again, Satan means advisory in Hebrew; Devil means slanderer in the Greek translation, and I wouldn't do that if I were you," said the professor.

"Why not?"

"Well for one thing, he's completely sealed in that chamber and isolated. In addition, I just don't think you can out-reason him; out of his desperation, he might try to trick you to get the key and get him out of there."

"The Hell with him, I wouldn't get him out of there even if I had the key," Tom replied.

"Don't be too sure; this guy is very crafty. Fear not them which kill the body, but are not able to kill the soul: but rather fear Satan, which is able to destroy both soul and body in Hell."

"Well, it's too late for that now, isn't it, Professor?"

"You're absolutely right, and I say it again, I don't like the way God does business," the professor replied.

"By the way, how long have you been here?"

"There is no time here, but I know that I lived in the twentieth century. And now if you excuse me, I'd like to talk to one of these tribulation-era souls."

"I'm coming with you, man," Tom said.

Renovated Earth

John and Jim were surveying earth after Armageddon had concluded and the Lord Jesus had established His Messianic kingdom on the earth and ushered in the era of the Millennium kingdom utopia. They were like two tenants eager to inspect their newly built home.

"All those years I recycled," said John, "which was my duty as a citizen in the kingdom of God, and now I see the Lord Jesus recycling the whole planet earth in no time. Jerusalem is the only city left standing after the horror of the tribulation—"

"Praise the Lord," a voice came from behind them. They both looked back and no one was there except the rocks. They looked at each other in amazement, and then the boulders started singing "Hallelujah. Hallelujah."

"Our Lord Jesus did say the stones will cry out," said John cheerfully, and then said to Jim, "Get yourself ready for a one Heaven of a time on this earth for the next thousand years and throughout eternity. Praised be His name. Going to Heaven was a temporary location. Now we're back on the newly renovated earth, where God intended for us to live in the first place.

"Here the same kind of rose with a different color smells differently. Cherries with different colors taste differently. We're seeing new colors in the rainbow. Is it possible that we always had this capability, but the devil busied our lives to the point where we didn't stop and smell the roses enough? We're hearing and singing new

Heavenly music. And that's just the beginning; after the thousand years are over, the Lord will create a new Heaven and Earth."

"What now then?" asked Jim.

"Well, we saw the Lord Emmanuel triumphantly go back to earth, split the Mount of Olives, then He marched down past the garden of Gethsemane, crossed the Kidron Valley, and entered the eastern gate which opened to Him! Then He sat down on David's throne where He will rule for a thousand years. The kingless throne and the throne-less king were united. He has returned to Zion, God is with us, and is dwelling in the midst of Jerusalem, the faithful City of Truth, at the mountain of the Lord of hosts, the Holy Mountain. Right now, the temple in Jerusalem is in the process of being cleansed for the next thirty days from the abomination of the tribulation, and then worship and the feast of the tabernacles will start. There is also the judgment of the nations that survived the tribulation that will take place shortly after."

"Didn't all the bad guys die in the bloodbath of Armageddon? Who will be judged?"

"Some of the Antichrist followers might still be alive, Jews and Gentiles, all the rebels and those who transgress against Him, God will purge them out and separate them from the surviving saints. They're the goats to whom the Lord will say, 'Depart from me, you cursed, into the everlasting fire prepared for the devil and his angels because of the way you treated My brethren, the Jews, during the massive anti-Semitism movement in the Great Tribulation.' On the other hand, the believers who survived, our brothers and sisters, are the sheep. And to those the Lord will say 'Come, you blessed of My Father, inherit the kingdom prepared for you from the foundation of the world' because they helped the Jews during the Great Tribulation. Remember, helping the Jews during that terrible time meant double trouble. Not only did the saints not carry the mark of the beast, but they also helped the most outlawed people, the Jews. It is a miracle that they made it to the end of the tribulation alive. Then there are the Jews who were hiding in Petra; they'll go back to their land and meet their other brethren in Christ, the 144,000 Jews who preached during the tribulation. They will make up the new house of Israel, a Jewish nation with a heart of flesh and a new spirit within them."

"Who would have thought that the Lord loved the Jews like that? We were taught that the Jews blew it, and Christ came for Christians only. You mentioned a feast earlier. Are we having another supper?" Jim asked.

"Four thousand years ago, the Jews celebrated the feast of the tabernacles when God brought them into the Promised Land, after forty years of wandering in the wilderness. In the Kingdom age, we'll celebrate every year in Jerusalem, the capitol city of the new world, by worshiping and participating in the feasts. We'll thank God for bringing us through six thousand years in the wilderness of Satan and a cursed earth, throughout the Old Testament Age and the Church age."

"I haven't seen the martyred saints and the 144,000 Jews since we landed here. Where will they be during the Millennium?"

"The martyred saints are the temple servants waiting on Christ and His bride, the church, in Jerusalem. They serve day and night because their glorified bodies don't tire out. The 144,000 Jews you'll see follow Jesus wherever He goes, just like His twelve disciples did when He was on earth the first time. And we'll be kings and priests during the Millennium."

"I wonder what the temple looks like. What happens after the cleansing is over?"

"The mountain of the Lord's temple will be established as chief among the mountains; it will be raised above the hills, and all nations will stream to it. We will go up to the mountain of the Lord, to the house of the God of Jacob, our everlasting Father and see it soon. The Lord will teach us His ways, so that we may walk in His paths," John answered.

"Will the Lord instruct us on what we do from here on?" asked Jim.

"The Lord will tell us what to do. The law will go out from Zion, the word of the Lord from Jerusalem. The earth shall be full of the knowledge of the Lord as the waters cover the sea. He will put His law within us, and on our hearts He will write it. He will judge between the nations, and will settle disputes for many peoples, a wonderful Counselor. The government will be on His shoulders, of the increase of His government and peace there will be no end. He will reign on David's throne and over His kingdom, establishing and upholding it with justice and righteousness from this time on and forever. The zeal of the Lord Almighty will accomplish this. See, the King will reign in righteousness and we, the rulers, will rule with justice as we walk in the light of the Lord. Yes, many people and strong nations shall come to Jerusalem to seek and inquire of the Lord of hosts, and pray for His favor. The Prince of Peace, will make sure that nation will not take up sword against nation. They will beat their swords into plowshares and their spears into pruning hooks. The God of Heaven has set up a kingdom that will never be destroyed, nor will it be left to another people, and we'll be kings."

"What the United Nations couldn't accomplish, the Lord will," Said Jim. "Imagine, all the earth and the human resources that were wasted on wars in the past will be spared. There won't be weapon-producing plants. The armed forces of Navy, Air Force, and Army won't exist in the new order. No more boot camp or military schools. They won't train for war anymore."

"Even the animal kingdom will obey His commands. The wolf will live with the lamb and feed together; the leopard will lie down with the goat, the calf, the lion, and the yearling together. The cow will feed with the bear, their young will lie down together, and the lion will eat straw like the ox! The infant will play near the hole of the cobra, and the young child will put his hand into the viper's nest. They will neither harm nor destroy on his entire holy mountain," John explained.

"Great, the animals will be tame. I used to like watching animal shows on TV, but didn't like the part where there were vicious killings and bloodshed. And now, there will be no more eating blood or shedding it. I haven't seen any mosquitoes yet. So if God decides to keep them, they have to suck on flowers. Vampire bats are probably eating fruit like their other cousins. All kinds of meat are off the menu, including the other white meat. Everyone is either a vege-tarian or fruitarian." Jim said.

"A fruitarian, that's a new word for the dictionary. As I was saying, the human condition will improve, too, for those who made it out of the tribulation with their physical bodies and for their offspring. Never again will there be in the Kingdom age an infant who lives but a few days—"

"Good bye to Sudden Infant Death Syndrome, SIDS."

"Yes, and no more old men who don't live out their years. For as the days of a tree, so will be the days of His people; he who dies at a hundred will be thought a mere youth. He who fails to reach a hundred will be considered accursed.

"Time has no meaning any more for the righteous. We won't hurry to get anywhere; instead, look, stop and smell every flower on the way. We have a lot of time for sightseeing a beautiful world. People won't say, 'life is too short, let's see what we can see, and build our wealth fast before we die,' anymore. Or say, 'let's eat and drink and be merry for tomorrow we die.' No more broken up lives. No more cancer, stroke, or heart attack." John thought, *No more migraine headaches or PMS*, then continued, "The undertakers and the medical profession might as well retire or find another occupation. We won't need doctors, nurses, pharmacists, medical schools and medical supplies, hospitals, or ambulances. Imagine being free to do other things we enjoy doing instead of having to do all the unpleasant things we had to do.

"We will build houses and dwell in them; we will plant vineyards and eat their fruit." John continued, "No longer will we build houses and others live in them, or plant and others eat. His chosen ones will long enjoy the works of their hands. We can plant if we want, but fruit is available for the picking. The saints with physical bodies will not toil in vain or bear children doomed to misfortune, for we and the saints with physical bodies and their descendants with them are a people blessed by the Lord. Before we call, the Lord will answer; while we're still speaking, He will hear. Every man will sit under his own vine and under his own fig tree, and no one will make us afraid."

"Goodbye to foreclosures and bankruptcy, and nobody will worry about the stock market crashing. I guess we won't even need money, credit cards, wallets, or keys. And the land is beautiful, there's no desert to be found. I really enjoy doing physical work rather than a desk job. There will be no disabilities," said Jim, "We shall bless and praise Him all day long. Is this our final destination then?"

"We have a Millennium to live on this renovated earth. We will rule on the same earth that Satan had ruled previously. However, the best is yet to come. We're looking forward to a new Heaven and a new Earth, the home of righteousness, and it will be spectacular. The Lord will destroy the atmosphere and the skies with a thunderous crash, where Satan, the prince of the power of the air, and demons lived and performed spiritual wickedness."

"Talk about a big bang. Ha!"

"Yeah, really. He will also destroy the earth and everything in it with fire and create a new one. Just as all of us saints were born again, so will the sky and the earth have to be born again. But before that, and when the thousand years is over, the devil will be released one last time."

Jim became disheartened and asked, "What for, why let him out?"

"To test those who will hear the gospel for the first time. The tribulation saints who survived the tribulation with their physical bodies, unlike us, will be able to procreate on the earth. They still belong to a fallen race, and the complete effects of the fall of Adam and Eve have not been wiped out from their blood. Therefore, their offspring will still have a human sinful nature. The scriptures say, 'Every inclination of man's heart is evil from childhood.' You don't need the devil to sin for sin is from the flesh. Satan only creates the environment that stimulates the flesh and exposes the rebellious heart. This will prove the Humanist wrong when they proclaim that they can change the world by changing society, and that evil is rooted in society. It will also prove conclusively that changing the environment doesn't change the world either. The only way the world can change is by changing the heart of man by the power of the Holy Spirit.

"In the end, all the people who will be born during the millennial kingdom would have equal opportunity to decide to follow God or Satan. They still have to choose whether they follow Jesus or reject Him, and Satan will be used to trigger the opposition. As for those who rebel before the thousand years is over, they will die at an early age of a hundred."

"Surely those who live when Jesus is among them would believe Him and reject the devil!" Jim said.

"Jesus lived among them for thirty-three years the first time. He loved them, healed them, and fed them, but they still didn't believe in Him and nailed Him to the cross."

"How does the Millennium end?"

"When Satan is released at the end of the Millennium, there will be enough evil resident in the heart of man, that many will reject Him. A thousand years of confinement doesn't change Satan's nature either. He will lead astray and deceive and seduce the nations, and give them an opportunity to rebel and organize war. They will follow him for one final revolt against the righteous government of Jesus Christ, and be destroyed and go to the final Great White throne Judgment. As for Satan, he will be thrown in the Lake of Fire for eternity."

"How would Satan convince the nations to rebel? The same tactic he used with Eve, maybe!"

"Perhaps through a conflict with God over power and leadership and maybe even a conflict over worship again. Also, when Moses was leading, his sister and brother wanted leadership and had conflicts and it ended disastrously for his sister. Even Jesus' disciples argued about who will be the greatest in Heaven. And just before the Rapture, denominations had conflict over whom would lead and who had the most power and influence. Each denomination thought that they had the best formula for salvation, even though there is only one faith, one God, and one baptism."

Jim said, "I think I'll be one of those who follow the devil to my doom."

John looked at Jim with astonishment.

"No...um..., I'm just kidding. I know that sin has no dominion over our glorified bodies. I was just having fun with you. I apologize."

"I should hope so; I mean, every resurrected saint should know the basics by now. Sin controlled us through Satan, our body, and the world. Satan is confined, our bodies have been resurrected, and the world is in perfect condition. Our eternity is secure," John explained.

While they were talking, one of the saints who had survived the tribulation and still had her physical body ran to Jim and hugged him. They had a joyful gathering and caught up on things.

John thought, *there won't be a need to ask anyone how he or she is doing any more. Everyone is feeling great in this world.*

"This is my cousin Kim," said Jim, "Her parents were atheists, never went to church or kept a Bible at home. We separated when she was a kid and haven't seen each other for ages."

"Hi, Kim," said John.

"Hi. Thank God for the angels He sent. I almost took the mark but they shared the gospel with me just in time," she said. Then she got some food out of her pocket and started eating.

"You sure seem to have a good appetite," remarked Jim.

"Listen, cousin, I have been starving for over three years and I'm going to eat whatever I want now. Look at me. I'm skin and bone. Plus, I can eat all I want and not worry about getting fat," said Kim as she smiled and seemed happy. "All the stupid diets I've been following before the Rapture to extend life for a couple of months, what a joke! I have an unlimited extension to my life now. Here, would you like some? There is plenty where this came from." Kim smiled as she handed him some of what she was eating.

"Thanks, I'm not hungry," replied Jim.

"Is it because of your new body?"

"No, I still eat just like the Lord Jesus ate with His disciples after His resurrection. John is also a pre-rapture brother, my best friend, brother in the faith, and my local leader," said Jim as he introduced John.

"Hi, John," said Kim, then she asked Jim, "What do you mean by your leader?"

Jim replied, "There is order in the Kingdom. I'm going to teach you and your children salvation through the saving faith of our Lord Jesus Christ. It will be a whole new world-wide educational system and I'll serve as one of the shepherds reporting to John here," pointing at John and continued, "who will be the mayor of this city. He, in turn reports to Bill, the governor, and so on. We all serve under and over others; the degree of authority is based on the faithfulness in the previous life. Then, we all report to and get our instructions from the one spiritual and government leader, the Lord Jesus."

Kim seemed troubled by the new order of things and said, "You know, I was the one who went through the three and a half years of Hell on earth while you guys were raptured before the big storm came and had a good time in Heaven. My best friend was beheaded in the tribulation period and she is assigned to be a judge in this city. I suffered the most and I should be the one having these privileges."

Jim said, "Why do you harbor evil in your heart? Be careful and get rid of these thoughts of resentment. There is still a sheep and goats judgment you have to go through before you enter the Kingdom age. If you keep this up, you might just not make it through that."

"Oh, I'm guaranteed to be a sheep for I helped the Jews at the tribulation, endangering myself. He already promised."

"Ok, so you'll live through the Kingdom age. But if you keep these thoughts and pass them along to your children and their children, one day at the end of the Millennium, Satan will be released and he'll use these thoughts to destroy you all, by rebelling against God's order. And you and your children will fall into his trap, and then you'll lose the little you think you have. You'll lose everything including your soul. Don't forget what happened with Moses and his sister when she wanted to rule too, and she was hit with leprosy."

"Yes, but Moses' sister saw the Red Sea part and she still sinned afterwards."

Jim sent a spiritual thought to John, *what's wrong with her, why is she talking like this, and where is this stinking thinking coming from?*

John replied back with a thought, *remember, when we lived in the sinful flesh and blood in the Adamic nature, we thought and acted similarly. So many times, I did and said things that later I wondered why did I just say or do that. And then I regretted and wished that I could take back or undo these things. I'm sure the angels wondered too, why we acted like that. But the Lord knew why and forgave. Blessed be His name.*

Jim sent back a question, *are the two cultures, the glorified and the physical saints, going to clash?*

John answered, *all I know is that Jesus will rule with a rod of iron.*

The spiritual messages went back and forth at the speed of light so that Kim wasn't aware of them. Jim looked at Kim and continued, "But she had the desert conditions and Satan was working against her. You, on the other hand, are living in a paradise regained and have dominion over earth, and Satan is in incarceration. So, you're living in a sinless environment. Moreover, when the Millennium is over we might all be equal in respect to our bodies and, possibly, position in the new world. All things will be new; we won't even remember this conversation."

John was also saddened by Kim's attitude, and thought, *oh my Lord, it is not over yet, and temptation and sin still abound.*

"I'm sorry, cousin, please forgive me. I don't want the devil to get me in the end! And I thank God in advance for the new me in the new world to come because I have memories and images in my mind from things I did before I was born again that I wish I could erase right now, but I don't seem to be able to. So, I really look forward to that day when I won't remember all the garbage that the devil had stuffed my mind with," Kim replied.

"Amen. You're on the right track, cousin. Just ask the King and God of Glory for forgiveness and obey Him, so you can enjoy His grace. Love Him with all your heart and strength, meditate on His words, bring your future children and come with us to Jerusalem once a year, and see the Lord, to get instructions from Him."

John was impressed by the manner that Jim handled his cousin, showing the traits of a teacher already. As he was thinking that, he noticed that Kim had fallen on the ground and her leg was bleeding. So he rushed to the scene where Jim was already bent down to help her and asked, "Are you all right, sister?" as he bent down, too.

"I don't know," she answered.

"Well, let me put some pressure on it," said Jim.

Then Jim looked at John in shock. Kim saw that and was alarmed and asked, "What, what's the matter?"

"Did you hear that?" asked Jim.

"Hear what?" asked Kim.

"You didn't hear a cry for help?" asked Jim again.

"No! Who cried for help?"

John looked at Jim and they spiritually communicated, *you know when Cain killed his brother, God said to Cain, 'Listen! Your brother's blood cries out to me from the ground.' Praise the Lord for a talking blood. There is so much significance in the blood that we never understood before. We knew that the life of the flesh is in the blood. But now we know that blood is alive. Thank God for the blood of Jesus in our lives.*

Kim impatiently said, "Ok guys, are you having a moment or what? Who cried for help?"

"Your blood did. It spoke and we both heard it," said John.

Jim kept the pressure on the wound with his hand.

"Well, how come I didn't hear it then?" asked Kim.

"I guess you need a glorified body with all the whistles and gadgets, to hear and see these things," said Jim, and then lifted his hand to check on the wound. The wound was healed completely. Jim smiled and sent out a spiritual communiqué to John, *I guess we have the gift of healing built into our bodies!*

John was overjoyed and said, "Hallelujah, I feel a psalm coming on. The Lord is my Shepherd. He gave me this paradise. He never stops to amaze me every day with new gifts and things to see, sounds to hear, and food to taste and smell." Then John looked at Jim and sent him a thought, *I just feel like going to visit with the Lord Jesus and thank Him for what He has done for us. I just want to sit by His feet and see what He is going to say and do next. The ideas of God go on for all eternity.*

Jim thought back, *I'm coming with you,* then he said to Kim, "I'll see you later, cousin." And the two disappeared.

* * * * * * *

Seventy-five days into the Millennium, John was surveying the lands of his territory from the sky, when he came across the remnants of Noah's ark. He stopped to inspect what most people thought to be 'a legendary boat'. A man came out of the ark, which he recognized to be Noah. John was happy to see him again at first, but then he noticed that a young T-REX was following closely behind him. At first, John was nervous to see a T-REX approaching, but when the T-REX reached for a fruit on a tree, on the way, and ate it, he remembered the lion eats straw now. Then said, "Noah, what are you doing with that once extinct dinosaur?"

"Hello, John. I had a baby behemoth for a pet before the flood," replied Noah.

"Is that what you call this carnivore, which seems to be vegetarian now?" asked John.

"Yes. When I told my grandson that there was a time, before the flood, when these creatures ate only grass and fruits like an ox, he didn't believe me either. See, when dinosaurs started eating other animals, after the flood, they became a threat to man. Actually, T-REX wasn't a predator; he stole other animals' kill, just like lions steal from hyenas sometimes. Nevertheless, civilized men didn't want them around their villages, so they drove the beasts away or killed them. Also, after the flood, God allowed us to eat meat, so some people hunted those huge animals for meat and ate them.

"I sure am glad to see earth having the same pre-flood conditions back. After the flood, we got out of the ark and saw that it was a different ball game. Things changed on earth and the atmosphere that surrounded it. There was a reduction in the amount of oxygen in the air. I noticed that we weren't able to run a long distance without getting tired. There was a reduction in the amount of air pressure, too, after the flood. Before the flood, wounds healed faster because the air pressure was doubled or tripled, which increased the blood circulation."

"We had to dive under water to get that same level of pre-flood high air pressure. Later on, they invented hyperbaric chambers, which had double the air pressure and concentrated oxygen, and they used these chambers to heal people," said John.

"In addition, there was a thin layer of water or canopy covering the atmosphere before the flood. This layer protected us by filtering out the ultraviolet light and harmful x-rays. But that layer collapsed after the flood. I met some brothers in Paradise who told me that man's days were shortened after the flood to a very short life span compared to my generation, who lived over nine hundred years. I also noticed my grandchildren didn't grow as tall; they were only six to seven feet, compared to I and my sons who grew up to nine feet."

"Do you know how long man lived in my time? Less than a hundred years."

"You don't say! How do you get to do anything and have children?"

"We got married at the age of twenty or thirty—"

"A babe!"

"Because people knew that they only lived a short time, they hurried to get things done. Tell me about the Ark, Noah," asked John.

"Well, I built the ark, and the younger baby animals came in two's and the ark was full. At first, it seemed as if I built the ark larger than needed. See, I didn't know how long the flood was going to last. As time went by, the baby animals grew up in size and filled the ark perfectly. Have you seen a baby alligator or a baby dinosaur, a couple of inches long, but they sure grow fast. The Lord thinks of every angle in every way; that is why I learned to trust Him. He gave me a mind to think, but He is the ultimate thinker and it pays to listen to Him. Amen."

Then Noah looked and pointed at the Ark and continued, "This piece of art sure brings back memories. You know one of the tribulation survivors told me that this Ark came drifting down the mount of Ararat at the time the sun melted all of the world's ice caps during the tribulation and landed here when the river dried up."

"I'd have liked to have seen the Antichrist explain away that one." Then John pointed at the T-REX and said," Unfortunately, the devil took advantage of the newly discovered bones of these dinosaurs and spread lies about their origin and existence. The End times generation was convinced, by seducing spirits, of a theory called Evolution. We Christians called it Devilution,"

"What's that?" Noah asked.

"Well, first they said that dinosaurs lived millions of years before humans ever existed and that they became extinct and disappeared before humans appeared on planet earth."

"Wait a minute! If the dinosaurs died before Adam sinned, then that would mean that there was death before sin," said Noah. "We know that sin entered the world through one man, Adam, and death through sin, and in this way death came to all men, because all sinned. Also, death reigned from the time of Adam and before Adam there was no death in the Garden of Eden."

"You're absolutely right, their theory is pure heresy. The Apostle Peter prophesized that in the End times false teachers and scoffers would come and mislead many. The devilutionists also said that the origin of mankind was a monkey, who evolved through millions of years," John explained.

"A monkey! Why did they think that? Did they see any monkey evolve? And, why didn't all the monkeys evolve? Why are monkeys still among us?" Noah went on.

"They knew that no one would buy this theory so they said that it took billions of years for the evolution to take place. Just a theory somebody dreamed up; and they were teaching it to our children at an age as early as five and six years old. Woe to them, in Hades now, those who caused one of these little ones who believed in the Lord to sin, by teaching them evolution, and that the origin of man was a rock. It would be better for them to have a rock hung around their necks and to be drowned in the depths of the sea."

"Did you live in a pagan kingdom or under a pagan king, brother?" asked Noah.

"No, they're mostly Christians! Yet, some doubted the story of Adam and Eve. The devil got into the government, and the government enforced the teaching that the world evolved millions of years ago and got the masses confused about the origin of mankind."

"My grandfather sat on Adam's lap, and he himself told me the story of Adam and Eve. And, before Adam, there was only God and the angels. Now you tell me, where are the big red waters I saw when we came down from Heaven?" asked Noah.

"I think the earth swallowed them back, reversing the effects of the flood. At the flood, all the springs of the great deep burst forth from the belly of the earth, and the earth has been asking for them back by groaning through earthquakes and volcanoes, which we'll never ever see again. It's like she got her lubrication back and she's happy. Those large bodies of waters we call oceans; they caused separation between continents and man. In the future new earth, there will be no sea at all."

"You know, the whales swam in shallow waters before the flood, but after the flood, we didn't see much of them anymore. It seemed as if they liked the deep waters," said Noah.

"The Lord has designed them so that their bodies can take different levels of water pressure. Because their body is so long, they could be in different levels of water pressure at the same time when they dive vertically. The various parts of its long body can miraculously adjust to the different water pressure zones."

"I don't know what all that means; I let the Creator worry about these design issues. As for volcanoes and earthquakes, we never had those before the flood either. And there also were no mountains before the flood," Noah explained.

"They disappeared, too, at the end of the tribulation. Maybe the earthquakes of the tribulation period leveled them down, it started with the splitting of the Mount of Olives and the others followed. Or maybe they just walked to the oceans and filled them. On the other hand, maybe the ocean's water level got higher from global warming and covered the islands, which are mountains in the sea. At any rate, they might come back when the Lord creates the new earth."

While they were speaking, a man, who was running fast, approached the two, and said from a distance, "You must be Noah."

"Yes, brother, I am. What can I do for you, brother?" replied Noah.

"Hello, I'm one of the tribulation survivors and I just ran fifty miles straight to talk to you."

John thought, *for a man who just ran fifty miles, he sure doesn't seem to be sweating much or running out of breath,* So John took a couple of deep breaths himself and it felt good because of the oxygen concentration. Then he thought, *this man had no trouble finding Noah. I guess from now on, men won't have to ask for directions.*

"Well, where I live, the sea has subsided, and the bottom of the sea has been exposed," said the man, "so we found massive graves of people who seem to be twelve to fifteen foot tall, and have a huge bone structure. I thought for sure you'd know something about these giants."

"Yes indeed, they were the reason for the flood. These evil giants had built the early monumental buildings of the early civilizations."

"You know, up until our time," said John, "we still didn't have any explanation as for how or who built these massive structures. Some people suggested that aliens came down to earth, built them and left."

"The only aliens I know of are the fallen angels," said Noah. "These fallen angels, the sons of God, left their glorified bodies which we were looking forward to getting, and cohabitated with the daughters of men and had children by them. They saw that the human females were beautiful, and they married any of them they chose. The product was a race of hybrid humans called Nephilim and they were on the earth in my days—and also afterward. They were the heroes of old, men of renown. These strange giants used the domesticated dinosaurs to help them build the large structures. The giants were so huge they could ride the dinosaurs like we ride horses."

"People in India have been known to use elephants to uproot trees and pull heavy loads," said John.

"Behemoth has about twenty times the amount of power that the elephant has. The demonized giants, themselves, had tremendous power."

"Like Hercules! Or was that just a Greek myth?" wondered John.

"I don't know who that was, but I met a brother in Paradise, an Old Testament saint, who had a blessing from God for incredible strength even though he wasn't a giant or had any relationship with the giants."

"You must be talking about Samson," said John.

"Did all the giants die in the flood?" asked the man.

"Yes, as you saw their bones," said Noah, "these giants were teaching Godly people of my generation, evil and wicked things. That's why God had to destroy them with the flood. When the giants died, their spirits were released and became evil spirits and demons and they dwelled on the earth and tormented mankind. The minute we landed on dry land, one of my sons, Ham the father of Canaan, started acting weird so I cursed him."

"More giants sprung up after the flood and the king, David, and his men finished off the last of the remnant giants," said John. "That's why Satan got angry and deceived David into taking a census and counting his men, which angered God because he depended on his might in numbers rather than depending on God. David killed the physical giants but Jesus, the seed of David, came along and defeated all of the supernatural seed of Satan; the spirits of the giants and evil spirits, demons, principalities, powers, rulers of darkness of the previous world, wicked spirits in high places of old. As for the original fallen angels, their body transformation was a one-way transformation and they got stuck in our dimension. They are locked up so that they wouldn't reproduce the Nephilim race again."

Then the man looked at John and asked, "Excuse me sir, don't I know you?"

John replied, "I'm not sure!"

The man asked, "Did you work for a marketing company? I was the vice president of finance there."

John answered with excitement, "Yes, I did! And I remember you now. My name is John."

"I heard you died before the rapture."

"Yes. Did you go through the tribulation? Of course you did, you still have your physical body."

"It was a terrible experience. You know, I was wondering why you didn't share the Lord Jesus with me."

John replied with shame, "You had the Hindu hat on and we were pressured by laws not to speak and share the truth of the Bible—"

"If you think witnessing was hard then, you should see what happened in the tribulation period. I ran to the countryside. Some days I wished that they'd just chopped my head off and get it over with. So I came out of hiding and, amazingly, they didn't capture me. After I ate a little bit, I decided that I didn't want to have my head chopped off. Then they ran after me and I hid again. I guess God wanted me to populate earth now. One time I managed to find a huge believers' camp where we had regular meetings and worshipped together. That's where I met my Christian wife. We marked our calendar daily waiting for the Lord's return. One day, while we were in hiding, a large army of GIA agents surrounded us. We ran to a nearby cave, but they flushed us out with tear gas and smoke. We, about a hundred of us, thought that this was it, we were doomed. All of a sudden, hornets came out of nowhere and attacked the GIA agents. They ran into the nearby woods, jumping up and down and swinging their arms around their faces. Later, we found them all dead in the woods. It was a miracle; the hornets only attacked the GIA agents and didn't come after us."

"Praise God, Are you married then?"

"Yes, a man named Jim, the greatest teacher in town, performed the marriage ceremony a couple of months ago."

"Yes, I know Jim. He reports to me."

"Are you the mayor of this town?"

"Yes, I am."

"There was a day when I was a VP and you were a clerk. Now I'm a citizen and you're the mayor. That's OK. Every day I live here on this beautiful earth, is worth a million days in the old heap of earth. You know what I'm doing now? I've become a florist; I love flowers. My wife, who used to be a doctor, is now the best vegetarian stew maker in town. You've got to come to our baby dedication and taste her stew."

"All right."

"Is it true that you guys can't have sex?"

"Yes, it's true. We have a new glorified body and mind and there is no Satan to influence our thoughts. God created sex and He can control it. I still love my wife like any other sister and brother, but the ultimate love is towards God..."

"What does a glorified body feel like?"

"It feels as strong as Samson, as wise as Solomon, and speaks like a child, innocent, no political correctness or hidden agenda in our speech. And we don't get sick..."

As they were talking, a group of people came out of the Ark and walked towards Noah. Noah said, "I was giving a tour of the Ark to my brothers, earlier. We're going swimming in the Dead Sea, next. I hear it's loaded with fish now."

John recognized a few of the brothers and thought, *praise God. Samson's hair isn't long now; Jacob isn't limping anymore.*

Adam was the first to approach them.

"Hello, Brother Adam, is this renovated earth as good as the Garden of Eden?" asked John.

"I have moved three times already," replied Adam. "I was downgraded from the Garden of Eden to the cursed earth. Later on, when I died in the body, my soul moved to Paradise, where I had a family reunion with Abel and Eve. Then one time, the Lord Jesus, whom I missed very much from the Garden days, came and moved us to a better place in Heaven to be with Him. Now I've come to this new and blessed place, and I'm told that this is still not the final destination, so I'm sure that I'll be moving again."

"How do you compare this to the Garden of Eden?"

"It's no Garden of Eden, not when mortals with their sinful nature inhabit it."

The death of Death

A thousand years later, in the dungeons of earth's center.
"Hey look, Professor. They're letting Satan out; he's unchained and at large. He sure is a busy character," continued Tom bitterly. "Did someone give him a get out of jail card?"

"Yes, the Millennium must be over and another blood bath is about to ensue. As for Satan, he's been given a short visa; we should be seeing him soon, in the Lake of Fire."

"This is some crazy world, man," Tom replied.

Then they heard a noise, felt shaking, and a very bright light started shining. The two covered their eyes completely. "What in the Hell is this blinding light, and where is it coming from?" asked Tom.

"We're being transferred to a new dimension, the Great White Throne and that light is coming from God's presence. We're going to be judged in His courtroom next."

"Can we go back to the dark place after that? My eyes can't take all this light."

"No, after the judgment we'll be transferred to our final destination, and that will be Hell, the Lake of Fire."

"You know what? I can feel my hands pressing on my face," excitedly said Tom.

"We have just been given a resurrection body."

"Now you're talking, I want a body already. I like this resurrection business, man."

Then, they slowly removed their hands from their eyes as they adjusted to the new light.

"Hey, at least this is a body I can feel, man. Even though it's not the greatest, it is still better than being in that freaky spirit state."

"Well, it turns out that we were always a spirit. The physical body we shed while we lived on earth was only temporary, but the spirit lives forever."

"What did you call this, resurrection?"

"This is the second resurrection. Actually, this isn't good news. We were born once and we'll die twice," replied the professor.

"I know that I died before, when my soul and body separated. What is the second death business?"

"The first death was physical. After the judgment, we'll be cast into the Lake of Fire forever, like Satan down there," the professor pointed down to the Lake of Fire. There, was the awful and fearful scene of divine judgment and the fury of burning wrath and righteous anger of God, which consumed those who put themselves in opposition to God.

"Would you look at that fire and sulfur," said Tom, as chills went down his newly resurrected body spine, out of fear.

"That is one fire that shall never be quenched. Death held the body, Hades held the soul, and now both soul and body go to the Lake of Fire."

"There is Satan again. Is this guy everywhere or what?" asked Tom.

"Actually, this is his first existence in Hell, contrary to the widespread belief that he was living there from the beginning of time. Look down there; this time he appears to be heading towards a special chamber in the Lake of Fire where he will be tormented the most. He has profaned his sanctuaries by the multitude of his iniquities and the enormity of his guilt. Therefore, God has brought forth a fire from his midst; it has consumed him. All who knew him among the people are astonished and appalled at him; he has come to a horrible end and shall never return to being."

"Who are all these winged ones with him down there?"

"These are multitudes of demons and fallen angels. These cohorts followed the demonic thug in his rebellion against the order of righteousness in heaven."

"Who are these?" Tom pointed at the only two humans present in the Lake of Fire, so far.

"According to the tribulation-era person we talked to earlier; the two men down there must be the Antichrist and the False Prophet, Satan's two human hooligans in crime."

Then there was another noise and shaking and a great multitude of people started dumping into the other side of the Judgment room.

"Boy, this sure is a busy place. Who are these now?" asked Tom.

"The Millennium must have just concluded. These are they who were deceived by Satan, rebelled against God, were killed by fire from Heaven and now they are coming here. The sea gave up the dead that were in it also, those who died at sea, or were cremated and their ashes thrown at sea. They're all joining us here in Hades."

The two watched the souls come in for a long time, for they numbered as the sand of the sea.

"Hey, let's talk to one of the Millennium-era people to find out what happened down there," suggested the professor.

"I'm coming with you, man."

"Excuse me, friend. Can you tell us a little bit about what happened up there, and how you ended down here?"

"My grand, grandfather was a survivor of the tribulation-era," said the woman. "He told me about the horrible judgment of God that took place at Armageddon. As I grew up, I was told that there were rules to follow and a God to worship and that we must go and see Him in Jerusalem every year. I particularly didn't like the resurrected saints; they thought that they were better than us and went around like they owned the place. I didn't care very much for the way they exercised their rod of iron ruling. I mean, we couldn't smoke some of the plants that gave pleasure—"

Tom interrupted, "Oh, how I miss these plants, and drugs, and—"

The professor interrupted Tom, "Would you let the woman finish!"

She continued, "There was no elicit sex to happen with His plan, no alcohol, no gambling, etc. Basically, no indulgence of the flesh whatsoever."

"What happened if you were caught?" asked the professor.

"The dictator had hordes of governors and judges, and they dealt swiftly and with no appeal with those who dared to break the rules. My brother, whom I'm looking for, died at an early age because he rebelled."

"What's an early age?" asked Tom.

"He didn't make it to hundred years."

Tom looked at the professor and with shock said, "A hundred! This is early."

The woman continued, "However, there was no other alternative to Him, so we put up with it. We praised Jesus on the outside but in our heart, we were seething with vengeance. Until one day our eyes were opened, and I and others like me from all the nations in the four corners of the earth felt that we didn't have to put up with this and gathered for battle."

"That was when Satan was released," said the professor to Tom. "I'm sorry, go ahead, and please continue."

"We marched across the breadth of the earth and surrounded the camp of God's people, the city He loves, Jerusalem. However, fire came down from Heaven and devoured us. And here we are."

"So, you're saying that God allowed you to have sex for a thousand years to populate the earth for this experiment, to see who would take the side of God and who would take the side of Satan, a testing ground for the good and the evil. When I see Him face to face, I'll tell Him that I don't like the way He did things," said the professor.

"Look, guys," said the woman, "I'm looking for my older brother who dropped dead suddenly. Have you guys seen him? He came here about twenty years ago."

"No, Sorry. Hey, Professor, that's my wife down there," said Tom while pointing down in the Lake of Fire, "what's her name...? What is she doing there?"

"The judgment must have started already. I see more people populating Gehenna. Hades is shrinking in size as Hell is being populated, and when Hades is emptied it will be thrown into Hell, too."

"Gehenna, what's that?"

"The Lake of Fire is also referred to as Gehenna in Hebrew. In Jesus' time, the occupants of the city of Jerusalem used to throw their trash in a valley just outside the city where it burned day and night. That's where the name came from, an old times sanitation technique."

"Well, that's just great, man." Tom looked at his wife, whose name was Elizabeth, and said, "Wife, I'm coming to join you, honey," but then he looked and saw his mistress there too and said, "Oh no, that's not good."

"Hey, what line is this?" asked the person in front of them whose soul had just come in with the new shipment.

"Judgment line," replied the professor.

"Why are you so worried? Did you do bad things?"

"No, I didn't. I didn't do good things, either. Even worse I didn't think God existed and here we are, ironically, in His courtroom," said the professor as the line of people moved forward.

"Hey, don't worry. I hear the old man is a merciful God. If God is good and fair, then He should overlook my sins. After all, I consider myself a good man. That Lake of Fire is for the devil and his demons only."

The professor thought, *how long is this guy going to fool himself? Doesn't he see all these people down in the Lake of Fire? He thinks that God is full of Grace and so eager to save him from Hell, that He will change His nature and universal principles.*

Then a man approached the two and said, "Do you guys know how to get to the good side? I'm trying to locate a person."

"What's your story, man?" asked Tom.

"On earth, I molested my daughter-in-law, Carol, and she left home and became a prostitute, bringing shame to my reputation. A couple of years later, she came home and told her mother what I did. Do you believe this lying tattle tale nasty kid?"

Tom was intrigued by what the man just said and asked, "No, what happened next?"

"Well, her unappreciative mother turned on me, after I'd been taking care of her for years. She took her daughter and hid at some Christian shelter. I looked for them for three days with no luck. I had a very high position in the government and if the news got out, it would have ruined my career. So when I heard from close friends that the news did get out, I blew my head up. I'd rather go to Hell than lose my position, and that's how I got here. I've been looking for them here to take revenge. I'll kill them and have the last laugh, but they're not here. Can anyone tell me how to get to other side?"

"There is a big gap between us and no one can cross over," said the professor as the two moved forward.

Later, Stephanie's father and the rich man from the hospital incident walked by. He asked, "Where is the nearest bank? How can I get to the other side where my wife and daughter are? I have influence; I'm a rich man; I have acquired wealth and don't need a thing."

"He left all that behind when he checked out," said the professor to Tom, "somebody should tell that man that there are no ATMs in here. It is easier for a camel to go through the eye of a needle than for a rich man to enter into the kingdom of God. What good will it be for a man if he gains the whole world, yet forfeits his soul? Or what can a man give in exchange for his soul?"

Tom looked at the professor and was surprised at what he just said.

Another man said, "I'm a Jew. How could I be here? I have connections with the judge who is a Jew also. Surely, He'll have mercy on me. How could the Gentiles be enjoying Heaven and not me?"

The professor said privately to Tom, "His blind religious leaders shut the kingdom of Heaven in his face, for these hypocrites neither entered themselves, nor did they allow those who were about to go in to do so. Then they would say, 'We ate and drank with you, and you taught in our streets.' But He will reply, 'I don't know you or where you come from. Away from me, all you evildoers! There will be weeping here, and gnashing of teeth, when you see Abraham, Isaac and Jacob and all the prophets in the kingdom of God, but you yourselves thrown out. People will come from east and west and north and south, and will take their places at the feast in the kingdom of God. Indeed, there are those who are last who will be first, and first who will be last.'"

Tom got frustrated and said, "Would you shut up with these Bible verses! Are you trying to get us killed here? Do you see anyone around here interested in what you're saying?"

"I'm sorry; it's a habit. I've become an automated Bible encyclopedia."

"Shut up, just shut up, man... This line seems to take forever, not that I'm in hurry or anything."

Then they heard some people's cheers, coming from the other side. The two went to see what was going on. They asked someone and he said that they were putting God on judgment.

Tom said, "All right, man. Let's go check it out."

The first man in the group spoke and said, "I was a Jew who was killed in the holocaust by the Nazis. I have a mark on my body to identify me as a Jew. Where was God then and what does He know about our pain?"

Another man said, "I was a slave. They took me out of my country and put me on a ship to a foreign land. I was ridiculed and taken advantage of. Has God suffered like me?"

Another man said, "Look at my blisters and sores; I was a child when they dropped the nuclear bomb on us. Where was God then?"

Another man said, "We're sentencing God to go down to earth and be born a man and live His life a poor man, betrayed by His best friend and killed by His own people."

The professor walked away and said, "These fools don't know what they're talking about."

Tom followed and said, "No, man, this is going good. What's wrong with that?"

"Don't you see? Whatever they are sentencing God to do, God did all that already. He was beaten, mocked, and crucified."

Tom was disappointed and asked, "So, tell me professor, what else did you do on earth regarding your strange career?"

"I wrote a book."

"What about? No, don't tell me. It's about God or the Bible!"

"Actually, it was about Jesus. I said that He was just an ordinary good man."

Tom's eyes opened wide.

The professor continued, "That His mother, Mary, was raped and Jesus was the product of that act."

Tom jumped out of his spot in line and said, "You did what?"

When he jumped back, he stepped on the toes of the person standing behind him. So he looked back to apologize and saw Adolf Hitler. Then, he jumped back three more steps this time, to get away from him.

"I don't believe this; I shouldn't be put in the same line with you freaks. There must be a mistake," screamed Tom.

Hitler spoke with an angry tone, "I'm looking for a few good men to bust out of here. What do you say; you're not a Jew, are you?"

"Shut up, man, just shut up. How can you, especially you, escape the damnation of Hell? What do you expect me to say 'hail whatever your name is'? Buddy, this isn't earth. Maybe you should go talk to that woman over there," pointing at the post-Millennium woman they just talked to. Tom lost it and got out of line and thought, *there must be a mistake here.*

"Wait, I wasn't the only one calling him a bastard, the Pharisees of his time called him a bastard too," said the professor.

"I don't want to hear from you anymore. You knew all the rules of salvation but you couldn't make it to the other side, the good side," said Tom as he started running towards the front of the line.

The professor started weeping and said, "I must be the most miserable man in the pits of gloom."

Tom looked back as he was disappearing in the crowd and said, "Not true; the devil and his demons were even closer to God than you ever were and still lost out on Heaven. They must be the most miserable ones here."

As he ran towards the court gate, he overheard voices of wailing and gnashing of teeth coming out of the dead, great and small, standing before the throne, waiting in line to be delivered up to eternal misery. One said, "You are a liar and son of a liar; you said there was no Hell!"

Another voice said, "You are the reason I'm here. I hated you and harbored so much animosity towards you that I couldn't forgive you. You empty-headed idiot!"

"I'm as good as the next guy."

And, "How would I know that my next door carpenter, who fixed our chair, is the Son of God? Who believes that?"

"I had all the children, two years old and under, of Bethlehem killed. The one that got away is going to judge me!"

"You killed my son, damn you. I hate you."

And, "I did the best I could."

"I was a lukewarm Christian—neither hot nor cold—He'll spit me out of His mouth."

"You stole my money. I still want my money back. It would have been better that you cut off your hand and cast it from you. I'll never forgive you."

"The one who got me addicted to drugs and got me here is on the other side. How is that justice?"

And, "I tried to live by the Ten Commandments!"

"I'm thirsty. Does anyone have water, water, water?"

And there was a lot of, "I hate God."

"I taught children that there was no God. There is no God!"

"I lived on the basis of the Sermon on the Mount. Why am I here?"

And, "Your tongue on fire has sent us to Hell."

"I couldn't stop lusting after the women and was addicted to sex. Is this torment ever going to end? It would have been better if I plucked my eyes out and threw them away."

"I couldn't stop lusting after the men." Tom looked back and noticed that a man said that. Tom started feeling worse after he heard all that and thought, *everyone blamed God and each other for their doom and misery, and nobody looked down at the Lake of Fire and accused Satan of what he has done to them, still.*

He ran for a long time and the closer he got to the throne door, the brighter it got. When he approached the Great White Throne, there were two angels guarding the court entrance. He slowed down and looked at them when he was just a few yards away. They were giants, and didn't look like two baby cherubs with their butts exposed holding a bow and arrow. It wasn't Tom's turn to enter, so his body started to rise up and got suspended in the air. He lost the feeling in all of his muscles except his mouth, eyes, and ears. He was terrified.

Tom said in a shaky voice, "Excuse me, sirs... Angels, but there must be a mistake. I don't belong in this line."

"Did you sin?" asked one of the angels.

"Yes, but not as much as these guys."

"You break one law you have sinned, period."

"So what man hasn't sinned?"

"Jesus Christ, an absolute perfection."

"So does that mean all humanity goes to Hell?"

"No!"

"Am I going to Heaven?"

"No!

"Where am I, and how did I get here?"

"This is the harvest of the end of the age, and the harvesting angels brought you here. It began when the Son of Man sowed the good seed in the field by creating this world. The good seed are the sons of the kingdom. The weeds are the sons of the evil one, and the enemy who sowed them, is the devil. Now is the end of the world and the Son of Man sent out His angels, and they weeded out His kingdom. Everything that caused sin and all who did evil, were pulled up and are getting ready to be burned in the fire. The fiery furnace is down there, where you see there is weeping and gnashing of teeth, compared to the righteous, who are shining like the sun in the kingdom of their Father."

"Who's making all the rules here?" Tom asked.

"God makes the rules, and He will measure all things through His Son's righteousness. Jesus is the only one that qualifies; there is no hope for anyone to escape God's judgment apart from Christ. Son of Adam, the blood of the lamb doesn't cover you; instead, your garment is spotted with the sin of the world. Thus, you don't have the right credentials, and your name will not be found written in the book of life. It has been removed. The Lord will verify that when you go in."

"What about the good things I did in my life, the good deeds? Don't they count for anything? Can't they be used in my defense?"

"Human goodness is the worst badness, if it becomes a substitute for the new birth. God will judge you on the basis of your works, recorded in the books, which will fail to measure up to His holy standard. All your deeds put together don't offset one sin you did; they are like filthy garments. Your works will be judged to show that the punishment is deserved. The same goodness that you think will save you, will judge you. You just don't see the seriousness of sinning. Sin is high treason against Heaven's King. It's like clinching a fist in His face. The only way that God can look at you without you being obliterated, is to see you through His Son Jesus."

"Hey, wait a jiffy here, just because I didn't give my heart to the Lord, doesn't mean that I'm His enemy, please!" Tom exclaimed.

"You can't be neutral, and there is no middle ground. He who isn't with the Lord is against Him, and he who doesn't gather with Him scatters. Every sin and blasphemy will be forgiven men, but the blasphemy against the Spirit will not be forgiven men, in any of the previous ages on the earth. When you rejected the free offer of salvation that the Holy Spirit presented to you over and over again, you blasphemed."

There was a pause while a screen opened up, showing the saints on earth and in Heaven. Tom looked up at the saints on the screen and they seemed very happy and having a good time.

"Hey, I know that guy. His name is John. We used to work together. He's a good guy; he'll help me. Hey, John...John...John," he started screaming louder.

"Don't bother; the saints cannot hear you."

"Now wait just a second here. I can understand John being a good man, belonging there. But Jim over there, he's no saint, for I knew the man. How could this be possible?" Tom asked.

"For nothing shall be impossible with God. One of the disciples asked the same question—"

"It was Peter," said the other angel.

"Yes, see all you had to do is follow the instructions the Lord gave to you in the Bible, and He would have taken care of the rest. He would have presented you to the Father, clean and blameless, like Jim here."

"How come they have different bodies than I do?" asked Tom.

"When the born-again Christians died, their soul separated from the body, which was no big loss for they have a new body now, designed to live in Glory. You, however, you remained spiritually dead and when you died, your soul also separated from the body. Now you're given a body, designed for the Lake of Fire where it will separate from the spirit of God Himself; this is the second death. See that guy over there; he lost his head after torture because he professed Jesus Christ as the savior. It isn't so easy to be a true believer, sometimes. The saints had to go through many hardships and sacrifices to enter the kingdom of God."

"What did these people do to get to Heaven?" Tom asked the angel, "Why can't I join them?"

"While you were having orgies, that guy over there was witnessing to other people and spreading the good news to sinners so they could avoid coming here. These saints had their ears openned to the words of God and listened to His message. They believed, trusted in, clung to, and relied on Him who sent the Lord. They possess eternal life now, and they don't come into judgment, nor will they come under condemnation, but they have already passed over out of death into life. It is by free grace and God's unmerited favor that they were saved, delivered from judgment, and made partakers of Christ's salvation through their faith. And this salvation wasn't of themselves or of their own doing; it came not through their own striving, but it is the gift of God; you obviously didn't want that free gift. By your callousness, stubbornness, and impenitence of heart, you were storing up wrath and indignation for yourself."

Tom looked at the saints and said, "I didn't know that it was going to be like this. No, man, I'll throw myself at His mercy. I'll do anything to get out of this mess."

"Unfortunately, it's too late for that; you had an opportunity when you lived your life on earth."

"I didn't have enough time on earth."

"What hindered you? Who changed your mind?"

"Nothing. I believed in God when I was a child, but as I grew up, I started thinking that these stories were fairy tales. You just grow up and life gets to you."

"Not to the saints they didn't. Why did you depart from the truth and follow seducing spirits and false teachings? The Lord said, 'unless you believe like children, you'll never enter the kingdom of God.' You walked in the counsel of the wicked, stood in the way of sinners, and sat in the seat of mockers. If you had believed, you would have seen the face of God in Heaven," pointing up to screen, "just like these saints are enjoying that privilege. As for you, you will see the face of Satan in Hell."

"So all they had to do is just believe in Jesus and they got saved!"

"Everyone related to Adam is born spiritually dead. When Adam disobeyed and sinned, he became a servant of Satan. You're his offspring, and a child of a slave is a slave. It is through the belief in the death, burial, and resurrection of the Lord Jesus Christ that a person became born again and their spirit became alive forever. While they were dead by their own shortcomings and trespasses, He made them alive together in fellowship and in union with Christ."

"Why should I be accountable for what Adam did? I have nothing to do with him."

"If Adam didn't have children, you wouldn't be here?"

"Yeah, but still I don't want to be held responsible for Adam's sin."

"Don't worry about Adam's sin; you have a lot of sins of your own to worry about. Moreover, if you were put in Adam's place, you'd have done the same thing."

"OK, so I see a variety of big-time sinners and some look-alike saints in here. I'm in between. Am I going where Hitler is going? But he is a horrible man, a child of Hell. Are there different sections within Hell?" Tom asked.

"Everybody will be judged accordingly when the books of works are opened. The degree of torment in Hell that you get at the Great White Throne judgment will be based on your works and the consequences of what you did in life. God, who knows the end from the beginning, will be a righteous Judge; His all-seeing eyes will reveal all truth about every man."

At that moment, his earthly wife screamed with terror from the Lake of Fire.

"You were supposed to be a spiritual leader at home, but you weren't," remarked one of the angels.

"I didn't know what church to join. There were so many denominations... I wished I was a Muslim, then I would have had seventy two black eyed virgins right now."

The angels looked at him and shook their heads.

"Well, what about this purgatory? Isn't there a place I can go to receive some suffering for my sins and be purified for an upgrade to Heaven? Hell shouldn't be forever; can't a merciful God change His mind?"

Again, the angels shook their heads.

"If I were a Hindu, I would be able to be reincarnated. I'd rather go back to earth as a roach than go to Hell. How about if I just disintegrate and be no more," pleaded Tom as he pointed to Hell, "I don't want to go there, man."

One of the angels answered, "Look, son of Adam, there is Heaven," pointing up at the screen, "and there is Hell," pointing his finger downwards. "There is nothing else anywhere, no virgins, no purgatory, no reincarnation, no deals you lose. Do you think that God is happy that you're going to Hell? Hell was prepared for the devil and his angels. God isn't sending you to Hell; you sent yourself by rejecting the Savior and His free pardon for you."

The other angel said, "It seems like you bought into every false idea except the truth. Why did you go to the wide and crowded gate and not to the narrow one? I'll tell you why, it's because you wanted to think and act like your father the devil. The Light has come into the world, and you have loved the darkness more than the Light, for your works and deeds were evil. Has the devil been so convincing that you followed him blindly?"

Then another man came in running and said, "Excuse me, sirs, I prophesied and healed people in Jesus' name, why am I here? Many people came to Christ through my ministry. I did more good than bad, yet I still don't have the right garment!"

Tom thought, *oh my goodness, I know this man from TV. If this evangelist couldn't make it to the good side, then I rest my case.*

One angel said, "Men were warned to beware of false teachers and preachers. You walked around in expensive suits and loved to be greeted in gatherings and conferences and had the most important time slot on TV for your program and the best places of honor on TV and radio. You devoured widows' houses and for a show, made lengthy prayers. You hypocrite. You had no self-sacrificing love and charity. God did use your ministry to save some people but your motives, He doesn't approve of. As for the other new converts to the faith you made, they are children of Hell and of wrath and disobedience and they stand in this line as you do. You were not a soul winner but a sheep robber; you stole from, and fleeced the sheep. You sent computerized letters to women living on social security, asking them to go to the bank to help you out in this emergency and that. You used scare tactics to force people to give offerings. Do you really want us to expose and reveal your private thoughts on a big screen for everyone to see? We have bookkeepers here, you know."

"No, that's all right. I'll wait my turn," the man turned around and walked away with his head down.

Tom asked the man, "Hey, preacher-man. What should I expect behind these doors?"

The man looked back and sadly answered, "A prosecutor and no defender, a judge and no jury, a sentence without appeal, and banishment with no parole."

At that time, the Great White Throne door opened up and a bright light shone out from within.

"You're next," said the angel to Tom.

"That's it then, He'll just throw me out and abandon me - ha! Some loving Creator He is!"

"You spent all your life wanting nothing to do with Him. God can choose not to fellowship with sinners that refuse to repent of their sins. If a smoker rides in your car, wouldn't you say, 'Hey, this is my car and I reserve the right to ask you to either not smoke or leave my car.' Well, God has made a place for those who have repented of their sins and don't intend to sin anymore. Anyone who doesn't repent and enjoys sinning will be excluded from Heaven."

Tom was ushered into the courtroom. His body was released, so that he could walk in by himself. And as the door started to close behind him, Tom was seen on his knees saying, "My Lord Jesus," And a voice was heard saying, "Where is your wedding robe, my son?" and Tom was speechless.

"They're not such chatter boxes anymore, once they are in the presence of the Lord," said one angel to the other. "Every knee shall bow before Him; every tongue shall confess that Jesus Christ is Lord, to the glory of God the Father."

"Another man will break the heart of the Lord, what a shame," said the other angel. "You know, I just can't wait until this judgment and dealing with sin is over."

"Before God can usher in His new Heaven and new earth, He must finally deal with sin. Once Hades, in the center of this earth, is emptied, the Lord can blow up earth and create a new one. Do you remember the first one?"

"How can I forget? We shouted for joy when we saw the wonderful creation. I'm sure the new one will be even more spectacular. And this time, the saints will be able feel and move in more than the three dimensions they were limited to before. Hallelujah."

"Amen."

When the judgment of the unbelievers ended, all those whose names were not found written in the book of life were thrown into the Lake of Fire. Hades was emptied out, then death and Hades were thrown into the eternal Lake of sulfur and Fire.

"Farewell, Grim reaper," said the two angels.

Then the two angels saw Jesus closing the door on the Lake of Fire with tears in His eyes. He looked at those who rejected Him and refused His love, which will suffer for eternity, for the last time.

One angel said, "He is withdrawing Himself from them; He must let them have their own way forever."

The other angel said, "Since God is necessary for every man's existence, when they decided to reject God they eternally plunged themselves into the most horrible sense of isolation a human being can know. Let's get out of here."

Then the black hole disappeared and the two angels took off.

Eternity with the Trinity

After Satan's last rebellion and World War IV, John and Bill were circling around the destroyed and desolate earth and saw that it looked like a big ball of mess.

John and Bill finally landed on a mountain and looked up at the new Heaven. It was brilliant with new light colors, planets, and stars.

John said, "Hallelujah, the Lord has made a new Heaven!"

Bill replied, "Amen, all we need now is a new earth, one that is cleansed from the devil's pollution."

And that was when they saw a very large pyramid-like shaped object coming down out of Heaven from God, prepared as a bride beautifully dressed for her husband.

"Look at that, brother, isn't that breathtaking. An angel told me that the Holy City was coming down and to expect it. I missed that awesome place where we spent seven years before the Millennium. The city foundation seems to be laid out like a square, as long as it was wide. I love the way it shines with the Glory of God. And its brilliance is like that of a very precious jewel, like jasper, clear as crystal. Look at the great, high walls with twelve gates and with twelve angels at the gates. He called it the New Jerusalem (N.J.). I call it a UFO and the final Frontier."

"It's magnificent," replied John, as the pyramid got closer, "look at the gates, the names of the twelve tribes of Israel are written on them. There are three gates on the east, three on the north, three on the south, and three on the west. The wall of the city has twelve foundations, and on them are the names of the twelve apostles of the Lamb. Did you say you call it UFO?"

"Undefiled Flying Oracle, UFO."

"I see," said John as he looked at something that caught his eyes. "Hey, look at that strange looking man on that mountain over there behind you, talking to one of our angel friends. My Lord, what happened to his body?"

"He is all wrinkly, like his body shrunk and his skin is bigger than his body," replied Bill.

"Look at his gray hair. What kind of a man is that?"

"You know, whatever space and time he came from, I wouldn't want to go there. Thank God, he put us on this Planet."

The old man was John the revelator continuing his tour.

"The angel seems to have a measuring rod of gold to measure the city, its gates, and its walls. Why does he need a measuring rod? I can tell the dimensions from here. Its walls are eighteen hundred miles in length, and are as wide and high as it is long."

"Maybe he's doing it for the sake of this strange looking man that he's talking to," said John.

"He's measuring the thickness of the wall now."

"Oh look! The N.J. is coming down closer. What do you say we go and meet her in the air?"

"Yeah, brother, let's go sightseeing and visit with our God. I miss Him, haven't seen Him recently." replied Bill.

"Praise the Lord."

The two flew in the air towards the pyramid, and hovered around it for a closer look. "I see that the wall is made of jasper, and the city of pure gold, as pure as glass," said John, "the foundations of the city walls are decorated with every kind of precious stone. The twelve gates are twelve pearls; each gate is made of a single pearl, with three gates on each side. Let's go in. I can't wait to see what's inside."

When they arrived at one of the pearly gates, the angel at the gate said, "Welcome, brothers, blessed are those who washed their robes that they may go through the gates into the city. The Lord our God made sure that nothing impure will ever enter it, nor will anyone who does what is shameful or deceitful, but only those whose names are written in the Lamb's Book of Life. The Lord wants to give you saints a white stone with a new name written on it, known only to him who receives it. Here are your stones; come and get it. Next—"

After the two entered the gate to the city, they ran into Adam and Eve who were just getting in through the same gate.

"Hello, brother and sister," the same angel at the gate welcomed Adam and Eve. "Hello, you two, and welcome back. This will be your last move and final destination. Jesus came here to prepare a place for you. And just like He promised you all, He came back and took you all to be with Him, that you also may be where He is. This is the Father's house and there are many rooms inside. The next time you see the Lord Jesus, ask Him to show you your rooms. The New Jerusalem is to eternity what the earthly Jerusalem was to the Millennium. Man and God will live together, for the environment is good for both of you. And look there," pointing to the center of the city, "I have guarded the Tree of Life for you. Look at it now in the middle there, in a new location. God has made everything new! Everyone have free access to it. How do you like it?"

The tree was about seven hundred miles in the middle of the city, but they could see it with their super vision, with no problem.

"Here are your new names, and just so you know, these gates shall never be closed by day, for there shall be no night here. Come in and visit anytime."

Then Adam and Eve picked up their names, thanked the angel and walked passed him as they went into the New Jerusalem city.

"I don't remember this angel. What was he talking about?" Eve asked Adam.

"I have no idea."

I don't blame you, thought the angel sadly; *it's good for you not to remember the former things. God's mercy has spared you from remembering the pain and suffering of the old world order and corrupt system. Here is a new world with no past history, where the second law of thermodynamics will be eliminated, information will never be confused, and created world won't deteriorate, a new creation for everlasting. Nevertheless, we angels won't forget what happened down there. No sir, my friends are in Hell suffering*

385

throughout eternity because the devil lied to them. As the LORD Almighty lives, whom I serve, from now on if anyone lifts up his head to proclaim himself as God whether angel or man, I will, by God's command, take care of it right away. No more experiments, we have seen the results of sin, and God would be justified in any action He takes against sin.

As more saints came in through the gates, the angel felt happy again and welcomed them. Then, John and Bill bumped into another saint who was amazed by the beauty of the city and said, "I looked forward to the city with foundations, whose architect and builder is God. This place sure beats living in tents."

John looked to see who this saint was, and his name was the saint who used to be Abraham.

"Do you notice that the city doesn't need the sun or the moon to shine on it," said Bill, "for the glory of God gives it light and the Lamb is its lamp. The Lord God Almighty and the Lamb are the city temple. We will not need the light of a lamp or the light of the sun, for the Lord God will give us light. Thus, there will be no more night."

"Yes, this is a great scene," said John, "the nations are entering the city through its gates and are walking by its light. The great street of the city is of pure gold, like transparent glass. And, the kings of the earth are bringing their splendor into it. The nations are bringing their glory and honor into it."

"I see over there the river of the water of Life, as clear as crystal, flowing from the throne of God and of the Lamb down the middle of the great street of the city."

"Come; let us also take the free gift of the Water of Life," said John.

After they drank the water of Life, the two saints ran like children to the Tree of Life, which stood on each side of the river, and ate from its leaves.

"It tastes great, everything is great," said Bill.

A voice said, "Blessed are those who washed their robes, that they may have the right to the Tree of Life."

Later on, the saints found out that the Tree of Life bears twelve crops of fruit, yielding its fruit every month, and the leaves of the tree are for the healing of the nations. No longer will there be any curse.

John said to Bill, "Eating a leaf a day keeps the doctor away," then they bumped into a man with a name written that said, "Previously known as John the Revelator."

"Hi, brother," they greeted him.

While the two were talking to the new JR, Bill pointed at a distant gate and said, "Look, it's that's strange wrinkly man again with that angel, and they are inside the city now,"

The new JR looked at where Bill was pointing at and said, "I don't know why, but I feel like I know that wrinkly man."

After the saints were acquainted with the New Jerusalem, they heard Him who was seated on the throne say, "I'm making everything new!"

An angel told the saints to go and look at the creation of the new earth. They looked through the gates and saw the word of God renovate the messed up earth, with fire. He made it into a new paradise resembling the original Garden of Eden. The curse of the Garden that was partially removed in the Millennium was obliterated now. The saints noticed that there was no longer any sea. They didn't miss it because the former things were not remembered, nor did they come to mind. The two were amazed at the handy work of God and His new beautified and perfected creation.

Bill said to John, "Praise the Lord, let's hover down there and check it out."

John replied with excitement, "Yeah, let's go!"

At that moment, their attention was directed towards the bright light of the SHEKINAH Glory of the Godhead inside the pyramid at the peak. The Godhead—Father, Son and Holy Spirit— started descending in new dimensions. There was silence, and all eyes of the saints were on that light coming down to their level. All eyes stopped blinking, mouths dropped open, and hearts missed a beat or two. It was a spectacular sight never seen before.

One saint standing next to John said, "I finally get to see His face. He talked to me from a burning bush once. Another time, I saw His back, but not His face. For there was an era when no man could see Him and live, but I said to the Lord, 'I beseech You, show me Your glory.' And God said, 'I will be gracious to whom I will be gracious, and will show mercy and loving-kindness on whom I will show mercy and loving-kindness. But,' He said, 'You cannot see My face.'

"So, He told me to stand upon a rock. Then He put me in a crack in the rock and covered me with His hand until He had passed by. He made all His goodness pass before me, and He proclaimed His name, Jehovah, before me. Then He took away His hand and I saw His back, but His face wasn't seen. And, that was a sight to remember. But this is the moment I have yearned for." John looked at the man to see who he was, and his name was "Previously known as Moses."

The Godhead descended to the saint's level and was visible and in their image. Jesus, God the Son, stepped out of the Godhead and became visible to them. They knew that in Christ the whole fullness of the Godhead dwelled in bodily form, giving complete expression of the divine nature. But now, all of invisible God was making Himself visible. So they saw God as He is and saw His face with pure hearts and His name was now on their foreheads and the old age mystery of the Godhead —Father, Son and Holy Spirit being one — was unveiled forever.

The angels sang again and the saints danced and chanted Hallelujah. Now the dwelling of God was with men, and He lived with them. They were His people, and God Himself was with them and became their God. The throne of God and of the Lamb was now in the city, the Lord God Almighty and the Lamb were the city's temple and His servants served Him. He wiped every tear from their eyes. There was no more death or mourning or crying or pain, for the old order of things had passed away.

Finally, John heard Jesus, the Root and the Offspring of David and the bright Morning Star, tell JR, "I'm the Alpha and the Omega, the First and the Last, the Beginning and the End. It is done." JR then got back in his time machine and returned to his world as his tour ended. Human history closed and the eternal day began, and, the saints reigned forever and ever.

The grace of the Lord Jesus is with God's people. Amen.